ENTHEÓPHAGE

ENTHEÓPHAGE

DREMA DEÒRAICH

Niveym Arts LLC

ENTHEÓPHAGE

ISBN 978-1-958461-00-6

Entheóphage is a work of fiction. Names, places, characters, and incidents either are the product of the author's imagination or are used fictitiously. Any similarity to real persons, living or dead, is coincidental and not intended by the author.

Cover illustration © 2022 Duncan Eagleson.
Cover and interior design by Corvid Design.
www.corviddesign.com

First printing 2022.

Published by Niveym Arts, LLC
Norfolk, Virginia 23509
www.niveymarts.com

For B, my biggest cheerleader

Chapter 1

SOUTH PACIFIC SUN STABBED ISOBEL'S EYES INTO A SQUINT. She cursed and slapped shades on her face as she headed for the ship's tender through air so salty its tang stung her throat. Travis, her crew liaison, looked up at her approach.

"Doctor Fallon. You ready to go?"

"Yes." Isobel rubbed sunscreen onto her fair skin. "Tell the divers to get started while we're gone."

"We aren't supposed to approach the reef until the Nlaantu give their final permission." Travis peered at her. "It took a lot of wrangling to get them to agree to this meet. If they find out you jumped the gun, they might send us packing."

Isobel grunted. "Picky, are they?"

"Something like that."

She grimaced. Gabe needed that coral. The medicine it would create. Isobel wasn't leaving here without it.

She stepped to the starboard railing. The Nlaan island chain consisted of a string of atolls—ring-shaped islands formed by coral reefs atop dormant undersea volcanoes—that stretched beyond what she could see. The closest one, a narrow cay that breached the Pacific's surface on the atoll's curve, lay in the distance off the *Pasteur*'s starboard side. Seabirds gathered there or flew overhead. Must be good hunting. She pointed.

"That's our target?"

"Yes, ma'am."

"And the island where we're meeting with the Nlaantu leaders?"

Travis appeared beside her. "You see that bigger island past the sand bar? The green one?"

"That's where they live?"

"No, ma'am. That little spit ain't big enough for a village." He made a circling gesture. "We're going past that one, a good ride on the other side. The Elder Council's on one of the four big islands, kinda dead center of the island group."

Isobel scanned the area. "Do they come out here often?"

"If they're fishing, they might. Why?"

"You said this arrangement was all but a done deal. I mean, they already have the boats we promised, even if they are primitive. Carbon fiber proa have to be better than wooden ones, so at least there's that. You'd think they'd want sonar and engines," she shrugged, "but to each their own. We've delivered the rest of the agreed items, too, right? Medicines, canvas, beads, bananas. What else?"

"Scrap metal."

Isobel frowned. "For what?"

"Fishing spears. Arrows. Knives. They've been using shaped stone, carved wood from trees with huge thorns, that sort of thing. They have a few knives from trade, but this'll level them up for sure."

North Sentinel Island's inhabitants also used metal that washed ashore on their island to tip their arrows, then fired them at outsiders who dared approach. "We aren't in any danger, are we?"

"No, ma'am. I think they want us here."

"Why?"

"Rumor is some of their folks are pushing for more modern items," he said, "like medicines. They'll need outside contacts to get those."

"Oh. Well, they have everything we promised them, right?"

"Yes, ma'am."

"Then what can it hurt if we start a little early? Except for this meeting, which we're about to complete, we've kept our end of the agreement. I don't need a full harvest yet, but I want a sample of the star queen by the time we get back. If they say anything, I'll take responsibility."

"You're the boss." Travis went to fill in the dive teams on the changed plan.

Isobel waited on the utilitarian ship's aft deck where crewmen worked. The rear wall of the main cabin, topped by two satellite arrays, cut off her view of the bow. Large cranes, once white and now some indeterminate color, loomed above stationary storage containers to port and starboard. Behind the ship, the South Pacific stretched in endless, undulating waves. Smaller ripples flashed and shimmered in the sun. Even a boat the size of the *Pasteur* bobbed on the bigger swells. She'd been aboard just over two days but still wasn't accustomed to that constant motion. She turned into the breeze and stared at the horizon to combat the slight discomfort.

Within minutes, Travis returned and the two of them climbed down into the tender. The boatman rounded the *Pasteur*'s bow and aimed inland.

Two days' travel from the nearest outposts of civilization, this isolated region shimmered with pristine radiance. Deep blue ocean filled the space between and beyond the islands as far as she could see, but closer to the shores its cobalt cast transitioned to patches of bright, clear aquamarine where the reef grew near the surface. Inside the characteristic pale ring of the nearest atoll, a turquoise lagoon rippled in the breeze. Vegetation in uncountable hues of green spanned the nearest large islet, while spots of vivid color flitted among the boughs on jewel-toned wings. A few dozen meters off the starboard side, a pod of dolphins raced their craft. She watched until they veered aside, bored and on the hunt for fresh entertainment. In the distance, a line of clouds bruised the horizon.

The wind felt good, cool against the heat. For a while, she took in their surroundings. Evidence of life in the limpid water around them registered as distractions, along with bird calls and the peaty smell of the thick ferny jungle on the uninhabited islet as they passed it on their left. She noted Nlaan's beauty, filed it away to consider another time. Right now, the small, jagged atoll behind them snagged and held her thoughts, along with all she had riding on this bet. This place could save her son's life. But if the Nlaantu denied her team's access—

Well. She couldn't dwell on that.

Spread before them, a few black and green islands hunkered above the ocean's surface like moss-covered pebbles strewn across a puddle. "It's smaller than I expected."

Travis's sharp amber eyes narrowed even beneath the brim of his hat. An old scar puckered the skin around his right eyelid. "Oh, this ain't all of it. Not by a long shot. The last count was sixteen islands. Four big ones with Nlaantu populations, and the rest too small to hold much." He leaned back in his seat and crossed his bared arms.

Why did ex-Marines always have tattoos? She considered the sun-browned visage of this man, Holschtatt Pharmaceuticals' best negotiator in these kinds of transactions. Sunlight gleamed in the small gold hoop in his ear and made his white Van Dyke beard glow. "What restrictions have they imposed? Anything that'll be a hardship?"

"No, ma'am. Little stuff. We can't go ashore on any island other than that closest green one. You and I are the only ones allowed to interact with any of their people. No hunting birds. A limit on our fishing. That sort of thing."

"And you've passed the word to the crew to keep this project a secret?"

"Yes, ma'am. Everybody knows not to talk about it in calls or emails."

"Good." A troublesome controversy, if the world learned of their activities on this Edenic snippet of land, would cost Holschtatt millions in recovery PR. The news would come out eventually, sure, but by that time she'd have developed a treatment for Milani Syndrome and could point to that as justification for the costs in any perceived environmental issues. Not that there would be any beyond the loss of a few chunks of reef and that didn't seem to be a problem at Nlaan, where the reefs stretched for miles and miles. If the crew dropped a little trash, that could be easily cleaned up.

The island dead ahead, much larger than the small strip behind them, boasted actual cliffs, sheer slopes of black volcanic rock that loomed above the water. Offshore, in the crashing surf and in between the emergent strips of land in the distance, smaller black crags jutted from the water. Some held feathered occupants and the inevitable white paint of guano from repeated use by generations of nesting seabirds. Grizzled squawking, audible over the roar of the engine and wind, drew her attention to the skies, where a growing collection of the birds circled the tender, dove into its wake, and rose again.

The boatman veered left, and Isobel shifted her focus to this meeting with the Nlaantu. Travis had all but finalized this crucial detail in the past few weeks, but the island's leaders had demanded one last formality, to meet her and "measure her spirit" before they approved her project. What would they be like?

The water around them paled as the boatman threaded the passage between the surrounding crags and atolls. Nlaantu islanders paddled past in their traditional and carbon fiber proa or drua and glowered at the noisy boat. It hit Isobel how far from civilization she was. Surrounded by a culture so alien to her own she didn't have any idea what to say or do, she suddenly felt very exposed.

Travis must have sensed her unease. "Follow my lead," he said. "Do what I do. But you should expect them to grant you more respect than they do me."

"Why?"

"You'll see." His mouth curved up at the corners in a secret grin. "Relax. Listen more than you speak. Nod and smile."

The shore drew nearer, and Isobel ignored the flutters in her stomach. Above the tide line, a group of women, both young and old, waited. Some wore what appeared to be hand-woven fabric in skirts and wraps around their chests. Others sported bright patterned pants with wide legs, and loose tops tied at the shoulders. One wore a beautiful fabric length tied like a sarong. Their gleaming black hair held beads, shells, feathers, and small bones in an impressive array of designs and styles. Everything about their presence screamed traditional Nlaantu culture, or what Isobel fancied that to be. None wore shoes.

To either side, small groups of men and children observed, fascinated by the strangeness of this loud, stinky boat and its peculiar occupants. They too were barefoot. Otherwise, their clothing seemed almost disappointing in its normalcy. Even here on isolated Nlaan, Western fashion had made its mark with t-shirts and everyday trousers or shorts.

Behind the islanders stretched a break in the trees and beyond that, a clearing. Large, lodge-sized structures with open sides and thatched roofs squatted above the ground on carved wooden pylons. Rolls of bright textiles hung below the roof at the sides Isobel could see, perhaps to be dropped as screens for protection from the sun, or for privacy. That must be the village.

The boatman dropped the engine to idle as they approached the beach. When the hull touched the sand, he cut power and jumped out of the boat with Travis to pull it ashore. Close as they were, the women did not give way. Instead, they stood with regal bearing as if they owned the whole damned island chain.

Which, of course, they did.

Travis helped Isobel out of the boat. On the beach, she extended a hand to the women, but Travis stepped forward.

He bowed, a shallow movement. "Mtuji, you honor us."

They never acknowledged him. Instead, they watched Isobel. Her gaze darted to Travis for guidance.

He flicked his thumb at the women in a subtle signal. *Do what I do.*

She mimicked Travis's action for the waiting group. "Mtuji, you honor us."

One of the women stepped forward. "I will translate your words for Mtuji, and Mtuji's words for you. I am called T'nei."

Isobel introduced herself.

One of the other women, a century old if she was a day, stepped forward and spoke in a language Isobel had never heard.

T'nei repeated her words to Isobel in English. "Why are you here?"

Isobel fought the urge to look at Travis. "To harvest a special coral from the reef."

"No," T'nei snapped. "Anyone could do that. Your men could do that. Why are *you* here?"

Isobel's mind raced. What was Mtuji after? "Because I am the lead scientist among these men. I know which coral to harvest, and how it is processed. Only I can do that."

"Only you? Among all your people?"

Isobel pursed her lips. "No. But I am the one who began this research, many years ago, in search of medicine for a very rare disease. I found what we needed in a special coral. I learned that this coral grows here." She paused. "I started this project. I came here because I intend to finish it."

T'nei regarded her, then translated her words for Mtuji.

The other women murmured among themselves, staring at Isobel as if they could see through her, see the truth of the matter. The elders among them wavered. Some argued. The younger ones held their ground.

Isobel's stomach knotted.

At length, the crone who stood front and center spoke aside to T'nei, who turned to Isobel.

"And if we say no, go home?"

Isobel's jaw tightened. "Then we will go home, and I'll start again. Find another way. But it took me years to find this coral. Thousands of children are born with this illness. None survive it."

Mtuji absorbed her words in silence.

"What would you do," Isobel went on, "if your children were born this way and I could save them? If you had to watch your children die because another nation's leader denied me access to their reef?"

T'nei hesitated, then translated Isobel's words.

Mtuji flinched almost as if she'd been slapped, looked Isobel up and down as if to determine her character by examining her bearing, her confidence, her stance. She said something to the others, all of whom blinked. They studied her with renewed interest.

The wind carried sounds of children playing nearby, along with a whiff of frangipani and bougainvillea. Calls of seabirds and the lapping of small waves against the boat behind them reminded Isobel of their precarious situation.

The other women spoke. Mtuji listened without taking her eyes off Isobel. They conferred before Mtuji spoke again.

T'nei translated for Isobel. "You may take coral from Vliat..."

Mtuji continued, and T'nei translated.

"...if you do so with care. Take only what you need. Do no harm beyond that you cannot avoid. T'nei will be your guide. Speak to no other Nlaantu. Respect our land, our people, our ways. We will be watching."

When T'nei finished translating, Isobel nodded to Mtuji. "Thank you. We—"

The women behind Mtuji withdrew in the direction of their village. Mtuji lingered. Isobel twitched beneath that piercing scrutiny.

"Thank you, Mtuji," Isobel said.

Mtuji lingered a heartbeat more, then followed the others past the trees.

Isobel walked forward as if to follow, but T'nei stepped between her and the other women.

"Outsiders may not enter the village." T'nei's stance discouraged any argument Isobel might have proposed.

She winced and retreated, prickles flushing her cheeks as if she'd committed some major faux pas but didn't quite know what it was. At the tender, she glanced over her shoulder. T'nei still formed a solid barrier between Isobel and the Nlaantu. Men and children had withdrawn into the trees, though a few of the youngest ones peeped out from behind tall ferns. She gave a little wave, then got in the boat.

Travis and the boatman pushed the bow off the beach, then hopped in. Once they were on their way to the *Pasteur*, Isobel let the tension go bit by bit.

"What is 'Vliat'?" she asked Travis.

"That's their name for that atoll where we'll be working."

"Ah. And this Mtuji, she's their leader?"

He grinned. "Technically, yes. But Mtuji isn't a name, it's an honorific. All those women, including T'nei, are Mtuji."

"They're matriarchal?"

"Yes, ma'am." He winked.

"You could have told me."

"Oh, I don't know. You picked it up pretty quick. Congrats, Doc."

His smile grew sad. Isobel cocked her head. "Is something wrong?"

Travis looked away. A second later he pointed. In the distance, a spray of water spouted up from the sea, droplets shattering the sunlight into a circular rainbow.

"What is that?" she asked

"I'd guess whales. Too far to know for sure. Several types pass through here in their migrations," he said, his voice distant, sad.

"Are you okay?"

"It's a shame, that's all. Such a beautiful, unspoiled place." He sighed. "Aren't many of those left in the world."

Isobel shrugged. "Don't worry. We'll just take the star queen and go home. Easy peasy. Besides, whatever small damage we might leave behind will be worth it to save those kids."

"I hope you're right, Doc."

"I know I am." A significant number of trials showed the coral protein would neutralize the Milani effect. It wasn't a cure, but it might mitigate the horrific symptoms, allow Gabe—allow the *patient*—to live a more normal life.

This project would be a success. It had to be. Anything else was unacceptable.

Chapter 2

Behn-Kaur Residence, Austin, Texas
Thursday, October 31, 6:00 AM

Number of infected: 1

KYNDRA WASN'T IN HER BED. A corner of her green blanket, grey in the dim light, hung from her bunk. She also wasn't at the cluttered desk beneath, nor in her yellow reading tent, where a stack of books had tumbled over to sprawl across its floor.

Lukas Behn rubbed sleep from his eyes and tried to remember the last time she'd awakened before him. This might be a first.

He padded to her bathroom. No light shone under its closed door. "Kyn?"

HVAC vents hissed in response as the system kicked in. Luk tapped on the door.

"Honey? You okay?"

Still nothing. He pushed open the door. His daughter's bathroom was empty, save for the dirty towel on the floor—how many times would he have to chide her for that?—and the jumble of bandaids, soap, toothbrush, and toothpaste on the vanity.

He went to the hallway.

"Kyndra? Where are you, kiddo?"

No response.

Maybe she'd fallen asleep on the couch. Luk pressed down the hall to the living room, then the den. No Kyndra. A tendril of worry threaded a prickly path through his calm.

Wide awake now, he checked his office, the kitchen, even the pantry. His mind wrapped around the empty spaces where she should be, and he shouted her name as he continued to search. Kyndra was not in the house. Worry blossomed into near panic by the time he jerked open the front door and barged onto the porch without switching on the lights.

At the edge of the sidewalk beside their street, his pajama-clad eight-year-old stared into the pre-dawn sky above a neighbor's house. She didn't move, not even in reaction to the noise he'd made.

Austin's early morning nipped at his bare chest with a chilly breeze, seasonal for late October in central Texas. He crossed his arms against the chill and stepped off the porch in her direction, peering up to see what had her so mesmerized. Kyndra loved the night sky, but she'd never before come out here on her own.

What was she watching?

He padded barefoot across the grass. "Kyn?" he called, keeping his voice low. Not all their neighbors rose this early.

She gave no sign she'd heard.

He touched her shoulder. "What're you doing, kiddo?"

She still stared at the skyline across the street. "The trees are burning," she said, her voice distant. Vague. "Like Mama's pyre."

Was she dreaming? Luk pulled her around, stooping down to her level.

"Kyndra, talk to me. What's going on?"

She blinked in slow motion, a glint of growing twilight in her eyes. "Dad?"

"Yeah," he said. "Are you with me?"

Kyn looked around. "What're we doing in the yard?"

Luk straightened. "I was hoping you could tell me. You don't remember coming out here?"

"No." She tilted her gaze skyward again.

Odd. She'd never sleepwalked before. He saw nothing in the direction she'd been staring. Only shadowy neighborhood houses and trees cast against ambient city lights rested there. "It's time to get our day started. Do you plan to ride your bike in your jammies?"

Her hands went to her hips. Her mother had done that.

"Dad."

She walked to the house, and he followed in companionable silence across the damp lawn.

In the foyer, she stopped to stretch. Her belly peeked out between her pajama top and pants that were too short. She needed bigger ones. Luk sighed. His little girl wasn't little anymore.

"Go get dressed."

She nodded.

"Five minutes."

"Okay," she said through another yawn.

Luk went to his room long enough to exchange his sweatpants for a pair of comfortable shorts, an old t-shirt, and a pair of socks. In the foyer, he plucked his runners from a semi-neat row of shoes and slid them on. Standing on one foot, he pulled the other up behind him, stretching his muscles. He held the pose, feeling the burn, before he swapped legs. Small sounds from deeper in the house told him Kyn was dressing. So mature, his daughter. Most people who met her had a hard time believing she was only eight. Losing her mother at such an early age might have had something to do with that.

He bent and flattened his palms against the floor, felt the stretch through his glutes and hamstrings, and tried not to think about Marin. Hard, that, since every time he looked at Kyn, he saw her mother. Same beautiful brown skin and eyes. Same low forehead, similar even to the tiny mole above her left brow. Same thick black hair, though where Marin's had hung past her waist, Kyn liked hers shorter. The main difference between their features was in Kyn's small, full mouth. Marin's had been wide, her smile as big as her spirit.

That familiar gnawing loss reared its toothy head, and he shoved it inside the cage he'd built to contain his grief. He needed to snap out of it. Marin had been gone two and a half years now. It was time he listened to the advice of friends and moved on with his life.

He leaned into a slow-mo lunge, first one leg, then the other. Kyn loved these morning outings. Sometimes she would offer thoughts on the latest BehnWerks game. She'd been testing Hyde and Seek for a few days and would probably have solid feedback by now. Marin probably would not have approved, but Kyn loved doing it so much she must have been born with pixels in her blood, same as he was. As a designer and the founder and CEO of BehnWerks Games, he'd been able to make a good living, and give his daughter some nonviolent entertainment in the process. Kyn had been one of his alpha testers for the last year, starting with LeapFrogge, moving up to Two-by-Two, and now Hyde and Seek. The child showed a clear aptitude for it. She often caught something he and the other BehnWerks crew had missed.

Kyn shuffled in from the hallway and stuffed her feet into her sneakers without untying them.

"You're going to break down the backs of those shoes if you keep doing that."

"I know."

"If you break them, you'll have to buy your next pair with allowance money."

He couldn't see her face, but he'd bet five bucks she had rolled her eyes.

She snagged her helmet from a wall hook and fiddled with the buckle. "You ready?"

"Yep." He gestured at the lightweight jackets hanging on hooks near the door.

"Nah, I'm good."

Luk let them out onto the porch. Kyn was as lightly dressed as he was, in jeans and a short-sleeved t-shirt with a Neil deGrasse Tyson slogan that always tickled him—"You matter, unless you multiply yourself by the speed of light squared...then you energy." He understood her refusal of the hoodie, though. They'd warm up soon enough.

He locked the door. Behind him, Kyn murmured. He glanced over in time to see her scoop something off of her blue Schwinn with her bare hands.

"What's that?"

"A spider," she said.

Just like that. Casual. As if this happened every day.

"A what?" Luk asked, eyes wide. Eight-legged creatures never entered Kyn's personal space without a minor display of hysteria. "Who are you, and what have you done with my daughter?"

Kyn shooed the arachnid into the shadows of the unruly shrubs and finished unlocking her bike. "Dad, you're so weird."

Luk grinned. "You should be proud. Getting over a fear of spiders is no small thing, child. But whatever shall I do with myself if I no longer hold the title of Spider Savior around here?"

She laughed, a giggly little-girl sound he loved. "You need another job, I guess. What about burger flipper?"

"I already do that."

"Oh yeah." She tapped her chin. "Maybe you could clean my room?"

"Hah. Nice try."

She shrugged, then sniffed, her nose wrinkling. "Ugh."

"What?"

"You don't smell that?"

Luk sniffed the air. "No. What does it smell like?"

"Like something died."

"You mean the crickets?" A few insect corpses had accumulated on the porch since he'd swept yesterday. At least cricket season was mostly over for this year, and he could soon use the porch lights again and open the door without being invaded. "I don't even notice that anymore until you mention it."

"No," she said. "This is bigger than crickets."

He regarded his daughter. Three odd behaviors in less than an hour cut through his usual morning fog like a beacon. He took in her stance, her attitude, her comments, but she seemed her usual self. Luk sniffed again. "Huh. I got nothing. Come on, let's go."

She pushed her bike down the steps and onto the driveway, then hopped on and pedaled into the street. Luk took a jogging position between her and the traffic lane. Most houses had at least one light on, but the inhabitants were probably still drinking coffee and trying to wake up.

They passed the time in silence for a bit, as usual. He liked the quiet of Hyde Park before everyone awoke. Kyn liked it too, even spoke in hushed tones as if she were reluctant to disturb the soundtrack of birdsong that accompanied these outings. Together, they'd pass through alternating patches of shadow and pools of light from streetlamps, moving down Avenue H to zigzag between lettered and numbered streets, working their way west and south toward Avenue B, where the owner of that little grocery was always arriving as they passed. Turn at 44th, loop around Shipe Park, and go home. Overall, it was nearly two miles every morning, great exercise for them both, and quality father-daughter time when they could talk, reminisce, or laugh, comfortable in each other's presence. Luk wouldn't trade it for anything in the world.

He ran beside her through early morning air scented with evergreen sumac, clematis, and Texas sage. This neighborhood boasted great gardeners, many of whom had planted devil's trumpets, jessamine, and other fragrant night-blooming vines and perennials. Some trimmed their yards into neat landscapes. Others surrounded their homes with mini wildernesses thick with ivy, herbs and flowers, or wayward shrubberies. It gave the whole area a character Luk loved.

Many houses sat beneath old trees. Here a cypress, there a live oak. He caught a whiff of desert willow. Marin had loved the way those drew hummingbirds.

Marin again. He grabbed at the first distraction that came to mind.

"How goes the testing on Hyde and Seek?" Luk asked.

"I like it," Kyn said. "Some of the trees are a little pixelated. And there's a bug in one of the scenes where the program lets a gate slam on my arm. Shouldn't it give me a flesh wound, or at least dent my skin?"

Luk squinted at her. "Is that the kind of video game you want to play?"

She giggled. "No."

"Whew. Thank the gods."

"You might wanna fix that glitch in the code, though. I mean, it's funny and all, but you should prolly edit out stuff that maims the players."

"Good point."

They were almost to the slight bend at Avenue F. "Even with the icky gate," she said, "I like that I can tell the game what neighborhood I want, and it sets the scenes with real-life backgrounds."

Luk grinned. Hyde was written to wrap around a Google-Earth-type street-view framework so it would resemble the real world, but it wouldn't be exact. Too much risk of enticing players to explore private property outside the game. He'd had fun with the idea. Simon Tanaka and the other three BehnWerks financial backers did too, except Luk wasn't moving quickly enough on its development to make them happy. He should pass it to the rest of his team, let them wrap it up, but he hadn't written a game all by himself in a while. These days his input was limited to offering suggestions or critiques on new games and strategies on how to make them work, then coding the finishing touches. The rest of his time was mostly consumed by marketing, business details, and boring minutiae. He missed those passionate early days when he was the one doing all the coding, but that wouldn't pay the bills anymore.

He wasn't too worried. Sometimes these things took longer than projected. Simon wasn't likely to complain about a couple of days. He and the others had made too much money on BehnWerks' creations in the past to get antsy now.

"It's cool," Kyn said, bringing him back to the moment, "because the settings are all familiar. It's like...I kind of know my way around, but the game makes me investigate things I might not notice in the real world. You know, peek under buckets, inside tree holes or up in the branches, like that. So I can find the things on my list."

"Good. What else?"

"You could make it more realistic."

"Tell me how."

She rounded the corner onto Rowena Avenue, Luk beside her. "I mean, the buildings and trees and all that seem real. But there's no trash on the streets or in the park."

"You want me to put litter in the game?"

"Why not? It'd be more real. I know we mostly ignore it outside the game, pretend like it isn't there."

Luk glanced at his daughter. "Has the homeschool co-op been talking about the environment lately?"

"Yeah, but I see it myself, too. Like that." Kyn pointed at evidence of a dumped ashtray beside a parking spot on the roadside. "Ick. That person shoulda cleaned up their mess. Birds might eat those cigarette butts and get sick."

She was right. All along the roadway lay small exhibits to support her argument. A soda can. A Woko Loko takeout box. The more he looked, the more he saw. A scrap of paper. A sliced zip tie. A broken balloon. None of it was enormous. Added up, it might fill a small trash bag.

"Hey, I know! You could design it so that when the player picks up a piece of trash and throws it in the garbage can, they find a prize. If they check the can without adding trash, they get nothing. Ooo! You could even make it a double prize for recycling bottles and cans!"

Luk offered a silent mantra of thanks. This was more like Kyn, following random rabbit holes of potential in his games rather than playing with spiders or sleepwalking. "Maybe I could throw in some random doggie poo while I'm at it," he joked.

"Yeah!" Kyn giggled. "That'd be cool! Add some doggie stations like we see at the park, with the little green bags and garbage cans, or even a compost station. Give the players points for trashing it. Give 'em more if they compost it."

He frowned. Gods knew getting adults to pick up their trash could be a never-ending struggle, as evidenced by what he could see from his current position. Coding in trash would make the game's world more authentic, but most players— especially the kids BehnWerks wrote many of their games for—wouldn't welcome that level of realism. Besides, Simon and the other investors would probably never go for it.

"Noted," he said. "What else?"

"Graphics are still a little jerky, especially when I first go to a new scene. If I've been there before, it's fine, but—"

She disappeared from his peripheral view. A heartbeat later, he heard the crash.

Luk whirled.

His daughter lay sprawled on her side on the asphalt, legs tangled in her bike frame.

"Kyn!" In a second, he was on his knees beside her. "Kyndra!"

Pre-dawn light turned her lips grey. A scrape on her chin oozed blood, beads of blackish-red against skin two shades paler than it should be. Sweat glistened along her hairline. She wasn't moving.

"Honey?" He stroked her cheek.

Her body jerked in a befuddled reaction. Her eyelids fluttered. She tried to speak.

He fumbled for his iPhone.

"Daddy?"

Phone forgotten, his hands hovered over Kyn's prone form, afraid to move her. Afraid he'd make it worse. "I'm here. Are you hurt?"

"Yes. Ow." Kyn rolled over and touched her chin with a hiss, then gripped her left shoulder. "What happened?"

"I don't know. One second you were riding beside me and the next you crashed. You stopped talking and fell. Did you hit a pothole?"

Her features puckered. "We were talking about the spider..." She trailed off.

Luk froze, staring at her. "That's the last thing you remember?"

"No, wait." She sat up. "You were telling me how you're gonna raise my allowance to fifteen dollars a week."

"Hmm. It must have been me that hit my head because I don't remember that at all."

"We were talking about the game. You said you're gonna put in doggy poo. I told you about the jerky graphics."

Relief rippled up the back of his neck and he let go of the breath he'd been holding. "So you're okay?"

"Yeah, just clumsy." Kyn got to her feet, brushing the dirt from her chin with a grimace.

Luk sighed. She'd have another scar there, a lopsided mate for the one on her brow from falling out of a tree a year ago. She'd been lucky to have only a few scrapes from that affair. Marin wouldn't have been as tolerant of those activities.

"Are you feeling shaky at all?"

"Yeah. A little."

Sugar crash? It would be the first time he'd seen that in Kyn, but she was getting older. Her body was changing. Tomorrow he'd see she ate something before they left for their outing. "Let's get some breakfast. That'll make you feel better."

She picked up her bike and remounted as if nothing had happened. "Yeah. I am kinda hungry."

That settled it for Luk. He took up a comfortable stride next to her bike. "I know what happened."

"You mean what made me fall?"

"Yep."

"Tell me."

"Gravity."

She laughed. "Dad!"

He belted out the first line of the "Gravity" song and she joined in. Together they sang the whole song, louder than they should have given the early hour, but so what? All he wanted right now was to get his daughter home, put some food in her belly, and bandage her chin. Everything else would sort itself out.

Chapter 3

Aboard the dive boat *Jewel One*, Vliat, Nlaan Islands
Friday, November 1, 11:45 AM
(Austin, Texas, Thursday, October 31, 5:45 PM)

Number of infected: 1

ISOBEL STRAIGHTENED THE STRAPS ON HER SWIMSUIT and sat to slide her feet into her flippers. She glanced at Travis, who'd joined them on this adventure.

"Sure you don't want to come along?"

His grin puckered the scar around his eye. "I've seen it. Someone has to stay topside."

"Your loss." Isobel shrugged into her tank harness, which was heavier than she'd expected, and cinched it snug around her chest. She grabbed her mask and went to sit beside Duvre, her dive leader, dangling her flippered feet in the warm water.

"Don't forget to spit-clean your mask, as I showed you," Duvre said, his English thick with Sami accent. He demonstrated the technique again.

Isobel spat on the faceplate and rubbed the saliva around before she dipped her mask into the water.

"Now you can put it on." Duvre secured his own around his eyes and nose.

Isobel followed suit and, at first, felt as though she were suffocating. She used to love diving reefs like this one, seeing all the diversity that lurked below the surface, an alien world right beneath her nose. The last time she'd dived, she and Jake had gone together in the nearby Solomon Islands. That trip had been all about fun, beauty, a new experience. She hadn't been a mother then. This dive meant far more.

Watching Duvre, Isobel mimicked his motions, feeling the familiar routine come back bit by bit. She pushed the breather into her mouth and took slow, normal breaths. She gave Duvre the thumbs-up sign, and the two of them lifted themselves off the platform and pushed forward to drop into the water.

Duvre had said the water temp averaged 27°C, and that they wouldn't need wetsuits, but it was still cooler than bathwater. Isobel took a moment to adjust, then nodded to Duvre and they dove.

Light filtered through the water with a bluish cast, yet as clear as it was, visibility stretched only a few meters. Murky silhouettes of schooling fish passed in the distance, scattering at the humans' approach. Longer, streamlined forms of barracuda passed close enough to see their blotched bellies and white fin tips.

As she and Duvre neared their goal, creatures grew more colorful, their forms more varied. A reddish-orange sea slug with ruffled edges waved and flapped along its way to whatever sea slugs might do. Striped bannerfish with their yellow backs swam past, their long white banner fins flowing out behind like a regal train. Ahead, the reef took shape in a solid mass of clustered life that writhed and undulated with the current. Schools of silvery fish passed, darting en masse in sudden changes of direction, bodies flashing in the filtered light. Smaller fish swarmed adjacent to the reef in clouds of bright colors and a wild variety of stripes and spots. The silhouettes of reef sharks haunted the waters, always moving, ever vigilant.

On the reef itself, corals and anemones in more shapes and colors than she could have imagined filled every centimeter along the angled surface. Tiny species filled minuscule niches between the larger animals. She recognized some—sea fans, brain corals, shelf corals that resembled giant mushrooms with flat caps, the star queen which was her target species—but there were too many for an amateur like herself to know them all. Some swayed in the current like clusters of grass or flowers. Others stuck up from the surface like naked, branching trees.

Above and to the right, clusters of white, feathery tentacles swished through the surrounding water and curled inward to feed. Down and to the left hung another that resembled mountain laurel flowers, some open, some closed. A group of orange anemones extended tiny white tentacles like delicate fingers that grasped at the water. At another section, a group of grape-sized puffballs pumped water in and out through their bodies in constant motion that made them appear to be breathing. A black coral stood out amid all the vivid colors, its thick fingers and tiny charcoal-grey tentacles filtering the water.

But the animals that made up the massive edifice weren't the only things living on the reef. Black and white striped sea kraits wove in and around the structure's layers. Clownfish hovered among the anemones. Sea snails, nudibranchs, and starfish crawled along the ridges. A giant clam, wedged in among the rest, siphoned bits of nutrients falling from above. Seahorses in vivid colors and ghostly pipefish—so tiny, so delicate—clung to branches of the coral or darted about in search of a meal. One animal looked something like a jellyfish but wasn't free swimming. Instead, it had attached itself to the crusty outer polyps of another species. What in the world was that? A lump she'd believed was part of the reef flushed a mottled red and brown, pushed out bumps and ridges, then darted away. An octopus.

In the gap between some of the mounds, where tall seagrass grew anchored to sandy ridges, swam a family of dugongs. The reality of their size came through much stronger here than in the photos and online videos. Most of them had been hunted to extinction in years past. This species, if she remembered her studies, was the sole remaining branch of that family in these waters.

Isobel pivoted, her movements slow and ponderous. All around her, life in a dizzying array of colors and shapes went about its business. Batfish she recognized, and a moray, its nose protruding from its hole in the reef. Another animal—an eel?—did the same, but that was no moray. Electric blue with yellow fins, this eel sported feathery protrusions on its nose, and tiny needle-like teeth in its open maw. Isobel gave it plenty of room.

The one thing she didn't see was trash. No plastic bags had snagged on the reef. No soda cans lay on the sandy ridges. No straws floated in the water to fool passing fish. Nothing marked the passage of humans. The animals present both here and in the Solomons ran similar, but the crystalline nature of the water and the immaculate sandy bottom surprised her. The way the Pacific currents circled, it seemed unlikely—if not impossible—to find such an unspoiled site. Every other South Pacific locale she'd visited, as beautiful as they all were, boasted trash. Perhaps this was part of the reason the Nlaantu wanted no outsiders in their territory? She'd have to take pains to hide any trash or waste from them so they would have no cause to complain. Her team could always run a clean-up op before leaving once the project was complete. Leave it as clean as they found it.

But that was an issue for the future. Right now, she focused on Gabe.

Duvre signaled and pointed, and Isobel followed his line of sight. Emerging from the shadows, a tiger shark glided into view. Isobel held her ground, as Duvre had instructed, but damn that was a big shark. Twelve feet, at least. Isobel's pulse hammered in her ears as it swam closer, investigating these intruders in its realm. Duvre's tap on her shoulder reminded her to breathe normally. She tried and failed. What a beautiful animal! So majestic and fearsome! It went its way in peace, cleaner fish keeping easy pace with its enormous mass.

They followed the contour of the atoll for a short way, both noting the locations of the star queen. Isobel swam close to one of the colonies, clusters of bubbles billowing around her from short, rapid breaths. Such tiny animals to shoulder the future of her son, the continuity of her career. She forced herself to take slow, regular breaths and observe in a clinical fashion. If she planned to use this coral to make the Milani treatment, she needed to know all she could about how to grow it in artificial tanks. Others would follow her down later, make further notes, but she wanted to see it for herself.

The star queen's distinctive form lay in patches along the reef, thick enough in many places that they had grown atop one another in layers like underwater condos. Each level of coral grew up from a central "core" support, leaving enough room for the lower colony members to feed. At first glance, the colony resembled one of those flat-topped mushroom-like structures. But on closer inspection, tiny details emerged. The overall mass formed from pale blue-lavender hexagonal cells, each topped with a veiny star design in iridescent blue. At the very center of the star, a spiked purple dot glowed, as if lit from inside. Tiny tentacles extended from the circumference of the purple dots, reaching out to filter the surrounding water and snatching morsels of food into that purple maw. Each of the small hexagons appeared to be a single animal. Yet this one colony consisted of hundreds, maybe thousands of them, their motions combining to make the collective present as a single creature.

She got as close as she could without touching the reef to find the star queen's base. She'd need to know how it attached, what kinds of foundations it required. But the surrounding animals were packed in too tight to see any gaps.

She backed up and scanned left, right. There—a scar where the initial dive team had taken a sample. She swam over to the gap. A small piece of the star queen had remained at the harvest site, missed perhaps, though the animals at the edge of the scar had been compromised and would probably die. The lifeforms around it, though, seemed to grow in such a way as to support one another. Further inspection showed that neighboring animals repeated at each star queen site. Companion animals, perhaps? Each helping the other in some obscure way? She'd let the dive teams know to take samples of those, as well, for planting in proximity to the star queen in Austin.

Closer inspection revealed that star queen had been anchored to the "bones" of older corals, bleached and lifeless. She broke off a piece for study. Perhaps it had a specific chemical compound they could include in Holschtatt's artificial reef structure, something that would improve their chances for successful growth.

She put some distance between herself and the reef again, taking in the whole. All that unspoiled beauty, save for the gouge where divers had pried chunks of the star queen loose. By the time they were finished here, pockmarks like that would mar the living ridge all the way 'round. If their holds allowed adequate space, she would claim from this atoll every piece of star queen they could find. The acknowledgment sobered her. But it isn't like she was killing the last of its kind. The animal would thrive elsewhere in Nlaan, and the protected Coral Triangle.

Besides, this was for Gabe. She pushed away the wisps of doubt about what she'd come here to do.

Duvre signaled the end of the dive, and they swam to the boat. In the distance, coming closer, swam an enormous manta ray, its motions as graceful as a dancer. A school of jellies drifted in the distance, visible because of the rust-colored ruffles beneath their bells. A group of barracuda passed below them, followed by a couple of ghost sharks. Even a sea turtle made an appearance before they surfaced by the dive platform.

Travis helped her aboard, then gave Duvre a lift. Her dive leader pulled his mask off.

"Well?" he asked. "Did you find what you are after?"

She nodded, a little out of breath as she doffed her mask and gear harness. "I did." She glanced at Travis. "The reef is wild with it. We'll have plenty for what we need."

He tugged on his hat. "So, we have a go?"

"Yes. The holding tanks are ready?"

"Almost. The frames are set up in both of them, but the water needs tweaking. While you were diving, I had them run tests to make sure we have the proper pH levels, temperatures, all the essentials. They're adjusting those now. You ready?"

"Yes." The sun felt good on her skin but fair as she was, she didn't dare stay out here long without sunscreen. She moved into the shade of the canopy.

Travis gestured to the pilot, and the dive boat circled around the way it had come.

Isobel slipped out of her flippers and let Duvre take her gear in exchange for a thick towel. She squeezed the water from her ponytail. "Tell the dive crews they can get started as soon as the tanks are ready. I want the live samples first, then we'll begin the harvest for my lab work. How soon can they make the first dive?"

"Thirty minutes, max."

"Good." Isobel dried herself, then wrapped the towel around her waist. "I've got a lot to do."

Travis's amber eyes gleamed. "I guess you do."

Behn-Kaur Residence, Austin, Texas
Thursday, October 31, 5:45 PM

Number of infected: 1

Luk inspected Kyndra's facepaint design, a sugar skull from Marin's tales of Mexican traditions. Flower petals surrounded the black eye circles. Twining vines curled from the corners of her mouth into the blackened hollows of her cheeks. An orange-and-red sunburst covered the bandaid at her chin. She'd dressed all in black, though Luk insisted she put reflective tape around her sleeves and pant legs. With her natural dark coloring, the effect was startling.

"Good job," he said. "You ready?"

"Yep."

"Alrighty then. Let's go." They stepped out onto the porch and Kyn's nose wrinkled.

"That smell's still there."

Luk sniffed the air. "I don't smell anything. Is it the same thing you noticed this morning?"

"Yeah." She sniffed the air like a bloodhound on a scent trail, then swung around the desert willow at the edge of the porch and started toward the corner of the house.

"You sure you want to do this now?" Luk jabbed a thumb at the neighbors' house. "Candy awaits."

Kyn glanced that way. "The other kids aren't there yet. We have a couple of minutes. I think that smell is coming from the side yard. The flowers over there are sick too."

Luk frowned. "The dahlias?"

"Mm hmm."

"Why do you say that?"

She shrugged. "Because they are."

"Okay." He followed her across the front yard and around the corner.

Along the outer wall beside their house, Marin had planted a row of black dahlias in the weeks before Kyndra's fourth birthday. Since then, the tubers had grown every year and spread to cover the whole side of the house. Every plant grew tall, too. Three-foot bamboo stakes provided support, but the dahlias topped them all. A handful of blossoms remained in the front, but withered flowers and plants lay on the ground at the rear of the mulched bed. This late in the season, the blooms would naturally be starting to fade, but this had to be some sort of disease. Many of the leaves had dropped, and the ones left were brown, or covered with fuzzy mildew. He never would have noticed this from the front of the house.

"That's weird. I fertilized them a month ago."

Kyndra stared at the dahlias, and at the other flower beds along the edge of the lawn. "Mom loved these gardens, didn't she?"

A pang tightened Luk's throat. "She sure did. I've let them go, haven't I?"

Kyn's gaze was even more piercing from that sugar-skull mask. "It's okay. We can fix them together."

Luk's brow inched higher. "You want to garden?"

"Sure." She indicated the wilted flowers. "The neighbors might appreciate us fixing up the yard, and it'd be fun. Maybe Sadie can join us, too. When she's not working at Perkatory."

He narrowed his eyes. "Are you playing matchmaker right now?"

She gave him her most innocent expression. "I would never do that, Dad."

"Right." Luk sniffed the air. At last, he caught a whiff of decay. "Oh, I do smell something now."

Kyn walked closer to the sick dahlias. "It's really strong here."

"No, honey, step back." He gestured. No sense letting his daughter find the dead whatever. He parted the drooping dahlia stalks to see the ground beneath.

A squirrel, or what was left of it, rested in the growing shadow beneath the flowers at the far end. Fur spread around the carcass like a puddle, rippled with evidence of insect industry. Exposed skin and what muscle remained stretched in stiff repose, taut against the animal's bony frame. The only thing intact was the tail, which lay separate from the rest.

He straightened. His inquisitive child had been peering past his guard at the remains. "Have you been playing over here?"

"No."

"Then how did you know about all this?"

"I smelled the squirrel."

"What about the flowers?"

"I just knew. I could feel them."

She could feel them? "What—"

From across the street, excited children squealed with laughter. Trick-or-treaters were gathering.

"We can talk about the flowers later. Let's go bag some treats."

Kyndra grinned, her real teeth gleaming between the painted ones on her lips and cheeks, and she took off running.

"Watch for traffic!" he shouted, following at a slower pace. How appropriate to find grisly remains on Halloween. He laughed. Tomorrow was trash day. He'd come out early with a shovel and remove the ex-squirrel to the bins before the truck arrived.

Kyndra waited for him on the sidewalk. They crossed the street in the slanting afternoon light, approaching the neighbor's house with its chunky pumpkin vines along the wall and verdant flora in raised beds, plants heavy with life all through the growing season. Rachel's rampant yard, one of the wildest green spaces in Hyde Park, trumpeted her love of gardening.

Behind their house, which was always in need of small repair, Rachel and Joy had transformed their two-car, two-story garage into the Central Texas Educational Cooperative, a small schoolhouse complete with bathrooms, classrooms, and a lab. The homeschool building never wanted for attention. Most subjects were taught right here, and Kyn loved everything about Cee-Tec. Joy and Rachel's twin boys, along with Kyn and a dozen other neighborhood kids, made up the student body.

The twins must have been at the window. Their door burst open and the boys practically flew into the yard, Zach dressed like a vampire and Oliver like a werewolf. Joy followed, her slender form dressed all in black, and laid down the rules for the group. Rachel came after, stepping over the creeping rosemary to meet Luk. Renegade strands from her red braid gleamed like a frizzy halo.

"You ready to go?" she asked.

"Yep. Some of us more than others." He glanced aside at the trio of costumed kids, Kyndra laughing as loud as Rachel's boys at some joke.

"Any other problems since this morning?" she asked

"Nope. I'll feed her tomorrow before we go out. It's strange though. That's never been an issue before."

"Well, she is about the right age to start her cycles." Rachel shrugged. "That'll change a lot of things."

Luk sighed. "Yeah. I thought of that. I may need your input when that drama begins."

She laughed. "You'll have it."

Joy approached them clutching a giant bowl of candy. Dark bangs hung in shaggy fringes over her pale forehead, strands of grey catching the light.

"Hey, Luk. Kyndra's makeup is fabulous."

"That's more due to her talents than mine, but thanks. You coming with us?"

"No." Rachel reached up to kiss her wife. "Joy's doling out the sugar stash while we gallivant the neighborhood."

All three kids whooped, jumping up and down as their friends approached. Other trick-or-treaters had emerged along the street. The scent of moonflowers drifted on the breeze. In the mulch beneath the sunflowers along the fence, crickets sang their randy come-on to no avail. This late in the season, potential mates had all moved on. A backyard fire burned somewhere in the neighborhood.

Luk waved a greeting to another woman who joined the outing. Behind her, trees rose in dusky silhouettes outlined by the glow from streetlamps beyond. Zach ran over, his vampire mask pushed up.

"Mama Rachel, come on! All the candy's gonna be gone!"

Behind him, a group of neighborhood kids approached with expectant faces and open bags.

"You're up," Rachel told Joy. "Don't forget our Samhain ritual starts at eight. Circle members ought to start arriving around 7:15 to set up the altar in the garden. We still have to eat dinner, too, so—"

"Go." Joy shooed her wife on her way. "I've got this." She winked at Luk and got busy with the candy.

Zach dragged Rachel past the herb beds and out to the street. Luk followed, trying to keep pace.

Their usual route for trick-or-treating followed the same path as his morning excursions with Kyn. Hyde Park was a pretty friendly neighborhood. Only a few porches stood dark, their stingy residents hiding behind closed blinds, segregated from all the fun. Laughing and singing, the co-op group worked their way around the first half of their circuit.

Rachel rambled on about Joy's new position scouting talent for Austin Power's expanded green energy division, then asked about Luk's latest game.

He shoved his hands in his pockets. "I'm behind schedule. Surprised my investors haven't already been hounding me, but I'll have a chance to work on it more this weekend. That's—"

A shriek snatched their awareness to the children twenty feet ahead of them. The group had clustered in the shadows between streetlamps, standing over someone seizing on the ground. He and Rachel broke into a run. The other adult in their group, who'd been further along with a few of the kids, ran over from the other side. All reached the cluster at the same time, and the kids retreated.

On the ground, Kyndra trembled and shook, neck arched at a strange angle. An unearthly strangling sound came from her taut, stretched throat. Both arms had drawn in to twitch and jerk near her chest, her fingers frozen into claws.

Luk cried out and threw himself on his knees beside his daughter, ripping the knees of his jeans along with the skin beneath them. Her eyes had rolled back, their whites visible against the black makeup that made them appear even more sunken. Painted teeth drew tight against her real ones. A trail of saliva ran from her mouth, tracing ghostly paths through layers of color. The smeared sunburst on her chin looked like blood, and her cheeks stretched in a frightening rictus made even more macabre by the skeletal image drawn there.

His mind raced, casting about for anything he'd ever read about what to do for a seizure before he grasped some distant detail.

Turn her over.

Without hesitating, he reached across her shaking body, grabbed her far shoulder and hip, and rolled her onto her side. He shouted, not caring who heard as long as someone obeyed.

"Call an ambulance!"

A thousand questions flashed through his mind, none sticking around long enough to explore, let alone answer. He focused on his daughter, watching for any change, any indication that things were getting worse.

Some part of his brain registered the other children weeping, voices muttering behind and around him as other parents came running to see what had happened. He blinked, and his tears dripped into Kyn's hair. Someone touched his back, said something. He shrugged them off.

"Come on, sweetheart. Come on. Daddy's here."

He murmured comfort as much for himself as for her. The seizure went on and on, lingering for what seemed like an hour. By the time the siren approached, she had calmed, but not awakened. Luk pulled her now limp form into his embrace and rocked her.

"It's okay, Kyn. Help's coming. It's all right."

Paramedics gently pried him away from Kyn. One of them shone a light in each of her eyes. No response in her pupils. Spittle still traced a sticky trail down her skin.

Luk described the seizure to them, his voice halting, aquiver. "Kyn, honey, can you hear me?"

Nothing. Her chest rose and fell in a shallow but steady rhythm. Thank the gods she was still breathing.

One of the medics placed his fingers against Kyndra's limp palm. "Kyn, if you can hear me, squeeze my fingers."

She lay still, so still. Like this morning. Luk's breath caught. This had to be related, didn't it? Oh, he should have taken her to a doctor right then. "Is she—"

The medic shook his head. "We need to get her to the hospital."

Luk's tears came harder. "What is it? Will she be okay? What's—"

"The doctors will figure that out. Are you her parent?"

"Yes," Luk said. She still wasn't moving. "Lukas Behn."

"Is this the first time she's had a seizure?"

"Yes." He gasped out the word, bit off the sob that threatened to follow.

"Sir, I need your permission to take her in for treatment."

"Yes. Yes." Luk rubbed his mouth. "Do what you need to do."

The paramedics slid a stretcher beneath his daughter, then lifted her into the ambulance. Luk climbed in beside her. No one objected.

Rachel finally got his attention. "I'll call Sadie. Have her meet you there."

He nodded until the ambulance doors closed, then watched as the paramedic worked on Kyn. Luk couldn't lose her. She was all he had left.

Come on, babe. Don't do this. Wake up.

He held her hand, prayed to Ganesh, and let the tears fall.

Chapter 4

Aboard the *Pasteur*'s Tender, Vliat, Nlaan Islands
Friday, November 1, 1:50 PM
(Austin, Texas, Thursday, October 31, 7:50 PM)

Number of infected: 1

ISOBEL FACED INTO THE WIND, her focus on the small knob of land that was their destination. She'd been too preoccupied earlier when she went to meet the Nlaantu. Now she'd see it up close. Put her feet in the sand. The idea of time spent on a deserted beach sounded like a little piece of heaven.

Except for Gabe. She missed her boy. Missed both her children. But Gabe was her reason for traveling so far, her reason for staying away so long. She had to come home with a way to help him, or it would all be for nothing.

Travis piloted the boat this time. He'd better know what he was doing. Even from here, she could see bright patches stretching across the dark blue water, shallows where the reef that formed the atoll lurked close beneath the surface. Cross one of those in the wrong boat and you'd be swimming the rest of the way to shore. Any shore.

Travel to the forested islet would take fifteen minutes, at least, because they had to go the long way around the atoll it shared with the harvest site to reach it, and because they couldn't anchor the tech-laden *Pasteur* any closer due to the Nlaantu's restrictions.

Rather than distract Travis, Isobel tried to make out details of their destination as they skirted its barrier reef. Coconut palms were obvious on the uninhabited strip of land, even from a distance. The rest was a tangled jungle. She'd never seen that many shades of green in one place before. The intoxicating fragrance of frangipani reached the tender, carried on the ocean breeze. Too bad it wouldn't reach the *Pasteur*. They could use a bit of perfume out there.

The pitch of the engine's whine dropped to a lower growl and the boat slowed. The surrounding water's hue progressed from cobalt to cerulean to turquoise to aquamarine as Travis decelerated further. At last, the hull scrape-bumped against the sand. Travis jumped out, shoes and all, and pulled the boat farther up onto the shore.

"Watch your step. I don't recommend taking off your shoes. Might be some sharp-edged shells and bits of coral around, and we're a long way from a doctor, Doctor." He winked.

Isobel laughed and allowed him to help her out of the boat.

"Okay," he said. "Now what?"

"What do you mean?"

"What are we doing here? What's our agenda?" He gestured around them. "I assumed you had a scientific reason for wanting to come ashore."

"No. But I'll go stir crazy on the *Pasteur* while we wait for the next load of coral to be brought up. I wanted to explore. Distract myself." She inhaled, breathing in the complex smell of this place, and peered at the jungle that lay not twenty feet in front of them. "Do you think there might be animals in there?"

"Some. Yeah. But nothing big. Too small an environment to support much of any size. Lizards, birds, bats."

She froze. "Bats?"

"Probably." One eye twitched beneath the brim of his hat. "Why?"

He was laughing at her. She was sure of it. "No reason." She scanned the treetops in search of furry flying rodents.

"They won't hurt you," he offered. "They see only the fruit. Or the bugs, depending on the type of bat. You aren't likely to see them anyway. They're nocturnal."

Good. "What kinds of snakes will we see?"

He walked a few steps, staring at the sand along the beach. "I doubt there are any. Not enough food for them to eat. But..." He pointed. "See that mark?"

Isobel joined him. "Where?"

"There." Travis squatted, indicating a swiped mark on the sand.

"Yes. What is it?"

"Flipper mark. Sea turtle." He swept his gaze along the shoreline. "Probably nests hereabouts somewhere."

"Is that a bad thing?"

"No. It's a really good thing if you're the local hoodoo doctor. Turtle eggs sell for big bucks as an aphrodisiac."

Isobel grimaced. "Really?"

"Yep. But it's illegal as hell to disturb the nests. They're protected, especially in this region. Best to leave them be."

She pointed toward the trees. "I'm guessing we don't want to go in there."

Travis shrugged. "It'll be hot. Plants and trees will block the wind. Probably some thorns, too, maybe even some south Pacific version of poison ivy. Not sure what kinds of insects and arachnids we might find." His eyes twinkled beneath the brim of his hat. "But I'm game if you are."

Isobel had worn a t-shirt, shorts, and plain canvas sneakers with no socks. Probably not wise to attempt a jungle expedition without dressing for the occasion. She smiled. "Thanks. I'll pass. What about the beach? No harm in that, right?"

He indicated she should take the lead and set the pace. For a while, they simply walked along the white beach without speaking. Isobel picked up a shell, incomplete, but pretty. She could bring it home for Claire. She turned it over and around, her fingers tracing the contours as she looked out over the lagoon this small islet shared with the tiny ridges of land at the harvest site, on the other side of this particular atoll. Those hadn't been emergent long enough to hold any plant or animal life other than small crustaceans that came up from the reef below, or perhaps a sea bird that swooped down to grab an unwary crab. This one though—

She glanced at the forested cay, then at the beach that stretched out behind them. No other people came here, except perhaps the Nlaantu, if there was anything worth harvesting among the trees and shrubs. What would it be like to spend a week in a place like this? Bring her family? She and Jake could have a second honeymoon? Claire would love the views and the snorkeling. Gabe would build sandcastle after sandcastle, assuming he didn't tremble too badly to put one together.

"You mind if I ask you a question?"

Her guard went up. Was that kind of intro ever anything other than a warning? "You can ask."

Travis seemed to choose his words as they walked. "I've known you a long time. Not on a personal level, of course. Strictly professional. I'd heard your name when you were still at Threet Research, but since you came over to Holschtatt, you've gained quite a reputation for success. As far as I could tell you were always content to do your work in the lab. I never heard of a situation where you went into the field to do your own negotiations or took an active part in gathering the resources for your medicines."

Isobel stopped.

"Why now?" he asked. "Why is this harvest different?"

"I thought you knew."

"I'm clueless. As usual."

Isobel took a few steps. The lagoon's center, that characteristic blue of the Pacific, lay surrounded by the paler color of shallows. How deep was the lagoon at its center? Was it open at the bottom to allow animals and fish to pass between this small, protected space and the wider wilds beyond? On the far side, beyond the sandy spits, the two dive boats floated at anchor, their captains taking advantage of the shade in the small cabins.

He moved beside her but did not pressure her to answer.

She smiled again. "Are you familiar with Milani Syndrome?"

"Can't say I am."

"What about Huntington's Disease?"

"I've heard of that," he said. "I know it's bad."

Isobel barked a laugh. "Yeah. Bad." She took a breath of perfumed air. "Milani is similar, but rarer, with some differences in the symptoms. In the early stages, it causes confusion, mood swings, myoclonus."

He frowned. "Myo what?"

"Involuntary twitching."

His expression cleared, but he didn't speak.

"Milani patients carry an aberrant gene which causes proteins to mutate and become brittle and toxic. They break apart into shards that damage the organs, including the brain." Out on the water, slender sandbars breached the surface above divers who even now harvested the star queen that might be Gabe's miracle. "As the disease progresses, voluntary muscle coordination decreases. They lose the ability to walk, speak, even read, since they can't control their eye movements. After that, the muscles begin to control the patient with unpredictable, sometimes violent spasms. Brain function declines, along with cognitive function. After that—"

Her voice pinched off the rest of her words.

"No brain function means no autonomic function." Travis's voice came low, barely louder than the waves and wind. "Patient death, I presume."

She nodded.

His features crinkled in a perpetual squint.

The cry of sea birds, indistinct from one another in her ears, carried on the breeze. Isobel had the crazy urge to take her shoes off and dig her toes in the pristine white sand.

"Which one of your kids has this disease?"

Her stomach dropped. "How did you know?"

"Because you're standing here on this godforsaken patch of sand, thousands of miles from your family. You're living and working on a boat in the ass end of the Earth with a load of guys who, in case you didn't realize, are on their best behavior due to your presence, not to mention my threats." He winked. "You're a scientist, yes, but unless I miss my guess, you'd much rather be at home every evening with your family."

Isobel wrinkled her nose. Talking about it hurt almost as bad as that helpless feeling that pushed her to keep trying, keep trying. "You aren't wrong."

"Which one?"

"My boy. Gabe."

"How old is he?"

"A little over five years."

"How long does he have?"

Isobel's head swung from side to side in slow motion. "I wish I knew. A year. Maybe two. Maybe less."

"Jesus wept." Travis took his hat off and ran fingers over his short grey hair before tugging the woven Panama back into place. "Huntington's is genetic, ain't it?"

"Usually, yes. Not always."

"Is Milani?"

She nodded.

"You've seen this before, then. A sibling?"

Miserable memories of her twin's slow decline and painful death stabbed as sharp now as they did all those years ago.

"Yes. My sister."

"And this coral will fix your boy?"

"There's no cure." Isobel swallowed the lump in her throat, amazed at the steadiness in her voice. "But it looks promising as a treatment that might let him live a more normal life."

"I sure hope you're right, Doctor Fallon. For his sake, and yours."

Across the lagoon, next to one of the boats, divers surfaced with a filled net. Her first test batch.

She pointed. "I think I'm about to start finding out. Let's beat them to the *Pasteur*."

He waved her on. "Lead the way, Doc."

**Rhue Children's Hospital, Austin, Texas
Thursday, October 31, 8:00 PM**

Number of infected: 1

Luk sat in the ER waiting room while doctors ran all the immediate tests—is the patient breathing? Is she bleeding? Is there a high fever? Is she in cardiac arrest? Is she in shock? Is her blood sugar too low? Is she hyponatremic?—and followed with questions for Luk. Has Kyndra been diagnosed with epilepsy, Tourette's, or other such conditions? What medications was she taking? What was she doing when the seizure started? Were there flashing lights or repetitive sounds that might have triggered the seizure? What had she eaten earlier in the day?

Luk batted at their questions like mosquitos, trying to see where they would lead, but then the doctors had disappeared without offering any answers. He sat reliving that awful memory, seeing Kyn on the ground, holding her while she seized, watching helplessly on the interminable ride to the hospital. He kept seeing her contorted form, her sugar skull smeared and ominous, as she lay on the ground in the dark. She'd been so excited to do her own makeup this year...

"Mr. Behn?"

Luk looked up. A middle-aged woman stood before him, her greying auburn hair pulled into a tight bun. He lurched to his feet.

"Yes."

"I'm Doctor Whitfield," she said.

Sadie rounded the corner behind Whitfield, and his friend quickened her pace to join them. Luk hugged her. "Thanks for coming."

"Of course." Her voice hummed in his ear before she withdrew.

"This is my friend," he told the doctor. "She can hear anything you have to tell us."

"Why don't we get comfortable?" Whitfield sat across from Luk. "I'd like to chat a bit."

Luk's heart sank. This didn't sound good. He perched on the edge of his seat, Sadie beside him.

"Mr. Behn, an MRI showed no cranial trauma and no abnormal mass or occlusions. There is no evidence of stroke. However, both the MRI and Kyndra's bloodwork show signs of an infection. We believe this may be affecting her brain."

Luk grasped Sadie's hand. "How serious?"

"We don't know yet. We need to run more tests to be sure. Because Kyndra's symptoms are different from what we'd expect to see in some very significant ways, we're treating this with care."

"Different how?" Luk leaned forward.

"Well," Whitfield glanced at her notes, "she has a fever, which is normal for an infection. But her pupils are dilated, and there's no swelling of lymph glands. You said there had been no vomiting or diarrhea, no fatigue. But her white blood cell count is off the charts, so we want to be sure what we're dealing with, for Kyndra's sake. Our resident infectious medicine specialists are working with epidemiologists in the health department to determine what, exactly, is going on. Once we figure that out, we'll know how best to help your daughter. All right?"

"Yes. Of course."

"Good. Let's start with a few questions. Has your daughter ever been out of the country?"

"Yes."

"When and where did she visit last?"

"India. February, year before last."

"Where in India?"

"Amritsar."

"How long was she there?"

The memory sprang to Luk's mind, fresh enough to hurt even after all this time. Encounters with Marin's parents, never an easy task, had been fraught with more tension than usual when he brought their daughter's body for the Antam Sanskar. She might have strayed from the strict Sikh path her parents had laid, but she'd always wanted a traditional funeral.

"A week."

The doctor scrawled on her tablet. "Did you stay in Amritsar the entire time?"

The sacred readings had already begun when he and Kyn arrived at Marin's family home, and continued in segments throughout their visit. The Shabads. Singing the kirtan. The recitations. Holding Kyndra close while Marin's father lit the pyre. Waiting for the collection of her ashes. Convincing her parents to allow him to keep a small container of them. It was all he had left of her.

Except for Kyndra.

"Yes," he said, his tone flat.

"Did you eat at any of the bazaars or drink anything out of an unsealed container?"

"We ate only food cooked in my in-laws' kitchens. We drank whatever they served us. It was not sealed."

"And she's not been out of the country since that time?"

"No."

"Well," Whitfield said, "I can't imagine that is the root of this problem. It was too long ago, but since we're unfamiliar with this malady, I want to be sure. Let's talk about more recent events. Can you give me a rundown of what she's eaten in the last few weeks?"

"Um," Luk started. He glanced at Sadie, then back at the doctor. "I mean, I don't..."

"A general idea will be a good start. Anything unusual?"

"No." Luk raked fingers through his hair. "Just the things we always favor. Pasta, beans, salads, veggie burgers. Pizza. Granola. You know."

"Have you eaten at any new restaurants?"

"No. We don't eat out much."

"And no chance she's eaten anything spoiled? No bad eggs or milk?"

"We're vegan. And I'm pretty sure she would have mentioned eating something 'ooky,' her word for spoiled."

"You're vegan?" Whitfield repeated. "Kyndra too?"

"Yes. Why?"

Whitfield gave him an accusing scowl. "She's very small."

"Her mother was small." Luk kept his voice even.

"I see." Whitfield's expression seemed to show exactly what she thought of Luk's defense. "You do realize that many conditions are exacerbated by nutritional deficiencies."

"She isn't deficient in anything."

"Has her doctor run a metabolic panel in the last year?"

Luk's jaw worked. "Well, no."

"I see." Whitfield tapped her screen. "I'll order one. Vegan diets are very restrictive. Adults can choose to eat those processed fake meats even knowing their high fat and sodium content, but we usually recommend that children have a more...complete diet."

Luk bristled. It had been important to Marin to follow a sustainable, vegan lifestyle. He'd gone along with it because he couldn't fault her arguments and because he already didn't eat much meat anyway. She'd always made sure their meals were healthy, nutritious. But he'd strayed into more convenient options, choosing from the growing number of meat and cheese alternatives. Maybe Doctor Whitfield had a point about the fat content. He'd have to research that.

"I will need a list of the foods she's been eating, after all. If they're processed, I'll want brands, quantities, everything you can think of. There may be an allergen in there that could have provoked this response."

Luk ground his teeth in a mouth gone dry. His stomach knotted at this rebuke. But when he drew a breath to defend his choices on behalf of his family, words fled. Sadie squeezed his hand.

"I'll start on it as soon as we finish here."

"Very good. Has Kyndra been sleeping well?"

"Usually, yes," Luk said. "But this morning I found her in the yard, still asleep on her feet."

Sadie's grip tightened. "She sleepwalked?"

"I take it she's never done that before," Whitfield said.

"No. Never."

"Has she been under a lot of stress lately?"

"No more than usual. Her homeschool co-op is reading for tests, but they do that every year."

Whitfield raised an eyebrow. "She's homeschooled?"

The knots in Luk's stomach jumped into his chest. "Yes."

"May I ask why?"

Luk forced a smile. "Is it relevant to her seizure?"

Whitfield's face closed even more than it had been before. "Mr. Behn, anything might help determine what's wrong with your daughter."

"Her mother liked the idea of a smaller classroom, more personalized instruction. We found one we liked and started her there as soon as she was old enough."

"Where is her mother now?"

Whitfield might as well have slapped him. "Her mother is dead."

At least the doctor had the good grace to look chagrined. "Was it from illness or accident?"

"She crashed in a helicopter." Luk's syllables snapped off at his teeth like crisp raw vegetables.

Whitfield scratched more notes.

"Could Kyndra be taking drugs or drinking alcohol without you knowing?"

"No!"

The doctor rested her tablet on her knee. "Mr. Behn, I apologize if some of these questions are upsetting. I'm trying to get to the bottom of what's happening with your child. Bear with me."

He made an effort to loosen his shoulders.

"Now. Has Kyndra had migraines at all?"

"No."

"Has she been doing anything outside her usual routine?"

"No."

"Has anyone else in her co-op shown signs of illness?"

"No."

"Is this seizure the very first sign you've seen that something is out of the ordinary?"

"No. This morning she sort of blacked out and fell on her bike."

At this, Whitfield perked up. "Why do you say she blacked out?"

"Because she was unconscious when I first got to her."

"How long did that take?"

"Three seconds. I was right there with her when it happened."

Whitfield frowned. "Does she do that a lot?"

"Fall on her bike?" He shrugged. "It's happened. She's a kid. But faint? That was a first. She was talking, everything seemed fine until she fell over."

"You were riding with her?"

"No. I run. She rides."

"Do you do that often?"

"Every morning."

"Does she eat breakfast first?"

"Not usually, but I'd planned to start." Luk winced. "Is it possible that she got this infection from that fall? From one of her scrapes?"

"Probably not," Whitfield said. "But I'll check it out. Is that the only unusual thing in her routine?"

Sadie nudged him. "What about the spider you told me about? From this morning."

"Spider?" Whitfield said. "Was she bitten?"

"No, nothing like that. But she's been afraid of them her whole life until this morning."

"What makes you say she's no longer afraid?"

Luk grunted. "Because she scooped one off her bike with her bare hands and put it in the bushes before we went for our outing."

"You're sure it didn't bite her?"

"No. She would have made it known. Trust me."

"And she'd shown no indication of overcoming that fear before then?"

"Nope." He couldn't begin to count the number of times she'd scared the daylights out of him with that little-girl scream. He'd come running to discover an eight-legged monster, sometimes barely visible, on the wall or floor or ceiling, and be obliged to carry it outside into the wild. "Never."

"Huh," the doctor said, almost under her breath.

"And she smelled a dead animal in the yard when I smelled nothing. And she told me the dahlias on the side of the house were sick. When I went to find the dead whatever, I found out she was right. About the animal and the flower bushes."

"Well, yes. But she could have seen the bushes. And some people have a much keener olfactory sense than others. That's probably unrelated."

Luk nodded.

She went on questioning him at length. Had anyone around Kyndra exhibited any of these symptoms? Had her sleeping patterns changed? Her appetite? Was she currently taking any medications, prescribed or homeopathic? On and on and on.

At last, Whitfield finished. "I know that was grueling, Mr. Behn, but if I'm going to track down what's ailing Kyndra, I'll need all the information I can get. If you come up with anything else, anything at all, please let me know."

"I will. When is she going to wake up?"

"I don't know, but I want to admit her until we know what's happening. The sooner she wakes, the better her prognosis. Besides, she might give us more answers. You're welcome to stay the night with her. Every room has a pull-out sofa bed and a full bathroom with a shower."

"They do?" Luk said, blinking. "I expected to be sleeping in a chair."

"Not these days." Whitfield stood. Sadie and Luk followed suit.

"Thank you, Doctor Whitfield," he said. "I appreciate everything you're doing for my daughter."

"It's no trouble. The staff will move her to a room shortly. I want to get to the lab and see if they've uncovered any additional clues. I'll be on rotation until 11:00. Please have someone page me if you have questions."

She walked away, leaving him no closer to an answer now than he had been before.

"Hang in there," Sadie said. She pulled a napkin from her purse and wiped his jaw. The paper came away black with greasepaint from Kyn's sugar skull mask. "They're gonna figure this out. We'll get through it together."

"I'm glad you're here."

"I wouldn't be anywhere else." She twined her fingers in his.

His cell phone rang, making him jump. He dragged it out and glanced at the screen.

Simon Tanaka. His chief investor.

Luk thumbed it on.

"Hello, Simon." He stuck out his tongue. Sadie grimaced at what they both knew was coming.

"Hello, Luk. I just came from a meeting with William Sato, Bob Rush, and Holly Muldin. They asked me to get an update on Hyde and Seek."

"I know I promised it almost a week ago. But my daughter had a seizure tonight. I'm at the hospital with her now."

"Oh, dear." Simon tsked. "I'm sorry to hear that. Is she going to be okay?"

"They don't know yet. She's still unconscious. They're admitting her to monitor her progress."

"How are you holding up? I know this must be a difficult time for you."

Luk almost laughed. "It is. My friend Sadie is helping a lot. I'm managing."

"Glad to hear it." Simon paused. "I don't mean to be indelicate, but what should I tell the others about your completion date for the game?"

Luk shut his eyes. "I'll work on it as best I can, but you have to understand that when I projected a release date I couldn't have known about this delay."

"I see."

"I would rather finish the game once I have some resolution on Kyn's medical issue. It's difficult to think about anything other than my daughter right now." Luk forced himself to remain calm. "I don't want to rush Hyde through completion and launch a buggy product."

"No," Simon said. "Of course not. But we're running out of time to finalize, promote, and sell the game before the holiday. Please don't misunderstand, Luk. BehnWerks is your company. I don't mean to press, especially during your family crisis. I'd appreciate it if you would keep me posted so I can inform the others. And please know you and Kyn are in our prayers during this trying time."

Sure they were. "Thank you, Simon. I appreciate that."

Luk ended the call. He did not need investors breathing down his neck, but he wasn't going to allow them to pressure him. Not now. They'd have to wait. He texted his assistant to let her know he wouldn't be in tomorrow, set the phone on vibrate, and shoved it in his pocket.

Sadie rubbed his shoulder, a calming gesture that needed no words. "You good?"

"Yes. Thanks again for coming." He hugged her and she returned the embrace. His cheeks burned, and he fought against the pangs of conscience that surged wraith-like in his chest.

Why should it be this hard to show his fondness for a friend? It's not like it was a new sensation. He'd hugged Sadie a thousand times before Marin's death. Of course, at that time, she was Marin's best friend, not to mention the manager of Marin's coffee shop, Perkatory. Sadie had been around so often she was almost a member of the family. Luk had no qualms about it then, but now he felt guilty every time as if he were being unfaithful.

He squashed the self-reproach, annoyed with himself. Hugging Sadie did not equal betrayal. Besides, it felt good to have someone's arms around him. They stood like that a few minutes before a nurse came to show them to Kyn's room. He pulled away, his solid world uprooted, anchored to the here and now by Sadie's hand, and the two of them followed the nurse down the corridor.

Chapter 5

Aboard the *Pasteur*, Vliat, Nlaan Islands
Monday, November 4, 3:15 AM
(Austin, Texas, Sunday, November 3, 8:15 AM)

Number of infected: 2

ISOBEL SAT UP IN HER BUNK AND GLANCED AT HER PHONE. In Austin, Jake and the kids would be starting their day. She flipped on a lamp, opened her laptop, and called home. Jake answered almost immediately.

"Hey." He leaned closer to the screen. "The kids have been expecting your call."

"I know. I wish I could budget for more than one damn call per week."

"No problem. You arrived in one piece, then? The Nlaantu gave their okay?"

"They did." Isobel yawned and stretched. "The divers began a few days ago."

"Good. The board's getting restless. They were hoping for a faster result. They aren't patient types."

She huffed. "That's unreasonable. You and I both know this trip is going to take at least two more weeks. And that's given ideal circumstances. If there are any storms—and there might be, this is the season, you know—that'll keep us out of the water. The teams need rest, too."

"Break them into units. Work around the clock."

"I'm already doing that. This might be my first field trip, but I'm not a total newbie at project management. Give me some credit."

"I know. But if you don't show some progress soon, they'll cancel the harvest. Recall the ship."

"I'm aware, Mr. CEO." She kneaded neck muscles strung tight as piano strings. What she wouldn't give for a good massage right now. "I've got the project in hand. Travis is pushing the crew as hard as he can."

"Travis's job isn't on the line."

Isobel jerked her gaze to his. "But mine is?"

Jake shrugged, broad shoulders straining the seams of his Eton shirt. "I've got your back, as best I can. Just don't let this go too far. We're already under the microscope as the only exception to Holschtatt's rule against fraternization. If the board has to hear me defend my wife too often, their tolerance will run out. Mr. Neillsen worries that you're letting your interest in this project cloud your judgment."

She recoiled. "*My* interest? What about yours, Jake? Gabe is your son, too."

"This is not only about Gabe. Try to keep that in mind."

"It is for me." She stared at her husband. "I understand Holschtatt's chairman might not have the same level of emotional investment, but this genetic disorder runs in my family." Grampa Ben's little brother, who she'd never met. Isobel's twin sister, who she'd watched die. Gabe, who—

Her racing thoughts stuttered to a halt. "My experience in this matter makes me an even greater asset on the project. I've had a detailed preview of our son's horrific future if this fails, and that's the greatest motivation to find a treatment I can imagine."

"Come on, Bel. Our family's stake in the project is undisputed but personal. For Holschtatt, it's business. The ball is rolling, sweetheart. You convinced the company— against their better judgment—to move forward on treatment for a disease rare enough that no one else would fund the R&D.

They've invested a lot of money already, on travel and fuel alone. Hell, putting the *Pasteur* out to sea for a trip like this costs the same amount as six months of my salary. We aren't talking peanuts. And every day it's operational compounds the bill. You're way out on a limb there, Bel. I sure hope that branch is going to hold you because if you fail they will eat you alive."

He shifted in his seat, his muscles gliding beneath the fabric of his tailored clothing. Amazing, how he could move her to laughter. To passion. To drink. She'd opened her mouth to retort when Gabe came into view.

"Mommy?"

Jake swept their boy up to see the screen. "Say hi, buddy."

"Hi, Mommy!" He pointed at the screen. "Mommy's on TV."

"Hey, sweetheart! I can hear you. Are you being a good boy?"

He began to chatter about his day, his toys, his friends…

Isobel frowned. What friends was he talking about? He had a few, but his life was pretty isolated because he'd never been able to go to nursery school or kindergarten. She didn't recognize the names he mentioned. She glanced at Jake, who shook his head, a small warding gesture, and she refrained from comment.

"Mommy, will you read me a bedtime story tonight?"

Jake's lips pressed together in a thin line. Isobel smiled at her son. "Honey, Mommy is at work. Remember? I'm on a boat, in the water. I won't be able to come home tonight. Daddy will be happy to read you a story. Won't you, Daddy?"

But Gabe wasn't going to be satisfied with that. "Daddy doesn't do the voices like you do."

"Oh, I'm sure Daddy can do the voices even better if you ask him to. Right, Daddy?" She glared at her husband.

"I'll do great voices, buddy," Jake promised. "You go pick out which story you want me to read, and we'll do it tonight after you have your bath and get into your pajamas. Okay?"

Gabe squealed and slid down from Jake's knee. Before he could run off, Claire came onscreen. She'd French braided her hair with pale blue ribbon wound in and...was she wearing makeup? She was ten! Isobel had wanted to be there when her daughter first experimented with cosmetics. Apparently, she'd waited too long.

"My turn! Hi, Mom."

"Hey, sweetie! You look beautiful."

Claire grinned. "Thanks. I'm just playing around. Nothing special. How's your trip going?"

"Slow. I'd rather be there with you. Or have you here with me. It's a beautiful place, with white beaches, pretty shells, and lots of stuff to see on the reef. Maybe we can take a family vacation over here sometime and you can see it for yourself."

"Really?" Claire squealed. "But I thought those people didn't want any strangers on their island."

"The Nlaantu don't," Isobel explained. "But there are lots of other islands where we could go. Fiji, New Caledonia, Tongo, the Solomons. You should do some research on South Pacific island vacations, and make a list of the ones you'd like to see." Those weren't as pretty. Still, they'd be new to the kids. Assuming Gabe was still around to see them.

"That would be amazing!"

They chatted a while longer about Claire's girl scout trip, the science fair project she had coming up next semester, her grades.

Finally Jake claimed some time with his wife. Claire blew Isobel a kiss and disappeared.

"She's growing up so fast." Isobel heard the note of longing in her voice.

"Tell me about it. Soon she'll be asking to borrow the car."

Isobel rolled her eyes. "Don't rush it."

"I'm gonna sign off. But listen. You be careful over there. Both on the island and with the project. I know how important this is, to both of us. But don't gamble everything. If you throw all your chips onto this one bet and it comes up zilch, you will have sacrificed any future chances to throw the dice. Keep something in reserve, hmm?"

"I feel like you have as little faith in me as Niellsen. I counted on you to support me, Jake."

"I do. I have complete faith in you and that's how I know it's all going to be fine. The project's going to be a success, and you'll develop a treatment for Gabe and all the other Milani patients. Think how many families this will save." He winked. "You always get nervous when you start a project. And if this one doesn't work the way you expect, I know you'll find another way to resolve the issue. Mark my words."

After she'd ended the call, Isobel savored a rare interlude of quiet. Such an ephemeral thing. External, always. She had yet to find the magic that would quell her internal drive, leave her feeling that no one wanted anything, needed anything, from her. Success with a Milani treatment could bring that. Hope, an ever-moving target always just out of reach, drew her forward. She closed her eyes and took a minute to herself before she rose, grabbed a jacket, and left the cabin behind.

Even at this hour, shipboard life never slowed. She followed the deck's open side passage to the stern of the *Pasteur* where the next diving team stood near the ladder, geared up and ready to leave. Even as she joined the group, Duvre followed the others down the ladder sporting a headlamp and additional nets. Travis directed a deck light down onto their crews.

"You got everything?" he called.

The dive captain yelled a response, and both engines on the smaller boats revved, sending the crew on their shift.

Travis looked up at her approach. "Hey, Doc. Didn't reckon I'd see you on deck at this hour."

She pulled her hoodie over bare shoulders. Even on this warm night, ocean breezes cooled her skin. "I needed some air."

Isobel watched the boats depart and sucked in a breath. All along the trail of their wake, the water glowed with vivid blue sparkles that shimmered and winked. "What is *that?*"

"Bioluminescent plankton. Lights up when it's disturbed. Pretty, ain't it?"

She didn't bother to respond, entranced as she was by the lights in the water. They lingered long after the boats had passed.

He gestured. "Here. Look straight down."

She went to the rail. Ripples of blue light ran alongside the *Pasteur* with every movement of the vessel. She laughed. Her kids would love this.

"You want to see something spectacular?" Travis said.

"Sure."

He called a caution to the deck crew, then murmured into his radio, and the entire ship went dark. Isobel stumbled and grasped the rail, blinded by the sudden darkness. "What the—"

"Patience."

Seconds later, pinpoints of light began to appear above the ship. Off to one side, she saw the distant glow of the dive crews' headlamps at the project site. A minute later, the sky twinkled from horizon to horizon. Isobel gasped. She'd never seen so many stars in the night sky.

"Look behind us," Travis murmured.

She did. An enormous streak of light, cloud, and darkness painted the sky above the western horizon. "Is that..." She paused, uncertain.

"The Milky Way. Yes, ma'am."

Isobel gawked like a child. "I've never seen it before, except in pictures or movies."

"You won't. Not in Austin. Too much light at night. Washes out the sky. You wouldn't have seen it here on a lighted deck." He gazed at the stars. "You ask me, a person could get used to a view like that. Grow to like it."

She watched with him until something out on the water caught her attention.

Another trail of blue luminescence, coming from the direction of the Nlaantu main islands, crept out from behind the small islet where she and Travis had explored a few days ago. She pointed. "What's that?"

Travis spun.

"I'm guessing a Nlaantu boat," he murmured. "Close your eyes. I'm gonna raise the lights." He lifted the radio again, giving the order.

Even through her closed lids, Isobel saw the flare of light. When she opened them again, the approaching boat was visible by the dim lantern it carried as well as by the trail of blue light in the ripples left by the boat and its oarsman.

"Do they come out here every night?"

"No, ma'am," he said. "This'll be the first time."

There must be something wrong. But what? She'd made it clear to Travis that the crew must follow their advisories from their hosts at all times. As far as she knew, they had.

So why the wee-hour visit?

Everything else was on schedule. Thus far, the live coral polyps had accepted the plugs and seemed to be happy in their new tank environment, an essential step since harvesting was the first of many pieces in this project. For long-term testing and manufacture, they'd need to establish a local Austin farm where the coral would thrive in an artificial environment. Isobel had already lined up two marine parks to establish enormous tanks and oversee the growth and maintenance of artificial reefs. In exchange, Holschttat would pay each park a cut of the proceeds from the finished drug. The board had signed with grudging approval. Sure, they stood to lose a lot of money if this treatment didn't work, but they weren't the only ones throwing the dice here. If this project failed, it would bury her son as well as her career.

Their skepticism made sense. Initial trials on any drug produced from the coral proteins were at least a year away. But creating the coral farm was the easiest part of this whole process. Environmentalists had been seeding corals in labs for

years now. Field tests required more time, more steps. Raw
harvesting. Initial sorting and processing. Refining and
sifting. After spending the last three days in the *Pasteur*'s lab
with her assistant, Seppo, they'd managed to segregate a
sizable sample of the coral proteins and could start binding the
Milani fragments tomorrow. Or rather today, in a few short
hours.

Unless the Nlaantu threw a contaminant into the works
and mucked up her plans.

The boat, with the translator and the oarsman, neared the
Pasteur. Isobel bit her lip.

At last, the boat reached them and the Nlaantu's
translator climbed the ladder despite wearing a skirt. Deck
lights lent an orange tint to her brown skin and pale clothing.
Shiny black hair fell in soft curls to her shoulders. Her bare
feet stood apart on the deck with accustomed confidence.

Travis greeted the woman. "You honor us, T'nei."

She glanced at him but spoke to Isobel without observing
the niceties. "You must stop working at once. Power down your
lights. Run dark after the sun sets."

Isobel frowned. "May I ask why?"

"Many of the corals are due to spawn within the week.
Your lights will interrupt their cycles. You must run dark."

Surely she wasn't serious. Isobel exchanged a look with
Travis. He gave a little shrug.

"We can't do that," she told the translator. "We need the
lights to continue our work in safety aboard the boat. And our
divers are blind at night without their lights."

"You must not dive at night. No harvesting after sunset.
This is a requirement of Mtuji. You will obey it, or you will
leave."

Isobel's breath stuttered. Leave?

Travis stepped forward. "If this is Mtuji's wish, we will of
course obey." He cautioned Isobel with a small flick of his
fingers. "But we risk harm to our people to operate without
lights on the ship while we stay."

T'nei listened, watched him speak, then responded to
Isobel. "You have coverings for your windows, do you not?
Hangings that will block the light, hold it inside the ship's
rooms?"

"Yes." Isobel considered the translator. "We can use those
for work inside the cabin. But that won't help workers on the
deck."

"Do your outside tasks in the sunlight. If we must repeat
this demand, we will withdraw our welcome. Mtuji has
spoken."

Without another word, T'nei retreated down the ladder.

Travis spoke at her shoulder as their Nlaantu visitors
departed. "Well?"

"Well what?"

"Should I recall the dive teams?"

Damn it. Mr. Neillsen would chafe at the delay. Jake's
comments about the daily expense of running the *Pasteur*
whispered in her thoughts. This would double the project's
costs, not to mention its timeline. How much longer could
Gabe hold on?

She gripped the rail, her knuckles white.

"Do it."

Travis spoke into the radio, passing instructions to the
surface teams aboard the dive boats, and the deck crew on the
research vessel.

Isobel heard his words, heard the commotion of the deck
crew as they secured their work for the night. At the project
site, dive lights came up to the surface one by one. Lights on
the deck went out except the one the dive boats needed to
navigate their way to the *Pasteur*. All the while, the glowing
blue trail of T'nei's wake receded into the distance until it
vanished around the bend.

Travis and Isobel stood a long while in silence, staring out
at the black water.

"It's gonna get dark out here in a few," Travis said. "You
wanna come inside?"

Her features twisted into a sour moue. Did T'nei have children? Were they ever sick? "No. I'm gonna stay out here a while. Watch the stars."

"You want some company?"

Isobel tried and failed to smile. "I'm fine. But thanks."

He withdrew on quiet feet. Moments later, the dive team tied up their boats, climbed aboard, and passed her without speaking. As soon as their equipment was stowed, and they'd gone inside, the lights went out.

She waited for her vision to clear, then lifted her face to the stars, and murmured a prayer.

Chapter 6

Rhue Children's Hospital, Austin, Texas
Sunday, November 3, 9:45 AM

Number of infected: 2

KYN WOULDN'T WAKE UP.

Nurses and orderlies came and went, first hooking Kyn to machines and an IV, then setting up systems to manage her body's waste. From the first day, the morning routine included bathing her and brushing her teeth, shifting her position in the bed, and working her joints in a slow, gentle way. Luk spoke to her as much as he could, chattering on about every sort of inanity as though she could hear every silly word. Through it all, she slept.

Several nurse stations positioned along the corridor meant all the patients in this wing were under twenty-four-hour observation. A curtain offered privacy when necessary. Natural light flooded in from the window where Luk glimpsed greenery in the sculpted grounds two floors below and across the street in Mid-City Park. A sofa positioned beneath the pane pulled out into a full-size bed.

Sadie had brought his toothbrush that first day, then returned every morning with a bagel, coffee, and fresh clothes. She would stay a while before she had to leave to manage her business, but she always came back. She kept Rachel and Joy in the loop and passed on to him their encouragement. She went by his house each day to make sure everything was in order and brought him a couple of battery-operated tea lights to use in his daily devotions. She even sat with Kyn while he checked in with his office. His assistant told him the web manager had put a message on their site about Kyn so BehnWerks clients would know why there was a delay in the latest game. He'd also placed a call to Simon with an update. The man asked about Kyn and told Luk they were all praying for her.

Hospital staff couldn't tell him why his daughter lingered in this near-coma state. Their furrowed brows, copious notes, and hushed conferences outside her door after every exam told Luk it worried them. Nurses had changed her IV a couple of hours ago and later came to take blood for another metabolic panel. When he'd asked why, the nurse said the first one came back normal, and Doctor Whitfield wanted confirmation.

That doctor's suspicion that he may have harmed his own child deflated Luk. Instead of trying to debate her points, he had chanted a mantra for healing. He had faith in Dhanvantari, and in Mariamman. They would watch over Kyndra and bring her to wellness.

Sadie brought his computer, too, and he'd tried to work on Hyde and Seek. All the rooms had internet access, but Luk hadn't been able to drag his thoughts from what was happening with Kyn. Instead of his usual desk set-up of coffee cup and computer, the counter and desk along one side of the room sported flowers, cards, and cheerful toys. Scrawled stickies that would normally be taped to the wall above his desk had been exchanged for colorful drawings and photos taken by her friends and classmates on the walls around her room. Gifts from all those she'd touched. Testaments to the joy his daughter shed on everyone around her.

Luk pulled himself off the sofa and drifted over to the cards, reading them again even though he'd memorized each one. Rachel and Joy and all the other families in the co-op.

Neighbors up and down their street. Sadie and her employees had signed a giant card that took center stage on the desk. Kyn had yet to read a single one.

He leaned against the counter. This was nothing like her cozy room at home. A row of electrical outlets, oxygen equipment, and medical apparatus stretched across the opposite wall. Multiple machines on a roll-around pole stood next to Kyn's bed, their readouts displayed on a digital screen atop a wall support. A special ceiling light hung centered above on a long, jointed arm. All this equipment and still his daughter was sick. Before this happened, all the tech she'd needed was her bike, an iPad for homework, and his iPhone for games. Four days ago, she'd been happy, laughing. Four days ago, he'd considered chiding her for leaving a towel on the bathroom floor.

Four days had changed his entire world.

Luk frowned, looking away from the equipment. He filled a cup with water at the sink and refreshed the vases beneath daisies, carnations, even one with bougainvillea that came this morning from Marin's parents. Their flowers had already begun to droop. Why had they sent such a fragile blossom? Maybe it was their way of saying he shouldn't hold too tightly to something that, by its very nature, was ephemeral.

He'd always respected Marin's family religion, even though they disapproved of his wife's openness to faith in all its forms. Marin had taught him and Kyndra both about world cultures and spiritual beliefs, and together they had developed a multi-faith family approach to the Divine. But he would never quietly accept what was happening with Kyndra, as he expected his in-laws would have done. He would fight it with everything he had.

Luk dragged a hand over his face. He shouldn't be hard on them. They might not agree with his ways, but at least they had accepted their daughter's marriage to an unbeliever. They'd accepted Kyndra, too, and loved her as much as they could from afar. It was more than he could say of his own parents, who'd renounced any connection to him when he married an Indian woman. They didn't even know they had a granddaughter. He was fine with that. They didn't want him, and he didn't want them.

His phone vibrated against the surface of the table near the sofa. Luk picked it up and thumbed it on.

"Hello?"

"Luk, we're downstairs in the ER," Joy said, her voice thick. "Zach—"

"He's sick?"

Pause. "Yes."

"Oh hell." Luk crossed the room and rushed into the corridor. "I'll be right there."

At the elevators, he stabbed the button even though it was already lit. Half a dozen people waited there. After a minute, he spun on the balls of his feet and took the stairs at a trot. On the first floor, Joy stood outside the ER corridor, her fingers toying with her pentacle necklace.

"Any change in Kyn?" she asked, her eyes red.

"No," Luk said. "Did Zach have a seizure too?"

"No. Not yet. I mean…" Her hand went to her mouth and she took a deep breath. "He fainted though. No apparent reason."

Luk tried not to wince.

"Came to with a bad headache and vomiting. Is that the same way it happened for Kyn?"

"Not exactly. Kyn didn't vomit."

"Still. After Kyn's fainting spell, we didn't want to take any chances. The ER staff assumed we were overreacting until we told them Kyn had fainted too, the same day she had a seizure and lost consciousness." She exhaled, short and sharp. "When they found out we knew you, and that we are vegetarian, they asked all kinds of questions about Zach's diet. They even took blood to test him for malnutrition. Did they do that to Kyn too?"

"Yes." He almost spat the word, then calmed and patted her shoulder. "Don't let it get to you. We know we aren't starving our kids. They'll soon know it, too."

"There's more. You said you found Kyn in the yard that morning, right?"

"Yes."

"I didn't mention it before because I didn't know it was important. But just before dawn this morning, Rachel woke to find Zach outside in the dark. He said he was talking to a fox. The thing is, there was a fox there." Joy wiped away tears. "Rachel saw it, halfway across the yard, which by itself is scary. Thank goodness it ran off. But what if it had been aggressive? Zach said the fox was his friend, that it was talking to him. Rachel asked him what it said. He shrugged and said it was hunting. He told it to come again tomorrow night and he'd leave food for it. Rachel and I made a talisman for him to wear to bed, a ward against that restlessness, but we hadn't given it to him yet."

Her words stirred Luk's memory of Kyndra in the yard. "Kyn said the trees were burning. But I didn't smell any smoke, thank the gods." He glanced down the corridor toward the ER. "How's Rachel holding up?"

"She's a rock," Joy said. "Solid as the Earth Mother. Nothing flusters her. At least not where anyone else can see. Her mom's watching Oliver until we find out what's going on."

It hurt to see Joy so afraid. Luk knew that special hell all too well. "You'll keep me posted, right?"

She nodded, wiping her eyes again.

"Good," he said, offering a quick hug. "Sorry, but I need to get back. I want to be there in case Kyn wakes up. We're in room 370. Find me if you need to talk."

"Of course. I just wanted you to know Kyn isn't alone in this. Goddess help them both."

Luk pressed his palms together, thanked her, then left. Two kids who spent a lot of time together. Both sick with similar symptoms. Didn't sound like a coincidence. Any number of ailments might cause someone, especially a kid, to hallucinate. But no, Joy said Rachel saw the fox too. Still, outside of movies and fairytales, foxes didn't talk to people. .

He exited the stairwell on his way to Kyn's room. Doctor Whitfield said this infection was messing with Kyn's brain. If that was the case, anything might happen—sleepwalking, hearing voices, imagining things. If their brains were compromised, it could cause permanent damage. Bile rose in his throat, along with the urge to scream. The prospect of Kyn in a persistent vegetative state made him want to climb the walls.

Was this his fault? If he'd brought Kyn to the ER the morning she fainted, would either of the kids be sick now?

He tiptoed into the room, but Kyn remained asleep, her chest still rising and falling, the machines still blip, blip, blipping with maddening regularity. What else could he have done to keep all this from happening? He hadn't felt this helpless since the call came in that Marin was missing. At least then, he'd been able to focus on Kyn's welfare. Keeping her fed and clothed and in school had kept him sane.

Now, there was nothing he could do. His daughter lay unconscious in a strange room in an unfamiliar bed, and the doctors had nothing more than educated guesses on which to base a potential treatment. Downstairs, his friends stood at their child's bedside feeling the same kinds of fears, the same sort of frustration. That same need to protect. But what the hell could they do? How did a father, how did any parent fight this sort of thing?

Luk pulled the privacy curtain across, then sat with his head in his hands. He was afraid to even close his eyes for fear Kyn would wake up and he wouldn't see. In the days that had followed Marin's crash, when he was waiting for news, he had been afraid to sleep, afraid he'd miss the call. That five-day search had lasted forever. A lifetime in which he had held out hope even though he knew. He knew they would find her too late.

Like now. He didn't know what was happening, but it prickled his skin and set his every sense abuzz as if he'd stepped too close to a high-voltage generator. A change was coming. Somehow, he knew it would flip his life upside down.

A sound at the door drew his attention in time to see Sadie push past the curtain, tiptoeing in even though Kyn hadn't given any indication of waking in days. His friend came closer, took one look at his face, and dropped to her knees to embrace him. At her touch, the tears finally started. Luk didn't think he'd ever be able to stop.

Chapter 7

Rhue Children's Hospital, Austin, Texas
Monday, November 4, 2:23 AM

Number of infected: 3

"MR. BEHN. MR. BEHN, WAKE UP."

Luk sat up with a start, blinked in confusion at the dim light in the room, and almost fell over himself to get out of the bed. "Kyn?"

"Kyn is still unconscious, Mr. Behn."

The nurse before him wore a mask and gloves. "What is it? What's wrong?"

"The doctors found a bacteriophage in your daughter's bloodwork."

"A what?"

"A bacteriophage," she said. "A special type of virus, but this isn't one they recognized. That's what raised her white cell count. Your neighbor's boy has it, too."

Luk's stomach sank. Zach's fainting spell had also been followed by a seizure, which left him in a bed a few doors down, near the entrance to this ward. Luk should have seen this coming. "It's contagious?"

"They aren't sure yet. We need to test your blood, see if you are carrying it, too."

"Okay."

She grabbed her kit from the counter and commandeered the roll-around chair from the desk for herself. Several tubes of blood later, she pressed a cotton ball to the needle site.

Luk watched her work while he mused on the ability of a blood draw to wake a person up. "How long before we'll know?"

"Not long. Tomorrow, probably." She taped a bandaid over the cotton.

"Do I need to wear a mask and gloves, too?"

"A mask is fine." She gave him a supply. "Someone will be in to sanitize the room and bathroom in about an hour, and we'll continue that practice several times each day as long as there is a chance of contagion. We ask that you keep the mask on at all times except when in the shower and wash your hands frequently."

"No problem." He'd do anything to protect his kid. "What about my friend, Sadie?"

"She'll be given a mask at the front desk when she comes in, as well as hand sanitizer. We'll want to test her, as well. Can you let her know?"

"Of course."

Luk hooked the mask over his ears and pinched the wire to seal it around his nose. "Like this, right?"

"Yep. Good. Any questions?"

"A million of them. But I don't think anyone has answers yet."

Her skin crinkled above her mask, and he guessed she had smiled. He followed her out into the corridor where Rachel talked with another nurse. Both were masked. When the nurse left, Rachel started into Zach's room. Her eyes met Luk's and held. Her fear for her child, her sense of helplessness, was evident in the way she carried herself. It matched his own. He held his palms together, a respectful acknowledgment of her angst. She held his gaze a moment, then disappeared into Zach's room.

Luk retreated to his cot and texted Sadie.

> This thing may be contagious. Need to get you checked. First thing tomorrow?

He hit send and stared into the shadowy room. Horrific images from epidemic-themed movies danced in his imagination, scenes in which isolation tents and hazmat personnel made up the daily landscape. If this thing was contagious, life was going to get a lot more complicated.

Aboard the *Pasteur*, Vliat, Nlaan Islands
Wednesday, November 6, 1:30 PM
(Austin, Texas, Tuesday, November 5, 6:30 PM)

Number of infected: 8

Isobel wound through the close passageways toward the lab. As she reached for the door, one of the crew called to her from down the way.

"Doc Fallon? There's a call for you on the bridge."

Frowning, she made her way forward. The moment she stepped into the command cabin, the captain cleared the room and left her alone.

Uh oh.

Isobel rounded the stations and came in view of the screen, where her caller tapped his fingers. Chairman Christoph Niellsen dominated the screen, his mouth pulled tight beneath that close-clipped grey beard, his blue eyes pinched down at the outer corners. Even though he had only a few inches on her in height, he always made her feel like an errant child. What was it about him that made him seem tall and imposing? Maybe it was the way he looked down his nose at everyone. Did he ever relax enough to dishevel his perfect grey hair?

Isobel met his stare with a smile. "Mr. Niellsen, this is a surprise."

"I'm sure it is. What's happening out there?"

She clenched her teeth. "We're doing what we came here to do, sir. Would you like a play-by-play?"

"Don't snip at me, Isobel. Why aren't you harvesting at night?"

Her whole body went cold. Someone told him. Travis?

"The Nlaantu have asked us not to. The coral spawn at this time of year. They worry the lights will interfere with the process."

"That's the most ridiculous thing I've ever heard."

Neillsen's typical response to anything that didn't fit his worldview. What would he know about coral or when they spawned? If the divers messed it up for one type of coral, they'd likely ruin it for the star queen too. Not a good result. "They might have a point, sir," she said. "I ran my own search after the Nlaantu gave us that directive. The evidence does support their claim. The coral times its reproduction by the first full moon of November. Our lights confuse that process. There are published papers—"

"Never mind." He glared at her as if she had been the one to reveal this to the Nlaantu, instead of the other way around. "How much longer is this going to take?"

She bit back the retort that sprang to her tongue. "I've been onboard a week. It took us two days to meet with the Nlaantu council, pull our first few loads, and set up the holding tanks to start the coral plugs. The rest is moving about as we planned, but the coral has to be hand-harvested, which is slow, careful work. Without the night dives, it will take a few weeks longer, sir. There's not much we can do about that." Unless he wanted to yank the plug and watch the money he'd already invested circle the drain.

Neillsen grunted. "The board won't allow you to drag this out indefinitely."

"I can't control this part of the timetable, sir." She shrugged. "The Nlaantu are our hosts. If they say wait, we wait."

His jaw moved as if he were grinding his teeth. Before he could speak again, she went on.

"I know an efficient schedule is important, but we also have to consider the safety of the crew. It would be imprudent to push the islanders into a show of force, Mr. Neillsen. We are a long way from help."

"Travis is armed. As is the crew. I ensured that."

"Even so." Easy for him to say, safe behind a desk half a world away. "If it comes to that, someone will get hurt, and Holschtatt will have to answer for any repercussions in the public arena. I'm sure the board would rather avoid such an incident."

His disgust shone through in the set of his shoulders, the way his fingers tapped at his desk. "I'm beginning to regret signing off on this whole project."

Her stomach dropped like she was in freefall. She hadn't had enough time. The tanks were full, yes, but not the holds. If he withdrew funding now…

"I'm sure it will be fine," she said, her voice sure as if she believed every word. "We both know every new project has its bumps, sir. Things will smooth out here. Give it a little more time."

Neillsen's features twisted as if he'd tasted something sour. "Very well. But the board's patience is not unlimited. You need to keep this project under control, Isobel. I'll expect daily status reports via email, and a weekly video update."

"No problem, sir."

Neillsen severed the connection and Isobel's legs began to tremble. She leaned forward, her elbows on the shelf, and waited for the reaction to pass.

Someone passed back-channel updates to the board.

But who? Travis? After she'd begun to let down her guard with him? Seppo, who she was training to take on projects of his own? Duvre or someone else on the dive crew? She was driving them pretty hard, but if that was problematic for them why would they report a lull in their workload? Could she trust no one on this boat? Should that be her conclusion?

She pushed upright and wove between the consoles to the door. The first mate lingered in the corridor.

"I'm finished," she said. "Where is Travis?"

"Aft deck, Doctor Fallon."

"Thanks."

He nodded and disappeared into the bridge.

Isobel crossed to the side passage, then turned aft.

Travis supervised near one of the cranes while the crew winched up another load. Divers stood amid their shift change, some shedding gear, others donning it.

She approached and stood to one side until his attention could be safely diverted.

"Travis, do you have a second?"

"Sure, Doc. Wait one." He instructed the winch operator, then came closer. "How can I help?"

"You can tell me the truth. Did you tell Neillsen that the Nlaantu halted our night dives?"

He muttered a curse. "I heard he called. Figured it was something like that. But no. It wasn't me."

"Do you have any inkling who it might have been?"

"I dunno." He swept his hat off, wiped the sweat with a blue-and-white bandana, replaced the hat, and stuffed the cloth in his pocket. "I've not crewed with everyone from this lot before, so I can't speak for them all. I know it isn't the captain or the first mate. But the rest, I can't say." He squinted at her. "You want me to find out?"

Did she? It's not like it would matter. Even if she knew, it wouldn't stop them from reporting on her every move. She couldn't afford to divide her focus right now.

"No. But I'm glad to know it wasn't you."

"No, ma'am. Far as I'm concerned, we're a team. Or that's the idea, anyway."

He held up a fist, and she bumped it with her own. "Good. I'll let you get to it, then."

He winked and resumed his work.

Rhue Children's Hospital, Austin, Texas
Tuesday, November 5, 8:05 PM

Number of infected: 9

A masked Sadie pushed past the curtain and bent to touch foreheads with him.

"I came bearing flowers and a stuffed frog, but hospital staff wouldn't let me bring them up."

"Why?"

"Something about the risk of infection on porous surfaces." She set her purse on the windowsill. "I guess they're trying to limit the spread. But Perkatory regulars wanted you to know they're thinking about you."

Luk nodded. "That's—"

The door swung open and the same nurse who'd taken his blood the night before last pushed through, maskless, carrying a tablet. "Ms. Schupert, Mr. Behn, your blood tests showed no signs of infection. You're clear."

"What about the Maxwells? The other children from the co-op?"

"All clear."

Luk let out a long breath. "That's a relief. It isn't contagious, then?"

"It's still likely that the virus is transmissible, but since no other patients in this wing are symptomatic, the doctors don't think it's airborne."

"Then how did Kyn get sick?" Sadie asked.

The nurse shrugged. "That they don't know. We're working on it. Someone will keep you informed but for now, you don't have to wear the masks any longer."

"Okay." Luk and Sadie both removed their masks. "Thanks."

"I do have some questions, though," she said. "The doctors need to begin tracking this thing to find the initial source."

"No problem."

He and Sadie sat while the nurse went through her queries. For the most part, her questions were identical to those the doctor had asked when Kyn was first admitted.

Where had Kyndra been, both in- and out-country, in the last six months?

What had she eaten?

Had she been bitten by any animal or insect that he knew of?

Had she been digging in the dirt, or playing in an area that might be used for dumping?

Had she been wading or swimming in any body of water in the last thirty days? Splashing in mud puddles?

Had she petted or come into contact with any wild or stray animals that he knew of?

And so on. By the time the nurse left, Luk sagged. Sadie wrapped an arm around him and pulled him close. The last thing he remembered was the warm smell of her hair.

Chapter 8

Rhue Children's Hospital, Austin, Texas
Wednesday, November 6, 11:10 AM

Number of infected: 17

LUK TAPPED THE KEYS OF HIS LAPTOP, tweaking the graphics code in new neighborhoods for Hyde and Seek. But concentration came hard when one's daughter lay in the hospital and no one knew what the hell to do for her. A week had passed since her seizure. Doctors were still mystified, but at least they had grudgingly admitted she wasn't malnourished.

He'd search "bacteriophage" online, and learned it was a special kind of virus that infected only bacteria. That was often good for humans since the bacteriophage killed the bacteria. Other times—like now—it acted in ways that harmed its host.

No one yet knew where the kids had gotten this thing.

The medical staff seemed baffled and kept asking him the same questions. A little over an hour ago, one of the nurses—a young man he didn't recognize—came to Kyn's room and started a third interrogation round.

On and on and on the questions went until finally Luk had almost shouted at the young man. "Enough! I answered these questions when Kyndra first came here and went through them again last night. That person even recorded my answers in an audio file. Why do you keep asking me the same things? Are these orders to question me coming from different doctors who aren't talking to each other? Do they suppose that sooner or later I might give you a different answer?"

The nurse flinched as if Luk had reached out to strike him. "I'm sorry for the inconvenience, Mr. Behn. We're trying to track transmission and isolate a source of infection. We're also questioning your neighbors, the Maxwells."

Luk kneaded the stiff muscles in his shoulder. He took a deep breath. "I know that. I understand you're trying to help. But you have to understand that this is getting old."

"Again, I'm sorry, Mr. Behn. We just have a few more questions—"

"Look." Luk struggled to maintain an even tone. "I don't know what I can tell you that I haven't already said. Unless you're going to ask me something new, can we stop with the repetitive cross-examination? If I think of anything else, I promise I'll let you know."

The nurse left clutching his tablet.

Guilt set in ten minutes later. Since then, Luk had berated himself for taking his frustration out on the nurse who was doing his job. The doctors were worried. Their manner and actions made him know they were as clueless as he was. And that scared Luk because if they didn't know what was going on, his daughter was in serious trouble.

The physical therapist came in and waved to Luk as she set up to work on his daughter. Today's therapist was the short woman he'd dubbed "Miss Green" because of the green tips in her hair.

"Good morning, Kyndra. Therapy time! We have to keep you in shape so you'll be ready to go home soon, right? Let's start with your feet. You ready?"

Luk watched Kyn, but she didn't respond. Not that he'd expected her to. Miss Green stood at Kyn's bedside, working his daughter's joints, chatting away as if her patient was awake and aware. Mostly she talked about all the gifts people had sent to Kyn.

Miss Green was right. The whole room bulged with tangible good wishes from Kyn's classmates, Hyde Park neighbors, Simon and company, even a slew of BehnWerks gamers. The hospital wouldn't let her have any new ones, but they'd left the ones already present. Hopefully, Kyn would wake in time to see the flowers before they all wilted.

Finished with Kyn's limbs, Miss Green shifted his daughter onto her side, then raised the head of the bed.

"Miss," Luk said, "do you know the latest on this virus?"

"We have five new cases here. Maybridge Children's and St. Ives also have a few."

A cold knot settled in Luk's stomach. "It's spread that far?"

"Unfortunately, yes."

The chill in his gut crept toward his chest. "Thank you."

Luk frowned. If this thing was contagious, why didn't he have it? Why didn't Rachel, or Joy? Or Sadie, for that matter?

He opened a browser on his laptop and ran a search for "Austin Texas sick children." At least a dozen articles and a few news videos came up. He popped in an earbud and played the first newscast.

"The mayor of Austin, Texas," said a serious female newscaster, "is calling for school closings in the wake of a strange new virus that has infected fourteen children in the last week."

Fourteen?

"Sources say the virus starts with fainting spells and progresses to seizures and coma-like vegetative states. No initial source for the infection has been found, and while doctors don't believe the virus is airborne, they advise caution. Officials urge parents to watch for early signs and to take their children to the nearest emergency room immediately if they suspect their child might be affected. In other news—"

He stopped the video and played a few others that repeated the same details. That chill had spread up his spine to prickle the hair on his nape. This would explain the morning's third-degree re-runs. Whatever was going on, it didn't sound good at all.

Sadie pushed past the privacy curtain carrying an overnight bag and a large coffee. She dropped the bag on the floor by the bathroom and set the coffee on the table.

He hugged her. "Have you seen the news?"

"I was going to ask you the same thing. I heard the nurses talking on the way in. They're scared."

"I am, too." He wrapped her in another hug and they clung to each other. After a few minutes, he let go.

Sadie pointed at the bag. "Clean clothes, enough to last a few days, and some fresh toiletries. If you want to shower, I'll sit with her."

He scratched at his stubbled jaw. In the last week, he'd showered a few times, and wiped his face with a damp cloth in-between. Shaved when he remembered to, which wasn't often. Brushed his teeth every few days. Changed clothes whenever Sadie brought them. It hadn't been enough of a priority for him to leave Kyn's side. "Thanks. I'll be quick."

"Take your time."

The prickly feeling wouldn't disperse. Instead, it crawled farther up onto his scalp. He stepped into the bathroom in a daze. When was the last time he'd gotten a good night's sleep?

Stupid question.

He set his care package on the shelf and opened it. Inside were two pairs of fresh jeans, half a dozen pairs of boxers, an equal number of t-shirts, and a week's worth of socks, plus a packet of wipes, a fresh sample bottle of shampoo, a fresh razor from his bathroom at home, and Kyn's favorite green blanket from her bed. Huh...maybe they were no longer forbidding this sort of gift? Luk shrugged and dug further into the bag. At the bottom was a nylon case with a new pack of flossers and a fresh tube of paste. He glanced at his reflection, his scraggly hair, shadowed cheeks. Bless that woman. She might keep him sane through all this.

He stepped under the shower's hot spray and washed quickly, scrubbing at his worry as if he could rinse it down the drain. After, he dressed in clean clothes. Brushing his teeth felt like a little piece of paradise. He hadn't even noticed the nasty taste on his tongue until it was gone. When he finished, he shoved his dirty laundry into the bag, plopped it on the floor under the sink, and left the bathroom behind to stash the rest of his clean clothing in the drawers in Kyn's room. He carried Kyn's blanket to the bed and spread it over the hospital linen. Maybe that one familiar thing would make her feel more at peace.

"Thanks for that." He pointed. "For everything."

"My pleasure." She patted the couch beside her.

"No. I've been sitting for hours."

Sadie kicked off her shoes and pulled her feet up before her. Her body curled in a relaxed crouch, arms wrapped around her knees.

Luk sipped his coffee and watched her. Freckles dotted her nose and upper cheeks. Her dark blond ponytail hung straight past shoulders tanned from hours in the sun. One of her tattoos peeked out under the scooped neckline of her sweater. It summed Sadie up in a few words. Though she was little, she was fierce.

She must have felt his scrutiny. She flashed that brilliant white smile at him. Her eyes crinkled at the corners in just the right way. She wasn't Marin, but to his surprise, he found that no longer mattered. She was Sadie. And he was coming to enjoy her company a great deal. She felt the same way, didn't she? He smiled back and almost bent to kiss her.

Until his phone rang. Its vibration on the table sounded like a bumblebee in a megaphone, and he grabbed it without checking the number.

"Lukas Behn."

Simon's smooth voice made Luk grimace. "Good morning, Luk. How is Kyndra?"

"She's stable. Thank you for asking."

"And you? Are you well?"

Luk huffed, an almost laugh. "I'm not sleeping well, to be honest." He gestured to Sadie and took the call into the corridor. "I have been trying to work on Hyde. I'm close, but it's hard to concentrate with all that's going on."

Simon's silence set Luk's defenses up.

"I'm ten days behind schedule, Simon. This is my kid we're talking about."

"I do understand, Luk. But we're a little concerned because the start of the holiday season is right around the corner." He paused. "Perhaps you could pass it to one of your staff."

"That may be best. I'll contact them immediately and have my assistant let you know who's doing the completion."

He finished with Simon and called his office. His assistant answered.

"Hey, Bea. Is the office still standing?"

"It is," she said. "But one of our coders called in this morning."

Luk's stomach clenched. "What's wrong?"

"Her little boy is sick with the same phage thingy Kyn has."

"Oh no." Luk covered his eyes. "Which hospital is he in?"

"St. Ives. That child's only two!"

Nausea raised a bitter taste in Luk's throat.

"His mother is beside herself, I'm sure you can imagine." Bea clicked her tongue, her number one sign of frustration. "I sent a card this morning from all of us."

"Who's left on the coding staff?" Luk asked, swallowing hard. He hated to bog anyone else down. They were all dealing with a lot.

"Tyler, Nila, and Val."

"Help me remember. Do they have children?"

"Tyler and Nila both do. Val doesn't."

"Are they already bogged down with work?"

Bea made a frustrated noise. "When aren't they? Why? Did you want help with Hyde?"

"I did." Luk blew out a long breath. "But no. I'll finish it. We'll get by somehow. Can you please call Simon and let him know one of our people has a sick boy and the others are already carrying heavy loads? Tell him I can't pass Hyde to anyone else right now."

"He's not going to like that news."

"I know. But we don't have much choice. He can wait, or he can sue. We'll deal."

"Luk—"

"Yes?"

Bea hesitated. "I'm sorry as hell you're going through this. You're right, though. We're a team. Don't stew about Hyde. We'll figure it out."

He ended the call and detoured by Zach's room. Rachel was on duty and came out for a minute to tell him one of the other co-op kids had been admitted at Maybridge an hour ago. The rest still seemed fine, but that didn't mean much, especially when this new co-op case tested negative yesterday. He couldn't have gotten it at Cee-Tec. All in-person classes there had been postponed after Zach had gotten sick three days earlier. No one had been there since. Doctors couldn't explain to the parents why some of their kids were sick and others weren't.

He paced to Kyn's room where Sadie perched on the sofa. She waved him over and tugged him down beside her.

"Are you okay?"

"No." He rubbed his chin. "Gods, I hate feeling so impotent. I've prayed, chanted mantras, lit the tea lights, but there must be something else I can do, some action to make her better." He gestured at the bed.

"Luk, even the professionals don't know what's going on."

"I know." He stared at the bed, willing Kyn to wake up. "But I'm her father. I feel like I'm failing her. I know that's unreasonable, but my heart can't shake this helpless ache."

Sadie regarded him as if she were thinking hard. "It's okay not to have the answers once in a while. You don't always have to know the right thing to do. Sometimes, all you can do is keep putting one foot in front of the other. Sometimes, you have to let someone else carry you."

Luk looked at Sadie's sweet face. "I don't know how to do that."

"I do. Let me show you how it's done." She slid closer, put an arm around him, and pulled his head down on her shoulder.

Luk's back stiffened for the briefest of heartbeats before he relaxed in Sadie's embrace. He breathed in her warmth, closed his eyes, and let her take the lead.

Parker Residence, Atlanta, Georgia
Wednesday, November 6, 4:30 PM
(Austin, Texas, 3:30 PM)

Number of infected: 23

Nadine sprinkled flour on the folded dough square and brought the rolling pin up into a two-handed grip. Starting in the center, she tapped the square with gentle blows, gradually working her way out to the edge and flattening the pastry as she went. One side done, she started again in the middle and tapped her way out to the next edge, until all four quadrants of the square had been tapped flat.

Another sprinkle of flour. This time she rolled instead of tapping, careful not to tear the surface. As she worked, Nadine whistled Christmas carols. Even though she was certainly not Christian—or any sort of believer, for that matter—she had no trouble engaging in the fun traditions of the holiday. Thanksgiving was a few weeks away, after all. She figured it was time to drag out the tunes. Start getting in the mood.

A closet door slammed in the other room. Minutes later, Barbara popped into Nadine's peripheral vision. "Which one?"

"Which one what?"

"Which table dressing? Nadine, will you stop for a minute?"

Nadine paused, rolling pin poised above the acquiescent dough square that was almost ready to fold. She shifted her attention to her wife instead.

Barb held out two options. Dark blue tablecloth with coordinated napkins in stripes of blue, grey, and maroon on the right. White tablecloth with bold border stripes in harvest gold, orange, and red on the left, with napkins bearing a matching autumn leaf motif in one corner.

"I like the blue." Nadine went back to her pastry.

"Why?"

Nadine shrugged. "It won't show stains."

"Details are important, Nadine. Jocelyn and Remy and all our friends are coming."

"Same as the last time," Nadine said to the pastry as she set aside the rolling pin and folded the dough in thirds to create the first turn. "And the time before that."

Barb huffed. "You never take these things seriously. I don't know why I ask your opinion." She flounced out of the kitchen.

"Neither do I," Nadine muttered under her breath with a grin. Louder, she added, "That kind of detail is your thing, honey. You're better out there in the rest of the house. I'm better in the kitchen." Got to know your strengths, her mom used to say ad nauseam. Nadine rotated the dough and folded it again, completing the second turn. She picked up the plastic wrap she'd set aside earlier and covered her folded pastry square, then transferred it to the fridge to firm up. Normally, she'd wait a day before the next set of turns, but she'd decided yesterday to make the Wellingtons for tomorrow's dinner party, so she'd have to finish the dough today. In between, while the dough was firming, she could prep the veggies and mixtures for the filling. Put them together tomorrow and refrigerate until time to bake for dinner.

Mmm. She hadn't made Wellingtons for far too long.

"Come here," Barb called.

"Just a minute."

Nadine stuck her hands under the faucet, watching the warm water rinse the flour and dough down the drain, rills of pasty white against the dark brown backdrop of her skin.

She grabbed the dishtowel and went to see the transformation.

There on the scuffed heirloom table, Barb had performed magic. That white tablecloth lay like thick, rich icing on a cake. Oval placemats woven from water hyacinths rested before every seat, each one holding a napkin and a sprig of fall berries pulled through vining silver rings, complete with tiny leaves. The chairs themselves sported harvest gold sashes wrapped and tied at the rear with festive brown ribbon. Along the center of the table rested a vintage black metal tray which held a careful hodgepodge of pinecones, decorative squash, and cream-colored candles in a variety of sizes and shapes. Between and around the rest, sprays of evergreen or fall foliage popped out almost as if at random.

The whole setup was stunning, as always, much better than the blue Nadine would have picked.

Barb studied the table as if hunting for the tiniest flaw. Nadine took advantage of the distraction to admire her wife. They were so alike in some ways—both loved good food, both loved to spend time outdoors, both loved goofy movies—but where they differed, the comparison was stark. Barb adored parties and crowds. Nadine avoided those things whenever possible. Barb's height of fashion awareness put Nadine's sensible drab clothing to shame. Barb stood two inches taller than Nadine's five-foot-five and was slender like a delicate flower. Nadine had some bulk to her, more muscle than fat, she told herself. Both sported greying hair, but Nadine kept hers natural, short, while Barb's fell straight and glossy to her shoulders. Barb's creamy Anglo skin almost glowed next to the brown hue of Nadine's. And her own blue-grey eyes might have been less noticeable in Barb's pale face, instead of the dark-brown-almost-black ones Nadine had fallen for. She and Barb fit together like puzzle pieces, one filling in where the other had gaps. The thought made her smile.

"It's beautiful, babe." Nadine wrapped an arm around her wife. "You always make things pretty."

"Thanks." Barb laid her head against Nadine's. "You always make things tasty."

Nadine laughed. "I do like to cook."

Barb pulled away to stare sideways at her. "No! Really?"

"I know it's a terrible shock," Nadine said in her best deep South voice, "but it's true, Ms. Parker. Bite my buns and call me Julia Child if it ain't."

Barb swatted Nadine's behind. "Don't you have vegetables to chop or something, Ms. Child?"

Nadine kissed her and resumed her task. In the kitchen, she grabbed her favorite cutting board and her best knife and began washing the vegetables. She'd put the first pepper on the board when Barb stepped to the door.

"I've been debating whether or not to tell you."

"What?"

After a long silence, Nadine looked up. "What is it?"

Barb grimaced like she was about to confess charging too much on the credit card. "Your mother called."

Oh. That. Nadine's mouth clamped shut. She should've known. Not like it was an unusual thing, this time of year. Still...

She focused her annoyance on the vegetables. "What did she want?" As if Nadine didn't know.

"She extended an invitation to Thanksgiving dinner."

"Uh huh." Nadine sliced a pepper in half and pulled the seed core free, tossing it in the sink. "Both of us?"

Barbara didn't reply, and Nadine nodded. "She can eat a passel of jalapeños then. I'm not going anywhere my wife isn't welcome."

"Nadine, she doesn't know I'm your wife." She paused. "Don't you think it's time you came out to them?"

"I tried. More than once. Soon as I would start, they'd overtalk me. Drown me out. They wouldn't shut up long enough for me to say a thing. Besides, even if she believed you were my roommate, which I doubt, the fact that she spoke to you and didn't invite you? They know. They don't approve. I'm done. And I'm not subjecting either of us to their sanctimonious scat." She pointed. "Pass me that bowl, would you?"

She began to slice and chop, pepper pieces tumbling to the board like warriors felled by her blade. Her mother had some nerve. She did this every year. Barb suggested they change their number, but Nadine would wear thigh-high stiletto boots and carry a whip before she'd inconvenience herself and her wife to avoid that one day every year when her mother mooned them.

She'd finished the pepper and started on the carrots when her mobile rang. Barb picked it up in the other room. Nadine listened.

"Hello?"

Carrot pieces piled up before her onslaught. It better not be her mother.

"Yes, she's here. Hold on."

Chopping sounds filled the silence. Barb appeared in the kitchen doorway.

"Who is it?" Nadine kept at the carrots.

"Work. Mitch, maybe?"

The knife stopped. Nadine took the phone.

"Nadine Parker." She laid down the knife. "Hey, boss." She listened, scraped the cut carrots into another bowl, carried the knife and cutting board to the sink, rewrapped the vegetables, and put them in the fridge. "Uh huh. Yeah. How many cases? Nineteen so far? Is this thing airborne? No? That's good news. At least isolation won't be necessary. Yeah. Yeah. Uh huh. Are my tickets all arranged? Or—" She glanced at Barb. "Good. What time's my flight?"

Barb pantomimed a giant "no way."

"Do I have a rental car set up? Uh huh. What about lodging?"

Barb crossed her arms, her eyes wide, her mouth tight.

Nadine had seen that display before. After almost twenty years together, she and Barb both knew the steps to this tango, but that didn't make it any more pleasant.

"Good. I've stayed there before. Who're you sending? Uh huh. Yeah, a few newbies are okay, long as you also send my usual team."

Barbara stomped away.

"Okay. Okay. Yeah. I'll let you know when I get there. Thanks. Bye."

"We have twelve people coming over tomorrow." Barb's voice carried down the hall. "You can't leave me alone with that responsibility."

Nadine sighed and followed her wife's voice. "The CDC is always on call, babe. You knew this when you married me."

In the bedroom, she found Barb sitting in the middle of their four-poster bed, her self-appointed preparatory observation post any time Nadine got called out on a case. "Where is it this time?" Barb asked

"Austin."

"Texas? Jesus, Nadine. That's worse than Atlanta. You're female. You're black. You're lesbian. You'll have three strikes against you before you even say a word."

"Well," Nadine called from the closet, "it's a good thing I've got such a great team. We'll run circles around those dadgum howdy boys while they're judging me. Not much I can do about it. I can't hide that I'm a woman, or that my skin's brown. But I do promise not to talk about our sex life." She came out with a compact suitcase and plopped it open on the bed in front of her wife. "Austin isn't bad, though. I've been there before. I liked it."

Barbara pouted. "I guess. Jocelyn once called it the blueberry in the tomato soup."

Nadine laughed. "Did she, now? She might be on the money about that. Not being from there, I can't say. I'll be fine. Let's hope I can figure it out and come home before you even know I was gone. My Wellington dough won't last longer than three days, even in the fridge."

"You're worried about your dough?" Barb rose to her knees on the bed. "What about me? Aren't you worried about leaving me for three days?"

Nadine climbed over the suitcase to push Barb down on the mattress and tickle her. "You're already spoiled, babe. You don't need three days."

Barb laughed and squealed about how tickling was torture, and after a minute, Nadine relented and lay beside her, both of them breathing hard.

"We're getting too old for that," Nadine said, still panting.

Her wife rolled over to look down at her. "Never." Barb leaned in for a long slow kiss.

Forty-five minutes later, Nadine smacked her wife's naked hip, untangled herself from the knot of covers and limbs, and climbed out of bed.

"I need to finish packing. Where are my black pants?"

Two seconds later, Barb's pillow thumped her in the back.

Chapter 9

Aboard the *Pasteur*, Vliat, Nlaan Islands
Friday, November 8, 5:30 AM
(Austin, Texas, Thursday, November 7, 10:30 AM)

Number of infected: 39

ISOBEL ROLLED OVER AND GLANCED AT HER PHONE. The sun would be up by now, or well on its way.

Rise and shine, Bel.

As if she'd been sleeping in the first place.

She pushed aside the light cover and sat up. In the shadowy cabin, she could just make out shapes of her small desk and chair, her shoes sitting by the wall, her jacket hanging on the doorknob.

Pushing against the bunk, she stood and padded across the small space to flip on the light. At the sink, Isobel splashed her face and brushed her teeth, still contemplating the coral tests from the last couple of days. The results kept coming up inconsistent. She'd separated the star queen's amino acids, as she'd done in her early experiments. In ninety percent of the material, resulting chains bound to the toxic Milani shards, as she'd seen in the throughput assays in Austin.

But yesterday she'd found some of the shards from the first set of tests aboard the *Pasteur*, completed a few days ago, floating free again. For some reason she'd not yet nailed down, the bonds on nearly twenty percent of the samples had failed.

She hadn't seen that in the Austin trials, and the difference baffled her. Could it be something about the different study environments?

She frowned, spit out her toothpaste, and rinsed the sink. It was conceivable that a variation in surroundings could cause this divergence, though she wouldn't have expected it to be this drastic. Neillsen had tasked others to execute the same experiments Isobel had run, trials using samples from that original harvest and performed in separate lab facilities at multiple Holschtatt offices. Any variations in those results had been well within acceptable parameters, thus both she and the crew were working by those final test notes, which summarized the best practice procedures. Still, it was conceivable that the environment aboard a ship could affect the results. They'd made the *Pasteur*'s labs as tight as they could for this trip, but they'd never approach cleanroom quality. This particular vessel hadn't been intended for this type of research. If they'd allowed her one of Holschtatt's more modern ships, with labs made specifically to cleanroom—or at least controlled environment—specs, she'd be better able to isolate what *wasn't* the problem. She'd have to trace the variables one by one to figure out the cause for the discrepancy.

Isobel opened her laptop and, while waiting for it to boot, traded her sweatpants for a pair of jeans and pulled a t-shirt over her tank. By the time she'd put on socks and shoes, her login blinked on the screen. She called up her email and new messages piled into her inbox. Several were from her assistant department manager at Holschtatt, who filled in for her while she was in Nlaan. There were trial results on several other projects she'd started for other new pharmaceuticals. A couple of messages were from friends. Twenty-odd spam messages screamed at her to buy now.

And one was from Jake.

She smiled and opened that one first.

Bel,

    Life around the house and the office proceeds as best we can in your absence. Your stand-in at the office lab is doing his best, although three of your scientists have gotten me aside to ask when you're coming home. Not sure what that's about. I'll see if I can dig up some details.

    Claire earned a new badge with her scout troop and came home with a class essay bearing compliments from her teacher. Also, she apparently has an admirer or two. She may be more forthcoming about those details with you than with me. You can ask her about it when you get home, then fill me in. She's growing up so fast!

    Gabe's news isn't that bright. Yesterday, going up the stairs with Claire, he seemed to lose control of his legs. He would have fallen but for his sister. At dinner last night, he wanted to know where you were. This morning, he didn't remember who Maria was. It only lasted a moment, but it caught us off-guard. I see Maria watching him sometimes. She's as worried as we are.

Her smile faded. Maria had worked as a housekeeper for the Fallon family since before Gabe was born. How could he forget who she was? But then, he had forgotten where Isobel was the last time they spoke, too. His memory lapses were happening more often. His condition deteriorated almost by the day. She needed to stay ahead of the Milani's progression. She didn't have the luxury of time to wonder whether or not that was a realistic plan.

Isobel stared at the words on the screen, remembering a conversation with Jake when she'd first begun campaigning with the board for this trip. They'd been in the den of their Austin home. Isobel held a wine glass. Jake had straightened the area rug to his satisfaction before sitting on the sofa and peering up at her.

"What if the board won't bite?" he had asked.

"Don't say that. Don't even think that."

"It's a possibility you need to entertain."

When he spoke like that, those ice blue eyes of his felt as cold as their namesake. At the time, she'd thought it was a stupid thing for him to say. She had poured herself another glass of shiraz, delaying her response.

Now that Holschtatt had finally agreed to her trip and she was on-site and actively working the project, she could admit the truth. Of course she'd considered it. She'd awakened in a sweat from disturbing dreams where she had to explain to Zoe the inability to find a treatment, or where Gabe fell down a hole and Isobel couldn't quite reach him. She'd seen all she wanted to see of Milani Syndrome. She refused to let Gabe die as Zoe had. Screw that.

> I know that harvest site is gorgeous, all the makings of an ideal island vacation. But don't forget that every day you're there raises costs and lowers Holschtatt's profits for whatever drug you create from this whole thing. Neillsen will want to see results soon.

She barked an unamused laugh. Her husband wasn't on the board—not yet, anyway—but he might as well be, from the way he reasoned. As far as Holschtatt's board was concerned, everything came down to money. Shareholder confidence. Market value. They whined about every penny, from the *Pasteur*'s mission and this trip to the set-up and maintenance of tank reefs to the sharing of profits as part of the cost.

Anything that cut into the balance sheet numbers and produced smaller returns raised their hackles, but the process of seeding and maintaining a reef upset them more than the rest. Isobel's long-term projections showed the establishment of an artificial source was the only viable option. When board members argued that wild coral would be cheaper, she'd had to point out the imprudence of that view. Yes, it would be cheaper, short term, to trade boats and other supplies to the Nlaantu. Yes, it might bring in a ton of profit in the beginning. But eventually, that natural resource would run out either because they'd harvested all of it or because the reef ecosystem collapsed, taking Holschtatt's opportunity for earnings along with it.

How could they not see something so basic?

Isobel huffed and rubbed her temple. There was no understanding the board's logic.

> Speaking of Maria, she said Claire's voice woke her around three in the morning. Maria went outside and found Claire squatting by the pond in her pajamas and bare feet. When Maria asked her what she was doing, Claire said she was talking to the frogs. Maria brought her back into the main house, wiped her feet, and tucked her in bed. I slept through the whole thing, but Maria told me about it this morning. She was frightened by the incident. I agree it's odd. Claire's never been one to sleepwalk.

Her husband could sleep through a bomb in the backyard. Her daughter's restless night made sense, she supposed. Claire worried about Gabe, too. Two nights before Isobel left for Nlaan, her daughter had come to her in the wee hours with concerns about her brother. Claire was very conscious of the fact that Gabe would eventually die from Milani. It hurt Isobel's heart to know that her ten-year-old daughter carried around that horrific fear day after day.

Isobel pursed her lips and saved the email for later. Gabe's illness had the whole family on an uneven keel. She and Jake were always snipping at each other. Claire's grades had slipped in the last few months. Maria seemed even more tentative than usual. The strain was even worse for Isobel. Between that and the constant concern about her job and this trip, Isobel's stress levels over the last few months had been stratospheric. She didn't dare show any signs of it, or Holschtatt would use it against her. As far as they were concerned, she was the expendable member of the Fallon family employed by the company. If she hoped to create this drug for Gabe, for all Milani children, she had to hold it together.

Chapter 10

Rhue Children's Hospital, Austin, Texas
Thursday, November 7, 1:10 PM

Number of infected: 43

NADINE FOLLOWED THE DIRECTIONS given her by Rhue hospital's front desk staff. She found her workspace on the fourth floor mostly set up and ready. Cagney Squires, her usual second-in-command on these off-site jobs, had co-opted a small conference room there, along with tables and desks they could use for workspace. A row of windows opened onto a small, landscaped courtyard. The room held a lengthy counter with cabinets emptied for their use and a handy deep sink.

Cagney had set the desks up the way Nadine preferred. Several held computers. One, with an enormous display, stood at the far side of the room, away from the windows.

Several other CDC investigators, all in various stages of doctoral studies and serving in the Epidemic Intelligence Service, were also present. Thom, Yuka, and Lara sat prepping their stations. Nadine greeted them. "Where are our labs?"

"One is right across the hall," Cagney said. "We have two others at our disposal, down and to the right. The clean room's down that way, too."

"Good. Thom, pull those blinds closed for me, will you? Cagney, did we get access to the data yet?" Nadine asked.

"Yep." His spiked red mop gleamed like a flame in the overhead lights. He'd probably been the first one on-site. He always liked being the one to scope out the landscape, even before he'd completed his doctorate. Now, he was practically a fanatic about it. "From all three hospitals. And I sent word to the other medical facilities in the city to let us know if anything new cropped up that might be related. It's all on that laptop," he pointed, "with your usual onsite login. Rhue Hospital staff are at our disposal for testing, running equipment, and other necessities."

"Thanks." Nadine logged in and noted the patient names, then perused their demographics. All came from various races, backgrounds, varying ages, no one gender more affected than another. No immediate similarities other than the fact that they were all preadolescent. No common environmental elements other than that they all lived in Austin. The usual antivirals had been tried in the first two cases and rejected as ineffective after days with no change in the patients. All the symptoms appeared similar, even to the commonality of seizure and unconsciousness. But in at least one case she saw a high fever. Two showed tremors or poor coordination in the early stages of onset.

"Cagney," she called.

"I'm on it," he said. "I already started the usual databases and set up an epi curve tracking program."

Nadine grinned. She should have known he'd have everything ready. They needed an overview of this thing, a way to see at a glance which symptoms were common to all and which were specific to some. That might help her track the bug down.

She opened the first file, Patient Zero. Kyndra Brooke Kaur. Eight years old. Daughter of Lukas Damon Behn, Greek and German ancestry, and Marin Jauna Kaur, Indian parentage. Unremarkable medical history. Common childhood vaccinations. Pretty standard stuff. Traveled to India two and a half years ago, which might be a little unusual for most Texas kids. Probably unrelated. The few conspicuous details found were in the onset of the phage effect. Nadine reviewed the physical symptoms, then opened a few of the other patient files and compared them. Even before the presence of the bacteriophage had been confirmed in each case, the similarities in the disease's emergence were too close to ignore. This didn't look like anything she'd seen before. She'd lay money on it being a new disease.

Still, as the CDC's lead investigator in this case, her first task was to confirm or rule out the obvious. Nadine spent the next hour poring over sample slides of the phage itself, then results reported from the tests on every patient. Despite finding the presence of the phage, doctors had tested for meningitis, encephalitis, West Nile, malaria, and other parasites, all the usual suspects as far as illness. Negative results across the board.

Test results for RNA and DNA analysis were still pending, but as far as she could tell, this was all related to the same unknown bacteriophage. The team could start compiling a working case definition. Meanwhile, she'd need to email Mitch with confirmation of diagnosis and get an official designation for the probable associated disease.

Nadine grabbed her earbuds and started the first interview with Zero's father in which he described the progression of the child's illness, including the seizure eight days ago. One by one she worked her way through the interviews but found nothing unexpected. Every parent's report matched the files she'd already read.

All indications led to the assumption that the phage was affecting their brains somehow. Every patient's PET scans showed elevated activity in scattered regions across the occipital, frontal, temporal, and parietal lobes. Other areas showed slight anomalies as if the readings had been shifted slightly to the left of center, enough to catch her attention but nothing she could pinpoint. But how was that possible? The organism itself was larger than most other phages she'd seen before—too big to cross the blood-brain barrier. Nor was it lipophilic. It couldn't be doing this by itself.

No. Something else was at work here.

"Cagney, order full metabolic and toxicology panels on these kids."

"All of 'em?"

"Yep. I want to know every detail you can give me about the breakdown, all of it. The phage can't get into the brain by itself, so we need to figure out how the little bugger is sneaking through the fence. Check for anything out of the ordinary. Anything there that shouldn't be. Also, anything that should be there and isn't."

Cagney squinted at her. "How am I supposed to test for something that isn't there?"

"You're a smart guy. Figure it out."

"You don't ask much."

She smirked over her screen before returning to her work. "And yet you always want to be on my team. I wonder if there's a connection."

His laughter echoed through the room and raised the briefest shadow of a smile on Nadine's face before she let it go. It wouldn't do to let 'em see too much of that side of her in the workplace. They might realize she was human or something. Ask her to join them for drinks. Barb might like that, but Nadine's idea of a fabulous evening was a night at home with her wife. Just the two of them, no matter what they were doing.

She sighed, scrolled to the beginning of Zero's file, and started again.

Chapter 11

Aboard the *Pasteur*, Vliat, Nlaan Islands
Sunday, November 10, 9:50 AM
(Austin, Texas, Saturday, November 9, 2:50 PM)

Number of infected: 97

ISOBEL SLAPPED THE LAB TABLE AND MUTTERED A CURSE. The bonding failure rate increased with every passing day. It made no sense. She snapped at Seppo.

"You checked the variables as I asked?"

"Yes. Double- and triple-checked. I don't understand it."

She twisted in her chair. He still reviewed the figures on his screen, his back to her. Seppo was a good kid. Well, not a kid, per se. Late twenties, maybe. He'd been her lab assistant before he even began his doctoral studies. She'd advised him during his coursework, consulted with him on his dissertation topic, guided him in his research, even attended the celebration when he was awarded his doctorate. Isobel closed her eyes. This was not his fault.

"Neither do I. But we need to figure it out."

A fine gleam of sweat coated her brow. Two bodies in this enclosed cabin produced too much heat, even with the ventilation and piped-in air conditioning. She twisted her hair into a bun and stuck a pencil through to hold it in place.

The proteins and other breakdowns seemed the same, so these numbers on her screen confused her. The coral amino acids wouldn't fuse with the Milani proteins for longer than a day or so. What were they doing wrong? She ran through the procedure in her mind, mentally ticking off each step in the process in comparison with what they'd done in Austin. She and Seppo had followed every step exactly as she had before. The single wild card was that in Austin, the coral had been cleaned, sorted, and processed before it got to Holschttat labs.

Could that be the difference?

No. Not possible. The *Pasteur* crew used the same procedure and followed the same steps written down in the summaries by Neillsen's confirmation teams.

She chewed her lip. It could be the origin of that sample. Or the season in which it had been harvested. For an animal that could tell the moon cycles even beneath the surface of the ocean to such a fine degree that they spawned by the first full moon in November, their physical cycles might wax and wane based on other factors she'd not considered. The corals in this harvest would spawn in three days, give or take a day. Would gearing up for that stage in the reproductive cycle, or even releasing their gametes, change their chemical make-up? That would be a real kink in the works. If the coral could only be harvested at a certain time of year to get the desired result, expenses on this project could well blow the whole thing out of the water, so to speak.

The truth was that she knew next to nothing about this animal. As rare as it was, not many people did. She balked at a potential need for further study. That could take years. Gabe didn't have that long. If this whole project proved nonviable due to something she hadn't taken into account, she'd probably lose her job, too. But that was beside the point.

The comm clicked, and Travis's voice came through into the lab.

"Doc, we need to break off diving for a while to dump our waste tanks. I wanted to give you a heads up before I recall the boats."

Isobel bolted upright in her seat. "Hang on, Travis. Don't pull the teams out of the water yet. I'll be right there." She pushed out of her chair and patted Seppo on the shoulder as she left.

"Keep trying. I'll be back in a few."

Several crew members passed as she made her way to the bridge. She nodded without seeing them. Instead, formulae, bonding processes, and protein chain diagrams danced through her thoughts. When she got to the bridge, she stood inside the doorway, reminding herself why she'd come.

The first mate stood duty alone. Travis, who'd been chatting with the crewman, came closer. His mouth twitched up at the corners. "Wrapped up, were ya?"

"A little." She shook off the distraction. "Where does the boat need to go?"

"The waste tanks are near full. We need to dump 'em."

"We can't do that here?"

"No ma'am." Travis pushed his hat back a smidge. "Regs say we gotta do that at least twelve nautical miles offshore."

"How will anyone know?"

"Can't do that, Doctor Fallon." The first mate tucked his hands behind him, his expression fixed. "It's international law."

She frowned at him. "It's treated, right? I mean, it isn't as bad as raw sewage."

"We'd still need to pull the divers," Travis pointed out. "Current runs toward the dive site."

Isobel grimaced. "Of course. Sorry. I'm trying to think of an alternative. I don't want them to stop if they don't have to."

"I know." He sucked at his teeth. "But it ain't safe to leave them with nothing besides the small dive boats. We don't expect to be gone long, but you never know. If they have an emergency while we're gone—"

She waved understanding. "No, you're right. Okay, how long will it take, do you think?"

"Couple'a hours, barring any difficulties."

"Could we set up a shore station for them on that far islet? The one where you and I walked last week? Would that be enough of a safety net for them for a few hours?"

Travis squinted, glanced at the first mate. "What do you say?"

The man shrugged. "Not up to me. Not up to the captain, for that matter. We're responsible for the *Pasteur*. The rest is your call."

"We'd need to leave a medic, too," Travis said.

"We have several, right?"

"Yes, ma'am."

"Okay, good." She could still see that tangled undergrowth from her last visit. Without venturing into the jungle, they'd be exposed to the full sun while the *Pasteur* was gone, assuming they needed to go to the island at all. "Do we have materials to set them up with a small shelter or pavilion for shade? Some bottles for water? A cooler or something to carry food?"

"I believe that could be arranged."

"What about a fire ring? Something they could use to contain a fire. It's early enough they shouldn't need one, but it's better to be prepared."

"The Nlaantu did say we could have a small fire if we were careful. But that beach is narrow. With the ocean breeze, it's a hazard for windblown sparks."

"If you're worried, cut a firebreak," she said. "Enough to create a safety gap. Nothing huge."

"You want me to cut down part of the jungle?"

She rolled her eyes. "You make it sound like I'm telling you to raze the whole damn thing. I'm suggesting we clear a swath big enough that we don't risk setting the trees afire. Surely the Nlaantu can't object to safety precautions. It'll grow again."

"Okay. I'll see what I can do." Travis swept off his Panama, ran fingers through his greying hair, and slapped the hat in place. "The divers might like having dry land beneath their feet for a change. Anything else?"

"What if we were to let the dive teams rest on the island every day between dives? As you said, it would give them a break, a change of scenery."

"That's a possibility. They'd need a waste pit. But you know that'll end up in the water."

"That'll happen anyway, right? I mean, it's not like there are any septic systems or sewer lines out here." How did the Nlaantu manage such things?

"True."

"Okay." She smiled. "Then we'll do that. Can you set it up now, before we go?"

"I'll take care of it."

Good. One less thing to worry about. Isobel thanked him and went back to work.

Rhue Children's Hospital, Austin, Texas
Saturday, November 9, 3:20 PM

Number of infected: 101

Luk drifted, as comfy as he could get on the sofa without folding it out. He listened for sounds from the bed as a memory rose to play like a beloved movie. Celebrating Kyndra's first November feast, their blended-faith nod to Thanksgiving. Lighting diyas, bathing Lord Shiva's icon, singing the Asa-di-Var, and preparing a special feast in Marin's typical cultural mix of traditions. Marin laughing when Kyn splashed her baby hands in the bowl of milk and honey, even though it meant they had to bathe more than Shiva afterward. Feeding Kyn little tastes from the traditional Indian and American dishes. How Kyn's face had puckered at that first bite of curry, and how she'd reached for more afterward. Her attention returning again and again like a moth to the beauty of the diya's flame.

Luk shifted his position, snugged the thin blanket closer. That feast repeated each year, as did others, ever since. Even after Marin's death, Luk had continued the best he could to merge their spiritual traditions with secular holidays.

Except they might not have a November feast this year.

A sound roused him and he opened his eyes. Sadie glanced at the bed, then at Luk, as she rounded the curtain. She gestured for him to come out in the hall.

Luk pushed himself off the sofa and checked his daughter. No change. He stretched and stepped out of the room. Rachel and Sadie stood a few steps from the door, and he embraced them both. Gods it felt good to hug Sadie, to hear that throaty hum she always made.

She pulled away. "Any change?"

"No." He looked at Rachel. "How's Zach?"

"He's still out."

Luk grimaced.

"I can't even burn candles in his room," she grumbled, "but my healing altar is set up in there anyway. One at home, too." She peered up at him. "How are you holding up? I mean, with the news and all?"

"What—" He glanced from one to the other of them.

Sadie winced. "I was going to tell you. The phage isn't localized in Austin any longer. It's all over Texas. Same symptoms as Kyn's. Some are even worse."

Warmth flushed his neck and cheeks.

"But you can't stress about them all, Luk." She touched his arm. "You worry about Kyn. I'll worry about you."

He managed a small smile for her, then searched Rachel's face. "Are you and Joy okay?"

Rachel pushed a lock of red hair behind her ear. "We'll be better once we get some answers."

"I know what you mean. We—"

A muffled sound from inside Kyn's room snatched the words from his mouth. He whirled and rushed into the room, shoving past the curtain. Kyn's head moved on the pillow, eyes squeezed shut. Her fists gripped the blankets, and a low moan rumbled in her throat.

Luk reached her side and stroked her hair. "I'm here, kiddo."

"Nonononono..." Kyn rolled onto her side, her muscles knotted, her body curling into a ball as if she were being attacked. "It hurts, Daddy..."

"Shh. Daddy's here."

Beside her bed, one of the monitors began to beep.

Kyn's body straightened, then arched backward, neck stretched out in a disturbing display of taut musculature. Her eyes flew open wide to gawk at the wall behind the bed, as terrified as if she saw monsters there. "Daddeeeee! DADDEEEE!"

Luk wrapped around his daughter. The first beeping monitor was joined by a second, their alarms sounding in concert with the elevated rhythm of his racing heart.

Behind him, nurses rushed in, a doctor on their heels. "Step aside, Mr. Behn. Let us help Kyndra."

He stared at them like Kyn stared at the wall, but he could not let go. "She... She..."

The doctor parted him from her with gentle but firm pressure. "We can't help her if we can't reach her, Mr. Behn. Step aside and let us work."

"It's BROKEN," his daughter screamed. "Those TREES! Daddeeee.... It HURTS! Fix it, Daddeee..."

Luk recoiled, sucking every breath through his teeth.

One of the orderlies pushed the bed away from the wall and stepped behind it to hold Kyn still. The doctor leaned over the bed, testing her pupil reaction with his penlight.

"Where does it hurt, Kyndra?"

"It's broken," she wailed. "All those trees, Daddeee..... You have to fix them! Nonononono...."

Her voice rose into a garbled scream. Luk's fingers curled into claws.

One of the nurses pointed at him and the doctor glanced up. "Get him out of here."

Two orderlies removed Luk from the room, shutting the door behind him. He fixated on the curtain drawn behind the closed glass door, his hands clenched at his sides.

Sadie stepped closer, her shoulder touching his. Beside them, Rachel said nothing.

Kyn's screams went on a few seconds more, each one pricking his heart like a tangle of thorny catbriar. Luk gripped his cheeks. What was happening?

It seemed an eternity before the doctor came out.

"Is she okay?" Luk asked, his voice shrill.

"We don't know, Mr. Behn. I'm encouraged that she regained consciousness, but this episode concerns me. She's sedated enough to keep her calm. We're going to run a PET scan. That will show us what's happening in her brain while she's feeling it, but that means we can't dull the pain completely. This infection isn't adhering to any normal parameters we recognize, but the mid-brain may have been affected, making her feel pain even though there's no physical stimulus. Once the PET is complete, we'll sedate her more deeply and run a CSF assay to test for any anomalies."

"CSF?"

"A cerebrospinal fluid analysis. A spinal tap."

Luk's jaw clenched. "Isn't that dangerous?"

"Every medical test has risks. She might get a headache, but the chance of a stronger negative reaction is extremely low. We'll know more after the tests."

Nodding, Luk drew a shuddering breath. He didn't trust himself to speak.

An orderly pushed aside the curtain and propped open the door. The doctor crossed his arms. "I don't mean to be contentious, Mr. Behn. But as I know you are vegan and that your daughter is on a vegan diet, I have to ask. What have you taught her about environmental issues?"

"I'm sorry," Luk blinked, "what?"

"I'm trying to put this as delicately as I can." The doctor hesitated for a heartbeat, then made a frustrated sound and cocked his head to peer askance at Luk. "Your daughter is screaming about someone killing trees, Mr. Behn. After being unresponsive for more than a week. Hallucinations like this are often based on something tangible, or the person's worst fears. Have you or her homeschool co-op been scaring Kyndra and the other children about the plight of the environment?"

Cold shock snatched at Luk's breath. "What?" he wheezed through a throat gone tight. "No! That's—" He couldn't even form words.

Beside him, Sadie stepped forward, every muscle taut. "We have taught her the science, as should any responsible parent. Nothing more. No doomsday scenarios, if that's what you're asking." Her eyes narrowed. "This is as much a mystery to us as it is to you, so back the hell up. Her father and I are scared enough as it is."

The doctor ground his teeth and might have retorted in kind, but was interrupted by two orderlies who pushed Kyn's bed out of the room and down the hall. The doctor followed in their wake.

Kyn's bed disappeared into the elevator.

Beside Luk, Rachel blanched and she whirled, burying her face against him as if to block out the frightful images. She was right to fear. She'd gotten a glimpse of her son's future.

Sadie embraced them both, then murmured something about getting Luk a coffee and some food. Rachel pulled away.

"I gotta—" She gestured and turned toward her son's room.

Alone and hip-deep in fear, Luk barely stifled the urge to scream.

Chapter 12

Rhue Children's Hospital, Austin, Texas
Sunday, November 10, 5:30 PM

Number of infected: 219

HER PHONE BUZZED, and Nadine picked it up without even noticing the number. "What?"

"Hello to you, too. You sound frustrated."

"Sorry, Mitch," she said. "Too many pies in the oven. What's wrong?"

"What makes you think something's wrong?"

"Because you're calling me. While I'm onsite with a case. Never a good thing."

He grunted acknowledgment. "First off, your official designation for this virus is Novel Juvenile Cerebral Bacteriophage or NJCB."

"That's a mouthful. Let's go with NJace."

"Whatever you say. Good idea, I suppose, since we'll be saying it a lot more in the coming days." He hesitated. "This thing isn't contained in Austin anymore."

"Yeah, I saw on the news that the chickens got out of the coop. Texas, Idaho, where else?"

"Virginia and New York, cases that all match the working case definition."

"Any luck in contact tracing?"

"Not yet. Tracking programs blew normal expectations all to hell. That initial case in Idaho—NJace's first appearance outside Texas—had no exposure we can find to an infected kid from Texas. But at least that supports the argument that it isn't airborne, which is a good thing."

"Yeah. It's already bad. Rhue discharged most of their non-critical cases, sent the patients home with medicines and a list of instructions on how to recuperate on their own. Phage cases are being lodged in every available room and Rhue staff even reached out to non-pediatric hospitals in the city looking for more space for future cases." Nadine pinched the bridge of her nose. "If we don't figure out how the dang bug's getting around, stopping its spread is gonna be harder than cracking a macadamia."

Mitch listened in silence, which made her twitchy.

"What else you got?" she asked.

He sighed. "The Department of Homeland Security is treating this as a possible terrorist attack."

"Well scramble my eggs. Are they going whole frittata on this thing?"

"Yep. Airports, borders, and hospitals are under heavy watch. DHS agents are on their way now to interview any medical staff who've worked with the patients."

"You know that's gonna get in our way."

"Not to worry. They might hit you up a couple of times, but we'll deal with most of their questions on behalf of the CDC and leave you folks free to do the fieldwork. Keep me up to date so I know what to tell them."

As many times as Mitch had tried to promote her, right now Nadine was grateful she'd never taken that bait. "I wouldn't take any amount of money to be in your shoes right now."

"You sure?" He sounded tired. "Because I'd gladly switch."

"You handle DHS. We'll handle the bug."

When they'd finished the call, Nadine stared at the wall and yawned. Sixteen- and seventeen-hour days took more out of her now than they had a few years ago. She'd divided the team yesterday, set everyone on 12-hour rotations. She should get some dinner, but somehow leaving felt like a surrender. She wasn't ready for that.

The most frustrating part was that she couldn't figure out what made this virus tick. It was a bacteriophage. Phages infected only bacteria so its effects should be limited to a predictable symptoms list, but the neurological manifestations present in these kids defied that rule. No strange substances showed up in the children's metabolic panels beyond normal levels of food additives, chemical pesticides, trace metals, and particulate matter—all the residual pollutants everyone carried these days. None of that would account for the neurological effects of this outbreak, which now included psychosis. Above and beyond the question of how the critter was getting from host to host, she needed to figure out how this phage was getting into the brain to cause these symptoms.

It baffled her. That didn't happen often, and never for long. She might be tired, but she was also annoyed. At herself. At the computer for failing to highlight and underline whatever it was she kept missing. At the dad-blasted bug. At the complications—like DHS—that never failed to manifest.

She rubbed her temple and sat up straighter. Working with DHS was rarely a pleasant task, but she could understand their concern. A fast-spreading disease made perfect sense as a suspicious event, especially since no one knew what in the crusty hell this thing was. She'd answer their questions if necessary and report her findings. Hopefully, any cooperation they might demand wouldn't drag her away from her computer for too long. She needed to figure this out. All the CDC's little patients here and in other hospitals in the affected cities didn't even know her, but every one of them was counting on her.

Nadine always believed, growing up, that she'd have a houseful of kids. She loved them, loved the unbelievable things that came out of their mouths sometimes, the surprises they brought into people's lives. But Barb never wanted the obligation of a family, so Nadine had made a choice. She'd never been sorry, but she still had a soft spot for children. Thus far, she hadn't been required to meet with any of those affected by the phage. Knowing they were sick was bad enough. Cram her thoughts with their little suffering faces and she'd land smack in the middle of an emotional minefield that would disrupt her process. Make her rush things that should be done slowly, however counterintuitive that might seem.

She puckered up and whistled the bass line from an old B.B. King tune, the lyrics keeping silent time in her head.

Why kids? Rather, why only kids? She couldn't see any reason why this bug shouldn't be affecting adults too. That had to be part of the key. She scanned the results of tests on the newest patients. Her fingers ticked on the keyboard to bring up the results of the tests on prior patients from the beginning.

Nothing useful popped out. Results differed from person to person but were close enough for most that this panel offered no new information.

She reviewed the digital chart. A couple of the kids attended the same schools, or maybe their parents were friends. Nowhere near all, though, not even in a specific region in any one city. Then how had it spread so fast? And so far? If the kids didn't all have contact with one another, then how was it being transmitted? She couldn't wrap her mind around its process, which was mysterious enough to give the impression it was spreading on its own, or by some outside intervention. But that made no sense at all. Unless DHS was right.

Nadine considered, then discarded the possibility. Unless they brought her proof, she refused to over-egg a recipe that was complicated enough already.

The thing that kept drawing her back, the one symptom that made the least sense, was the psychosis. Zero and thirty-seven other early patients had awakened from their unconscious states screaming, hysterical, claiming pain from some outside source. Yes, the phage appeared to be affecting their brains somehow, so it was conceivable the patients would encounter audial, visual, and experiential hallucinations. She re-read the reports on the psychotic episodes. Each child's exact phrasing differed. For Zero, it was something about trees. For another, it was dying elephants. Yet another claimed to feel the fear of thousands of fish in nets. No matter what else they might say, all the patients babbled that everything was broken, or that the sickness was spreading— which it certainly was.

A few also said they felt the pain of other humans around them as if it were their own. None of these children had ever shown any signs of a purported empathic connection. Their words sounded, at times, almost as if the children were in the throes of some form of ekstasis. She'd heard of that before, cases where mystics experienced spiritual visions so intense that they caused pain. But that possibility made no sense here. Even if she wanted to connect this to a religious origin, ridiculous as that was, all the patients were from different backgrounds. Religions never agreed on anything, certainly not on this scale.

Regardless, it was unproductive to drag God into the mix, even in a theoretical way. She must be more tired than she'd realized.

When her phone buzzed she glanced at the screen and answered, glad for the distraction.

"Hey, babe."

Barbara's voice tickled her ear. "Hey yourself. How goes the battle?"

"Hold on. Yuka," Nadine called across their makeshift office, "I'll be right outside if you need me."

At her workstation, Yuka gestured acknowledgment, and Nadine stepped into the corridor. "Okay. I can talk now. I hate to say it, but we aren't making much progress. This thing's got me stuck."

"News folks are saying it's not just in Austin anymore. Is that right?"

"Yeah." Nadine leaned against the wall. "Four states. Today. Tomorrow, I predict it'll be more."

"I hope not." Barbara sounded concerned. "Thanksgiving is coming. We'll have a whole houseful of people over that day."

Nadine rolled her eyes. "I remember." What a tragedy it would be if she had to miss *that*. But she did hate being separated from Barb during the holidays. "I'm working it as fast as I can."

"Well, you tell Mitch if he slows you down, he'll have to deal with me."

"Boss-man's gonna boss, babe. Can't help that. Though I suspect, tough as he is, he'd never survive your wrath."

Barbara laughed, a musical sound Nadine loved to hear. "You'll need to get down our tree and decorations from the attic before that. Then we can set it up in time for the party."

A grin played at the corners of Nadine's mouth. "This thing runs on long enough, you might have to get it yourself."

"I can't fit," Barbara said, her voice prim. "I'm the tall one, remember?"

"I'll give you a tall one," Nadine teased. "Let's hope this will be over soon and I can be home in plenty of time. Though you might want to call someone to clean that attic anyway, or I'll need to bring hazmat gear from work before I go up there. It's like somebody busted open a couple dozen bags of flour up there."

"It is kind of yucky."

"Yep. I know crud when I see it." She let a pause fall between them and pictured her beautiful wife.

"Nadine?"

"Hmm?"

Barb paused. "You're okay, right? You're safe?"

"Yes. Whatever this is, it's affecting kids. In case you hadn't noticed, I left puberty in my rear-view ages ago. But I have to run. It's almost the end of my shift, and I'm starving. I'm gonna go grab a bite and get some sleep if I can."

"Yeah, I need to go, too. But I wanted to tell you I love you."

"I love you back."

Nadine ended the call as her belly growled loud enough to be heard down the hall. She ducked into the makeshift office for a few last-minute details and sent in an order for yet another round of bloodwork on Zero so Nadine could test it herself. There had to be something, some clue she kept missing. Before she left, she messaged Thom to set up a half dozen cultures seeded with NJace, and a half dozen with common bacteria and no introduced phage, each one isolated in a glove box. Maybe she could see how fast this thing multiplied. Document its method of growth. See if it would spread from one petri dish to another despite isolated environments.

She hung her lab coat on her chair and pointed herself at the elevator. But even when she'd passed the lobby and walked out into the evening air, those numbers from the bloodwork followed her like a fog. Tomorrow she'd get the results from Zero's PET scan and CSF. Hopefully, one or both of those would hold the answers she needed to solve this mystery before more kids got sick.

Chapter 13

ISOBEL CHOSE 4X FOR A PLAYBACK SPEED and set the video in motion on her screen. She couldn't follow every detail at that rate, but she watched it anyway, waiting—

There.

She stopped the vid and reversed it ten seconds, then ten more, scanning the image for that critical moment, then ten more. Setting the playback at one-half speed, she started again, her attention pinned to the screen. There—the joined amino acid and Milani protein fragment twitched in the sample fluid. The bond began to decay, and she slowed the speed another notch. What had seemed a solid attachment greyed and withered, the line between one substance and the other peeling off in particles barely visible on the scope as if something in the solution was dissolving it.

A growl built up in Isobel's throat. She bent over the keyboard, shoved her fingers into her hair, and propped her elbows on the table. All this time, all this money, all this effort, for nothing. Nothing! And Gabe—

She surged to her feet, grabbed the sample, and threw it across the lab with all her might. The glass smashed against the wall, shattering into dozens of tiny shards that flew in all directions. Seppo, at the other table, ducked and threw his bare arms up to protect his face with a startled cry.

Isobel trembled, her fingers clamped to the edge of the table as if to hold herself upright. What had she just done? She needed that sample! What if it had held some vital clue?

"Damn, Doctor Fallon." Seppo's voice was hushed, shaken.

All the strength drained from her legs, and she collapsed into her chair. "My apologies. Are you hurt?"

He inspected himself. "I don't think so." He glanced at the floor and shelves near the smashed test. "But we're gonna need a cleanup before we can do anything else."

She dropped her head into her hands. She should have been in her bunk an hour ago, at least. But the thought of resting before she'd resolved the issues with these tests clenched her jaw and drove away any possibility of sleep. Something was wrong, with the samples, with their test equipment, with their process, with some other element of the procedure. The problem eluded her, hiding like a tiny white grain of solvent on an otherwise pristine white lab floor. Isobel knew it was there. Now she needed to find it.

She straightened. "My mess. I'll sweep up and resanitize. You keep working on whatever you can in the meantime."

"You know," Seppo said, then paused as if he'd reassessed his words.

"Spit it out."

Seppo scrunched his nose, his expression cautious. "Maybe the Austin tests were all flukes."

"No way. One test, even two, I could accept that possibility. But I wasn't running those experiments alone, Sep. You even ran one, if I recall. As did others Neillsen engaged, people we don't even know. In different labs. I don't see how they all could have come to the same conclusions by any coincidental means. The science was solid."

"Then something about the lab here, or this particular variety of star queen, or —"

"I'm aware," Isobel snapped. "I've been asking myself those same questions. I feel like I'm chasing my tail here."

"I know." Seppo's tone bespoke sympathy.

Isobel stood up. She couldn't take compassion right now. She'd lose her grip. Not a very professional thing to do. But then, neither was throwing a bad test across the room. "Keep at it. I'll only be a few minutes."

She set out to find cleaning cloths and supplies. In the mess hall, Travis sat backward at a table, staring at his tablet.

"Still awake, I see." His eyes twinkled in the overhead lights.

Why did he always look like he knew a secret? "Yeah. Can't sleep."

"How're you all doing in the lab? Any breakthroughs?"

"Not yet, but we're close." Isobel didn't want to talk about it again. "Where can I find a broom or small lab vac and some cloths and bleach?"

He jerked his chin at the galley. "Probably back there. But the cleaning crew can mop up if there's a mess."

"I'd rather do it myself. Tight quarters in there. A third person might make it too difficult for Sep to keep working."

Travis nodded, though she could see he didn't really understand. "Dive teams say they're almost dry in that one spot they've been working. I'd expected them to fill a hold by now. I guess these tests take more of the coral than I realized."

That's what she needed...yet another reminder of her failures. "Don't."

"Sorry." He set his tablet down, propped himself against the table. "I didn't mean to upset you, just statin' a fact. I don't know how your process works."

"It'll take as much as it takes to get it right."

He peered up at her. "I'll put the dive teams on a new spot tomorrow. They tell me there's plenty o' coral down there.

She pointed at the colorful image on his tablet's screen. "What's that?"

Travis held it up. "Photos from the dive team."

"Can I see?"

He gave it to her, and she scrolled through the images. She remembered from her own dive the color and variety of life forms. These photos could have been a different reef altogether. Wide patches of white and grey veined the brighter areas, making them stand out like islands in a flooded river. Along the edges of the gouged sections, anemone drooped. Tall branching corals lay in scattered pieces. Some of the shots showed swarms of bright blue and green parrotfish mobbing the broken segments.

Isobel frowned. Plenty of reef remained. It would heal. She passed the tablet to Travis.

"You'll figure this out, doc."

She stuck her hands in her pockets. "Aren't you going to advise me to get some sleep? That it'll all be clearer in the morning?"

"Would you listen?"

It was good advice. She knew it as well as he did. But she was glad he hadn't suggested it. "Probably not."

"Didn't think so." He gestured toward the galley. "Ask the kitchen crew where you can get what you need. Pretty sure someone's still on duty. G'night, doc." He got to his feet and slid past her in the direction of his cabin.

Isobel watched him go before she went back to her search.

Rhue Children's Hospital, Austin, Texas
Monday, November 11, 8:19 AM

Number of infected: 764

Luk roused with a start.

"I'm here," Sadie murmured. "It's okay."

He focused on her, seated beside him on the sofa. Light coming in through the blinds behind them told him it was much later than when Sadie had arrived. He must have dozed off and slumped over onto her shoulder. His restless night mitigated any guilt he might have felt. Kyn had tossed about, muttering in her sleep. He'd alternated between pacing in the hall outside her new ICU room with her door open, and standing over her bed awaiting any sign that she might awaken screaming again.

"Your coffee's probably cold. Do you want a fresh cup?"

Luk pushed himself up straighter on the sofa and brushed at his hair. "No. Even cold, Perkatory's coffee is better than the brew from downstairs." He retrieved the cup and swirled the contents before he drank, then walked over to lean on the bed's side rail. Kyn had gotten so thin she seemed lost in the sheets. Sunlight coming in the window cast shadows over the sharpened angles in her sleeping profile, darkness that gathered beneath her cheekbones and in the hollows beneath her eyes to add age and a hint of wisdom to her features. She looked peaceful, lying there. Almost as if she were in a deep, normal sleep.

A tickle made him rub his face. To his surprise, it was wet. Again. He'd not even realized he was crying this time. Doctors were no closer to a cause for what was happening, and the uncertainty was wilting him like the fungus on Marin's dahlias. He stroked his daughter's hair.

Kyndra woke. "Hey, Dad."

Sadie appeared at his side, and he smiled. "Hey, kiddo."

"Why are you crying?"

Luk's smile faltered. "I'm fine, sweetie."

She closed her eyes again. "We said we weren't gonna lie to each other."

He winced. "You got me. I'm not really fine."

She breathed evenly and he thought she'd gone to sleep.

"I saw Mom in my dream."

"Really?" He glanced at Sadie. "What did she say?"

"I don't remember. But she looked different."

"How so?"

"Her skin was a pretty green, like the grass or the leaves." She opened her eyes. "I feel it, Dad."

"Feel what, babe?"

"All the yucky stuff."

"Yucky stuff is kind of general," he teased. "Can you be more specific? Does it still hurt?"

"Yeah." Kyn paused, as if trying to put words to her feelings. "The water makes me want to throw up. The air's all wrong. It hurts the trees. It makes the birds cry." Tears leaked out, but she made no attempt to wipe them away. "It hurts so much, but I don't know how to make it stop. None of us do."

"None of who?"

"The phage kids." She blinked, her movement slow. Dreamy.

Her words clouded the air between them like the rainbow powders at a Holi festival, and he peered at her through the murk of his confusion. "How do you know about the others?"

"I just do. They feel the pain, too, same as I do. The worst part is that no one cares except us kids."

"Of course we care! All the parents are worried sick—"

"It isn't us you should worry about."

A chill slithered up Luk's neck.

"No one else feels how we're cutting down too many trees," she went on, "and what that'll mean for the birds or for us. We're changing the weather and we don't even care. Everything is messed up. Like that island. Nobody even knows how bad that is. How bad it will be." She yawned.

"What island?"

"It's a reef like the ones we saw on those videos about the ocean in the co-op. Except this one's tall enough to stick up out of the water. I don't remember what it's called."

Luk stared down at his daughter.

She smiled in apparent wonder. "Can you imagine it? A whole island that's alive like a tree, with roots that spread out under the water and all kinds of little animals living on every piece of it. Everything's alive, though, isn't it? Even the dirt in our yard."

He hung on her words. Where was this coming from?

"But they didn't care," she went on. Her smile twisted, her features contorting as if she were in pain. "They tore off big chunks of it. Messed up the water so the animals on the reef can't see the sun. They can't breathe right. Their food died and now they're hungry."

The doctor's accusations echoed through Luk's thoughts. "Kyn, who's telling you these things?"

"No one. I told you, I feel it.

He brushed at her tears, and she flinched.

"It's all wrong. Everything's broken. The game isn't working like it should. You put in too much trash."

What was she talking about?

Kyn took a deep breath and let it out slow, as if it hurt. "Maybe the players don't even see it anymore," she said, her words slurred. "They're too used to it. They don't see the brown air or the dirty water either. If the game costs them health points when they miss clues and gives them health points when they fix the problems, clean up the mess, it could work."

Luk took a breath to ask what she meant when it hit him. Hyde and Seek. Her suggestions from almost two weeks ago to put trash in the game's world. His eyes widened beneath raised brows. He hadn't had a chance to talk further to her about that before her seizure. But the sort of realism she talked about now was a level or two up from what they'd discussed before. He shrugged at Sadie, who looked as confused as he was.

"I know you don't believe me," Kyn said, her words slow.

"Kiddo, I believe you believe it. But what you're saying doesn't make sense."

She nodded. "This morning while you were sleeping, one of the nurses—Alicia—killed a spider outside my room. My curtain was closed. I didn't see her do it, but I felt her fear. I felt the spider die. Go ask her about it."

Luk tried to grasp her words.

"I felt it. I feel the other kids like me, too. The ones here. The ones in the other hospitals. Other countries." She seemed to search his face. "Am I gonna die?"

"No." He grasped her hand. "The phage isn't deadly."

"Not yet." She blinked in that slow-motion way.

There was that chill again. "The doctors will figure this out any day now. You're going to be fine."

"Nobody's gonna be fine if we can't make people see what they're doing. Make them stop."

"What do you mean?" Luk tried to keep the fear out of his voice.

"You all think we're sick. The phage kids." Kyn's breath came slow. Even. As if this was the kind of conversation they had every day. "But we're the ones who are getting well. It's everyone else who's sick."

"I'm not sure I understand, kiddo."

"That's because you're sick, too." She watched him a little longer, then curled into a ball on her side.

When her breathing evened out he turned to Sadie. "Can you stay with her a minute?"

"Go," she murmured. "I'll be here."

He slipped past the curtain and stepped to the nurse's station. The attendant on the desk finished her call and smiled up at him. "Can I help you, Mr. Behn?"

"Is Alicia still on shift?"

The nurse glanced around. "Yes. Over there."

Luk thanked her and stood in the corridor while Alicia finished with her patient.

As she exited, she saw him. "Mr. Behn," she said, clutching files to her chest. "Is Kyndra all right?"

"I'm not sure. Alicia, did you kill a spider outside her room today?"

"Yes." Her eyes widened. "How did you know?"

A new chill rushed over him so fast Luk could swear the temperature dropped five degrees. "I didn't. But she did. Was the curtain open?"

"No. But even if it was, she was sedated. There's no way she could have seen."

"Tell that to Kyndra," Luk murmured. He told her what had happened. Did this signal a change for the better? he asked. Only the doctor could tell, she said, but she'd pop in on Kyndra, be sure everything was stable.

Luk wandered to the window down the hall. He stood for a while, staring out at Austin. How did she know these things? It had to be the medication. The illness, which the doctors said was messing with her brain. Right?

Kyn's words replayed in a confusing medley with her comments from that morning she'd first passed out. Add trash to the game indeed. Games were distractions from reality for his customers. They'd be unlikely to pay money for a game that reminded them of their shortcomings. She didn't know what she was asking. She couldn't. She was a child, with no concept of marketing and business details essential to building a product's appeal. His nose had wrinkled at adding a few pieces of trash. Now she was talking about brown air and dirty water? What would she recommend next?

Even if he wanted to, he was already too far behind schedule with Hyde to make sweeping changes to the code and change the whole essence of the product. Besides, Simon and his investors would never go for it.

He'd never simply disregarded Kyndra's suggestions about his games, once she made them. He wanted her to feel as though her contributions had value because they did. Not only was she scary bright, but her input was usually market worthy since many BehnWerks games were written for players Kyn's age. Still, those weren't the sole reasons he listened to her. He wanted his daughter to grow up strong in a world that was often unfriendly to women and girls. He wanted her to be secure in her self-worth from the start. So he seriously considered her ideas.

This one though...

He contemplated the city outside the window, a distraction from his distaste. The healing garden with its pond and labyrinth sat below and to his right. Gibson Drive skirted the outside edge of the Rhue campus. Across the street, city residents took advantage of Mid-City Park's lawns and paths. Residential rooftops backed up to the park on the other side. In the distance, Hyde Park waited for him to bring his daughter home. Beyond that lay all of West Austin, its rolling landscape receding into the distance.

Luk's gaze skittered along the tops of buildings in an offhand way to the skyline, where his attention snagged. Just above the horizon, a brown haze tainted the morning view. He'd never noticed that before. Had it always been there?

The air's all wrong. It hurts the trees. The players don't even see it anymore.

He frowned and retreated to Kyndra's room.

Chapter 14

TRAVIS STEPPED INTO THE LAB. "Doc, can I see you a minute?"

Isobel groaned. It had taken her two hours to clean up her mess, and another hour to clean herself up after. Four hours of sleep left her exhausted. She'd finally gotten started again and now he called her away?

She followed him into the corridor. "What is it?"

"Sorry to bother you." He pushed his Panama back. "T'nei's here. She has a complaint."

"Can't you deal with it?"

"I tried." He shrugged. "She insists on speaking to you."

Isobel muttered an expletive. "Fine. She's on deck?"

"Yes, ma'am."

In the two weeks since they'd arrived, Isobel's failures approached monumental. She couldn't lead the testing and deal with the crew and the islanders, which was why she'd brought Travis along in the first place. She'd clear that little item up with T'nei first thing. She stomped down the corridor and emerged onto the side deck, Travis in her wake.

T'nei stood tall and proud near the aft ladder, feet apart and apparently sure on the bobbing deck. Her shiny hair had been braided against her scalp in an ornate design incorporating beads and shells. A green cloth wrapped around her chest and tied at one shoulder. Wide-legged pants in multi-colored stripes sat low on her hips. Her expression might have been carved from stone. She acted for all the world as though she were the one in charge.

Isobel gave that little bow Travis had taught her. "T'nei, you honor us. How can I help you?"

T'nei pointed an accusing finger at the dive site. "Your people foul our waters."

Isobel forced herself to pause before she responded. "In what way?"

"They spew coral dust from their work. Their boats piss oil. It will take us many days to right this after you have gone. The council is reconsidering their decision."

No! Isobel's heart lurched. She looked to Travis.

"T'nei," he said, stepping in, "we will have our people float booms behind the boats while they're stationary, and skim the oil out of the water each day. It won't be a perfect solution, but it will capture about eighty percent of the oil."

"And what of the coral dust?" T'nei pressed.

"Won't that disperse on its own?" Isobel hated the pleading tone in her voice.

"That will take too long." T'nei stared at Isobel, her body rigid. "You must take more care, work at a slower pace, and give the dust time to settle before you create more."

"Slower?" Isobel gaped. "We have already doubled the time we will be here by not working at night. If we delay further, it will take a month to finish."

T'nei stepped closer, pale green eyes flashing. When she spoke, her voice had dropped ten degrees.

"That reef has taken uncountable generations to grow this large. Many of my people have lived and died while it grew here. The fishes and turtles and kraits and jellies depend on it for survival. My people depend on it and the others like it.

What is one month of your time compared to that? Three months? *Six* months?"

Travis cleared his throat. "T'nei, what if we can filter the coral dust from the water as we work?

Her gaze never left Isobel's when she answered. "You cannot. It is too fine. Already your work here has disrupted our waters and our lives. We do not need your boats or foods or supplies badly enough to warrant disrespect of our demands. Will you heed?"

Isobel glanced at Travis, who moved not an inch as if he were afraid to exacerbate the tension. She nodded at T'nei. "We will."

T'nei turned to go, but Isobel wasn't finished.

"One more thing."

The translator spun on the balls of her bare feet to listen.

"Our people often delegate—"

"I do not know this word."

Isobel stopped. Started again. "—share a portion of our tasks with one another. As I am the scientist, I must be the one to perform the work in my lab. Travis cannot help with that. He can, however, act as your liaison. I would like you to please speak to Travis about these things in the future, so that I need not leave my delicate experiment at a critical stage.

"It is acceptable among your people to shirk their duties?"

"No," Isobel protested. "Not shirk—"

"Among ours, it is not. I will speak to you." Once more, T'nei approached the ladder. This time, no one stopped her.

Isobel, still sputtering at the woman's gall, watched her go. The Nlaan boat pulled away from the *Pasteur*, the oarsmen pushing the traditional proa through the water with hardly a splash.

Travis stood rooted to the same spot where he'd been standing all along.

"I would swear she's pushier now than when we first started." Isobel squinted at him. "Is it my imagination?"

"No, ma'am." He scratched at his stubbled jaw around his usual white Van Dyke beard. "The Nlaan are a proud people, and fixed in their ways, from what I hear. Maybe asking them to deal with an underling is an insult to their honor or some such thing." He quirked an eyebrow. "Or maybe it's 'cause I'm a man."

"Whatever." She loved the concept of a living, matriarchal culture. Right now, though, it was damned inconvenient. "Is there any way we can continue the same pace and hide it from them?"

He shook his head, a slow motion that declared his hesitation. "I don't see how. Water's too clear."

"Keep thinking about it, will you? If we can manage a way to keep up our pace without getting ejected from the site, I want to know."

"Yes, ma'am."

She huffed, staring toward the dive site. This was taking far too long. "I guess you should radio the dive teams, tell them to slow down, let the dust settle from time to time around the worksite until we can come up with a workaround. And have them set up that baffle, or whatever you called it, to catch the oil. We don't want that to affect the samples."

"Ma'am." Travis touched his hat and moved off, already speaking into the radio.

This whole trip was fast becoming a thorn in her side. If Gabe didn't have Milani Syndrome—

But her son *did* have the disorder. This trip *would* be worthwhile. She would do anything, endure any difficulty to save him from Zoe's fate.

Isobel cast one last nasty sneer at the distant Nlaantu boat. She would not let those people spoil this for her child.

Rhue Children's Hospital, Austin, Texas
Monday, November 11, 2:45 PM

Number of infected: 1,176

"You told me two weeks ago that Hyde and Seek was nearly ready."

"Yes, Simon. I did. But have you not seen the news?" Luk said, louder than he'd intended. Other parents in the family room gave him an annoyed look, and he lowered his voice. "My daughter's not out of danger yet. None of these kids are."

Simon's sigh conveyed a combination of the man's frustration and annoyance. "We're aware of that. But this game is nearly a month overdue. If it isn't completed soon, we'll miss the chance to make Hyde and Seek a top-ten seller on the market for this season."

Luk picked up his laptop and left the family room. "I need to save my daughter first."

"That is out of your control. BehnWerks is not."

"I know you don't have kids," Luk said through clenched teeth, "so it isn't such a personal issue with you, or with William Sato. But what about Holly Muldin? Bob Rush? They both have little ones. I assume their children are phage negative, or we wouldn't be having this conversation. But what if they weren't?"

"I know your family is in crisis now, and we're trying to be patient." Simon's terse tone said more than his words. "But we invested in this game with the expectation of a profitable return. As much as I feel for you, I can only afford to take a limited loss before I will be forced to seek redress. Nothing personal, this is business. I'm truly sorry for your daughter's difficulty, but if you don't show some revenue on our stake soon, I'm not sure I can convince the others to fund you again."

"I don't mean to be rude, Simon. You've been very supportive of my company's growth, and I appreciate it more than you'll ever know..." Luk stood beside a window in the corridor. An approaching storm darkened the skies, much like the one within him right now oppressed his thoughts. His jaw worked with the effort of being polite. "But our families are more important than any game or your funding. BehnWerks can be rebuilt. Our kids can't. If you or the others feel the need to withdraw support because our children's life-threatening illness is costing my company some points on an already fickle market share chart somewhere, then do what you need to do."

He waited, but Simon didn't respond.

"I'll call you when we have a finished product," Luk said. "If you still want to do business after that, we'll talk. If not, I'll find a way to repay you and the others for your investment, and then locate another patron. Now please forgive me, but I have to go."

He thumbed off the call, still peering out the window.

"Simon?" a voice sounded at his shoulder.

He whirled, his skin prickling.

"Sorry," Joy said. "I didn't mean to startle you. I figured you could use an ear. If that was Simon."

"Yeah." Luk slid the phone into his pocket.

"Forget him. He's all bark. And if he isn't..." She shrugged. "Well, you'll figure out what to do after Kyn comes home."

Luk nodded, still chewing on the words he hadn't said. "How's Zach?"

"Hanging on, thank the Goddess. Kyn?"

"A little better, maybe." Luk breathed deep. "I'm still scared."

"I know."

"Taking a walk?"

"Yes," Joy said. "Need a change of scenery."

"Me, too. Want some company?"

"Sure."

They walked down and around the halls on the second floor, taking their time. Luk glanced aside at her as they passed the playroom. A sign on the door said, "Closed until further notice."

"How's Rachel?" he asked.

"She's holding her own. Sadie?"

"The same. Honestly, I don't know what I would have done without her."

They paced to the end of their wing and veered left, strolling in silence for a bit. Other parents walked these same halls, lost in their concerns, their faces stretched as thin as his from the stress of their child's illness. He knew what they felt, or some part of it.

In the crook between wings, a window overlooked one of the healing gardens. Through the foliage of trees, he glimpsed flashes of the city beyond the campus grounds, reminders of the world that still revolved outside these walls. He'd been so caught up in his own fear he hadn't been present for any of it.

They continued to the corner and swung right by unspoken agreement, then left at the end to follow the inner hallway loop.

"Can I ask you something?" he said.

"Of course. We've been friends a long time."

"Has Zach said anything..." Luk hesitated. "...strange?"

"You mean crying for the world? Yeah. He woke up a little while ago and made some...odd claims. Kyn, too?"

"She said she felt one of the nurses kill a spider outside her room yesterday. I asked the nurse. It checked out. How did she know that?"

Joy's eyes narrowed. "I don't know. Zach keeps saying he 'feels' things, too. They aren't alone in that. A lot of people are talking about it."

"Why do you say that?"

"It was on the news, a special report on the phage kids last night." She hooked her thumbs in her jean pockets as they reached the corner and meandered to the right. "You didn't see?"

"No, I missed it."

Joy came to a standstill just shy of the chapel. "The news anchor said that the phage kids all claimed similar things, the ones that woke up, anyway. All related to environmental issues. One even said that the rain forest in South America was dying and that it's almost too late to prevent it."

"Last I heard, they were still selling pieces of that for farmland."

"Yep." Her lip curled. "Even though the land won't be productive. Without that old-growth forest, there aren't enough nutrients in the soil. Shortsighted bastards."

An image rose in Luk's mind, Kyndra standing in their yard when this whole thing started, saying something about burning trees. Was this what she'd meant? The slash-and-burn in South America?

No, it couldn't be that. She'd been facing northeast, not south. He tried to dismiss the image of his child gazing into the darkness that morning.

Joy started walking again, still speaking. "—kids talked about how clean water and air would be big problems before they even grow up. I mean..."

He heard Kyndra's words again. *No one knows how bad it is. How bad it will be.* He puffed out a long breath and rubbed his arms. "I keep thinking this must all be some enormous mistake. That the kids have it wrong, and once they get better, they'll stop talking like this."

"I hope you're right. But I've got a bad feeling about it."

That conversation replayed in his memory, his daughter calm, yet weeping. "Kyn said the phage kids were getting better, that those people without the phage were the sick ones. She asked me if she was going to die. I told her no, she was going to be fine. And she said—" His voice caught.

They passed a closed office and several other parents as they strolled. Joy made a sympathetic sound.

Luk tried again. "She said no one was going to be fine if the phage kids couldn't—and I quote—'make people see what they're doing.'"

"Damn."

"I know. Gave me a shiver." They passed another hallway, the one that led to their wing, but they kept going. This end of the corridor was clear of others pacing. He tried to swallow the lump that had tightened his throat. "What if they're right?"

The angle of light shifted the dark circles under her eyes into bruises and accentuated the lines of fatigue there and along her neck. Her spine curved in a slouch that defied her normally erect posture. She'd aged ten years in the last week. Is that how he looked? Bags under his eyes and a sag to his shoulders?

"If they are, we're screwed, and our kids are in for a bumpy future." She shivered. "I wonder how many corporate leaders' kids are sick with the phage? They wouldn't be as eager to continue business as usual if they suspected even for a second that they're hurting their own children." She scowled at Luk. "They wouldn't, would they?"

"I dunno." Simon's words echoed in Luk's mind. He refrained from voicing his qualms. That for some of them, watching their kid suffer might be a small price to pay to have whatever it was all that money and power gave them that their kids couldn't. Some of them didn't have kids to worry about.

Maybe he was being too harsh but right now, his every emotion throbbed like an open wound.

Joy shook herself as if to snap out of her melancholic funk and gestured. "I should get back. You coming?"

"Yeah."

They returned at a faster pace past the family room where adults hunkered around a television, and Joy left him at the first nurse station in their corridor. He kept seeing Kyn in the front yard the morning of her blackout. Something about the image haunted him. What was she really seeing?

He continued past two other stations and into Kyn's room to find Sadie resuming her seat on the couch.

"Was she awake?"

Sadie patted the cushion. "For a minute. Are you okay? You're awfully pale."

He told her what Joy had said.

"I heard some of that report, but not those parts." Sadie bit her lip. "Do you suppose the kids are trying to tell us something?"

Good question. "The day this all started, I found Kyndra in the yard before dawn, staring into the sky."

"I remember. You said she talked about burning trees?"

"Yeah." His voice trailed off. "It's like she knew something we didn't know."

His friend's features pinched. He saw when the idea occurred to her. "What if..."

"What?"

She put her foot on the couch in front of her. "Weren't there wildfires going around that time?"

"Yeah, but that's nothing new."

"Granted. But does your daughter always talk about them in her sleep?"

Luk felt the color drain from his cheeks. He snagged his laptop from the desk and opened a browser.

Halloween, the same day as her seizure. *The trees are burning, like Mama's pyre.*

He ran a search for fires on that date. Clicked on a few links. Brought up a map of Texas wildfires for October 31. Gaped at the screen, as unable to breathe as if he were himself caught in their smoke.

Centerville.

Anderson.

Tyler.

Nacogdoches.

Madison County.

All northeast of Austin. Of their house. That's what Kyn had been looking at, even though they were all far too distant to put a glow on Hyde Park's horizon.

"Luk, what's wrong?"

Sadie's voice filtered in through the buzzing in his ears. She peeked over his shoulder and gasped, covering her mouth.

He raised his eyes to the bed to find Kyn watching them. Her face, calm at first, took on a wistful, sad expression that brought a lump to Luk's throat.

"Now do you believe me?" she said.

Luk stared at his daughter, trying to form words. At last, he managed one.

"Yes."

Chapter 15

Rhue Children's Hospital, Austin, Texas
Monday, November 11, 4:05 PM

Number of infected: 1,203

LUK APPROACHED THE NURSING STATION closest to Kyn's room and waited to be noticed. At last, one of the staff smiled in his direction. "How can we help, Mr. Behn?"

"I need to speak to the doctor, please. Can you let him know?"

"Of course," the woman said. "Doctor Whitfield is just coming on duty. I'll call her."

Whitfield. Luk grimaced. She's the one who had insisted Kyndra was malnourished because they were vegan. "Isn't there another doctor I can speak to?"

She hesitated. "Doctor Sarsby is going off duty. Would you rather speak to him?"

"Which one is he?"

"Tall, slender, white hair, glasses. Big booming voice."

That's the doctor who'd been on duty when Kyndra woke screaming. The one who had accused him of frightening his daughter with environmental nightmares. Luk groaned.

"Is there no one else?"

Voices rounded the corner as Whitfield, Sarsby, and another doctor Luk didn't recognize walked toward them, conferring in jumbled, overlapping voices, almost as if they were in disagreement.

The nurse called to them. "Doctors? Mr. Behn would like to speak with you."

Whitfield and Sarsby stopped, their expressions resigned. The third doctor, a tall woman with very short hair, offered her hand.

"I'm new on staff. Doctor Molly Engan. Pleased to meet you."

Luk shook her hand. "Doctor." He nodded at the other two physicians. "Do you have time to speak with me?"

"Of course," Engan said at once.

The other two agreed with reluctance.

Luk told them about the things Kyn had said. How she'd described an island being damaged by careless actions, the spider incident with Alicia, how she wept for the water and air, and claimed to feel the pain it was causing.

Whitfield all but rolled her eyes. "Mr. Behn, Kyndra is sedated. I'm surprised she was able to speak to you at all. She's probably delirious. You shouldn't take anything she says seriously right now."

Engan frowned. Sarsby checked his watch as if eager to be anywhere but here.

"You don't understand," Luk said. What was it going to take to make them listen? "It isn't like Kyn to make outrageous statements. Listen, the morning of her seizure, I found her in the yard shortly before dawn. Do you remember, Doctor Whitfield? We talked about this. You asked if she had ever sleepwalked before?"

"I might have," she said. "I'd need to see her file to be sure."

"She was staring northeast into the dark sky and talking about burning trees. A little while ago, I realized what she was staring at. That's the same night as those wildfires out Nacogdoches way. That has to be what she was looking at. Don't you see?"

Sarsby made a visible effort to be polite. "Mr. Behn, you can't even see Nacogdoches from Hyde Park. How could she be watching a fire there? How would she know about it?"

"That's exactly my point," Luk said. "How did she know? How did she know Alicia killed a spider? How does she know about some island that's been damaged? I don't—"

"Mr. Behn," Doctor Whitfield said, "what you're suggesting isn't possible. She's delirious. But I do wonder where she is getting this from. Is her homeschool teaching about environmental issues?"

"Dr. Sarsby already asked me this, but yes. Probably." Luk bristled. "It's a relevant enough topic it's taught in all schools, public and private."

"Yes," Sarsby said, "but *how* are you teaching her these things? Are you sticking to the science, or are you using alarmist language and examples?"

"Alarmist?" Luk fumbled for a suitable response. "No! We teach her the truth of the matter, but we don't sugarcoat it."

Whitfield and Sarsby exchanged a glance heavy with some meaning Luk couldn't untangle.

"It's not healthy to share adult issues with children," Sarsby said, his face a twisted moue as if he'd bitten into a lemon. "They aren't equipped like we are to deal with the stress of speculation or the ramifications of acting in haste. Teaching her things like that puts her in a tenuous position. It isn't good for her emotional state or her body."

"Wha...I don't..."

"It's also not smart." Whitfield glared at him. "One of my young patients was removed from his parents' care by the Department of Family Protective Services when DFPS found out his parents were expecting him to carry an adult load in the household, and shoulder some of the family's emotional burden."

Luk's mouth opened and closed before he latched on something to say. "But this isn't my doing. I mean...I would never..."

Whitfield tsked. "Then perhaps you'll want to explore who is exposing Kyndra to this fear-based philosophy."

"But Kyn isn't the only one saying things like this. They all are. Shouldn't you at least investigate?"

Sarsby looked askance at Luk. "Are you talking about what they said on that news special about the infected children?"

"Yes," Engan said, eyes wide. "I saw that special."

"You can't listen to everything you hear on the news." Sarsby gave a gruff snort. "Courts declared years ago that television news is nothing but entertainment. Those newscasters can and will say whatever might boost their ratings. Now if you'll excuse me, I need to finish rounds with Doctors Whitfield and Engan so that I can be on my way."

The three of them moved around the nursing stations, pausing at each room while Sarsby caught the others up on the day's events for each patient. Over her shoulder, Engan offered him a sympathetic smile before she followed the other doctors.

How could they not see the significance in this? No matter how smart they were or how much schooling they'd achieved, doctors didn't know everything. Science learned new things every day. And yet they'd talked past Luk's concerns. Made him—and his child—sound ridiculous. Maybe he needed to watch the news more often, keep up with the news sources online, see what else he could find. If Joy had been right about all the phage kids making comments like what Kyn had said, that had to mean something, right?

Not that Whitfield and Sarsby would accept it.

In Kyn's room, Sadie closed her book.

"What did they say?"

He sat beside Sadie and turned away from the bed. He didn't want Kyn to hear this.

"They blew it off. Said she was delirious, that I shouldn't pay any attention to it."

Sadie's jaw went slack. "You're kidding."

"I wish I were. They even said her comments could be based on ideas I had put in her head."

"Like that jerk doctor did when Kyn woke screaming?"

"Yep," he said. "He's one of the doctors I just spoke to."

"But Marin told me she was the one who convinced you to be more green. She convinced me, too." Sadie sat back with a huff. "Hell, she was so eco-conscious she insisted on researching our coffee suppliers herself. If she hadn't gone to Kibukwo—"

Her mouth clamped shut so suddenly her teeth clacked together. She reached out, then withdrew as if afraid to touch him. "Oh honey, I'm sorry. I didn't mean to bring that up."

Luk tried to speak, but the words wouldn't come. Sadie was right. When Marin wanted to start Perkatory, he'd helped her to make it fit her dream vision of an inclusive, green, community business, including investigating the coffee sources herself.

But even before Perkatory, Marin had started their family on a fairer, more inclusive, greener way of life. Recycling, composting, reusing things he would have thrown out before, all of those were changes Marin instigated. They'd both driven more sustainable vehicles, done everything they could to be heedful of their waste.

They'd moved to Hyde Park because of the "feel" of the place. Marin had liked the gardens and natural, uncultivated appearance of many of the yards and houses. At her urging, they'd installed solar panels on the house soon after they bought it.

After Kyn was born, he'd gone along with Marin's ideas on nursing, raising their daughter to be fair-minded, finding a homeschool co-op. Marin had been a real eco-warrior. Kyn had picked up on that and followed her mother's example.

None of it had ever been initiated by Luk, but he was happy to go along with it because Marin wanted it. She'd always explained why she did what she did, and Luk began to understand and agree with her reasons. He kept following them, although to a lesser degree, after Marin was gone. When Kyn got a little older, she took up the banner, pushed their lifestyle back to where it had been before.

But he wasn't about to tell the doctors all that. It was none of their business and besides, he refused to shift any "blame" onto Marin, or Kyn. He didn't see any blame to be had here, except for the blind spot in the doctors' perception.

He patted Sadie's knee. "I know. It's okay."

He had to admit, though, that instead of getting angry at the doctors, Marin would want him to try and see it from their perspective. Why were they refusing to even listen to him?

What would his claims have sounded like to them? Six months ago, even six *weeks* ago, he wouldn't have bought it either.

"I guess I can understand that it's hard to swallow. I mean, it sounds like we're saying that the phage has made these children psychic. The logical response is to ask what would be the purpose of that, right?"

"I suppose." Sadie didn't sound convinced.

"Everything in nature has a point to its existence, right? To its place in the grand scheme of things. Even if it's something as basic as providing sustenance to higher orders of animals. Like mosquitoes."

"The bane of my summers." Sadie's lip quirked up at one corner.

Luk focused on some distant spot behind Sadie. "Even when an animal's purpose is harder to define, everything fills an ecological niche. Every species has a reason for being here. A reason for its nature. Its behaviors. Its peculiarities. Right?"

"Right. Where are you going with this?"

"If all that is true," he mused, "what would a virus have to gain by evolving to imbue its victims with extra-sensory perception?"

Sadie twitched, a little wrinkle between her brows. "It sounds crazy when you lay it out like that."

"I know." He wasn't sure what to make of it either. Nor how to find an answer.

"It doesn't matter, though, does it?" Sadie said. "Kyn says these things like she's seen them herself. She isn't guessing here. I believe her. I know you do, too."

Luk smiled. Sadie loved his kid. He could see it in her face. The realization warmed him, untangled one or two of the knots in his stomach.

"Yeah. I do."

"Okay." She nodded as if she'd made up her mind. "What are we gonna do about it?"

What indeed. If the reactions of Whitfield and Sarsby were representative of the wider professional opinion on the matter, how could he hope to get anyone else to listen?

Luk sighed. "I have no idea."

Chapter 16

Rhue Children's Hospital, Austin, Texas
Tuesday, November 12, 7:00 AM

Number of infected: 4,156

NADINE STUDIED THE SCREEN where Zero's latest bloodwork, drawn an hour ago, was displayed.

Cagney appeared at her desk. "They're ready for you."

She locked the screen and followed him to the small classroom they'd been using as a breakroom for the last week. All the members of her team sat waiting for her update.

"I know you're tired. Sorry I had to call some of you in off the regular rotation, but the home office has upped our game. NJace has jumped U.S. borders. The WHO has declared a global pandemic."

Everyone reacted except Cagney. He'd cussed and fussed in typical colorful fashion when she'd told him earlier. That young man knew words that might've made her blush if she'd known what they meant. Now he watched the others in silence.

"Is that why DHS hasn't been around?" asked one of them. "I mean, if it's global—"

"That doesn't mean squat," said another. "Some isolated nutjob could still have set this menace on the public with the hope it would eliminate everyone but their own faithful. You never know these days."

"Yeah, but only affecting kids doesn't serve that purpose," said the first.

A young blond man, the newest member of their team, bent to rest his elbows on his knees. Nadine could never remember his name.

"Really?" he said. "What better way to bring a populace to its knees than by threatening its children? If someone came up with a cure tomorrow, most countries would probably pay whatever price they demanded."

"That's enough," Nadine said, her voice even. "We aren't here to debate or presume motive. We're here to figure out how NJace works and how to stop it. The DHS isn't gone, and they aren't likely to be anytime soon. Leave them to me. Thom, did you get those cultures set up?"

"Yep. They're in lab three."

"No results yet, I presume?"

"No. But we didn't expect any this soon, did we? I mean, it's been less than thirty-six hours."

"True that. Keep me informed." She crossed her arms and leaned against the edge of a counter. "The blood draw on Zero a little while ago showed an interesting new curiosity. There's a change in the phages. I haven't measured exactly yet but nearly a third of them now appear dormant."

"As in inert?" Cagney frowned. "Sleeping?"

"Yep."

The others fell silent for a moment.

"Then," Yuka said, "why isn't the kid's body flushing them out?"

"That is the mystery of the hour, and whichever one of you can answer it for me gets a one-hundred-dollar bottle of wine. My treat. I suggest you start by examining Zero's normal gut flora."

"We still need to know how it's affecting the brain. That's the key," said one of the newbies. "I'd lay money on it."

"Maybe it's attaching to their hormones," Lara said. "Wouldn't that allow it to pass the barrier?"

Cagney straightened in his seat. "Or maybe it's producing a toxin that mimics a hormone. That would do it."

"Elaborate," Nadine pressed.

Cagney's face brightened. "Once it gets past the barrier, it'd be free to wreak neurological havoc. That could explain the seizures."

Nadine pursed her lips. "That agrees with my line of thinking. Here's what we need to accomplish today. Cagney, reexamine the bloodwork. Scan for neurotoxins or anything that might be in the same zip code as one. Also double-check anything that resembles hormonal presence. Make sure it is what it says it is. If it's camouflaged, unmask it. Get me a clear identification.

"Lara, I want you to review all the research we have on environmental effects on blood-brain barrier permeability or any new findings on that front. Anything that might be relevant. Also, reach out to our contacts at the Clinical Research Society, the International Coalition on Health Research, the World Health Organization. Plumb any other resource that might be helpful. We don't know all there is to know about this. Let's find out if someone else has an answer for us.

"Thom, start working on a medical countermeasure."

"Okay," Thom squinted. "Which MCMs would you recommend to start?"

"Normal pharmaceuticals did nothing, so go stronger. Much stronger. Start with whatever we haven't thrown at this bugger and go from there. Improvise and see what you can come up with. I'll want to see your test results by five o'clock tomorrow."

Thom sat forward in his seat. "That's not enough time, Nadine!"

"Then you'd best get busy." She glanced around. "Everybody else, help where needed. Any questions?"

No one spoke up and Nadine sent them on their way. She remained by the counter, tapping one finger against her chin. She might not be infected, but this bug had crawled under her skin. Those inert phages made the initial symptoms seem like smoke and mirrors. That, coupled with the disease's effect on the brain, raised her skin into goose flesh. Despite huge advancements over recent decades in the areas of neuroscience and neuroanatomy, scientific study of the human brain was still a nascent discipline, poorly understood in many ways. NJace melted into that nebulous region without a care for whether she and her investigators or any of the doctors could follow.

Truth be told, that made her more nervous than anything else.

She entered their communal office and brought up the list of reported infection sites. Cities in Russia, China, Liberia, Brazil, Papua New Guinea, and India all reported infections, and the chance they'd all had a common thread of contagion, though extant, was slim. Thus far, no cases had been reported in Europe, but she doubted that luck would hold. It made no sense. How was this charbroiled beastie getting around so fast?

The odd thing was that some of the listed cases were not located in large urban areas, but in low-population-density regions where she would not have expected to see them. Not this early in the program, anyway. The emerging pattern, or lack thereof, set her spidey senses tingling. Something was going on under the surface with this organism's invasion of the kids, and the longer it took her people to find it, the greater the chances that permanent damage would already be done before they could stop it.

"Hey." Cagney stood next to her desk. Lara, too.

"We were talking about that dormancy twist..." he said.

"And?"

Cagney and Lara exchanged a look.

"If..." Cagney fidgeted, blew out a breath before making eye contact again. "If the phage has been actively working in the children's bodies all this time and now suddenly decided to take a break..."

Nadine peered at them. "Go on."

"It sounded to us," Lara said, her words slow, considered, "like they've finished what they started."

The prickles started at the nape of Nadine's neck and crawled down her spine like a big ol' Joro spider, dragging a shiver along with it. She hadn't thought of it that way before.

Now she couldn't unthink it.

Chapter 17

Rhue Children's Hospital, Austin, Texas
Wednesday, November 13, 4:15 PM

Number of infected: 10,013

IN THE MAIN CORRIDOR BETWEEN WINGS, Luk stared out the window into the late afternoon. Sunlight pierced the thick clouds to shine like moving spotlights on the healing garden and, beyond, the park across the street. In another hour, those clouds would blaze with orange, crimson, indigo. He and Kyn had always loved to watch sunsets when time allowed. Each one held its own special beauty and, like their morning routines, gave them great bonding time when they could talk about the day or sit quietly in each other's company. Marin had started that habit, and they'd kept it up after she'd gone. Maybe... maybe he'd invite Sadie to join them when this was all over.

His phone vibrated. He snatched it up. Simon. Luk groaned, then sent the call to voicemail. He didn't need that drama right now.

Kyn had awakened twice in the last two days, though she'd not been as alert as before. Both times she had mumbled what sounded like similar comments, that she felt pain for the reef, the trees, the fish. He and Sadie had rolled it over and over in conversation that first evening but had come to no conclusions.

If the doctors wouldn't investigate why Kyn had been saying those things, how else could he figure out what it meant?

Luk started back, his steps slow, ponderous, his shoulders bent. There had to be something he could do.

Outside Zach's room, Sadie and Rachel chatted. "Rachel says Zach's still making claims like Kyn has," Sadie said. "Did you know?"

"I knew he did a few days ago." He glanced at Rachel. "He's still talking that way?"

"Yep." Rachel's hair, more frizzed than usual, had been pulled into a haphazard bun. Her features showed the same strain Joy's had two days ago. "Mostly about how animals we never even knew about are dying, or that we're taking away their homes. I'm not sure what he's talking about."

"Hell, that's happening every day, isn't it?" Sadie grumbled. "The more of us there are, the more land we need. And the more we take, the less there is for them."

"I know." Rachel's face crinkled in a perplexed frown. "But the more I think about it, the more I think he's talking about something specific."

"He's been awake again, then," Luk said.

"A couple of times. Not for long. And he's always groggy. Doesn't always make sense. I'm starting to wonder if the doctors are right. That this talk is coming from the drugs and we should ignore it."

"Let me guess," Luk groaned. "They made light of your concerns?"

"A couple of them."

"Whitfield and Sarsby, I'll wager."

"You too, huh?" Rachel grumped. "They're the senior docs on this ward. I tried telling one or two of the others, but they steered me to those two every time."

Sadie muttered beside him. "If it were one of their kids up in here, they'd pay more heed."

Luk's phone buzzed. He read the text.

Have spoken to the others. If you haven't finished Hyde by
Sunday, we will seek a refund with interest, or a judgment
in Court.

Luk tsked. He wanted to say something unkind. Instead,
he shoved the phone in his pocket and murmured a Shiva
mantra.

Sadie didn't miss it. "Simon?"

"Who else?" He waved it off.

Rachel gestured. "I'm going in. See you later?"

"You know it." Sadie hugged her, then Rachel disappeared
behind the curtain in Zach's room.

"She's scared."

"We all are," Luk murmured. Whitfield walked by the far
end of the corridor, souring his expression. "Most of us,
anyway."

Sadie followed his gaze, then puckered like she might start
spitting nails. "Don't worry about that. I have an idea, but I'm
not sure you'll go for it."

"Tell me."

She glanced around. "Let's get to Kyn's room. In case she
wakes up."

She took his arm as they walked. Inside, he sat. But Sadie
ensured the door was closed and the curtain drawn before she
fidgeted around the bed.

Luk squinted at her. "You aren't usually this reluctant to
speak your mind. What's going on?"

She pivoted in place and gave him an unreadable look, her
lips pulled to one side as if she'd reconsidered. At last, she sat
beside him.

"I've been thinking."

He leaned in. "Clearly."

A smile flashed across her face and was gone. "If the
doctors won't listen, maybe other people will."

"What 'other people'?"

"Anyone. Everyone. Enough kids are sick now that I bet
you'd get a lot of attention."

"Because I'm going to...." He opened both hands, waiting.

She peered at him, clearly torn, before she plunged forward. "Let me interview you and Kyn and put it online."

Luk recoiled, his mouth dry. On occasion, as the founder and CEO of BehnWerks Games, he'd had to speak in public. It took him days to work up to it and although the actuality was always easier than he'd imagined, he still feared it every single time. But at least he could see those people, or most of them anyway, and could judge their reactions to his presentation by their behavior. This, where he couldn't see the viewers, would be ten times worse.

"Don't say 'no' yet. Just...sit with it a while." Sadie drew her knee up before her like a shield. "If both you and Rachel are having this same issue where the doctors aren't listening, then there's got to be dozens more. Hundreds. If it were one or two in every hundred kids talking like this, then it would be reasonable to assume it's the drugs."

She laid her hand on his arm, a gesture of friendship, closeness, comfort, probably meant to soften his reaction. "But you and I both believe something else is going on here, and I'm betting we aren't alone."

"Then there must be plenty of parents online, already discussing these things." He peered at her.

"There are," she said. "But your name is known in every household where children play video games. If you add your voice to theirs, it would help reassure them that they aren't crazy, that their kids aren't spewing random drivel. Besides, your word's more likely to be taken seriously. You could lend credibility to this argument."

He eyed her. "For them? Or for the doctors?"

She shrugged, a slight trace of grin on her lips.

Her eyes had that gleam they always got when she was managing a difficult customer at Perkatory—patient, determined, canny. She did have a point. Several, in fact. Still, the notion of airing his family's private drama online felt like an extreme reaction.

He rested his hand over hers. "Marin would hate that plan."

Sadie's mouth opened, then closed. She drew a long slow breath. "Luk, Marin no longer gets a vote. She's gone. This decision is all yours."

Her words, almost whispered, pierced his heart like a thorn.

She squeezed his arm and pulled away, leaving a warm spot where she'd touched his skin. She checked on Kyn, then left the room.

By the time he got up to follow, she was gone.

HomeSpace Suites, Austin, Texas
Wednesday, November 13, 6:30 PM

Number of infected: 11,078

Nadine sat in her hotel eating fried rice takeout from the box and staring at her laptop screen. China, though reluctant to reveal exact numbers, reported cases in most cities in the eastern region of that country. India's numbers were all over the map, literally. Not one major city in India remained unaffected, but even the smaller cities and outlying villages showed phage-positive cases, all of which were following the same pattern as cases here in Austin.

At least that much she could understand. Dense population centers often aided the quick spread of viral contagions. In those instances, these numbers fit traditional models.

But those predictions didn't hold. Far inland, Nepal also showed a smattering of cases. She did a quick population count on its areas of infection. All lay in districts with fewer than two hundred thousand. One had fewer than one hundred thousand.

Infection sites in India showed the same thing. No consistency with regard to population density.

Still, was it conceivable that it was being carried from the more populous regions to the smaller, outlying areas by—

By what? Food, maybe?

No, that didn't make sense. Entire families here in the States had eaten the same meals, yet only one child was affected. A few rare cases saw more than one child in the same family, but that was the exception.

What else?

The wiley bugger wasn't airborne. It wasn't traveling in saliva or sputum, no evidence of transmission via fomites. It wasn't in the water. No animal trace genes showed up in the phage's makeup, so it wasn't animal-to-human transmission. That seemed unlikely anyway, since it didn't appear to be spreading from human to human. Transmission from insect bites was out for the same reasons. If all the patients were isolated to one region, it might be reasonable to investigate environmental reservoirs—soil, water, vegetation—but that made no sense given the spread of the virus.

She took another bite of her rice and scanned the other infection sites. Russia reported cases in Moscow and Saint Petersburg. Brazil's infections, though mostly in Sao Paulo, also popped up in isolated areas to the north and northwest. All infections in Papua New Guinea reported by aid workers fell into remote areas. Liberia was the sole African nation thus far to be affected, but Nadine didn't expect that to hold.

What in the rainbow-spotted tarnation was going on with this critter?

She pushed the rice box aside and looked out the window. Below and to the left, soft lights shone through moving foliage along the paths in a cemetery. To the right, cars dotted the sixth-floor roof of the hotel's parking garage. Beyond that, yellow-tinged lights illuminated a nearby stretch of I-35, the main feature in her suite's view, and filled with endless flows of white and red lights in constant motion. Past the interstate stood some sort of stadium, which was dark, and a couple of sports fields, both lit as if for some sort of game. Farther afield, neighborhood streets of central Austin lay in logical grids that satisfied her sense of order. It would be hard to get lost there. Every street led inexorably to the next block, and the one after that, and they all connected with neat precision.

Not at all like the mess on her plate, as it were.

Nadine liked things orderly. Everything in its place, so she knew where to find it when she needed it. She and Barb had that in common, at least. This danged bug didn't follow the rules, which annoyed her no end.

She stretched her neck, hunching her shoulders before letting them fall slack. The knots were still there. Standing here staring out at the city lights wasn't going to help her figure it out, she supposed, but it had been worth a try.

With a sigh, she sat down and reviewed the data once more.

Chapter 18

Aboard the *Pasteur*, Vliat, Nlaan Islands
Thursday, November 14, 7:15 PM
(Austin, Texas, Thursday, November 14, 12:15 AM)

Number of infected: 13,914

ISOBEL SAT IN THE MESS WITH HER NOTES, ignoring the few crewmen who talked over coffee, and compared the steps between harvesting and final analysis to the process they'd followed in Austin. Every detail matched. Only the results differed. She had to be missing something. But what?

She went over the values from the post-Austin tests reports—again—hoping to find any discrepancy, no matter how minor.

Maybe it was something done to the coral in the samples before it got to her. Travis said the crew swore they followed every step of those transcripts with exacting precision. She double-checked anyway. Sure enough, every value fit the way it should, from the minute the coral was harvested to the final sample.

She closed her eyes and massaged her temples, trying to ease the ache that had started there over an hour ago. Saline quantities, pH levels, and proportion values danced together behind her closed lids, as they did in her dreams. She'd read these reports often enough that she could probably quote them in her sleep. The thought of admitting to Jake, not to mention

Neillsen, that she'd been wrong to such a spectacular degree nauseated her. But it was Gabe's sweet face that cramped her gut, his laughter that tightened her throat so that she couldn't speak. Her boy wanted nothing more from her than to play with him in his sandbox or read him a story and yet he, more than anyone else, would pay the price for her failure.

The good part of being wrong was that she could go home sooner. See her boy. See Claire. Spend time with them together as a family before—

Well. Before.

She sighed and reviewed, once more, the latest set of failed tests. Her mind, melded into habit, went through a routine assessment of the solution values and quantities, the mixture of chemicals in the testing fluid. That post-Austin processing report, still lying on the table beside her, overlaid the edges of her own test results, and her gaze flicked over the numbers for the umpteenth time. She'd need to tell Travis they were finished. Stop the dive teams from making another run. They—

Isobel frowned at the earlier processing report, which said they'd used a solution with a pH of 7, neutral, to clean and prep the coral base. But if that was the case, her initial Austin tests wouldn't have worked. The coral's normal environment, seawater, held a pH of 8. If they'd used a neutral baseline, the coral extracts wouldn't have held up in a test solution of 7.4, the same as human blood. That slight rise in acidity would dissolve any post-processing bonds the amino acids tried to form.

She stared at the pages, mentally running through scenarios using the lower pH, but couldn't see any other result. Those first coral samples *had* to be processed at 8, not 7. The report prepared by Neillsen's people was wrong.

A laugh bubbled up in her chest and spilled out of her mouth. All this wasted time and money because of a typo.

The nearby crewmen looked up. "What's wrong?" one asked.

"We were." Isobel ran through it once more, but it made sense. She lurched to her feet, already running, and burst through the door into the lab. Seppo almost jumped out of his seat.

Isobel went straight to her computer. "I think there's a mistake in the reports from Neillsen's processing teams."

"You're kidding."

"See for yourself."

He came over while she explained her reasoning, then pointed to the screen. "I gave this to Travis as the procedure to follow for prepping test samples. But this pH is too low. That's why the tests all failed."

Seppo paled. "All that coral is already tainted?"

"No. They've processed what we wanted to use here in the lab but the rest should be okay. We need to run another sample load through with a pH of 8, or 8.01, like what they used for the holding tanks with live specimens. Then we can test another series." A tingle started at her fingers and worked its way up. This would work. It had to. "I bet you a steak dinner those won't fail."

"I'm not taking that bet," Seppo said, "but we can still celebrate if it works."

The radio on the table chattered before Travis's voice came through. "Doc, you might wanna go up on deck with the binocs."

Her smile evaporated as she picked up the handheld. "Aren't you on the atoll?"

"Yes, ma'am."

"What's going on?"

"Someone found us."

Isobel stumbled out of the lab, Seppo on her heels, and ran to the bridge to grab the binoculars. On deck, she passed Seppo the radio, looped the cord around her neck, and searched the surrounding water. The only boats she saw were those of the dive teams. "Where?"

Seppo sent the question to Travis.

"This direction," Travis replied. "Up high. Above the treeline."

She swung the binoculars toward the island until she saw movement and latched on, allowing the visual to clear and focus.

Was that a drone?

"What the hell—where'd it come from?"

Seppo sent the message.

"I glassed the horizon. Found a boat about a mile off, pretty big one. That logo on their banner looks familiar."

"Who is it?"

"If I'm right, it's an environmental activist group, The Gaian Protectorate, or some such thing. Guess they got word we were here and wanted some footage."

The drone flew behind the trees on one side of the atoll, then reappeared on the other side of the remaining jungle. It zipped past the beach camp where the crew had cut down a wide swath of trees and dug their latrine pit, hovering long enough to get some good footage of the site, then flew a slow path along the atoll's curving underwater ring in the direction of the dive boats. Isobel already knew what they'd see there.

No, no, no, no...they could throw a kink into everything. "Ask if he has his gun with him."

"What?" Seppo said, startled.

Isobel dropped the binoculars and grabbed the radio. "Travis, do you have your gun with you?"

"Yes, ma'am. Always."

"Then shoot it down."

"Doc, it's too late for that. They're probably livestreaming."

"Irrelevant. This is a proprietary work site where privately funded research is underway. We can't allow them to see any more. Shoot it down, *now!*"

Isobel raised the binoculars again in time to see the drone dip. A moment later, the device jerked hard to seaward as bits of metal and plastic popped off it with explosive speed. The whole thing disappeared from view. She found it again a moment later, in a flurry of splash and ripples, along with floating bits and pieces that revealed its fate.

"This should be the immediate fate of any further drones attempting to film our work site," she snapped into the radio. "Am I clear?"

"Yes, ma'am," Travis said.

Wide-eyed, Seppo blanched.

"Good," she muttered to herself. She shoved the radio and the binoculars at Seppo and spun on her heels.

"What are you going to do?" he asked, following her.

"Keep working."

"But," Seppo said, "they have video of our site. The trees, the coral dust, everything."

"Doesn't matter." Isobel's jaw worked.

"It kinda does." Seppo's soft voice made her stop.

"Why?"

Seppo's mouth worked as if he struggled to find the right words. "What if the news gets hold of it?"

"They probably will." She shrugged. "Can't worry about that now."

"What are you gonna tell Neillsen?"

"Nothing. And neither are you. Because Neillsen will pull the plug, and we can't let him do that. Not yet. Not when we finally had a breakthrough." The longer she could keep Neillsen in the dark, the more coral she could collect. She spun toward the lab again. "Call the crew to get us another small sample in here. I want to process it myself this time."

Rhue Children's Hospital, Austin, Texas
Thursday, November 14, 8:15 AM

Number of infected: 19,342

Nadine hunched over Thom's glove box experiments, peering through the lens into the sterile containment system, observing the test's results thus far. Even in what she'd considered ideal conditions, the sample showed negligible growth. Bust. Blipsky.

Her phone buzzed.

She straightened. "Nadine Parker."

"You might want to take a peek at the news." Cagney sounded out of breath.

"Which service?"

"I saw it on Newsy, but it's probably on every single one. Three kids have died from the phage."

Her heart picked up its pace. "Where?"

"Austin," Cagney said. "St. Ives hospital."

Nadine stormed down the corridor and into the makeshift office, where she dropped into the chair at her desk and ran a search.

At least a dozen news services ran the headlines.

"Phage Claims First Victims."

"Austin Mourns."

"Entheóphage Patient's Prediction True."

She opened that last one first and skimmed the text. One of St. Ive's little patients—six years old—had predicted he would be the first, but not the last, to die. He'd been proven correct when he succumbed at 4:16 this morning. Two others had followed in the next three hours.

Ouch. His parents must be a mess right now.

She gave herself a mental smack. *Stop it, Nadine. Focus.*

She reviewed the other articles and sat back, one hand wrapped around her mouth. No doubt the little bugger was slimier than raw okra, but its new nickname jerked a snort of wry laughter from her lips. Entheóphage, the reporter called it. "God in the phage." Where did they get this stuff?

Nadine snorted and pulled up one of the news videos to watch the whole program for anything else that might be related. More than fifteen thousand known cases. All under the age of puberty. Global pandemic. Blah blah blah. Most of the details they shared were old news, and the rest came from their overactive imaginations. The ticker tape at the bottom of the screen reported outdated numbers for the various affected countries. News anchors moved on to the next story, something about habitat destruction on a South Pacific reef.

Video footage from above flicked past and drew Nadine's eye. She tuned one ear to their story of a pristine reef being harvested by an unknown company, and how the activist group claiming the footage, the Gaian Protectorate, planned to investigate and release the name of whoever was destroying this blah, blah, blah.

She tuned out again and switched from the news services to the CDC's latest infection reports. All fifty states now boasted infections. Canada, Vietnam, Sierra Leone, Gabon, France, and Italy all joined the ranks with cases reported since she'd checked last night. Again, the confusion. Sierra Leone she could understand due to its proximity to Liberia. Even Gabon didn't seem like such a leap, being on the same coast. But how did it make the leap to Europe? Unless it was spreading by traditional means, which they already decided it was not, based on a plethora of other disproving factors.

None of this made sense. Much as she wanted to hate this pestilential beastie, she had to admit grudging respect. She hadn't felt like such a goose-witted newbie since her early days in university. A yawn caught her off guard and she stretched muscles stiff from long hours at the computer or in the lab, followed by long hours of restless rehashing when she should have been sleeping.

She crossed her arms. When the possible is ruled out, one must consider the impossible. So what impossible factors might be in play here?

Spontaneous global evolution of a common virus over a period of two to three weeks? No. Were that the case, they'd have seen signs long before now.

Escaped biological warfare experiment? Possible, but not plausible. Otherwise, with the way this thing was spreading in unpredictable ways, someone would have offered an antidote or MCM by now. She hoped, anyway. Besides, even if that were the case, the disease would still depend on traditional methods of transmission.

Some ecological reservoir element common to all these sites? No. No way. Climates were too variant. Even at the extremes of their seasonal swings, none came close to being similar enough for this to be a factor. If that were the case, then reported infection numbers would rise and fall with the seasonal change. She hadn't seen any evidence of that, though it was still early in the game.

Aliens?

Nadine laughed aloud.

Across the room, Thom peeked over his monitor. "Something's funny?"

"Yeah. Me. I'm a laugh a minute." The chuckles faded. "Where's my MCM that was due yesterday evening?"

Thom rolled his eyes. "I'm working on it. I'm good, but I'm no magician. Now stop distracting me." He waved in her direction. "My boss is waiting for this formula."

Rhue Children's Hospital, Austin, Texas
Thursday, November 14, 8:45 AM

Number of infected: 22,527

Luk sat at a sunlit table outside the cafe, his fingers hovering over the keyboard as he tried to work on Hyde. He'd managed to tweak a few lines of code, but his concentration always wilted after a few minutes. Sleep had come in short bursts for two weeks now, and last night was no exception. He'd dozed just after dawn and woke an hour later to find Sadie there with a Perkatory cup and a bagel. She couldn't stay today. Her manager had called in sick, but she'd be by later. She encouraged him to get out of the room, walk the grounds, enjoy some sunshine, for a few minutes at least.

She'd been right. Luk took in his surroundings. Bright swirls of blue tile mirrored the undulating shape of the patio, which followed the path of a small stream meandering between patches of grass through the lower level of the courtyard. The four-sided enclosure around the courtyard meant blocked breezes and pleasant warmth even in the shade.

He took a deep breath of fresh air perfumed by sweet alyssum that crowded through the railing in thick clusters on the garden's second-floor tier. There, trees still green with foliage threw shadows across the pathways. Phoebes, waxwings, and wrens twittered and chirped in their branches. Even the bright yellow flash of a goldfinch flitted from tree to tree. The serene sounds, along with ubiquitous traffic noise on the streets at the outskirts of the grounds, set a nice soundtrack as he searched for a sprig of peace.

Maybe if he played the game, he could get into the proper mood for final revisions. He brought up Hyde and Seek and started a game. Every few minutes, he made a note for changes, then continued active play. When his phone vibrated against the table, he jumped, snatched back to the real world. He picked it up. Sadie.

"Hey."

Her voice soothed him. "How's Kyn?"

"Sleeping, last I saw. I'm in the cafe garden. Decided to take your advice."

"Good." She hesitated. "Have you seen the news?"

A chill curled up his spine. "No. Why?"

"The morning report I saw was on KAST, Channel 14. You need to see it. Should be online. I'll hold."

Luk opened a browser and went to the station's website. That morning's broadcast topped the page, and he hit play.

"Good morning, and welcome. I'm Ian Stewart," said the anchorman.

"And I'm Madeline Cowan," said his co-anchor.

"Later in our broadcast," Stewart continued, "we'll show exclusive footage of coral harvesting on a delicate reef near the protected Coral Triangle, driven by an international corporation with headquarters right here in Austin. But first, our top story," said the newscaster, a brown-skinned man in his mid-forties, "is the Novel Juvenile Cerebral Bacteriophage, otherwise known as the entheóphage, the mysterious new disease sweeping the globe. Children in more than a dozen countries have been affected, and experts say this is only the beginning."

Luk gaped at his computer, his phone forgotten at his ear.

The camera switched to the female anchor, an attractive woman with a fair complexion and blond hair. "That's right, Ian. An estimated twenty thousand children around the world are currently afflicted with the alleged empathy bug, whose young victims weep for the pain of other people, including other phage patients, as well as animals, birds, fish, even trees."

Luk muttered a mantra of strength under his breath.

"Doctors say the entheóphage starts small with pupil dilation, low-grade fever, and fainting," said the man. "Later symptoms include headaches, nausea, elevated fever, dizziness, and seizures, followed by extreme pain with no apparent physical cause. So far, specialists have no idea how the disease is spreading, nor have they found any solution other than to treat the symptoms and keep the children sedated. Doctors believed that was the worst of it, until yesterday."

"That's right, Ian," said the co-anchor. "According to our sources in the National Centers for Disease Control, seven patients reportedly lapsed into comas within the last forty-eight hours. Since early this morning, three of those—"

Both anchors paused, exchanged a look, then the woman faced the cameras.

"—We've just received word that there are now four reported deaths from the empathy bug, all right here in Austin. International airports remain open but are under constant watch. Many European nations have closed their borders. In Austin, where schools have been closed for the last week, officials now have shut down all public parks and playgrounds. Parents are under notice to keep their children close to home until this illness is resolved. Local residents are being advised that—"

He paused the video and slammed the lid on his laptop, already rising. "I gotta go."

"Luk, wait. There's more."

"What?" He tucked the laptop under his arm and left the cafe.

"Did you hear the part about the reef at the very start?"

"No." In the stairwell, he took the risers two at a time.

"When you get to Kyn's room, play the rest of the report, especially the footage of the island. It's almost exactly like what Kyn predicted when she woke up and started talking crazy. Remember her comments about the entire island that was alive?"

"Yes."

"Well." Sadie's voice squeaked like it always did when she got excited. "Watch the footage. Think about what I said last night." He heard customers and Perkatory background noise coming from her end of the call. "I have to go. Call me later."

In Kyn's room, Luk restarted the news program. The island footage ran up to the moment where the feed went dead. Stewart reported the company behind the harvesting crew as Holschtatt Pharmaceuticals. Luk had driven past their big shiny building more times than he could count. They were a landmark in this town, employing hundreds, possibly thousands, of Austin citizens. What were they after on that island?

Didn't matter, he supposed. But how had Kyn known about this three days ago? No one could have told her because no one in Austin knew until now. He could still see her, still hear her voice. *They tore off big chunks of it. Messed up the water so the animals on the reef can't see the sun. They can't breathe right. Their food died and now they're hungry. I feel it.*

Even the news anchor spoke about the phage kids crying for the pains of others. Kyn had also known some of the infected children would die. Maybe his theory that the virus made its victims psychic was right. But if that was true, then these things the children said gave him pause. Kyn had claimed no one would be fine if the phage kids couldn't make people stop what they were doing. It almost sounded like a doomsday prediction, as if the clock was ticking down.

Was that possible? How could they know that?

More to the point, how could they prevent more deaths among the children? How could he keep Kyn safe and alive?

Sadie's suggestion about the video dangled in front of him. If the news anchor was correct, and all the phage kids were claiming these things, then Sadie might be right. Speaking up about his and Kyn's experience might help embolden others to do the same. If enough of them demanded the attention of the doctors on this piece of the puzzle, they might finally listen to what the children were saying, and act on that information.

But post an interview online? Simon and the others already loomed large with their threat to sue him for a refund of their investment if he didn't finish in three more days. This might push them into reaction mode. And Marin would never have allowed it. Their family's private business remained private. Period. End of story.

But Sadie was right. Marin wasn't here.

"Hey, Dad."

Luk spun. Kyn, awake, lay on her side.

"Hey, kiddo!" He took her hand, his thumb stroking her fingers. "How're you feeling?"

"Okay, I guess," she said. "Better. A little tired."

Relief threw a cool splash on the heat of his angst. "You don't feel the pain anymore?"

"I still feel it." She took a slow breath. "But I'm getting used to it."

His relief shut down like someone flipped a switch. "How do you mean?"

She took a deep breath and rolled her shoulders, twisting her body in the bed. For a moment she peered at the ceiling. "Remember Grampa Singh told us how he fell down the stairs when he was a kid and broke his knee?"

"Yeah."

"And how it still hurts all the time even now?"

Luk nodded.

"I guess it's like that for me, too. It hurt so bad at first that I couldn't stand it, like when Grampa first fell. I didn't know what to do. Except with Grampa, the doctors fixed him. I know the doctors can't fix me. I wanted them to. At first, I wanted them to make it stop. But now, I guess it feels like Grampa's knee all these years later. It aches, but I'm getting used to it."

"It isn't that bad now?"

"It's still pretty painful," she admitted. "But we're getting better at coping."

"'We'?" His throat went dry. "You mean the phage kids?"

"Mm hmm." She eyed him. "What's wrong?"

He opened his mouth to say nothing, then reconsidered. She would know. "You were right about that reef. It was on the news today."

Kyn said nothing at first. Her fingers toyed with the edge of the blanket. "How many have died?"

Luk hesitated. "Four."

"You're confused. Worried."

"Yeah."

Her attention shifted from her fingers to his face, her gaze peeling away the screen he'd erected to shield her from his fear.

"But there's something else. Tell me."

It occurred to him to wonder why she didn't know already, but he did not give voice to that uncertainty. Both of them—all three of them—were still finding the boundaries of their changing reality. Luk's brow creased, and he smoothed a strand of her hair.

"Sadie wants me to speak about all that's happened with you and put it online."

"And you don't want to."

He raked his nails over the stubble on his cheeks. "I don't know, kiddo. I really don't. What do you think?"

"Can I do it with you?"

He grimaced. "Oh, honey, I'm not sure that's a good idea. You've been through a lot."

"That's why I should do it. You're going to talk about me anyway, aren't you?"

"Yes," Luk admitted. "But why do you want to? It might be upsetting."

She wrapped her fingers around his. "There's a lot of kids like me."

"That's right."

"And a lot of worried dads and moms."

"No doubt."

"Would it make them feel better if I talk about what happened? What I feel?"

"That's not your responsibility, kiddo. You worry about getting back on your feet." He'd almost said *getting well*, but according to Kyn, she was already doing that.

"I dunno," she said, her mouth puckered. "Maybe it is up to me. Maybe the world would be a nicer place if we helped each other more."

That sounded like something Marin would have said. He took a deep breath. How bad could it be, anyway? It was Sadie. He trusted her. He could endure an hour's awkward discomfort to help all those kids.

He gripped the bedrail. "Are you sure you're only eight years old?"

She grinned.

Marin might have engaged their daughter in social causes even sooner, if she'd been around. He supposed it was past time Kyn got involved, especially in this case, since the cause affected her along with tens of thousands of other kids and, if their predictions were accurate, humans of all ages as well. Luk pursed his lips.

"You're sure about this?" he asked.

"Positive."

"Okay." He nodded. "I'll set it up."

Chapter 19

Rhue Children's Hospital, Austin, Texas
Thursday, November 14, 3:30 PM

Number of infected: 35,914

SADIE PUSHED PAST THE CURTAIN and glanced at the bed.

Luk followed her gaze. Kyn lay quiet, her chest rising and falling in gentle rhythm as if nothing were wrong.

"How is she?"

"I'm better, I think." Kyn's voice snagged their attention.

"Hey, sweetie." Sadie hugged her.

Luk joined them. "She wants to do this interview with me."

Sadie looked at Kyn. "You sure you're up to it?"

"Long as I don't have to do anything but talk."

"You want to be an internet star, huh?" Sadie winked.

Kyn grinned, then shrugged. "I have to start somewhere, right?"

"She's smart enough to know her own limits," Sadie said. "Let's include her."

"I agree." Luk turned a stern face to Kyn. "But you've been through a lot lately. If I even suspect you're stressed, your part's over. Sadie and I can continue later."

"Got it." Kyn stretched.

Luk adjusted the bed to a semi-upright position and helped his daughter sit up straighter.

Sadie fluffed and plumped the pillows behind Kyn, brushed her hair, and tidied her blanket, probably eager to get on with it before Luk changed his mind. "Ready?"

Luk hesitated. "We should check to see when the docs are going to make their rounds again. I don't want them to walk in on us quizzing Kyn about the environment."

"Why?" Kyn looked from one to the other of them.

"They're convinced you're delusional." Sadie leaned on the bedrail. "That you're saying the things you are because we made you afraid."

Kyn rolled her eyes.

Luk winked. "Give me a minute."

He stepped to the first station. "Excuse me."

"Yes, Mr. Behn?"

"Which doctor is on duty this afternoon?"

"Doctor Engan."

Whew. At least she'd seemed compassionate. "Do you know when she'll make her rounds again?"

"Not for at least another hour. Why?" The young man got to his feet. "Is Kyndra in pain?"

"No." Luk hoped his answer didn't come too quickly, or sound forced. "She's fine. I was curious. That's all."

The nurse's expression showed his uncertainty.

"I had some questions for her. But I can wait. It's no emergency. Thank you."

In Kyn's room, Luk ran quick fingers through his hair, bracing himself to step in front of a camera. "The coast is clear," he said. He'd do this, and anything else, for his daughter. For the other phage kids.

"Then let's get started." Sadie pulled her phone from her purse and prepped it to record. She straightened Luk's shirt, tidied a strand of his hair. "Luk, why don't you first introduce yourself, tell viewers who you are, introduce Kyndra, and tell us why you're doing this. Not the whole thing, just that Kyn's infected with the phage, and I'll take it from there. We'll get into the deeper reasons later. 'Kay?"

He swallowed his fear. "Got it."

"Good." Sadie lifted the phone and started the recording, then pointed at him to begin.

Luk's stomach flipped. He tried to smile but failed. Instead, he stood by the bed and addressed the camera. "I'm Lukas Behn, founder and CEO of BehnWerks Games. This," he laid a gentle hand on Kyn's shoulder, "is my eight-year-old daughter, Kyndra Kaur. We're talking to you today because Kyn is infected with the phage, and there are things about this disease you may not know. We want to tell everyone what it's like to be neck-deep in this thing."

He paused. Sadie took the verbal baton and ran with it.

"Kyndra," Sadie said, "can you tell me how it feels to be infected by something new, something no one understands?"

"I dunno," Kyn said. "Weird? I didn't like it much in the beginning."

"Do you like it better now?"

"Mmm," Kyndra hummed to herself. "Maybe. I think so."

"Can you tell me why?"

"It's cool to be able to feel that stuff. Even if it hurts sometimes."

"Do you still feel pain for animals and fish? Like the ones on that reef that's been in the news?"

"Yeah."

"Luk," Sadie said, "when did Kyn first mention animals dying on the reef?"

"Three days ago." He touched Kyn's hair. "I didn't know what she was talking about until today when I saw the drone footage on the news. It was exactly like what she'd described."

"Kyndra, did anyone tell you about the reef?"

"No."

"How did you know?"

"I can feel it. Like I'm an animal on the reef and it's happening to me."

Luk spoke up. "When all this first began, I found Kyndra in the yard shortly before dawn, staring northeast. She told me the trees were burning, but I only realized a few days ago that was the same night as all those wildfires up Nacogdoches way."

Sadie spoke to Kyndra. "Do you remember that morning?"

"I didn't at first," she said. "But now I do."

"How did you know about the fires? Could you smell the smoke?"

"No," she said. "I could feel it. Like when Dad and me have a campfire in the back yard, and I get too close to the firepit. It made me feel too hot, and I knew it wasn't me, but I still felt it." She wrinkled her nose. "I don't know how to explain it."

"You're doing a fine job. Do you still feel the reef? The same kind of pain? Or is it better now?"

"I still feel it, but it doesn't make me so scared now. I know what it is, and I know I have to tell people about it."

"Is that why you're talking to me today?"

"Mm hmm." Kyn nodded. "'Coz if I talk to you, I'm really talking to a whole lot of people. If I tell you we have to stop hurting the trees and the reefs, they'll hear me too. Right?"

"Yes, they will. Kyndra, do you know what being psychic means?"

"Mm hmm. Knowing stuff before it happens, or before anyone tells you."

"That's certainly part of it." Sadie paused. "Were you psychic before you were infected by the phage?"

Kyn smirked. "No way."

"Are you now?"

Luk watched Kyn's reaction. Her fingers fiddled with the blanket. Her mouth pulled to one side as if she were considering her response. "Maybe. I do know stuff sometimes. Like I know that we've messed the environment up so bad we'll have to work hard to make it right again. We haven't destroyed everything yet, but if we keep making it worse, the phage kids are gonna pay."

Sadie tossed Luk a sharp glance over the camera. "Do you think you know these things because of the phage?"

"Definitely."

"Can you feel it inside you? Does it talk to you?"

"No. Not yet, anyway."

"Do you think it will?"

Kyn shrugged.

"Did it infect you and the other kids for a reason? I mean, do you think it knew what it was doing?"

"Sure."

"Why do you think it did that?"

She sat quietly for a minute. "It wanted to heal us. To connect us."

"Why do you say that?"

"Before, we couldn't hear each other. We couldn't feel the animals, so we didn't know what we were doing to them." Kyn rested her head against the pillows and smiled into the camera. "Now we do."

Luk gestured, and Sadie paused the recording. "Okay, kiddo. I'll take it from here."

She reached for him. "Don't leave though?"

His eyes misted over. "You sure you don't want to rest?"

"I will. I'll listen and not talk if that's okay."

He kissed the top of her head. "No problem." He faced Sadie again.

Sadie resumed the recording, aiming the camera in his direction. "Luk, what has been the hardest part of this whole ordeal?"

"Well, all of it's been hard." Luk looked down at his daughter. "Seeing her in pain and knowing there was nothing I could do. Nothing anyone could do. Not knowing what was going on. Trying to get the doctors to take me seriously when I tell them Kyn's feelings and sensations are real. It's tough to pick one thing."

"The doctors won't hear Kyn's claims?"

Luk gave an annoyed grunt. "No. They assure me it's the medicine, that Kyndra is delirious." He indicated the bed and its occupant. "Does she act or sound delirious?"

"What do you think is happening, then?" Sadie smiled encouragement at him.

"I didn't know at first. But she's my child. I saw her struggling. I heard her screams. Those weren't faked. Is she psychic?" He took a deep breath. "I don't know. I'm not a scientist. But she's told me things she could not have known. Like those wildfires. Like that coral harvest that's been in the news. So I believe her. I also know she's not the only affected child saying things like this, and I think we should start listening to them and stop doing whatever causes them pain."

"I can understand that," Sadie said. "Has Kyndra spoken to any of the other phage kids since she was admitted to the hospital?"

"No. She's been unconscious or sedated much of the time."

"Does she know where they are anyway? How they're feeling?"

"Yes," Luk said, "mostly in a general way, not specific to any one person."

"What would you say to the parents of children who have recently contracted this disease?"

A million possibilities clamored to be first, and Luk tried to pick and choose between them. "First, tell your kid every day how much you love them. Even if they're asleep or drugged or unconscious, and you think they can't hear you. They hear more than you know. Second, enlist help. You cannot do this alone. And third, buckle in. It's a rough ride, but I truly hope you come through the crisis with your family intact."

"BehnWerks was scheduled to release a new game in October, though I'm sure this has pushed back all deadlines for you until Kyndra is home and well." Sadie winked at him over the top of the phone. "Any projections as to when players might see that hit the market?"

Luk wanted to kiss Sadie. What would his investors say about that question? "Not yet. Hyde and Seek is almost release-ready, but every employee at BehnWerks has been affected by the phage. I'm sure the gaming public will understand that we have to put our families first. We appreciate the continued patience of our customers during this difficult time."

Sadie gave him a thumbs up behind the camera. "One last question, Luk. How do you expect this crisis to affect your gaming business? Do you have a plan to move forward, and is BehnWerks going to take any action in response to the events of the last month?"

"I haven't thought that far ahead yet. But it's possible. Watch our website for announcements and news. That's all I can say for now."

Sadie ended the recording and came to the bedside. "You wanna see?"

Kyn pushed up a little higher on the bed.

Sadie replayed the video for her interviewees.

"Well?" she asked when it finished.

"Brilliant addition about Hyde and Seek." Luk grinned. "That was a nice opportunity to personally ask the gamers for their patience. Simon's not going to like this, but hopefully, now his argument won't stand."

"Do you want to post it now?"

"I say do it, Dad."

Kyn slid down on the bed, and he lowered it so she could be more comfortable. "You think I should?"

"Mm hmm," she said, her eyes half-closed.

He glanced at Sadie, who waited for his answer.

His stomach fluttered. It'd get a lot of response, no doubt. Luk didn't for one minute suppose it would all be positive. Putting anything online, especially something like this, was fodder for the trolls. His biggest hesitation came from the fact that he wouldn't deal with any fallout alone. Kyn, the other BehnWerks employees, BehnWerks itself all would be targets. But hopefully, the video would do more good than harm. If he could reach other parents who were struggling with this same issue, if he could raise enough awareness that the doctors would take the parents' claims seriously and investigate, then it would be worth it.

Luk glanced at the bed again. Kyn slept. Her chest rose and fell with slow, even, reassuring normalcy.

He closed his eyes in a long blink, gathering his nerve. "Yes. Let's do it."

Sadie sent the file to his cloud account. When the upload was completed she gave him a thumbs-up.

Luk sat at his laptop. A few minutes later, he uploaded the video to his personal blog with a "phagepandemic" hashtag. He reviewed the draft post, then published it.

"Okay. Done," he said, his stomach in knots

Sadie sat beside him and twisted around so her knee bumped his. "You did the best thing."

"I hope you're right."

Her mouth twitched at the corners as if she was hiding a smile. "Do you want to give it an even larger number of hits?"

He frowned. "How?"

"We could get the local greenies in on it. Have them post links to it on their pages. A lot of them knew Marin. They've known Kyn since she was a baby. I'm sure they'd help."

Luk shoved both hands into his hair as he sagged against the sofa's cushions. "If they knew Marin, they'd know she never would have allowed me to do this."

Sadie wrinkled her nose. "I disagree. They would know Marin would do whatever it took to help her daughter, especially if it helped everyone else's kids, too."

This was deeper than he'd intended to go into exposing his family's personal business. But he'd already decided to do the video. What was one more step down this road?

"Do you know how to reach them?"

"Yes, I have the mobile phone number for the spokesperson of their group."

He offered a thin smile. "Okay. Make the call."

Chapter 20

HomeSpace Suites, Austin, Texas
Friday, November 15, 2:00 AM

Number of infected: 52,097

THE RINGING PHONE INTRUDED INTO HER DREAM, inserted itself in that disjointed way dreams sometimes melded with the reality surrounding the dreamer.

I should get that. She foraged through rooms in an enormous, unfamiliar house filled with more shadows than light. The ringing came from everywhere. Every room.

Nah, probably a telemarketer.

Still, she couldn't ignore it. Might be important. She'd been working on something...what—

Another ring jolted her into the darkened hotel room. She jerked upright, almost falling out of the bed, and snatched her mobile.

"Whazzit?

"I found something."

She blinked dream-filled eyes in the dark. "Cagney?"

"Yeah. Wakey wakey."

Nadine rubbed her face, trying to kick her brain into gear. She squinted at the clock. "Ugh. This can't hold for a few hours? My brain is burnt toast."

"Trust me. You'll wanna see this right now."

"Okay," Nadine sighed. "But I warn you. I'm shower-free. Give me ten, no fifteen minutes."

"See you then."

She rang off and switched on the bedside lamp, then dragged her feet over the side of the bed. Why did these momentous discoveries never happen in the bright light of morning, after breakfast and coffee? If the world ever ended, it would surely happen in the wee hours of the night. At least that she could sleep through.

Her clothes from the day before lay neatly folded on the chair, and she pulled them on piece by piece, shoved her feet into shoes, and unplugged her charging laptop. She slipped it into her backpack and grabbed her keys. Ten minutes later, she re-entered the conference room where Cagney sat waiting for her. She dropped her pack on the floor at her feet and examined his computer screen. "What am I looking at?"

"Results from Zero's bloodwork. You told us to search for neurotoxins or anything like hormones?"

"I remember."

"Well, I'm pretty sure this qualifies." He circled an area with his cursor. "This section in particular."

The structure of the beastie on the screen twanged a chord in her memory. "Intermedin," she said through a yawn. "So?"

Cagney made an annoying buzzer-like noise. "Wrong." He enlarged the image. "Look closer."

She did. "Oh. The structure's flawed. There's an extra amino acid. Can't be intermedin." She straightened. "That doesn't belong."

"No, it does not. It is, however, lipophilic enough to transit the blood-brain barrier." He winked at her.

"Our first clue. Good catch, Cagney." She hunched over the desk again, near enough to smell his shampoo. Patchouli. A hint of vanilla. Much more pleasant than her own fragrance right now, no doubt. "Have you isolated a testable quantity yet?"

"No. I wanted to show you first. What do you think it is?"

"I have no idea." Wily little sneaks, these phages. What in the weird world of wonder were they up to? Nadine pushed away from Cagney's station and hustled over to her own, whipping out her laptop as she went. She typed in commands to bring up Zero's PET scans, even though she'd reviewed them a dozen times. If something was there, she'd have seen it. Even so, she zoomed in on the graphic, then zoomed in again. Still not good enough. "I need a bigger display."

"Main station," Cagney said right behind her.

Nadine jumped. "Mother of all white hairs, Cagney. Warn a person when you sneak up on them like that, would you?"

He laughed, the impish jokester.

Nadine suppressed a grin and carried her laptop to the main station where Lara sat engrossed in her assigned research.

"Switch to another station for a bit, would you?" Nadine said. "I need this one."

"Sure." Lara closed her work, gathered her notes, and grabbed her coffee.

Nadine sat and pulled Zero's scans up from the server. On the huge screen, she zoomed in on the graphic. She finessed the touchpad, jockeying the enormous image bit by bit. She drew back to see the whole image better.

"What are you looking for?" Cagney asked, watching the screen.

"I'll know it when I see it."

Lara joined them. "What's going on?"

Cagney caught her up, his words rapid, breathless.

Nadine ignored them, scouring and analyzing every inch of the brightest area on the image until—

Her fingers froze. She might have squeaked. Barb teased her for making noises when she got excited about something. Like a new discovery.

Nadine dragged the cursor over the anomaly she'd found. A random spot on the screen, really. Until she maxed out the system's zoom capacity.

There it was. She must have made some sound to alert her coppertop assistant.

"What?" Cagney prompted.

"Our second clue." Nadine pointed at the object on the screen. "See that?"

"Yeah."

Lara sucked in a breath. "What is that?"

"That, my friends, resembles a fresh batch of cells in little Zero's anterior insular cortex. Probably VENs."

"VENs?" Lara frowned.

"Von Economo neurons. Special neurons specific to social mammals, or so the hypotheses assume. I expect these will be spindle neurons, but I can't be sure yet. You know anything about the brain? Which parts control different functions?"

Lara's perplexed expression answered for her.

"I know the insulae are thought to be involved in consciousness," said Cagney. "But that's basic theory. This is beyond me."

"Don't feel bad. I don't completely grasp it either. This is the stuff of specialists. But I do know that neuroscientists believe the insulae are also linked to emotions like compassion. Empathy."

Cagney's face scrunched, pinching his pale features. "I'm following you, barely."

"You know how sometimes people with brain injuries, epilepsy, or good drugs feel like they've had a mystical experience? Sort of a reunion with God?"

"Yeah," Lara and Cagney both said at the same time.

Nadine waved at the screen. "Researchers theorize that's the insulae. The spindle neurons firing overtime in the insular cortex. Especially in the anterior region."

Lara glanced at the monitor. "But wouldn't a mystical connection to God produce euphoria, not extreme pain?"

Cagney shrugged. "That would depend on interpretation, wouldn't it? Couldn't NJace or this byproduct, if that's what it is, be crossing the pathways? Confusing the signals?"

"I don't know about all that," Nadine said. "It's been a long time since I studied neuroscience. But I know Zero isn't supposed to have that intermedin lookalike in her blood, and her brain isn't supposed to produce new VENS on this scale. I'd lay tomorrow's lunch against the possibility that those two things are connected."

"Maybe the intermedin thingy is some sort of catalyst," Cagney said, his eyes shining, "causing the new growth. This is the first break we've had. We need to get on it pronto, right?"

"You bet your bold and shiny hairdo. We need PS3XG brain scans of Zero. Pronto. In fact, do two—one overall image and one of the anterior insular cortex, complete with contrast. Put a rush on both. Also, order another lumbar puncture. I want to see if your 'catalyst' is present in the CSF and compare it with her prior results. Make sure her parent is there, though. She's already had one, but that's a scary test. We want him nearby in case she wakes up."

"Got it. Anything else?"

"Not yet. Let's see what those tests say first." Nadine closed her laptop and shoved it in its pack.

"You're leaving?"

Nadine paused, peering up at Cagney. "You telling me you can't handle these instructions without me here to supervise?"

"No, I got it. Just collating data."

"Good. 'Coz I'm going to shower and change clothes." She slung her pack over her shoulder. He'd done well. Without that catch, she might not have examined Zero's bloodwork again for a while, at least. Cagney had his heart set on a promotion. He seemed all kinds of ready. Worth every penny they'd spent to train him. He'd make a great lead investigator in the next year or two, but she'd be sorry to lose him on her crew.

"I'll be an hour. Call me if anything else comes up before then." She pushed through the door and left the lab. Somehow, she no longer felt sleepy.

Chapter 21

Aboard the *Pasteur*, Vliat, Nlaan Islands
Saturday, November 16, 6:20 AM
(Austin, Texas, Friday, November 15, 11:20 AM)

Number of infected: 79,442

ISOBEL GRABBED A BURNT COFFEE IN THE MESS and started toward the lab. Last night, for the first time in more than two weeks, she'd slept the night through. A yawn stretched her jaw and she covered her mouth, even though no one was around to see. She tipped the cup to take tiny sips of the hot brew and tried to wake up.

It helped to remember that last set of tests. The bonds still held, as she suspected they would, and close examination showed no degradation. Pity, all the time and resources they'd wasted because someone made a mistake in their lab notes. She'd have to track down who'd done that so she could share the blame from Holschtatt—from Neillsen—with the person who'd almost ruined her hopes.

But there would be time for that later. Right now, it tickled her to know that the medicine she hoped to create for Gabe, for all Milani children, could finally come to fruition.

She made it to the lab compartment before a short, brawny deckhand in dungarees and a thin grey tank that had seen too much wear stopped her.

"Doctor Fallon, there's an urgent call for you on the bridge."

"Thank you. I'll be right there." She ducked into the lab and left her coffee on the desk before following him down the corridor.

On the bridge, only the captain and a single crewman remained. As soon as she stepped into the cabin, they gave her the room. Not a good sign. She moved into view of the vidscreen where Neillsen glared out at her. Isobel's stomach dropped.

"What the hell is going on out there, Isobel? For god's sake, your worksite is all over the goddamned news! Holschtatt's taken over a hundred calls this morning. Goddamned protestors are blocking our entries. This is the biggest mess I've ever seen in my whole goddamned life."

"They came out of nowhere, Mr. Neillsen," she said, "a big ship maybe a mile off our site. Travis didn't notice them until they sent that drone over the atoll. He—"

"He? Where the hell were you? Why didn't *you* see this goddamned ship? Why didn't *you* do something to stop them from getting that footage?"

She fumbled for words like a berated teenager. "M-Mr. Neillsen, I was in the lab, sir. I couldn't see anything topside from there. Travis and I agreed—"

"I don't give a damn what you and Travis worked out. This is on you, Isobel. You told me you had an agreement with those backwater boongas."

"I did, Mr. Neillsen. We've done everything they asked of us, even when it slowed down our production."

"Well, clearly you missed a few details. For all we know they're the ones who sicced those goddamned climate nazis on your people. And you shot the son of a bitch down! They're suing us for destruction of property!"

"Wha—" Isobel's mouth worked faster than her brain. "They were attempting to video proprietary work, sir. I thought—"

"You are paid to think in the lab. Not in international political arenas." Neillsen muttered something she couldn't catch, then gestured at someone off-camera. "This has gotten out of control. It's a matter of time until the Nlaantu lodge formal complaints about the alleged damage you're doing there. Either way, you're done. Those envirofreaks have enough clout to make Holschtatt listen to them, so now you will listen to me."

Isobel's heart tried to leap from her chest. She staggered and clutched the edge of the table as if the floor had dropped. "No, you can't—" She forced a calm tone to her voice. "Mr. Neillsen, don't shut us down. We finally started making some real progress, and if we leave now, all this was for nothing! I'll meet with the Nlaantu again. I'll find out what they want, figure out a way to satisfy them while we still keep working. I'll—"

"You'll pack up Holschtatt's shit and get the hell out of there. You have twenty-four hours. Am I clear?"

The edge of the table bit into her hands. She let it go and stood on shaky legs. "Yes, Mr. Neillsen. I'll take care of it."

"Do a better goddamned job of clearing out than you have of running the harvest. That's all I ask. Report directly to me as soon as you get to Austin."

"Of—" she began, but the screen went dark. "—course," she finished. Isobel closed her eyes and drew a slow, calming breath. Tears squeezed out and she dashed them away.

A tap at the door drew her attention. Travis stood in the corridor outside the bridge. She turned aside while she regained control.

His quiet words told her he knew everything. "You okay?"

"Hah," she breathed. "Um. Sure. The project I counted on to save my son just got flushed down the toilet. My job may be dangling by a thread. And oh yeah, Holschtatt got sued for property damages for that drone, which means they'll probably take any settlement out of my salary, assuming I still have one by the time we get home." She hugged herself. "Yeah. I'm peachy."

He came in without asking and rested his elbows on the table across from her, peering at her over the equipment. "What can I do to help?"

She met his gaze, saw the sympathy there, which thickened that lump in her throat. Isobel looked down and blew out a heavy breath.

"I don't know what we can do in a single day. I guess we could get the dive teams out there once more, but I'm not sure it'll be enough to do any good. Waiting for the coral dust to settle before harvesting more slows us down too much. How many more loads can they get today?"

He shrugged. "Three? Four? I know that's not a lot, but it's better than none."

Unless they could speed up the process. An idea took root, a desperate measure to match a desperate situation. Big risk. But if she succeeded...

"What if we could get more?" Isobel pitched her voice low, secretive. "A lot more?"

Travis squinted at her. "How?"

Isobel hesitated, measuring the depth of her commitment. Shouts came from the deck. A crewman passed by the bridge compartment on his way to some obscure duty elsewhere on board. The boat's gentle motion in the water felt almost natural to her now.

At last, she took a breath, glanced aside, and leaned closer. "Are there any explosives on the ship? Small ones?"

"Explosives?" He gaped at her. "That would piss the Nlaantu off even more!"

Of course it would, but she didn't have much of a choice. "The Nlaantu are ready to banish us anyway, and Neillsen's said we can't continue. What's one more offense?"

"Using explosives would destroy the star queen," he pointed out.

"Not if they're small," she said. "If they're big enough to knock loose those segments with the star queen, but not so big they destroy the harvest. Afterward, we gather the detached bits and bring them aboard. Much faster than pecking at the reef piece by tiny piece. Right?"

"I'm pretty sure that sort of thing's..." He frowned. "...illegal."

"That may be," she said. There were ways to fuzz the lines into debatable shades of grey, and she intended to use every one of them if need be. "But we could claim we didn't know. Besides, as little as the Nlaantu deal with technology, I doubt they'd have actual laws about explosives."

Travis seemed to be reevaluating her, ticking through pluses and minuses. "We'll have to be ready to gather and go. We won't get a second chance."

Isobel watched his mouth form the words, her heart beating faster. This would cause Neillsen more trouble, but he wouldn't care as long as they got the coral. Once she could establish the artificial reefs for a steady supply of the material with which to manufacture the drug, the proceeds would provide ample payback for any restitution expense this project incurred.

"Good. Let's do it. Meanwhile, we should have the rest of the crew prepare to depart."

"Yes, ma'am," Travis said. "I'll get on it right away."

Rhue Children's Hospital, Austin, Texas
Friday, November 15, 12:30 PM

Number of infected: 86,715

Sadie stood at the bed while Kyn slept. Luk watched them both, a warmth spreading through his chest. Marin had told him Sadie could never have kids. Some accident or injury when she was young, if he remembered correctly. The way she looked at his daughter now, the way she had bonded with Kyn and stood by her all through this, Luk would never have known Sadie had no experience with kids of her own. She'd make a great stepmom.

The thought startled him, and he sat up straighter. True, he'd grown much fonder of her over the last year, and especially in the last few weeks. But stepmom seemed a bit premature when he had yet to discover whether she reciprocated his growing affection. He hadn't even tried to kiss her. He'd considered it, but...

He dug into his feelings, peeped under the rocks in his emotional passages, shone a light into corners left dark by Marin's passing. Had anything new sprouted there? Had those old vines blossomed again?

His phone buzzed. Simon. Luk let it go to voicemail while he watched Sadie. Her hair, unbound today, tumbled halfway to her waist, locks of it swinging forward when she reached over the bed. Her teal sweater hung down past her hips and had slid off one shoulder to reveal the grey tee-shirt beneath, probably her BehnWerks shirt. That thing was old. He should get her a new one.

A second buzz from his phone told him he had a text. He picked it up and read the message.

Video on your blog has gone viral. Reposted in numerous forums. Did you know? Urgent that we speak.

He must have made a sound.

"What is it?" Sadie said.

"A text from Simon." He held out the phone for her to see. "Our video has gotten a lot of views."

She read the message. "Do you want to check it out?"

He almost said no. But he should know what he was dealing with before he spoke to Simon. "Yeah."

She grabbed his laptop and sat beside him. Together, they opened his blog. They'd left the comments on at the time, not anticipating any problems. Now he scrolled and scrolled, trying to find the end. In fewer than twenty-four hours, hundreds of comments had been posted. At first, Luk's spirit soared. Until he began to read them.

> What an idiot. Does BehnWerks' board of directors not vet their people?
>
> This is a hoax, a grab for attention before they release their next game. Don't fall for it.
>
> You're a criminal, pushing your child to do something like this, then airing her face and personal drama online. Shame on you. I hope they take her away from you and put her somewhere safe.
>
> Getting sick makes people psychic? Where do I sign up?
>
> Hey Kyndra, what's my dog trying to tell me?

Sadie read with him and muttered in frustration.

Luk kept reading, his stomach sinking lower with every post. A few supported him, other parents who'd seen the same sort of reactions from their own sick children and thanked him for speaking out. Those were in the minority. By far, most derided his comments, ridiculed him and Kyn for believing such things, or dismissed him outright as a fool. He'd never been so embarrassed in his life, not as much for himself as for what Kyn would have to deal with when everything opened up again. And BehnWerks...

He felt sick. No wonder Simon was calling. Luk would be lucky if they didn't drop him like a venomous snake. BehnWerks may not survive this kind of publicity.

"Oh, Luk." Sadie's soft voice pierced the gloom building around his head and heart. "I didn't know this would happen. I'm so sorry."

"No." Luk scowled. "Don't be. This isn't your fault. It was a good idea. I just...I hoped people would be surprised, call for more action with regard to the actual problem, not point fingers, and accuse me of harming my daughter. I guess I expected too much." He disabled the comments feature, even though that was a bit like closing the barn door after the horse was out. Still, perhaps it could stanch the wound.

He ran a search. Dozens of other sites had shared his post. Comments on every one fell into the same—or worse—categories. After a few more pages, he shut the laptop. He'd seen enough.

"I need to call Simon." He got to his feet and grabbed his phone.

In the hall, he found Simon's number. His thumb hovered over the "call" command but someone called his name. Two strangers approached, a brown-skinned woman of about fifty-something with her hair in short twists, and a tanned, bearded man in a designer suit. Luk tensed.

"Can I help you?"

The woman spoke first. "Mr. Behn, I'm Aimee de Verlaine, Director of Rhue Children's Hospital. This," she said, gesturing at her companion, "is Jorge Schirru, Director of Public Relations."

Luk nodded. "Nice to meet you."

"I'm afraid this is not a social call." De Verlaine clutched a file to her chest. "We are here about the video you posted to the internet."

"Yes? And?"

"And I must ask you not to do it again. Not while your child is a patient in this facility." Her full lips clamped down on her words, almost as if they pained her to speak them.

"May I ask why?"

"What you have claimed in that video casts the hospital and our medical professionals in a bad light," Schirru said. "Rhue is funded by public resources, as well as private ones. We do a lot of good for our little patients. This video, or others like it, could damage our credibility, cause us to lose our funding. Try to comprehend how that would affect the sick children we help every year."

"Not to mention several of our doctors have lodged complaints that your video was barely shy of a personal accusation." De Verlaine struggled to keep her voice civil. "Our staff is chosen from among the best and brightest, Mr. Behn, but their reputations are everything, both to them and to us. We can't allow you to cast shade on their professional integrity. Now I'm afraid I must insist that you do not make any more videos while you are on the Rhue campus, nor any that mention Rhue Children's Hospital or its medical staff, or I will be forced to have security remove you and ensure you remain off the premises. Our legal department is already reviewing this matter. Please don't give them further reason to make your life more complicated than it already is. Focus on your child. She should be your concern right now."

Luk stared at them. "I *am* thinking about my daughter. That's why I made the video. Doctors Sarsby and Whitfield refused to take me seriously when I told them things about my daughter's actions and behavior, details that—"

"Enough," de Verlaine said. "This is a very fine line, Mr. Behn. I urge you not to cross it. Leave the medicine to the doctors. I have complete faith our staff is doing the best they can for your child, and for all the others here who are sick with this virus." She gestured to Schirru and they left.

Luk blinked. The phone rang. He started, saw the number, and squeezed his eyes closed.

He thumbed it on and raised it to his ear. "Hello, Simon. Let me see if I can guess why you've called."

Before he could say more, Simon interrupted. "Luk, what were you thinking? Have you seen the reactions online? This has made a laughing stock of BehnWerks. You didn't sacrifice only yourself, you yanked your employees and your investors down with you. The company is tanking. Why would you do such a foolish thing?"

"You haven't seen her. You haven't heard the things coming out of her mouth. Every word I said in the video is truth."

The investor muttered at the other end of the line. "I've gone as far as I can," he finally said. "Will Sato is out, too. You'll be hearing from our lawyers."

"Simon, come on." Luk spoke louder than he'd intended, and one of the nurses shushed him. "Don't do this," he said, his voice softer but no less urgent. "You know this will pass. Don't pull out now."

"I'm sorry, Luk. I truly hope Kyn will recover soon. Goodbye."

"No, Simon!" But he was gone.

Damnit. Luk grabbed a clump of hair in his fist and tried not to scream. He called Bea, his assistant, but got no response at the office or on her mobile. He left her a voicemail to call him, then pocketed his phone.

Joy appeared at his side. "Hey. Need a friend?"

He sagged. "Yes. Yes, I do."

She threw an arm around his shoulders without speaking. Having her nearby helped. Joy and Rachel had been friends for years. They'd never abandon him. Neither would Sadie, but those three, and Kyn, might be the last ones left who supported him. "Thanks."

"No problem."

They stood there a while before he asked about Zach and Rachel. She asked about Kyn and Sadie. Both kids held their own. Both had experienced the odd "feelings," though Zach's hadn't played out in the news yet. Joy didn't mention the video. She didn't need to.

While they stood there, another stranger approached, a solitary woman this time, slender, pale-skinned, glasses. She carried a small notebook. Luk braced himself. What now?

"Mr. Behn?"

"That's me," he said, his voice sharper than he'd intended.

"I'm Rory Eppstein, with the Department of Family and Protective Services, Mr. Behn. I wonder if we might have a word?"

"Oh for..." Luk bit down on his words. He took a breath as if he might draw strength from the air. "Yes. Please feel free to speak. This is my neighbor and friend, Joy Maxwell. I have no secrets from her."

"Very well." Eppstein's posture revealed nothing. "We have received several complaints from concerned citizens that you are exploiting your young daughter for your gaming company's monetary gain. Are you working with a child specialist in this matter to ensure she's not overworked or pushed to say or do things that make her uncomfortable?"

Joy dropped her arm.

Under his breath, Luk murmured a mantra of self-control. "This is about the video we put online yesterday, isn't it?"

"I haven't seen a video. I'm here to investigate a claim against you as the father of Kyndra Brook Kaur," she said, after glancing at her notes, "but if you put a video of your child online, one that compromises her in any way, that would explain why someone called in a complaint."

"My daughter speaks her mind, Ms. Eppstein, as I have always encouraged her to do." Luk had to work to remain calm. "I doubt I or anyone else could convince her to claim something she didn't believe for herself."

"I'm going to need to speak to Kyndra for myself." Eppstein peered over her glasses at Luk. "Without you present."

"No problem," Luk said. "But it can't be now. She's sleeping, and she's been very sick. You'll have to come when she's feeling better."

"Ms. Maxwell," Eppstein asked, "how long have you known Mr. Behn and his daughter?"

Joy glanced aside at him, her demeanor skittish, her hands clasped together in front of her as if to ward off this regrettable encounter. "Several years."

"I see. Are you here visiting Mr. Behn or his daughter?"

"Not exactly." Joy shifted on her feet. "My son is also sick with the virus."

"I'm sorry to hear that," the woman said, her voice flat. "Was he also in this online video?"

"No." Joy's response came so fast it caught Luk by surprise. "No, he wasn't."

"Good to know. Is there a time when I might speak with you on this matter? Perhaps when you and your husband would both be available?"

Joy cast a hurried glance at Luk, which begged forgiveness for something she hadn't yet done, then offered Eppstein a small smile. "Perhaps when our son is better, my wife and I can find time to help. If you'll excuse me." She walked off with staccato steps, as jumpy as if she were being stalked.

Eppstein's jaw fell open for an instant before she recovered.

Behind her, Joy gestured to Luk, slicing the air in front of her as if to say "I can't get involved." Her expression filled with sorrow and she ducked into Zach's room.

Of course. A lesbian couple might not want to be under investigation by DFPS for any reason. Yes, Joy and Rachel were legally married. Yes, both of them were listed as parents of their boys. Yes, they were model citizens of Austin and had no real reason to fear—except bias and homophobia. Even if DFPS couldn't legally seize their children, they could stir up trouble for their family. With Zach already sick, they did not need that grief as well.

He heaved a sigh and realized Eppstein had spoken. "I'm sorry, what did you say?"

"I said I'd like to come in. If Kyndra's sleeping, I won't wake her, but I'd like to see her before I leave."

Luk's shoulders slumped. He held the door open for Eppstein and followed her into the room and past the curtain.

Sadie rose from the couch in one graceful move and came forward to greet Luk in subdued tones. He introduced them, showed Eppstein that Kyn was, indeed, sleeping, then took the

DFPS worker's card and promised to call her when Kyn was awake.

When the woman was gone, and Luk had explained all that had happened with Simon and the hospital staff and now DFPS, Sadie pulled him down on the sofa.

"I'm sorry, Luk." She tucked an errant lock of hair behind her ear. "I'm so, so sorry I talked you into doing that damn video. It was a bad call."

"Why?"

Kyn's voice from the bed sounded distant, sleepy, as if she were still half dreaming.

Luk went to her side, Sadie right behind him. "It's nothing. Don't bother yourself, kiddo. Rest."

She reached for his fingers. "That lady thinks you're a bad dad, doesn't she?"

"She doesn't know. Someone else told her I was, though, so she has to make sure you're okay. She's doing her job."

"I know." Kyn paused. "I can talk to her now if it would help."

"Do you feel up to it?"

She shrugged but didn't answer.

"Then no. She can wait."

She paused, watching him with eyes that looked older by far than her eight years. "Don't worry about this. You didn't talk me into anything. We did the right thing. They don't understand. Not yet. But they will."

Luk smiled. But inside, he trembled at what he had done, and the price they might all pay for that one act. Hopefully, Kyn was right, and everyone else would figure that out before the state tore apart what was left of his family.

Chapter 22

Rhue Children's Hospital, Austin, Texas
Friday, November 15, 1:15 PM

Number of infected: 98,952

NADINE SAT AT HER DESK EATING HER SANDWICH, her feet up on an extra chair. "What kind of nonsense?"

Blondie barked a laugh. "All kinds. You name it, they're claiming it. There are some real weirdos out there, man. Some say this is God's punishment or some such thing. Others insist it's a weaponized biotest gone wrong. One guy's even suggesting that the virus is making his kid psychic. He put her on camera and everything. Trolls are hounding him."

"Shame, that." Nadine took another bite of her sandwich.

"Why?" Blondie squinted at her. "You don't suppose that nut is right?"

"Any one of them could be right, for all we know. I'll remind you that we, the professionals, aren't sure what's happening either. We've already ruled out the possible."

"It's sad." Yuka plopped down across from Nadine. "These people's kids are sick. They're dealing with a lot, especially since some of them began to die."

"You think they're losing it?" Blondie looked almost eager.

Nadine pursed her lips. That young man was far too intrigued by drama. He'd need to shed that if he was going to make it in this field.

"No." Yuka scowled. "I think they're grasping at anything that might explain what's happening to their kids. That's all. I feel for them. Don't you?"

Blondie sat up straight and tugged at his collar as if had been askew. "Well, yeah. But we can't get emotional. We can't allow ourselves to indulge fantasies, right?"

"Why not?" Nadine said.

"Well, this is a medical issue." Blondie shrugged as if it were obvious. "Science will solve it, sooner or later."

"You do know that many new scientific theories were once considered fantasy, right?"

He scoffed. "Don't tell me you believe these whack jobs."

"I haven't heard them. I can't say. But it isn't smart to automatically discount something simply because it doesn't fit known parameters. Stepping outside the box is how we learn new things." Nadine sipped her soda. "Okay, let's get to it." She sat forward, popped the last bite of sandwich in her mouth while the others went to their stations. There wasn't much they could do that they hadn't already done, at least not until they got those test results. Should be soon.

But Blondie's comments made her wonder. She Googled #phagepandemic. Numerous hits filled the page, many of them apparent repeats of the same video of the kid and her dad. She scrolled down to the bottom where a couple of new images from a different setting made it into the results. At the top of the page again, she clicked the first link, which took her to a personal blog for someone named Lukas Damon Behn.

Why did that name sound familiar? Her eyes widened. Wasn't that Zero's dad? She paused, confirmed against Zero's records, and switched back to the interview.

The video began to play, and she listened. Near the beginning, the mention of the reef sounded familiar, somehow. Where had she seen something about that? She paid closer attention to the rest, noting how the child first commented about the reef three days before it hit the news. According to the father, doctors dismissed his claims that this was a symptom. She probably would have too.

But then how did the kid know about the reef?

Wait a minute. Hadn't she heard something else about one of the phage patients knowing something before it happened? Something had made the reporters name this bug the entheóphage. Was this it? She dove into her browser and followed the other #phagepandemic hits. Post after post talked about kids weeping for harm to animals, insects, marine life, or trees. They babbled about poor air quality, fouled waters, even poisoned earth.

Each post she read added depth to her frown. Sure, there were plenty who dismissed the parents' claims as ridiculous. But to the scientist in Nadine, a clear pattern began to emerge. She opened a document on her desktop and made notes of specific claims. Next, she reviewed her list of infection sites with high numbers and began digging for details on environmental destruction taking place in those regions.

China and India, where the first major overseas infections began to occur, were the two biggest users of coal-burning power. She dug a little further. Yep. Many countries or regions most reliant on coal had high infection numbers.

She scanned the global spread indicators. Brazil had especially high figures. Deforestation and development in that nation's delicate Amazon rainforest rose by 85 percent that year alone. Vietnam had a multitude of hits for habitat destruction, but also for trade in wild tiger skins. Nepal's use of pangolin scales in its traditional medicines had pushed the animals to the brink of extinction. Many coastal areas had high infection rates, as well as news articles about overfishing in the local seas.

The U.S. cities on her list each had their claim to environmental damage. In Austin, the first city hit by the phage, air quality had grown steadily worse for the last year.

Studies found fecal matter in more than half the city's freshwater sites, as well as pollution in the estuaries and wetlands from local industry. Other eastern and central U.S. cities relied on coal.

No. No, she couldn't conceive of any way there might be a real connection between these infected children and what was happening in the environments where they lived. Not like that, anyway. Maybe if they drank the polluted water, or showed signs of respiratory distress due to poor air quality she could see it.

She tried a new tack, searching areas of low infection rates for environmental pollutants or other activities deleterious to Nature. Among the lowest numbers, Iceland's capital city of Reykjavík had fewer NJace cases than other cities its size. Tasmania, Finland, Norway, Greenland, all had lower cases than many other nations, but even those were not untouched. Was it due to smaller populations? No. Several similar-sized cities had very different infection rates. Were those places less affected by habitat destruction, environmental damage, and animal poaching? She'd probably be hard-pressed to find a single region on the entire earth unspoiled by pollution or damage caused or exacerbated by human activities.

Nadine watched the interview with Zero and her dad again, stopping it at the mention of the atoll. Where had she heard that before?

Oh yes. On the news. Yesterday, right after she'd heard about the first NJace deaths. She sifted through reports of atoll damage and found the same footage she'd seen yesterday of an otherwise pristine island chain fouled by reef harvesters. From the air, she could see the clouds of coral dust, rainbow sheens of oil from the dive boats, a wide swath of trees leveled, presumably for the harvesting teams. One segment showed a trash pit with water seepage and what appeared to be human waste on the narrow strip of land near the dive site. Dead fish and birds floated in the water nearby. Could those deaths be connected to the rest of the site damage?

The article below the video stated this atoll was outside the protected Coral Triangle, but still labeled a delicate area, a motherload of marine biodiversity that could well collapse because of these activities. The group responsible for the video claimed there were threatened corals on these reefs, found in few places outside the Triangle. The company being blamed for the debacle, Holschtatt Pharmaceuticals, had not made any statement that Nadine could find.

But Holschtatt's main office happened to be right here in Austin, the very city where Patient Zero lived.

A thought struck her, its impact wrinkling her brow. Further digging revealed that work on the reef project had begun on November 1. Nadine paused. That would have been in the South Pacific, though. She checked online for the location of the international dateline. Yep. November 1 there would have been October 31 here in Austin. She switched back to Zero's records. Her initial seizure happened—

—October 31.

Nadine replayed the video of Zero and her dad, up to where he said he'd found her in the yard before dawn that same day, talking about burning trees. She looked up Texas wildfires for that date.

Hammer? Meet Nail.

She sat back, blinking at the screen. She'd laughed at the notion of aliens at work behind NJace. Good times. Now she wasn't laughing. Even aliens seemed more credible than a virus that made children psychic, or at least empathic. Yet she couldn't deny the picture taking shape right in front of her, a pattern of children knowing things they shouldn't. Things they couldn't. One had accurately predicted his own death, for Pete's sake. She'd read about *that* yesterday.

The image of that tiny patch of elevated brain activity in Zero's PET scans flashed through her mind. Would a lively batch of new spindle neurons in the anterior insular cortex of Zero's brain explain this?

Nadine tapped her lip.

"Yuka?"

"Yes?"

"Call down and find out when Zero's tests will be ready. Then get the rest of the team in here to view them with us, especially that cynic, Blondie. We'll want all hands on deck for this big reveal."

Yuka grabbed her phone. "You got it."

Nadine barely heard her over the buzzing in her own ears. If even a tiny piece of her suspicions were true, NJace was going to upset everyone's applecart.

Chapter 23

"Perfect timing," Nadine said as Cagney reentered the lab. The rest of the team awaited. "They just sent up the 3XG on Zero."

"Good." He shuffled over to the large screen where a compressed file was uploading on the desktop. Everyone crowded in around him.

"Let's see what we've got." Nadine double-clicked the icon. The file took almost a full minute to open. Greyscale images fanned out, one atop the other like a stack of cards in the hands of a gambler. What she saw took her breath away.

Zero's brain, "shaved" by the 3XG scanners that then lit up active sections on each slice, looked like an overdone Christmas display so bright Nadine squinted in its glare. Gasps and exclamations sounded behind her.

"Whoa," Cagney breathed.

"When were Zero's first images?" Nadine asked. "The ones we've been using for reference."

"Um... Two weeks ago, I think," Cagney responded.

"Those didn't even come close to *this*." Thom reached past Nadine to indicate a particularly bright spot on the image. "What the—"

"I don't know. But we need to find out." Nadine selected an anterior slide in the region with new growth and set the system to dive into the scan, all the way down to the microscopic level. No one spoke at first as the image recalibrated, redrew, and recalibrated again, over and over. This would take a few minutes.

Nadine frowned at the working screen. "I've seen results like this before."

"Where?" Cagney said, breathless.

"Before I joined the CDC, I was working my way through school by taking jobs in all sorts of experimental testing labs. You name it, we probably tested it. For a while, the university used neuroimaging in experiments to see how different sorts of behaviors affected brain activity."

The image rendered and the system kicked in to blow it up even more.

"One of the test series proposed to determine which parts of the brain lit up during spiritual practice. You know, meditation, prayer, chanting, that sort of thing. Sometimes they would dose the subjects with cannabis or some other substance. Once, if I recall correctly, they even used LSD, but I'm not certain about that. It was a long time ago."

"How can a test like that be valid," Yuka asked, "if they're doping the subjects?"

Nadine shrugged. "Well, the control subjects got no drugs, of course. And some of those who were more heavily medicated showed results that couldn't be reproduced. If you don't take the test to both extremes, you can't know where the boundaries lie for what you're testing."

"I guess," Yuka said.

"All the subjects who prayed, meditated, or chanted during the test showed elevated brain activity. But the subjects who regularly participated in those activities outside the test showed a far stronger response."

"Like this?" Cagney gestured at the screen.

"No. They were bright, but this is a whole different kind of shine."

"Then...." Lara said, but the same unspoken question was mirrored on every face.

Nadine's features scrunched to one side, remembering the first time she'd seen a similar image on a PET scan, a few decades ago. The 3XG with its ultra-high resolution and greater detail didn't exist until many years later. She'd wondered if the subject were tripping, but no drugs had been administered in that session.

"A little more than halfway through the experiment, a man signed up to participate. He answered the questionnaire, said he followed a regular spiritual practice, but claimed no association with any one religious faith. He always smiled, never seemed to get agitated or impatient. And we ran this same test on him at least five times. We all assumed it was a fault in the equipment."

Cagney raised an eyebrow. "His brain lit up like Zero's?"

Nadine nodded. "Just like Zero's."

"Was he drugged?"

"Nope. We showed him the image after the fifth run. He wasn't surprised. You know what he said?"

Cagney shook his head. Everyone waited, holding their collective breath.

Nadine pictured that man's serene countenance, his calm demeanor, his almost beatific glow.

"He told us that when he prayed, God talked back."

Thom scowled. "Was he...sane?"

"Much as I am. Much as you are. He was a regular guy. No one special. Nothing physical to explain his...results." On the screen, small images were becoming visible in the selected field. "Turned out he's not a solitary case. On rare occasions, other tests found the same or similar results. Every time, the subject claimed to be in regular communion with God."

"I can claim to talk to fairies," said Cagney. "That doesn't make it true."

"I'm no believer either, my redheaded friend." She peered at the developing image on the screen. "But those people? They had complete faith in their claims right down to their million-watt brains. Something tells me Zero does, too. Look."

The final image finished rendering. Everyone crowded in to see the monitor.

Zero's insular cortex teemed with new spindle neurons highlighted by the special contrast dye.

"That's not normal, is it?" Cagney said.

"In a developing fetus, yes. Not in an eight-year-old. Not at this rate." Nadine pulled up the 3XG's recording of electrical activity in the brain during Zero's test. It wouldn't show which specific neurons were firing, but it would show which regions were active.

The insular cortex shone like a beacon.

No one said a word.

"Wasn't she sedated during this test?" Nadine asked.

"Yeah," Cagney confirmed. "So, what the hell? If that's what a conversation with God does to a person's brain, Zero must have a direct line. All the time."

A direct line. Right. Channeled by a bacteriophage no one had ever seen, accomplishing in weeks a significant and profound change to Zero's brain that would normally take years of meditation. Or generations of evolution.

"You realize what this could mean?" Nadine murmured. She wasn't even sure she bought it herself.

"That we should give Zero our Christmas wish lists instead of Santa?" Blondie said.

Such an enormous modification to the child's cerebral architecture suggested a conclusion Nadine didn't want to entertain. But what else could it possibly be? "What if Zero's not sick?"

"You lost me," said Cagney.

"What if she's changing?"

Cagney paled more than usual. His lip curled. His nostrils flared. Nadine would swear he'd begun to breathe faster. She glanced around. Similar reactions colored them all. Yuka pressed fingers to her mouth.

"Into what?" Cagney croaked.

"That," Nadine said, "is a very good question. Yuka, contact the lab. Right now. Make sure they have the data on our intermedin lookalike and tell them to hunt specifically for that in the CSF. Also, let them know what this is about and that I need the results of that puncture test put in front of everything else on their plates. And run the same tests on at least three other patients who've been infected for more than a week."

Yuka raced off, stumbling over her own feet.

"What else?" Cagney asked.

Nadine leaned back, tapping the chair's armrest with a muted thumpity thump noise. What else, indeed?

These phages and masquerading intermedin buggers were unlike anything she'd encountered. She'd already decided it couldn't be something environmental, or it would be confined to the region where conditions were ripe for infection. Except it *did* seem connected to each patient's individual region, only not in any way familiar to disease trackers. Maybe…

What if it had started as some ordinary bacteriophage common around the world?

And what? Mutated? Worldwide? Simultaneously?

But she'd already ruled that out. Doctors, and certainly the CDC, would have seen evidence of this long before now if that's what was behind NJace. Wouldn't they?

Not unless it drew attention to itself. Like now. Because come to think of it, there had been a few environmental changes common to all the affected countries that might have played a part in such a modification. What if…

Thumpity thump.

"Nadine?" Cagney waggled fingers in her field of vision. "What's going on in there?"

Thumpity thump. "Any results on those glove box samples?"

"Not yet." Thom fidgeted as if afraid he'd made a mistake.

Nadine sat up straighter. "Let's revise the experiment. Leave three of the cultures as they are. For the other three—the ones without NJace—set one up with an environment ten percent richer in O_2 than is the norm. Set the second one up with increased CO_2. In the third, amp the CH_4. Increase the ambient temperature for all three by .17 degrees centigrade."

"Why?" Cagney asked.

She shrugged. "A hunch. Probably nothing."

Thom hurried out.

"Cagney, skim through the patient files. I could swear I saw something in them about the patients sleepwalking and talking to animals. If there are no mentions in the files, we need to talk to the parents directly. If they all have this as a sign of NJace, I wanna know. Make me a list."

Cagney skedaddled to one of the other stations.

Nadine examined the screen as the others chattered in excited voices around her. The story she'd told them was true, every word. But Nadine had never bought into those earlier subjects' explanations. The fact that Zero's brain was lit up like Rockefeller Center at Christmas didn't mean she was talking to a God that didn't exist. Neurological events like this were natural results of a chemical reaction displayed in living color across one's grey matter.

Yet clearly something unusual was at work here, especially given the emergent patterns she'd begun to see an hour ago. Evidence of the stimulus displayed before her shouldn't be possible. Infecting children in such a way that they became empathic to the plight of ecosystems and living things around them would appear to be a purposeful act taken—or at least driven—by a sapient being who could, in turn, empathize with its victims. But...a conscious, sentient, purpose-driven virus?

Or was there something behind the virus's mutation? Some would no doubt see this as proof of God. Like here God was, laying cable for a new high-speed communication network in these kids who had become God's new receivers.

She chuckled, a flat mirth that felt forced. The sound splatted against the heavy air around her and died without a whimper. In the relative silence that followed, Nadine remembered how she'd laughed when that man said God talked back to him.

Somehow, it no longer seemed funny.

"Give me the room for a bit, folks." Once everyone cleared out, Nadine called her supervisor on video chat. She poured a pile of paperclips out on the desk while she waited for him to connect.

Soon his grizzled mug popped up on the screen. "Please tell me you have news."

Nadine toyed with her paperclips. "I do."

In his Atlanta office, Mitch hunched forward at his desk. "Am I going to like it?"

"I can't speak for you, boss. But any answer at this point is a step closer to resolution."

"That would be a 'no,' then," he said. "You like stirring the pot, don't you?"

"I didn't make this gumbo. I'm just serving it up. You want some or not?"

Distant city landscape rippled beyond rain-spattered windows on his left side. Behind him on the far wall, a giant digital screen displayed NJace "hot spots" on a global map. The thing looked like someone had bled over every landmass.

"I'm not sure I do," he said. "But lay it on me anyway."

"Zero's anterior insular cortex is crowded with new spindle neurons, all firing at once." She watched him twitch.

"How old is the patient?"

"Eight."

Mitch's jaw clenched and released. "Have you confirmed this finding in other patients in Austin?"

"That's in the works."

"Do you think this is temporary?"

She fidgeted with another clip. "Can't say yet." She dropped the clip, pushed it parallel to the side of her laptop on the desk, and pulled another out of the pile to lay it end-to-end with the first. "You have to admit it might be the most intriguing thing you've seen in a long while."

"I'll withhold judgment on that." His voice sounded tired. It wasn't even three p.m. in Atlanta. Mitch was a couple of years from retirement. He used to be excited by new finds. Now he wanted things to flow without a hitch. He still lusted after a cabin in the mountains. Good fishing up there, he'd said. "Give me the rest."

"I told you yesterday that about a third of Zero's phages have gone dormant, but her body isn't flushing them out."

"And?" he prompted.

"We found prophages in Zero's normal gut flora."

"Holy crap." Mitch covered his eyes and rocked back, his leather executive chair creaking. "It's flipped to a lysogenic mode. Great. Exactly what I wanted to hear."

"For the record," she said, her fingers working the paperclips almost unconsciously, "it was Lara who found that clue. Cost me a hundred-dollar bottle of wine."

"You can't claim that as an expense."

Nadine half-smiled before sobering again. "There's more. We found a new peptide in Zero's bloodwork."

"A new peptide?"

"New. As in never seen before."

He tapped his lip. In the hall outside his office, someone called to a co-worker, their words muffled by the closed door. "You believe it's part of the disease?"

"Yep."

"Why didn't we find it sooner?"

"It mimics intermedin. That's what we thought it was, at first. Cagney figured it out. That boy's gifted in this business. He shines."

"Noted." Mitch scratched on a pad at his desk, then played with the pen, staring at her through the conference screen. "It's connected to the neuron growth?"

"I'm eighty percent convinced it's actively promoting that growth," she said, "though that's a hunch. We're gonna need to run serious testing before we'll know for sure. We first found the peptide in the bloodwork, but I have a hunch it can cross the blood-brain barrier the same as intermedin. I've requested a fresh CSF sample from Zero to be sure."

"Is NJace producing the peptide?"

"My money's on yes, but I can't be sure." She poured out another pile of clips. "Our cultures aren't producing any results at all on that front yet, but the experiment's still in the primary stage. We're still clueless on how this bugger is doing any of this."

"Then start testing ways to kill it."

"We've tried. Used everything we could think of that would be safe in pediatric use."

"Try something new."

She smirked. People always wanted to kill what they didn't understand. "Listen. Maybe that's not a good idea."

"For Pete's sake, Nadine," he said, his voice raised as he flung one hand toward the display and almost knocked over his coffee. "We're trying to eradicate a phage that's incapacitating and killing children around the world!"

She didn't answer, and he shook his head.

"I want us to fix it," he said, "and move on. Keep putting one foot in front of another, filing reports, and tallying results until time for retirement. You're rocking my boat within view of the shore."

Nadine knew that frustration. She'd felt the same way. Until now.

"Mitch..."

He muttered something she was sure she didn't want to hear.

"Boss—" Her mouth worked, fingers clamped down on the paperclip. "We can't unbake this cake. The phage has already spread around the globe."

"I still want to know how that happened."

Nadine said nothing.

"You know something about that?" he asked, features twisted in that shrewd, sideways expression he always got when he knew he was right.

She snorted. Good thing she wasn't in the espionage business. Her face was too loud to keep secrets. "Not enough to offer an opinion yet. I'm working on something."

"Lay it on me."

"Mitch, it's speculation on my part. I've got no—"

"Don't care." He flapped his fingers in a "gimme" gesture. "Talk."

She cursed under her breath. For the love of deep-dish pizza. Why had she said anything? "I'll tell you the general gist. That's it."

More finger flapping.

Nadine ground her teeth. Paper clips stretched out in two lines on her desk. She nudged a crooked clip to straighten the row. "I suspect NJace is the result of an epigenetic modification."

Mitch froze. Raindrops coalesced into rivulets against his window. "Induced?"

"I couldn't swear to it, but no. I'd guess it occurred naturally."

"How?"

"Uh-uh. That's all I'm saying until—"

He slashed a hand through the air. "Unacceptable. This is not your private project. Conjecture or not, give it to me so that I can get people working on it in every lab we've got. The sooner we figure this out, the sooner we can make these kids better."

"Make them better how?" Her skepticism slipped through in her voice despite her efforts to keep it neutral. After all these years, she and Mitch might be as comfortable together as an old married couple, but he was still her boss. "If Zero's pattern is repeated in every phage patient, and if they survive the modification, we could be dealing with the next level of development in the human race. Trying to 'fix' that is like sending a high school sophomore back to third grade because he got a woody in class."

"What are you talking about?"

"These kids are *changing*. And I'm not talking about a simple thing like puberty. If this trend continues, it could reshape everything. For all of us." She braced her elbows on the desk, her nose inches from the screen. "But there's more to it than the changes in the patients. When was the last time we could organically stimulate neuron growth in the brain at this level?" She heard the clipped tone in her voice, the accelerated pace of her words. Didn't care. For the first time in years, she stood on the brink of something massive. Life-altering. World-changing. "Imagine the breakthrough this peptide could herald in neuromedicine. In neurotrauma recovery. We could repair damaged brains. Mitch—"

He slapped the desk. "This is the goddamn CDC. Not some big pharma company." Mitch sat forward, elbows planted, fingers clasped together. "You'd suggest that we call their parents and say sorry, we choose not to fix your kid because— why was that again? Because we want to make money on the phage's peptide?"

"Oh, come on." Nadine threw the paperclip at her display and Mitch blinked as it bounced off. "You know me better than that. Step back. Take a breath. We're both tired here."

Mitch huffed and rocked his office chair. "Sorry," he grumped. "I guess I am a little shell-shocked. This whole thing has everyone here breathing down my neck."

"I get it. But we're going to figure this out. Together."

"Right." He pulled himself together. "Where were we? Oh yes, you were going to tell me why you think the phage is epigenetically modified?"

She didn't want to reveal that until she had supporting evidence. It sounded crazy even to her, at least to a degree. But Mitch was right. This wasn't her special project, and the more people he could get testing it, the sooner they'd find out if her suspicion was correct.

Nadine plucked the tossed clip from her keyboard and started a third row. "What if this bug began as a common phage, but has been modified over the last decade or two into this latest version by significant environmental changes?" She laid another clip end-to-end with the first.

"A climate-change superbug?"

She shrugged. "That's the only constant factor in every case. I mean, if it was tagged to specific bacteria or any other environmental variable, the number of cases would be regionally predictable. Right? But these are showing up all over the place in kids who've had no contact with other victims, or who haven't traveled at all. Ever. I've got a few cultures growing in tricked-out glove boxes with different conditions in each one. But I don't know what good it'll do. There are so many things to check, I'm swinging a wedge in a sand trap the size of the Sahara while blindfolded."

Mitch rested his chin on his fist, one finger stretched over his mouth, which did not move. He said nothing. The silence stretched out for at least a minute. Nadine began to twitch. She plucked another clip from the pile and fiddled with it while she watched him.

"I told you it was a long-shot hypothesis. I—"

"Why do you believe this?"

She threw her hands up and let them fall on her lap. "It's a hunch. But here's what I'm basing it on. We know that epigenetic shifts can be—and have been—caused by changes in environmental conditions. Remember that article that came out a couple years ago about the increase in ocean temperature and the related adjustment to gene expression in fish?"

Mitch nodded. "We talked about that over lunch, as I recall."

"Early flowering in Thale cress was tracked to elevated levels of CO2. Consumption of chemical-laced food caused heritable pathologies in mice."

"Point taken. But those usually take time to effect such a transformation. This has happened rather suddenly."

"Has it?" Nadine said. "We don't know. All we've seen of the process is what happened when NJace interacted in an infectious manner with human victims. That part has happened pretty quickly, true. But we don't know when this modification—if that's what it is—began."

"What else?"

Nadine wrinkled her nose. "You'll say I'm off my Betty Crocker."

"I've already said that."

She chuckled, then sobered. "From everything I've seen, I can't help but infer that this phage is—" She hesitated. The smell of Thai food wafted through the lab, then dissipated. "I'm starting to wonder if—"

"Spit it out, Nadine."

She wasn't normally this reticent to share an opinion, and Mitch knew it. But this sounded crazy, even to her. She scowled, part of her wishing it'd never occurred to her.

"Remember, this is all conjecture on my part," she said. "But hear me out. The phage's development and evolution or mutation or whatever you want to call it could have been caused by ecological divergences that are happening around the globe. Water and air temperature differentials, acidity in the oceans and soil and even the rain, elevated levels of carbon dioxide and methane and a host of other pollutants. Weather patterns and habitats are changing too fast. The flora and fauna are having trouble keeping up. We can't expect that sort of global change to have predictable effects."

"I never knew you were a climate activist." A siren passed the office at his end, red lights flickering in the window.

"I never have been. I'm speculating here. But I find it intriguing that the phage—one that we suspect was provoked into its current form by environmental changes, mind you—affects humans in this specific way so that those who are infected become emotionally attached to said environment, even physically pained when others of their kind harm it. Feels too contrived to be a coincidence."

"That would imply intelligence," he said. "Viruses are not intelligent."

"As far as our current understanding of viruses, that's true. But if this one is the result of an epigenetic shift, how do we know that hasn't changed?"

He gawked. "Please tell me you aren't serious."

"I kinda am."

Mitch stared at her.

"You think I don't realize how crazy it sounds?" She steeled herself for a "no freaking way."

"I don't know. It's a stretch."

She drew a breath.

"But," he said, gesturing, "I'm not going to dismiss it outright. I want to chew it over with some of my colleagues here. Give me a day."

"You—really? You're going to consider it?"

"What did you expect?"

"Honestly?" she said. "A padded room."

"I haven't ruled that out. Don't get your hopes up, though. Keep after a way to stop this thing. Just in case."

She sighed. Inertia presented the biggest stumbling block to proof of her theories. CDC tradition said find it, kill it, move on. But what if befriending it would provide more benefits for them all? If they destroyed this opportunity, they'd never know the answer. Convincing Mitch and his superiors of the potential value in a new, untried solution might be the biggest challenge she'd ever taken on. She wasn't at all sure she wanted that task.

Chapter 24

Aboard the *Pasteur*, Vliat, Nlaan Islands
Saturday, November 16, 9:30 a.m.
(Austin, Texas, Friday, November 15, 2:30 PM)

Number of infected: 125,002

TRAVIS AND A FEW OTHER CREWMEN helped the divers aboard and winched the dive boats into their davits as a precaution during the blasts. Isobel paced the deck, wringing her hands. What she had proposed could destroy the rest of the star queen. But if she didn't at least try, she would lose the last chance they had to get more of the coral for her trials in Austin. Either way, her time was almost up. Every minute she debated ran the clock down that much more.

If they were lucky, the Nlaantu wouldn't even know her team had done this. She hadn't seen any of the islanders the past couple of mornings and Travis said the blasts would be small. Isobel shifted the binoculars to the islets where the reef crested the water near the harvest sites. Sea birds congregated there in large numbers, pecking at slow crustaceans or small particles of food washed up on the narrow shore from the dive boats' passage. They squabbled and squawked, lifting into the air only to set down again a few feet away.

Isobel looked farther afield, toward the open sea. She could have sworn she saw a whale fluke in her peripheral vision. If she had, it was gone now. Most whales would have passed through here a month or more ago, but Travis said stragglers came through late some years. Maybe she'd gotten a lucky glimpse.

Travis spoke to his mates and came to her side, long legs carrying him in a confident stride. She tried to keep from fidgeting like some nervous newbie—which, of course, she was in this particular scenario—and affected what she hoped was a relaxed expression.

He touched his hat. "Everything's set."

"Good." A few other crewmen watched as if gauging how she would handle this rebellious move. Isobel gritted her teeth. She'd hoped to leave a lesser mark of their passage when they'd gone. But in truth, she'd do whatever it took to get what she came here for. She didn't have much choice. Gabe needed that coral.

"Is the *Pasteur* at a safe distance from the blast site?"

"Yes, ma'am." He held out the radio. "Whenever you're ready, say the word."

She glanced from the radio to his face as realization set in. She'd expected him to give the order. But no, of course it would be her. This was her project. She took the radio, raised it, and paused.

"Everyone's accounted for? You're sure?"

"Yes, ma'am. Double-checked it myself."

Behind him, Seppo arrived on deck. He seemed as nervous as she was.

Isobel aimed the binocs at the blast site and spoke into the radio.

"Do it."

Before she could lower her hand, a muffled boom preceded a screeching exodus of seabirds lifting as one in a frenzied mob, followed by a shock of water that rose in graceful arcs perhaps as tall as she was along the curve of the atoll. Morning sunlight sparkled atop the aquatic surge that crested, then fragmented, its droplets falling like jewels back into the sea, along with feathers and carcasses from birds that delayed long enough to grab that one last morsel and did not make it off the islet in time. Waves hurtled out from the blast site both across the lagoon and seaward, on approach to the *Pasteur*.

"Might wanna hold on, ma'am." Travis's voice filtered through the distraction of those birds in the air and the ones in the water. Her mind still saw them on the reef, fighting and pecking over scraps.

The deck beneath her feet pitched and she stumbled. Travis grabbed her arm, steadied her until the swells evened out and the *Pasteur*'s yaw calmed.

"How long before we can dive again?" she asked without looking at him.

"Just need to drop the boats. Five minutes."

"Good." She passed him the radio and binocs. "I'll be in my lab."

Rhue Children's Hospital, Austin, Texas
Friday, November 15, 2:30 PM

Number of infected: 125,002

News on the family room television held Luk's focus. One report covered protesters in front of the Holschtatt building, their signs calling for the pharmaceutical company to cease operations at the reef in the South Pacific and invest whatever it took to clean up the site and its surrounding waters, as well as make reparations to the islanders, whose food source had been fouled. Another followed up on the special report about the entheóphage kids, and Luk decided he'd seen enough.

Reporters were everywhere. Sadie said they were relentless, that they'd harassed her every time she came to see Kyn. Hospital security had started keeping them away from the doors the last few days. News crews had also haunted

Perkatory and his office and sat in front of his house awaiting a chance at an interview with him. They'd love to get a shot at any of the parents, but his being the founder of BehnWerks Games and the maker of that video interview made him a prime target. His cell had buzzed so many times he'd almost switched it off. He didn't know how they'd gotten his number, and he didn't care. He didn't want to speak to them. His single concern was his daughter.

In her room, he found Kyn awake, propped more or less upright. She had awakened brighter this morning, more like herself than she had been since Halloween and now smiled her thanks to one of the nurses, who'd brought her a cup of broth. A kernel of warmth sprouted in his chest, spreading until it pushed out every lingering doubt and carved a grin into his cheeks that he couldn't have suppressed even if he'd wanted to. Let the trolls say whatever they wanted. He knew he'd done the right thing in supporting his child, even though it might cost him plenty.

Sadie beamed at him from the bedside, and Luk joined her. "Wow," he said. "Real food? That's huge, kiddo."

"Mmm hmm," Kyn hummed, preoccupied with her cup. Her hands trembled with weakness. She'd been in that bed far too long. "Best veggie broth ever." The cup tipped once more and she sipped the hot liquid, Sadie standing by to help.

"Gods forbid I should interfere with the process," Luk teased. He crossed to the sofa and took a seat. Midday sunlight poured through the window behind him, casting his shadow across the floor between the sofa and the bed.

There had been talk earlier this morning of moving Kyn to a step-down unit. That had to mean they were encouraged by her progress. Maybe he'd ask the doctors when they made their rounds later whether she could go home soon. Of course, that might be rushing things. She still slept a lot, and got that pained expression sometimes, or flinched for no apparent reason. Each time she did that he wondered what had caused it, but talking about it seemed to make her even sadder. He'd stopped asking.

Sadie brushed her fingers through Kyn's hair while his daughter held her broth. The two of them giggled together over some secret. Whatever it was, Luk didn't care. His heart felt as full as the day he'd married Marin. Or the day he'd first held Kyndra. Moments like this didn't come every day. They should be treasured. He offered a silent mantra of thanks.

"What's so funny over there?" he finally asked.

"It's girl talk, Dad," Sadie said. "You wouldn't understand." She winked at Luk. "Something about a boy."

Kyndra blushed all the way to her ears. "Sadie!"

"Oops," Sadie said with mock horror. "Me and my big mouth. Not another word, I swear it."

They giggled again, and Sadie's eyes shone. He hadn't seen her that happy and relieved in a couple of weeks. She had come to love his daughter. How lucky could a guy get?

Kyndra's giggles turned strange, twisting into hiccups. Brown broth sloshed over the sides of the cup onto her blanket.

Sadie grabbed at the mug. "Hey, now, don't get too excited," she said, a note of surprise in her tone.

But Kyn didn't stop. Her grip on the mug tightened. Her head bent back, neck muscles straining, her whole body jerking with that sound that came out like hiccups.

Luk's smile slid aside as he lurched to his feet. His knee bumped the table and sent it skittering a foot across the floor. "Kyndra?"

Machines began to beep in frantic, discordant rhythm.

His daughter's face flushed beet red. Her legs stiffened. Her arms spasmed, muscles drawing them to her chest and spilling the rest of the hot broth across her torso. Before Luk could get to her, the room was full of doctors and nurses.

"Please step into the hall," the doctor said. "Give us some space."

An orderly pushed them out of the room. He and Sadie stared through the glass at the sudden crowd working on his daughter. One of the nurses jerked the curtain forward, but the motion pulled its other end away from the wall to clear a view of the monitors. Their numbers skewed so far beyond wrong Luk's world tilted. His heart thrummed in his ears. Breaths came in short, wheezing gasps. His fingers tingled with pins and needles as if he'd slept wrong.

"What's happening?" he cried.

Sadie shook him. Pointed. "Luk. Look."

He finally saw her. Registered her gesture. Lifted his gaze to the rooms on either side and down the hall. Doctors, nurses, and orderlies crowded all three staff stations down the corridor, while others rushed in and out of every room, pushing medical equipment or carrying medications. Parents stood outside each door, holding one another, weeping, acting as scared as he felt. At the other end of the corridor, an ashen Rachel watched Zach's room in horror. Panic spread through the entire wing like spores cast on the wind, thickening the air and lending a surreal gleam to the whole scene. Luk's breath hitched.

Luk murmured a prayer to Ganesh, repeating the mantra under his breath. What—

A single sound sliced through the tumult and snatched his attention to his daughter's room. All other noise receded, the gap filled by a single, flat tone from the one visible monitor, where a solid green line bisected the top of the black screen over other jagged, irregular readouts. He'd grown so accustomed to the machine's regular blip, blip, blip he'd stopped hearing it until it wasn't there anymore. Now, he couldn't hear anything but its absence.

More nurses appeared from somewhere. One pushed aside the curtain around Kyn's bed. Between the press of bodies surrounding her, glimpses of action pierced him. The doctor pressed on her chest in a rhythmic cadence that went on and on and on for what seemed like hours. Someone administered an injection. A nurse snatched aside her clothing. The doctor held paddles against her chest. Kyn's body jerked, then lay still. Jerked, then lay still. Again. And again. His own heart lurched each time, his body flinching in synch. Luk's breath caught, held.

An orderly rushed into Kyn's room, leaving the door to swing slowly shut.

"I'm calling it," the doctor said. "Time of—"

The closing door cut off the rest of his words.

The world around Luk wavered, slipped sideways. He stumbled. Almost fell.

Sadie grabbed him, stepped in front of him, shouted at him. Shook him. Her lips moved in her pale, pale face, but her words never made it past that unchanging tone—

—the sound of his world ending.

Chapter 25

Rhue Children's Hospital, Austin, Texas
Friday, November 15, 2:35 PM

Number of infected: 126,027

THE HOSPITAL PA BLARED outside their makeshift office as Nadine prepared to sign off with Mitch.

"Code blue. All floors. Medical staff report to your stations at once. Code blue. All floors. Medical staff report to your stations at once." A three-tone signal followed, then the whole thing repeated twice more.

"What's going on?" Mitch said.

"You got me. I'll find out and let you know. Bye." Nadine disconnected the call without further explanation.

The other team members congregated in the corridor. Nadine nudged them out of the way and called to a staff member who hurried past.

"What happened?"

"I don't know yet," the woman said as she ran. "On my way to find out now."

Nadine stepped forward. "Where's your station?"

"Second floor. ICU." The staffer called as she dashed around the corner.

Nadine waved at the rest of her team. "Stay here. I'm gonna find out what's happening."

She hustled around to the stairwell door and pushed through to walk down. No sense tying up the elevator in a crisis. She didn't want to be in the way.

On the second floor, she pushed out into a madhouse. Even from where she stood she could hear the beeping monitors from wards right and left, see staff rushing to some crisis, but not all moving in the same direction. What in the half-baked hell was going on here?

She picked a direction and walked over to one of the corridors, staying out of the way. Parents and medical staff crowded the passage between staff desks and rooms all around the horseshoe-shaped ward. Palpable tension and fear rolled out to soak through even Nadine's thick skin. She watched, her breath shallow, ragged. It looked like every single kid in the ward had gone into crisis at the same time. And this code had been called for all floors. But that didn't make any sense.

Unless—

She checked other wards down the main corridor. Every single one reflected the same level of panic. Parents wept and clung to one another, medical staff worked over beds, nurses at the desks hustled with grim expressions or spoke with urgent voices on phones or to each other. If this was happening throughout the hospital...

Her frown gave way to slack-jawed realization. If she was right about what this virus was doing, then something major must have gone down in the last few minutes. Some eco-disaster or environmental event with sweeping repercussions.

Nadine spun to the stairwell. Going up took longer than going down, and she'd not done any stair-stepping in a few years. Okay, probably more than a few. By the time she reached the top, her breath came hard and fast. She stumbled to their office and pushed through to become the focal point of every other team member.

"Well?" Cagney asked.

"Get...online..." she gasped. "Run global...searches...for eco...disasters...that just...happened."

Cagney came closer. "Are you okay?"

She stopped, hands on her knees. "Fine. Go. Do." She staggered to her computer and started her investigation.

"What are we looking for, Nadine?" Yuka asked, her eyes glued to her screen.

"I'm not sure," Nadine said. Words came a little easier now. "But something big. Every Njace kid…in Rhue Hospital is in crisis right now."

"And this is connected to eco-disasters how, exactly?" Blondie asked.

Cagney scowled at him. "Do it, man."

Blondie gave in with an "okay, but this is weird" attitude.

Nothing showed up on the news sites. Disappointing, but Nadine guessed it made sense. If something *just* happened, it would take a while to make it onto the news, unless it happened in or near a big city.

"I can't find anything." Lara sounded frustrated.

"Widen the parameters." Nadine threw her a glance. "Try major eco-events over the last two weeks. Don't limit your search to here. Check everywhere. Concentrate on the areas most hard-hit by NJace."

"You're serious?" Blondie gawked at her.

"You are welcome to go to your hotel if you feel this is a waste of your time," Nadine said. "We can discuss your career change after this crisis is over."

"Geez." He went back to work.

Nadine ran additional searches for anything she might have missed earlier. While she worked, muttered exclamations came from every occupied desk in the room. She said nothing, waiting. Would they see it too?

"This is weird." Yuka sounded confused.

"What?" Blondie asked.

"Well…" Yuka trailed off, as if afraid to say what she thought.

Nadine peeked at her over the laptop screen while the younger woman struggled with whether or not to share.

"This sounds crazy, but—"

"—there appears to be a correlation." Cagney finished for her. "Am I imagining things?"

"No," Yuka said. "I see it too."

"So do I." Lara spun in her seat. "Air quality alerts went out in New Delhi in early November, less than a week before the first cases showed up there."

"Don't forget China," Cagney added. "They're one of the first countries to be hit after the U.S."

Nadine gave him a verbal poke. "What did you find for them?"

"Hah." He leaned forward, still reading as he spoke. "They pushed forward on a big road construction project, even though it'll go through sites with critical biodiversity, not to mention the groundwater pollution and industrial waste it'll leave behind." He looked up from his screen at last. "They took the first steps on that project two days ago. Their infection numbers jumped by almost a thousand the same day."

Nadine jerked her chin in Yuka's direction. "What did you find, Yook?"

"An uptick in construction in Liberia. They broke ground on a new water treatment plant on the ninth. Three days later, construction waste and groundwater pollution prompted health alerts, and they showed a hundred new cases."

Nadine let them sit in silence for the pattern to sink in. "Anyone care to comment?"

Blondie regarded them. "I see what you're getting at. But a connection between environmental destruction or crises and this virus isn't possible." His expression almost begged her to agree. "It isn't, is it?"

She held his gaze. "Do you have a more acceptable explanation for what we are seeing here?"

No one said a word. A clock on the wall above the counter ticked in the silence, keeping tempo with Nadine's heartbeat. She gripped the chair's armrests. Cagney finally broke the dam.

"How long have you known about this?"

"I don't *know* anything," she said. "But I noticed the pattern right after our lunch conversation about the gaming guy and his kid. I watched their interview, did some hunting, and found that Zero's symptoms started around the same time as that atoll project that's been in the news. I read the comments on their video from the other parents about how their children said similar things. I read through the #phagepandemic hits and found more of the same. That made me do more digging. Areas of the world that use dirty energy production like coal have high infection numbers. Countries where animal poaching is a big thing also have more cases. Brazil got hit hard, too. They—"

"Deforestation." Thom sounded surprised at his participation in this conversation. "In the Amazon."

"You got it." Nadine jabbed a finger at him, then shook it at the others. "This kind of problem isn't limited to other countries. Every state in the U.S. has major ecological issues. Coal use, water pollution, industrial waste. Oh, and don't drink the tap water in Austin. I'm not saying their treatment plants aren't up to snuff, but there are traces of human feces in most of the freshwater sites." She shrugged.

"Ew." Lara made a gagging sound. Another researcher developed a green hue.

"Yeah. Right here in the good ol' U.S. of A."

"Still, this goes against the science we know." Blondie snorted. "How can it even happen?"

"Did you happen to note the names of the man and child in that video you were laughing at earlier?"

Blondie shook his head with a frown.

"That was Zero and her dad." She watched his eyes go wide, watched the others react in realization, then turned back to Blondie. "You saw the slides of Zero's brain. We all did."

"Yeah."

Nadine raised an eyebrow. "Then we have to consider the possibility that her brain, and thus the other patients' brains as well, are more sensitive than ours. This is new territory. Unknown science. Old criteria and presumed rules may no longer apply. We don't know yet."

"Then...how...the hell..." Thom asked, his features puckered, "are we gonna fix this?"

"How, indeed." Their shock mirrored her own when she'd made this connection for herself. "I suggest you sit with this. Let it marinate. We're gonna need some good ideas soon."

They gawked at her like she'd asked them to cure cancer in three hours.

With what she suspected, Nadine wished it were that simple.

Chapter 26

Aboard the *Pasteur*, Vliat, Nlaan Islands
Saturday, November 16, 10:45 AM
(Austin, Texas, Friday, November 15, 3:45 PM)

Number of infected: 150,997

ISOBEL WORKED AS FAST AS SHE COULD, running final tests to tweak the Milani formula closer to perfection. Seppo worked at the other station, separating the resolved solutions into packets. Neither of them spoke, but Isobel's desperation infected her assistant, pushing him toward an edgier mood. On a normal day, she'd take a break to calm them both with a relaxed chat.

Not now, though. Today was all about Gabe.

Isobel finished another batch of solution and passed it to Seppo. Before she could reach for another measure of the processed coral, the radio crackled.

"Sorry to bother you, Doc," Travis said, "but you might wanna get up here."

"Can't you deal with it?"

"The Nlaantu have come."

Isobel frowned. "You mean T'nei?"

"Yes, ma'am, but this time she brought friends."

Seppo made a choking sound. "How many friends?"

It took Travis a second to respond. "I'm gonna go with all of them."

Seppo paled.

Isobel swallowed hard. "Keep working." She left the lab and walked as fast as she could without running down the corridor until she came out onto the side deck, and an unrestricted view from that side of the ship.

The sea around the *Pasteur* bristled with weapon-toting Nlaantu, their proa bobbing in the water like prickly coconuts. Dozens of them. She turned aft and kept going, trying not to stare.

Travis met her at the access, his whole body tight as a coiled spring, his expression guarded. "They aren't happy, Doc."

Isobel's heart danced in her chest. "Are we in danger?"

"Hard to say. But we aren't defenseless. If this gets ugly, you drop to the deck. You got me?"

"Yes." Her breath quickened. "Where are the divers?"

"Still out. Nlaantu boats have them surrounded, too."

"Are *they* defenseless? The dive boats?"

"No, ma'am. But they are outnumbered, and the divers are vulnerable in the water. We need to keep this peaceable if you know what I mean."

She nodded. Together, they made their way to T'nei, who stood with regal bearing before a bevy of warriors, their group crowding out the crew. The dance in Isobel's chest picked up its tempo.

"T'nei," Isobel said, "you honor us."

"And you betray us." T'nei's voice rang out over the water. "You should not have come. We were wrong to welcome you. Leave. Now."

She went on in her own language, and Isobel could guess what T'nei had said.

Isobel glanced at the Nlaantu faces, all of them as hard as ebony. "Our people are still at work, T'nei, gathering our latest harvest. At least allow us to collect what we already broke loose from the reef. I wouldn't want its sacrifice to be wasted."

T'nei's voice grew colder. "You have brought a curse to our people with your noise and your foolishness. You care nothing for the damage you do. Our children sicken while you linger here, poisoning our waters and our lands. We want no more of your plague."

Travis stepped forward, and Isobel could see the concern in the squint of his eyes. "Plague? You say your children have sickened. How, T'nei?"

She kept her glare on Isobel. "They scream in pain for the *le'uuté*, the water village, and the *basaad*, the sea birds you have killed. For every blow you strike here, a child weeps among our people. Now they all suffer. Some have died. No more. You will leave."

Thoughts of North Sentinel Island roiled Isobel's stomach. She fought to concentrate on T'nei, instead of the women behind her holding sharpened spear tips made from the metal Isobel's people had provided in exchange for the Nlaantu permission to harvest from the reef. Behind T'nei's group, more proa surrounded the *Pasteur*'s stern. Some of them were provided by Holschtatt as payment for their harvests.

"I see the metal scraps we gave you on the tips of your people's weapons, our boats in which some of them stand, our payments for your permission to work in your waters. Yet we have not finished the harvest we bargained for." At least her voice didn't tremble, thank goodness for small favors. "Will you take our gifts, yet send us away?"

Travis sucked in a startled breath beside her, a small sound he cut off as quickly as it started, but T'nei's angry glower snapped to him before coming back to pin Isobel to the spot where she stood.

"Please let us complete what we started. We won't harvest any more of the reef but let us claim what we've already broken free." Isobel gestured behind herself. "Our people are already packing and preparing to leave. We will be gone in less than a day. You have my word."

"Your word is worth less than a bottomless boat." T'nei's lips curled down as if she would spit.

"You say your children are sick," Isobel said. She sounded calmer than she felt. "I understand your fear for them. My child is sick, as well. That's why I've come. This coral will make him better. Stronger. Will you deny him that chance?"

In her peripheral view, Isobel saw a crewman come forward on tentative feet. The young man spoke into the silence that followed. "Doctor Fallon?"

Isobel did not shift her focus from T'nei.

Travis snapped at the crewman. "What is it?"

"I'm sorry sir, but there's an emergency call for the doc. I tried to tell them she couldn't come now, but they said it's urgent. Something about the doc's daughter."

Isobel whirled, T'nei forgotten. "Claire? What's wrong?"

"I don't know. They wouldn't tell me."

A chill flashed up her spine. She spoke aside to the Nlaantu translator. "Give me a minute." She raced to the bridge and took the satphone, her heart in her throat.

"This is Isobel Fallon."

Jake's voice came through, tinny but strong. "Bel, Claire's in the hospital, in critical condition."

Isobel's legs went weak, and she stumbled against the counter. She fought for a breath. "What happened?"

"She had a seizure and lost consciousness. We don't know for sure what's wrong, but they're saying it's some new disease. The ER was a madhouse. It took them almost an hour to get to her." He huffed at his end of the call. "You need to come home. I'm sending a Holschtatt jet to pick you up in New Caledonia. They'll be ready when you get there."

She blinked. Did he say 'leave'? Now? They needed time to collect all that coral, or the blast would have been for nothing. And Gabe—

"Jake, I'm in the middle of nowhere, on a boat that will take me at least two days to get to someplace resembling civilization."

"I know," he lamented. "I'd send a helicopter if there was any way for them to retrieve you from the *Pasteur*."

"We're in the middle of a crisis here, too. I can't leave for at least twelve hours."

"Why the hell not?" Jake shouted over the phone. "What could possibly be more important than Claire? You weren't there. You didn't hear her screaming, Isobel. Come home. Now. Your daughter needs you. *I* need you."

"Gabe needs me too, Jake. I'm already neck-deep in this harvest. No one else can do it. If I leave, that's it. They won't let us finish the job later."

Jake cursed at his end. "Claire has always come second with you, hasn't she? Gabe has been sick all his life. You've known he was going to die since he was born. Well, now his sister might die, too, Bel. Remember this conversation if you get home too late to see her before that happens."

Isobel opened her mouth to respond, but Jake had gone. She gave the satphone to the crewman, Jake's words echoing in her mind.

His sister might die, too.

She ground her teeth, clenched her fists. How could she choose between her children? If she stayed, she was doing that anyway, wasn't she? A groan rose from the depths of her soul and spilled past her lips. She bent and dropped her elbows to the table, staring at its scarred surface.

Stay for Gabe. Leave for Claire.

She already knew she had to leave before she wanted to. Before they finished what they started. But if she left now, she'd lose all the coral they'd blasted off the reef, materials that the divers hadn't yet collected. How much more could they gather in a few additional hours?

Her brain flipped to the other side of the equation, her fears whispering that if she stayed, and anything happened to Claire, she'd never forgive herself. Neither would Jake.

She inhaled, long and slow, stood up, and smoothed her hair. Crewmen working the ship looked at something else as if they hadn't been staring at her the whole time. "You okay, Doc?" one asked.

"No," she said in a wooden voice.

She retraced her steps to the deck.

"You win, T'nei." Isobel wondered that her voice did not echo in the hollowness of her chest. "As soon as we can get our people aboard and our equipment stowed, we'll leave."

"Doc?" Travis's voice reached her, steadied her. "You sure about this?"

"Yes." Her voice squeaked out the sound, and she cleared her throat. "Now both my children are sick. I'm needed at home."

T'nei's chin lifted another notch. "Your actions sicken even your own children, so far away."

In a heartbeat, Isobel's cheeks burned. Fists clenched, her body coiled to step closer to this woman who knew *nothing* about her situation. How *dare* she!

Travis stepped in front of her. "Not a good idea, Doc," he said, his voice pitched low, calm. He raised an eyebrow and indicated the armed boats around them.

Isobel took a shaky breath, her jaw clenched, and gave a curt nod. "Call our people back."

"What about the rest of the star queen?"

She flicked her fingers as if to dislodge an insect instead of what they were actually doing—abandoning the means to Gabe's treatment—and forced the necessary words through clenched teeth. "Leave it. Whatever they already loaded is what we have."

Travis walked off with the radio.

"We'll leave as soon as our people are aboard," she said, working hard to keep her voice civil.

T'nei's features twisted as if she'd swallowed something nasty. "We will wait and watch."

Without another word, she and her warriors left the deck and climbed down to their boats. When they had rejoined their fellow Nlaantu, Travis stepped up beside Isobel.

"What about your son?"

She drew a breath to answer, but her words tripped over the lump in her throat and emerged as a sob. Isobel clapped both hands over her mouth to stop that awful sound. She heaved a few shaking gasps before control returned in brittle pieces.

"I'll have to find another way." She hiccuped another sob before she went on. "My daughter is in the hospital."

"Aw hell." Travis's gruff voice sounded even more gravelly than usual. He swept his hat off and held it in one fist at his hip. "Do they know what's wrong?"

She shook her head and swiped at a tear. Sunlight glinted on the waves and sparkled in the ripples between the Nlaantu's proa. At the worksite, the islanders had withdrawn a short distance from the dive boats. She thought the divers were pulling in their nets, but she couldn't tell for sure without the binoculars.

"How long before we can leave?"

"Everything else is pretty much battened down or stowed. We knew we'd be leaving soon anyway. I'll tell the crew to finish the job. Soon as the divers get aboard and we winch up the boats, we can set out. Maybe half an hour? Forty-five minutes?"

"Good." She looked from the water to Travis. His apparent compassion made this hurt worse. "How long until we can get to New Caledonia?"

He sucked air in between his teeth. "At least forty-eight hours. That's at the *Pasteur*'s best speed."

"Then let's get to it. What can I do to help prep for departure?"

"Nothing." Travis slapped his hat on. "Go back to the lab. I've got this."

She nodded. In the distance, the dive boats were coming about. The deck would soon be alive with activity. But Isobel couldn't take her eyes off the sandbar where those birds had sat this morning.

Chapter 27

Rhue Children's Hospital, Austin, Texas
Saturday, November 16, 7:05 AM

Number of infected: 219,738

NADINE ENTERED THE GLASS-ENCASED FOYER, its colorful slatted artwork arched across the ceiling, scattering light and heat. Plants of all sizes and shapes lined the walls on either side in gravel gardens. She noticed them, perhaps for the first time, as she moved into the bustling lobby past parents and other family members on their way to or from a visit with a sick child. Footfalls echoed against bare terrazzo floors where patterns and colors shifted with the light cast through multiple stained-glass windows.

Past the intersection with the giant green guitar, she approached the open elevator, waited until it emptied, then stepped aboard with a yawn. She'd gone to bed early and slept late enough to put her almost an hour behind schedule. Images of those parents during yesterday's crisis had haunted her dreams all night.

At her floor, she trudged toward their temporary office in a daze.

Cagney turned a corner at the other end of the hall. He grinned. "Good morning, sleepyhead."

"Sorry I was late. You can take off if you want. I've got it from here."

He shrugged. "No big. I'm not tired. We got Zero's CSF results, along with two of the other early cases."

"And?"

"That peptide's present, as you suspected."

She sighed. "It's such a burden, being right so often."

"Four more kids died in Rhue's ICU during yesterday's crisis." Cagney rubbed his eyes. "Seven at St. Ives. I heard about it after you left last night."

Nadine stopped as if she'd hit a wall, her face twisted like she'd guzzled chunky milk. She needed to be right more often. She and her team needed to move faster on this.

He came to nudge her shoulder with his own. "Have you seen the news yet?"

"Not since dinnertime. Why?"

They approached the shared office and he paused outside the door. "You need to see it for yourself."

Nadine went inside and dropped her backpack on the desk. She pulled the laptop out, opened it, and sat. A minute later, her screen filled with a local news broadcast about that pharmaceutical reef project she'd seen mentioned before. Only this time, Holschtatt had blown the lid off the pressure cooker. Drone footage, taken at a safe distance, showed some sort of explosion along the curve of the atoll, followed by footage of smaller boats setting out once again to the blast site. The broadcast replayed footage from the earlier report showing prior damage to the islet nearby, as well as water clouded with some whitish substance and coated by rainbow slicks of oil that stretched at least a mile.

The news anchor came on screen to say that according to their contact in The Gaian Protectorate, the blast had taken place the prior day around 9:30 in the morning island time and that in a weird coincidence, here in Austin hospitals, children all went into medical crisis at almost the same moment—2:30

p.m. Austin time. Online chat forums buzzed with conspiracy theories and predictions of end times, and blah blah blah.

This whole thing scared Nadine. Of all ingredients she might have expected in a recipe for disaster, a virus that made children empathic to harm inflicted during ecological devastation would not even have made the list. But her imagination projected the ramifications of such a thing into a future she did not like at all.

She glanced up at Cagney, who came up beside her to watch the broadcast again. "Are you convinced yet?"

He straightened, one hand to his chest. "Hey, you had me yesterday."

The others had all taken seats nearby, watching her. Blondie and one other new person were absent. "What do you all say?"

"Maybe," Thom said in his slow, thoughtful way, "Zero and her dad are onto something."

Yuka squinted at him. "Maybe?"

Another guy shrugged. "Hey, until we have some sort of scientific proof, we can't say for sure, can we?"

"I hate to say it, but he's right," Lara said through a yawn. "No matter how strong a circumstantial case we have, no one will listen if we can't find some strong provable connection, something better than coincidence."

"Then let's find one." Nadine frowned. "We need to figure out how it's doing this. We know it's promoting new growth in the insulae. I'm betting that's the connection we need to isolate."

"It's the interneurin," Cagney said, his tone energetic, excited. "That's the key."

"The what?" Nadine peered up at him.

"The interneurin." He looked around. "Sorry, that's what I've been calling our weird new peptide."

Nadine shrugged. "That's as good a name as any. Elaborate."

"We already postulated that the virus produces the interneurin, and the interneurin provokes the new spindle neuron growth, right?"

Everyone else leaned in closer.

"Go on," Nadine said.

"What if we can intervene at a critical point in that process?"

Yuka sat straighter in her seat. "Yes. Like either keep the virus from completing its formation or prevent it from entering the brain."

"What if we could put together an agent that would interrupt the interneurin's cohesion?" Thom said. "It's possible we could neutralize it so that it could no longer affect the brain."

"You could do that?" Nadine said.

Thom's eyes widened for a split second. "I could try."

"That's all I ask." She pointed at him. "After you get some sleep."

He blew a raspberry. "Nah. I can get some tests started first, let them run in the background. Besides, sleep is for wimps and old people." He sprang to his feet and bolted for the door.

"Wait up." Yuka followed. "I'll help. That way we can be working the samples 'round the clock. Both shifts."

"Good idea. Get Blondie on that, too," Nadine called after them. The more people they had working on it, the faster they'd find something. She swung to face Lara. "I want you to experiment with isolated phage samples. See if we can get it to produce the peptide outside the body. I want to know," she held up a finger, "one, can it survive isolation from the phage. Two, will the isolated peptide still provoke neurogenesis. And three, does that neurogenesis follow the same pattern of spindle neurons in the insulae, or can it be redirected."

"That's more than I can accomplish in a week," Lara said.

"You got someplace else to be?" Nadine winked at her. "At least we can start."

"Okay," Lara breathed. She rushed out, dragging everyone but Cagney with her. She'd need all the help she could get.

"Cagney," Nadine said, "where are we on the sleepwalkers and the Doctor Doolittle stuff?"

"Found it in most of the cases I scanned. Either the patient exhibited odd behavior while sleeping or claimed to speak to wild animals in their yards, or both. Foxes, coyotes, snakes, birds, you name it. I'll send you the list of patient names."

"Please do. And make a separate one for the families where there is no mention. We need to canvass them for the sake of thoroughness and consistency but now is not the time. We don't want to intrude while they're dealing with a crisis unless it's urgent. This can sit for another day. I'm pretty sure I'm right about this."

Cagney trotted to his desk, leaving her alone with her computer.

She watched the newscast once more, then called Mitch. He should be in the office by now. He always did get there before everyone else.

He picked up on the first ring. "Donaldson."

"Mornin', boss. You had your coffee yet?"

He grunted in response.

"That's a 'no,' then." She paused. "Have you seen the latest about that atoll?"

"Yeah. Why?"

"That explosion happened right when the emergency hit here in the hospital. Every kid in ICU and a few in other wards went into some sort of crisis."

Mitch's breath came through the earpiece before he spoke. "And?"

"It supports what we talked about yesterday," she said. "Think about it. A reef is a delicate ecosystem. If they detonated explosives, even small ones—"

"That's enough."

She stuttered to a halt. "Excuse me?"

"I've heard enough of this wild-assed theory."

"You said you were going to consider it."

"I did. I've decided it's ridiculous."

Nadine sat with her mouth open, unsure how to respond. In all their years of working together, Mitch had always been open to hearing new theories. As science evolved and knowledge expanded, he'd been willing to evaluate potential new explanations that fell in line with their evolving field. He'd never dismissed her conjecture this way before.

"I agree with you," he said, his tone a touch less abrasive, "that this phage is probably a new strain, maybe even epigenetically modified as you suggested. But I don't buy that it's intelligent, nor do I believe it's causing its victims to become empathic. If we go spewing that nonsense to the public right now, we'll panic them for sure. The CDC has to be the voice of reason. Logic. Hard science. If you find absolute proof, we'll talk about this again. But we can't upset this already tenuous situation with babble based on suspicion."

"If I'm right, there may be no way to prove it beyond circumstantial supporting evidence."

"Then stop wasting time and effort on a pointless dead-end theory and find the real source of this virus. Nothing happens without a reason, Nadine. It might be obscure, but this phage had an origin. A catalyst. Find it, and you'll find the cause. Follow CDC-approved procedures for testing and confirming theories on the spread and treatment of the virus, and for god's sake start testing ways to kill the damn thing."

"Already doing that." Her voice sounded about as flat as a pot of soup with too many greens and not enough salt.

"Good. Keep me informed."

She hung up and stared at the phone. What in the blot-nosed hell? Sounded like he'd had a fight with the missus, or like someone slipped a little extra bitters into his breakfast beer.

Whatever. She couldn't spare the brainpower it took to figure out Mitch Donaldson right now. Nadine slid the phone in her pocket and opened the list from Cagney.

Chapter 28

Rhue Children's Hospital, Austin, Texas
Saturday, November 16, 1:30 PM

Number of infected: 279,501

LUK FOCUSED ON KYN'S CHEST. Its rise and fall. The musical sound of the blip, blip, blip kept him glued to her side. He wouldn't admit it to anyone, but he half-feared that if he got out of earshot, it would stop again and never resume.

Sadie had barely left him until an hour ago and hadn't ordered him out of the room once. He'd eaten what she brought, at least he thought he remembered chewing and swallowing something, but he couldn't have told her what it was afterward. Doctors came, checked Kyn's pupil reaction, made sure her IV was properly set. Told him how lucky she was.

He'd believe that if she would open her eyes.

He couldn't shake the idea that she was now connected to the world around them in a way he couldn't understand. His dreams had begun to echo her words that everything was alive. That things were changing. *Nobody knows how bad it will be.*

Was this why she'd started talking about putting trash in Hyde and Seek? No, she'd started that before she got sick.

Or had she? The first time she mentioned it was the day she fainted. The day of her seizure. Was it part of her illness? It fit the things she'd said since then. The water made her sick. The air was wrong. Loss of trees and changing weather and damage to that atoll. How could he protect his child from that kind of harm? The very concept felt so overwhelming, and he was only one man.

He got up and paced in the open space between the bed and the coffee table, both hands in his hair. That gut-twisting feeling recurred, the one he'd felt when he'd made the connection with the wildfires, swirling his agitation into an even tighter coil. This was uncharted territory, unfamiliar ground over which he had no clue how to navigate. The uncertainty plagued him, kept him from taking a first step as surely as if it were a twelve-foot fence through which he could catch confusing snippets of events or actions, but could not pass. All he could do was stand before this barrier like a lion at the zoo, trying to understand what was happening outside the pen. He was as stuck as Kyn, unable to move forward, unable to turn back.

He needed to do something while he waited for her to wake up, anything to keep him occupied. Even under sedation, her face twitched. He couldn't stop what was happening to her. But maybe he could help to fix the causes of her pain.

What if a game could retrain those who weren't afflicted by the phage? Computer and video games were already used in educational ways. They made learning fun, and the lessons stuck with the player long after the game was over. Besides, great games became escapes. People dove into them, lived them even when the game wasn't on. A game whose goals included environmental remedies and sustainable living within the game setting could encourage players to solve the extant problems outside the game. If he started now, then by the time the phage kids grew up and took over, the healing would have already begun.

Luk sat on the sofa, opened his laptop, and started a text document. In that original conversation with his daughter about making the game more realistic, the morning this whole nightmare began, she'd first said he should add trash. He put this in his document, with the idea to credit players for picking it up.

What else?

Kyn had suggested he make the game cost the player health points when they missed something—clues or trash— and give them health points when they saw and fixed the problems. He added this to his notes as a good starting place.

She had also talked about dirty air and water, how no one sees it anymore. He remembered how he'd noticed it himself for the first time that same day, and how shocked he had been. The game could start with the player's avatar sick and require them to regain health in order to continue playing at all, or to extend more cleanup effort to win the game.

Yeah…Luk typed as fast as his fingers could fly, so caught up in this new project he didn't hear the visitor enter the room.

"Lukas Behn?"

The stranger, a man in his thirties with a neat beard and brown hair gathered into a ponytail, waited.

Luk set aside his laptop and got to his feet. "Yes. Do I know you?"

With a smile, the man gave him an envelope. "You've been served."

Luk frowned at the packet. "What is this—" He raised his gaze, but the man had gone. Luk opened the envelope. Inside he found a citation and a summons that listed both Lukas Damon Behn and BehnWerks Games as defendants. Named plaintiffs included Simon Tanaka and William Sato.

Luk stared at the papers while his mind reeled. The bastards were suing him for two hundred thousand dollars while his daughter lay unconscious in the ICU.

He dropped down on the sofa. His fingers curled into a fist, crumpling the papers into a wrinkled mess. What kind of person would do such a thing? At least Holly and Bob hadn't joined the suit. Luk hoped that didn't mean their kids were sick with the phage. No one deserved to go through this kind of hell. He made a mental tickler to call them as soon as he could to see how they were holding up.

Kyn moved, restless in the bed, and he lurched to her side. But she didn't wake.

He resumed his seat on the sofa and glared at the rumpled papers on the table before he smoothed them out and took photos of each page with his phone, then sent them off to his lawyer with an e-mail about the situation. It'd been quite some time since he had needed legal assistance. He hoped this would be settled amicably, but he wasn't going to count on that.

Oh, how he wished Sadie were here. No matter what was going on, she always made him feel better.

Rhue Children's Hospital, Austin, Texas
Saturday, November 16, 4:10 PM

Number of infected: 348,622

Nadine stepped out into the corridor and wandered down the hall to the courtyard door. Enclosed on three sides, and open on the fourth, this small balcony garden held a few benches along with several small trees, herbs in large pots, even a hummingbird feeder, though there were no takers for the sweet nectar at the moment. Late afternoon sunshine cast slanting shadows across the courtyard. Pathway lights came on.

She walked to the railing. Every level had its piece of garden, each extending farther out than the one above it like steps that descended toward the first-floor patio. There, the pavement curved along a winding waterway outside the cafe. From her vantage point on the fourth floor, she could survey this green space where Rhue staff called on Nature to assist in the healing process. Many details, geared specifically for the facility's young patients, teased the imagination, like the bright puzzle pieces woven into the groundcover on the second floor, or the colored swirls in the walkways. Rhue hospital worked hard to engage all the senses for their little patients. She'd seen a sign in the lobby a few days ago that said healing was not just about the body, but also about the mind. The spirit. That explained why the facility's corridors and grounds were filled with light and color and art.

She contemplated the brick facade in front of her, the four-story outdoor wall to whatever portion of hospital lay inside. Even there, architects had built in artistry. Colored windows in random-sized rectangles scattered across the bricks to admit panels of hued light into the interior, like those in the lobby.

Shadows deepened. Nadine pulled her phone from her pocket and dialed her wife, who picked up on the third ring.

"Nadine!" Barbara sounded overjoyed. "I'm glad you called. I miss you something fierce."

"I miss you, too, babe." Nadine grinned. "I wanted to call and let you know I'm still breathing."

"Well, whew. Thank goodness for that." Barbara's tone grew serious. "How's it coming?"

"To be honest," Nadine said, "it's gotten weird."

"How do you mean?"

Nadine hesitated. But if she couldn't talk to her wife about this stuff, she might lose what little sanity she had left. "I think this virus is sentient."

"You mean..."

"I think it knows what it's doing. I think it's acting with a purpose. I think it's got an agenda other than simple replication."

Barb's silence made Nadine twitchy. "Hello?"

"I'm here." Barb paused. "I'm just...taking it in. Are you serious?"

"As serious as you are about the table decor before a dinner party." She filled Barb in on her theory, and how yesterday's crisis had cemented the idea in her perception.

"Holy cow, Nadine. That's...I don't even know how to respond. What did Mitch say?"

"Hah. At first, he said he'd consider it. But today he told me it was ridiculous and that I should stop wasting my time on it." Lights along the path and in the garden patches illuminated each level of the courtyard. A ruddy glow lit the western sky above the hospital roof. "He's lost his edge. He used to be more open to stuff like this, but now, I don't know."

"Honey, if you tell me that this is true, I trust you. But you have to admit, it is far-fetched."

"Only because we haven't seen it happen before."

"Yeah." Barb gave a little laugh. "Ever. Like, in the entire history of the human race, never. I can see why he'd balk at putting all his oomph behind it."

"I suppose. But he should also know that I wouldn't suggest it unless I was pretty damn sure I'm right. Because I am. It's wacky, yes, but it's the truth. I'm convinced any effort to find another source of the infection will be wasted time that could have been spent in pursuit of this theory." Nadine gripped the railing. "I mean, think about it, babe! A sentient, maybe even sapient virus that connects people—connects *kids*—to their environment in a way never before seen. It'll change everything. But that's not all. If this peptide is promoting the neurogenesis, and we can harness it, we could repair damaged brains. Heal Alzheimer's patients. Fix brain tumors."

Barb hesitated. "There's a lot of 'if' in that, Nadine."

"I'll admit that. But I'm telling you the potential is there. It's real. Mitch wants to kill it before we even explore the good it could do. But if it's sapient, and doing this with a purpose, I have no doubt it'll fight for its survival. I'm not sure it's a smart move to go up against a virus that can affect our brains in unforeseen ways."

"Just..." Barb tsked. "Don't do anything we'll regret later. Okay? Promise me."

"Like what?"

"Oh, I don't know. Like defy Mitch's orders, put him on the spot. Don't risk your career on this one situation. You're so close to retirement, and we're both old enough that we'll need every penny of your pension, not to mention the medical benefits."

Barbara spoke truth, but Nadine wasn't sure she could stay quiet about this for long. At least one parent had spoken out already. Others might soon follow, especially now. Reporters had begun to make the connection for themselves. How long before others drew the same conclusions? How angry would they be if they knew the CDC had suspected but did not follow up on this theory because it sounded crazy?

"I don't wanna talk about Mitch anymore. Tell me about your day." Nadine listened while Barbara prattled on about her friends, Atlanta's politics and social scene, her plans for Thanksgiving if Nadine made it home, her alternate plans for celebrating without her wife, if necessary.

Nadine wanted to forget, for a while, the tiny beasty that jeopardized her future. She listened, smiling, as her wife's voice soothed her, lulled her into a sense of well-being, and replaced thoughts of sick children with memories of home.

Aboard the *Pasteur*, En Route to New Caledonia
Sunday, November 17, 5:20 PM
(Austin, Texas, Saturday, November 16, 10:20 PM)

Number of infected: 468,929

Isobel paced on the bow of the *Pasteur*, her ponytail swinging. Between the serious wind from their accelerated pace and her state of constant motion for the last few hours, she may never get the tangles out. She squirmed from one regret to another—all that coral on the seafloor instead of in her holds on its way to help Gabe, Claire seizing and afraid without her mom there to help, Jake's accusations of how she favored one child over the other. Logic argued there was a limit to what she could accomplish at any given time. Obsession insisted she could at least try to exceed that expectation.

She wrapped her hands around the prow's rail, staring over the ocean around them. A large pod of dolphins tracked the ship's port side, keeping up and even passing the boat as they leaped and frolicked in the water. Seabirds followed, swooping and diving for bits of food churned up by the passage of both cetaceans and humans.

Isobel closed her eyes. If only she could find peace, instead of more regret, in the sound of the wind. At last, she gave up and crossed the deck to the bridge, where Travis assisted the captain. He smiled and pushed the Panama back from his face. "Hey, Doc."

"Can't we go any faster?" Her tone sounded sharp, maybe too sharp. So what?

"No, ma'am. We're already pushing it past the safe limit, for a longer time than we should. Sorry."

"How long 'til we get to New Caledonia?"

Travis consulted the instruments. "Tomorrow morning. Nine or ten o'clock."

Isobel cursed under her breath. "Then let me use the satphone. Please."

He passed it to her and she stomped away down the side deck without even thanking him. By the time she made it to the aft end, she'd added yet another regret to the list. She stepped into the lee of the cabin and called Jake.

He answered, his voice haggard.

"Hey."

"Isobel! Where are you?"

"About sixteen or seventeen hours from port." She leaned against the outside wall of the structure, watching the dolphins. "Travis says we'll get there before lunch tomorrow. Are you at the hospital?"

"Yeah."

"How's Claire?"

"That seizure nearly killed her."

A tortured sound escaped Isobel's throat. She touched her fingers to her lips as if to keep them from quivering, and squeezed her eyes shut.

Jake's report continued. "They managed to stabilize her, but it was close."

"Have they determined the cause for any of her symptoms?"

"They called it right. It's some new bacteriophage that's gone pandemic. They're calling it Novel Juvenile Cerebral Bacteriophage. It's affecting her brain somehow. The news is full of stories about it."

T'nei said something about sick children, too. Isobel forced herself to stay calm. "How many infected?"

He sighed. "Last I heard it was something like four hundred thousand."

That number sucked all the moisture from her mouth. "Which..." She cleared her throat and tried again. "Which hospital is she in?"

"St. Ives. It was the closest. They have a top-notch pediatric facility. She's getting the best care possible."

"How's Gabe?"

"He's fine. Maria's watching him."

"How're you holding up?" she asked.

"I'm upright. You?"

"I don't know," Isobel said. "All right, I guess. Is everything okay at the office?"

"No. It's a rout."

"What? Why?"

"Kids all around the world went into crisis the minute the *Pasteur* detonated that blast on the reef. That's about the time Claire had her seizure, too." His voice trembled. "She's luckier than some. Three of the kids in this ward died."

"You—" Isobel gulped. "How did you know we used explosives?"

"That Gaian Protectorate got it on video by drone. The whole world has seen it. They're calling the virus the enthéophage, claiming it's God working through the children to hold us accountable for our actions, or saying Holschtatt's responsible for starting the whole mess."

"That's ludicrous."

Jake grunted. "Of course it is. Pure coincidence, those things happening at the same time. But they want a scapegoat. The board's been fielding calls all afternoon. A dozen countries are demanding intervention against Holschtatt, even sanctions. One of their leaders is a military dictator. His two youngest children got the phage. His son didn't make it. He seized control of the Holschtatt facility in his country and is holding our employees hostage. He threatened to start executing them if we didn't cease operations in Nlaan immediately."

Isobel's whole body went cold. "You didn't mention that before."

"I didn't know until a little while ago. But I'm glad you left when you did. Corporate sent word for employees at our other facilities to evacuate, to get to the U.S. Embassies in their region immediately. I think I heard one of the directors say something about the U.S. military being on high alert." He blew out a long breath. "And, oh yeah, Holschtatt stock plunged today. That small fortune we had in company securities is worthless now. I suppose we can hope for a rebound, but that won't happen anytime soon. Not until we can drag the company out of the garbage heap, if that's even possible."

She felt like she'd eaten a lead weight. If Neillsen fired her, how would they pay the kids' medical bills? How would she save Gabe?

"Don't talk like that," she said, forcing a confidence she didn't feel. "Neillsen and the others will figure something out. They always do. They're as unsinkable as corks."

"I know." He went quiet for a couple of seconds, and she could hear the weariness in his silence as much as in his words. "How's your work on the boat coming along?"

Oh, that. "I finally figured out what caused our first week's worth of tests to fail."

"What was it?"

She explained the typo. "Once we resolved that small detail, everything else fell into place like I knew it would. We'd started to make progress just before we got word we had to leave."

"Well, at least this trip wasn't a waste, then."

"True. Even if there isn't enough raw coral left after trials to manufacture a market supply of the drug, we'll have the live samples. It'll take a few years for an artificial reef to grow large enough to harvest it in any significant quantities, but it's a start." She didn't add that they'd left at least as much on the seafloor as they'd loaded or that, had she stayed another twelve hours, she could have filled the rest of their holds. Seemed senseless to dredge up that argument when neither of them would benefit.

Instead, she promised him she'd call again when they reached the port, then hung up. She slid down the wall to the deck and put her head in her hands.

Chapter 29

Rhue Children's Hospital, Austin, Texas
Sunday, November 17, 10:14 AM

Number of infected: 902,561

CAGNEY POPPED IN AT THE DOORWAY. "You got a minute?"

Nadine glanced up from last night's test results. "What are you doing here? You should be sleeping."

"After we talk. You're gonna want to hear this."

He ducked out before she could ask why not talk here. Everyone else was in the lab hunting for viable ways to interrupt the phage. She closed her computer. She'd already reviewed the data twice anyway. Thom's attempts from last night showed no promise. Would, in fact, either exacerbate the extant issues or be deadly to the patient. Or both. It wouldn't be easy to stop this virus, much less kill it.

In the corridor, Cagney tapped his foot, his laptop tucked against his chest, his lips pulled together in a thin line. His red hair lay flat on one side, the top still reaching for the ceiling but not as well-tended as usual. The freckles stood out more than usual on his pale skin, and his green eyes held a hard glint Nadine didn't recall seeing before.

She frowned. "What—"

"Not here." He took off down a corridor she'd seldom used.

Nadine followed, worry nibbling at her calm like a mouse on a peanut.

Around the corner, he led her into a separate room with a window on one side, a sofa, a few comfortable chairs, a couple of tables, and a second door at the far side that must open into the auditorium. Nadine had seen such prep rooms before, a small quiet space where presenters would gather their thoughts or notes before entering to deliver their lecture.

Once they were both inside, Cagney closed the door and sat on the sofa. He patted the cushion beside him.

She sat, waiting for him to explain, but he opened his laptop, connected to the wi-fi, then spun the computer around, and pushed it at her.

"Read."

The article, which dominated the screen on Fortune Report's website, pictured a couple of top CDC officials seated at a table with two men she didn't recognize. The headline read "Holschtatt Pharmaceuticals in preliminary talks with CDC and FDA over potential Milani Syndrome treatment."

The brief article first explained the horrific symptoms of the rare childhood disorder, then went on to say that no treatment had ever been found, until now. Holschtatt admitted trials had yet to be completed but that initial results showed promise. The whole thing hinted that a deal was all but reached for the sharing of non-proprietary portions of Holschtatt's medical research on the Syndrome in exchange for the CDC's collaborative genomic testing and FDA's support in seeking swift approval of the drug.

"That's Anuka Brine," Nadine said, "and Justin Kirkland. Since they top the CDC's org chart, should I assume these other guys are her peers from the FDA and Holschtatt?"

"Yep." Cagney retrieved the computer and scooted closer to share the screen. "That gorgeous piece of humanity," he indicated the slender, distinguished man to the left of Anuka, "is Cristoph Niellsen, board chair for Holschtatt Pharmaceuticals. He's the one responsible for Holschtatt swallowing all those smaller pharmaceutical companies in the last fifteen years. His efforts and leadership since he took control raised their stock value and spiked the company into the top five of all medical research facilities worldwide."

"But he's the chair." Nadine squinted at the man's image. "Not the CEO."

"I don't know their inner workings." Cagney wagged his eyebrows. "Maybe he's the hand inside the puppet, ya know?"

The other man in the photo sat taller than Neillsen. A hank of greying hair crept past the man's receding hairline onto his forehead. "This the FDA guy?"

"Bingo. Meet Bernard Geldart. Works in drug safety and approval channels for the FDA. I couldn't find much on him, except he's newish to their corporate chart. Been in the medical field for a while, though, even did some time as a doctor."

Nadine skimmed the article once more, then checked the date. "This is from yesterday morning."

"Yeah."

"Did you find any other references to this alliance on other sources?"

"A few environmental watchdog groups mentioned it," he said. "They all had similar photos, probably from cell phones."

"Any of them dated before this article?"

"Yeah. Most of the watchdog pieces were timestamped the night before. Why?"

"I'm trying to pinpoint when the actual meeting took place," she murmured.

He shrugged. "Probably the same night as the first piece showed up. The greenies wouldn't have held onto this. They're waving it like a flag, though they don't have a lot of hard info to add yet."

Interesting. She tells Mitch her theory on Friday afternoon. Friday night, Mitch's superiors have a sit-down with Neillsen and Geldart. Saturday morning Mitch says

Nadine's eggs are scrambled and orders her to abandon her cockamamy theory.

"Uh oh." Cagney waggled his fingers in front of the monitor. "You see connections. Come on. Spill."

Her mind still racing, she quickly outlined her last two conversations with Mitch.

Cagney's face grew hard. "Oh snap! He must have gone to Anuka Brine with your theory, and she shot him down."

"Probably."

They stared at one another.

At least Nadine knew the why, though it still didn't soften the bite in what felt like a betrayal of sorts.

"I guess it makes sense, to them anyway," Cagney said. "If they have this deal in the works, they can't let us blow it out of the water by revealing connections between Holschtatt and this latest fiasco with the phage kids."

"That would add a pinch of hypocrisy to the stew." Nadine looked at the photo again. "When I first mentioned this theory to him and he wanted me to kill it, I suggested we experiment with the new peptide in neuromedicine as an aid to repair damaged brains."

"Wow. That never occurred to me." Cagney blinked. "What did Mitch say?"

"He almost came unhinged, accused me of choosing to not fix the problem so that we might make money on it."

"You're kidding."

"Nope."

"When did that happen?"

"Day before yesterday."

Cagney's expression shifted. "The morning before this dinner, then." He indicated the photo. "And when did he tell you to let it go?"

"After the dinner." Nadine slapped the couch cushion. "Exactly my point. Now that the CDC stands to gain something, he's not willing to listen to anything that might challenge that possibility."

"I dunno. This might not be on him, Nadine. He's probably following orders. Like we are. He may not have any choice."

"That never kept him from pushing the limits before."

"He has a lot more to lose than we do, I guess." Cagney closed his laptop with a yawn. "Anyway, after our conversation the other day, and given Holschtatt's involvement in that reef wreck, I wanted you to see this."

"You could have e-mailed me the link."

"I know." He got up and clutched the computer to his chest. "But you might not have seen it for a while. Besides, I wanted to hear your take on it. I'm glad I did." He yawned again.

"Me too." She pushed to her feet and gestured. "Now go. Sleep."

He preceded her into the hall, waved as they parted company at the next corridor, then disappeared in the direction of the elevators.

Thom's first set of tests, exploring ways to destabilize the peptide had proved fruitless. It wasn't a dead proposition yet, but she'd instructed him to move on to other ideas while that one percolated in the background. Next, he'd tested ways to disrupt the interneurin's production or progression through the body and into the brain. On the plus side, one of the treatments killed the phage. On the minus side, that treatment, as well as all the others in which the peptide proved resistant, would have prompted serious negative reactions in the patient.

On a whim, Nadine instructed Blondie to set up new glove boxes and try treating the phage and the peptide with a cocktail of sex hormones. It couldn't hurt and since the virus only affected pre-adolescent victims, it's possible their physical changes at puberty would make them immune. If so, those hormones could be toxic to the virus.

The whole time she worked, Cagney's revelation spun on instant replay, a constant distraction like a TV playing in the next room while she tried to accomplish a thought-consuming project at the hotel.

She sat at her desk and popped open her laptop, searching out those sentinel sites Cagney mentioned and reading them one by one. Though none of them theorized on the Holschtatt fiasco as a catalyst for further spread of the phage, they all predicted that the reef destruction would soon be old news. Once Holschtatt could produce some new miracle treatment, no one would remember the explosion or destruction in the South Pacific, nor the devastating effect it had produced in the phage patients.

This had to be what made Mitch change his tune. Disappointing as that was, Cagney was probably right. Mitch had little or no control over what orders got passed down from on high. And with his retirement looming, it was almost understandable why he'd give in to pressure from his bosses. He had kids, yeah, but they were grown. Even though one had a child of her own, that kid was past puberty. If Mitch came down here into the trenches and saw what she'd seen, he might make different choices. Then again, maybe not.

In the end, it wasn't Mitch's theory. It was hers. Was she going to box it up, as Mitch said?

She crossed her arms. Okay. She needed to treat this theory like any other. Examine its weak and strong points and let logic dictate how to proceed.

Why was she convinced she was right? Easy—the spread numbers, along with the crisis coincident with that South Pacific explosion. Strong point, though admittedly circumstantial.

Where was the scientific proof? She had none, except perhaps for the fact that phagey retaliated when they tried to interrupt its process. "Phagey?" she muttered to herself, then shrugged. Why not? If it was sentient, and acting en masse as she suspected, it needed a name.

What's worse, she may never be able to prove her theory. Science still had no way to determine beyond any doubt the presence of sapience or self-aware intelligence in animals, outside theories based on observation of behavior and reactions to their environments. Even though Nadine had followed that same process to reach these conclusions, those kinds of studies came from a whole different branch of science, one unlikely to convince CDC leadership of its veracity. Weak point.

What if she was wrong? Then she was back to square one. No predictable or even traceable means of transmission, no clue where the organism itself came from, and if they couldn't find a way to interrupt the peptide, no means of ameliorating its effects. Weak point.

What if she was right? How could she "cure" something like global climate issues in time to save all these children? Simple answer. She couldn't, not by herself. But if she were right, and she could make enough other people see and accept it too, then they could work together to find the solution. Maybe the answer lay in a different scientific field altogether, as its "proof" did. Perhaps this wasn't a simple medical issue at all, but something far deeper.

She caught herself and stopped short, snorting in self-derision. Next thing you know, she'd be believing in God or some other ridiculous notion. Why, minutes ago she'd called Mitch a hypocrite, and here she was doing the same thing.

Nadine locked her hands behind her head and tilted her chair. She'd always been a person of science. How had she come to this? Listening to some religious nut muffin and his kid talking online about a mystical connection between the phage kids and the virus, and being *convinced* by him, was crazy.

So then...was Mitch right?

Logic said yes. He was right. But her gut said no, and her gut was correct more often than not, logic be damned. After all, Cagney, Thom, Yuka, and Lara had recognized the same patterns she had seen. Did she think they were seeing what she wanted them to?

Doubtful. While Lara and Thom might agree with her even if they were unsure she was right, Cagney and Yuka had both called her on past mistakes more than once. Matter of fact, Cagney took pride in catching her flawed theories and taunting her about them, always in private, for months after. He was twisted like that and thus made a great second.

She circled once more around the idea that Phagey might be something other than a typical virus that could be cured by medical science. She hadn't said it out loud or even admitted it to herself until now, but she was more excited over the possibilities presented by this study than she had been about any other medical dilemma in many years. No one had ever seen anything like it. No one knew where to go with it. None of them knew how to cure it or stop it or even if they could. Or should. That was a very new feeling for her. For most of them. The scientist in her almost wished it would remain an enigma they could delve for years to come.

Except for the sick kids. That poked holes in the dough for sure.

She closed her eyes and saw again the ICU in chaos the night of the explosion—there she went again, assuming this theory was credible—watching the anguish of the parents, hearing the equipment alarms, seeing the staff rushing to help their small charges.

She tapped the back of her skull, her thumbs keeping time with Ray Charles in her brain. Mitch might demote her, even toss her out on her ear if she didn't follow his orders. Barb would peel Nadine like a banana if she put her job, her retirement, and her benefits on the line. She supposed the real question was this: Was she going to allow more kids to die without uttering a single word that might help them in order to avoid the personal fallout?

Her fingers tingled, and she straightened. She called up Zero's records, perused them, closed her laptop, and left the office behind.

Chapter 30

IT HAD TAKEN AN HOUR LAST NIGHT TO CALM SADIE after Luk told her about Simon's lawsuit. She'd wanted to call the man, give him a piece of her mind. Or better yet, pay him a visit. In Florida. Right then. Luk talked her down, convinced her that wouldn't help and might even hurt matters, and assured her that his lawyer would take care of it.

This morning she still steamed over it, though she sat curled beside him on the couch. She hadn't said anything more, but he could see her fretting over it like a cat outside a mouse hole. Gods help Simon if he ever stepped into the room with Sadie again.

He reached over and took her hand, hopefully distracting her from private revenge scenarios. She pushed her hair behind her shoulder. "I'm okay."

"I know."

"He makes me so damned mad," she hissed.

"Who does?" Kyn asked.

Luk flew to the bedside as if he had wings, Sadie right behind him. Luk stroked his daughter's hair. "Hey, kiddo. Welcome back."

"Thanks." Kyn offered a tired smile. "Who are you talking about?"

"Nothing. Grownup stuff. Nothing for you to worry about."

"Nothing for you to worry about either," she said.

He hoped she was right. "Thanks. I needed to hear that."

Kyn wiggled her fingers at Sadie. "Hey."

"Hey yourself. How do you feel?"

"Mmm. Better. Stronger, kind of. If that makes sense."

"Are you hungry?"

"Yeah. But I can wait until after."

"After what?" Luk said.

A tap sounded at the door. He spun to find a stranger peering around the curtain. Grey eyes, high cheekbones, and full lips made her seem friendly. But after his last visit by a stranger, Luk felt disinclined to offer a welcome.

"Mr. Behn?"

"Who wants to know?"

"Dad," Kyn murmured. "Be nice."

The woman stepped into view. Dressed in practical slacks and a sensible shirt and shoes, she wore no jewelry or makeup. "I'm Doctor Nadine Parker. I wonder if I might speak with you and your daughter about her illness.

Kyn's sweet voice piped up. "Sure you can. I'm Kyndra."

"Nice to meet you, Kyndra. And thank you, but we should probably get your dad's input on that, too. Right?" Doctor Parker winked at Kyn, then looked to Luk.

Sadie stepped out from behind Luk. "No offense, Doctor Parker. But it's been a rough few days. What's this about?"

The doc shifted her gaze from Luk to Sadie. "I've been researching the viral spread and patterns of transmission in phage cases. I saw Mr. Behn's video—"

Luk raised a hand. "I'm sorry, I'm not interested in hearing your critique of my interpretations—"

"—and his theory raised a few questions for me about how I was pursuing that information. His words, and Kyndra's, made me see the data in a different way." She watched Luk, her manner more open than he'd seen in the other doctors. "Mr. Behn, I believe you."

"You...You do?"

"Yes. I'd like to get more details if that's okay with you." She gestured over her shoulder. "If it's a bad time, I can come later."

Luk glanced at Sadie. "Can you sit with Kyn?"

Kyn tugged at his sleeve. "No, Dad. She needs to talk to me, too. Stay. Please?"

"Oh, kiddo," he said, "you just woke up after a pretty bad few days. I'm not sure you're up to this."

"Please? I promise to tell you if I get too tired."

His daughter had many variations of that beautiful smile. This version, the one she flashed at him in this moment, was the one best calculated to change his mind. His heart melted. How could he say no to her after everything she'd been through?

"Okay," he said, hesitant. "But if she gets too tired, we're finished."

"Of course." Doctor Parker came to the foot of the bed. "I understand. Mr. Behn, would you please recount for me every step of Kyndra's illness since you first noticed anything out of the ordinary to now? Leave nothing out, no matter how unimportant you think it might be, even if you never mentioned it to the other doctors."

Luk groaned. Not again.

Doctor Parker placed her hands in her pockets. "I know it's asking a lot, but I'd like to hear it directly from you, without the filters that might have colored or obscured any of the facts. I don't want to risk missing any details that might not have made it into the file."

"Hah." Luk fought the urge to sneer. "I imagine there are quite a few little things that never made it into the file. They never took us seriously."

"What do you mean?"

Luk related his attempts to get Doctors Whitfield and Sarsby to listen to his ideas, and how they discounted what he said.

Doctor Parker listened to his concerns. "I won't do that. I swear on my Alton Brown recipes."

Kyn laughed.

Luk frowned. "What?"

She smiled, wide and warm. "Sorry. Old habits. I give you my word I will listen to everything you say and take it seriously."

He'd never seen this "doctor" before. Who was she, really? Kyn watched him twist with a little smirk on her face. Would she know if this person was on the level? The only way to find out was to allow it to develop and see what happened. He waved toward the sofa. "Would you like to sit?"

"I'm fine, thank you."

Luk started his and Kyn's tale for what felt like the thousandth time, including everything he could think of...the sleepwalking, the dahlias, the spiders, the fainting, the seizure, the connection he'd made to the wildfires, the suggestions she'd made for his game-in-progress, the things she'd said that made sense, the things she'd said that didn't. He included the responses of the doctors and hospital staff to his video, and how Child Protective Services had been called on him by someone. By the time he stopped talking, his voice had gone hoarse. Sadie brought him a glass of water.

Doctor Parker took it all in. Never once did a doubtful expression cross her face. Luk felt hope set roots in his heart.

"Kyndra didn't sleepwalk or talk to animals before that first day?"

"Not that I recall," Luk said. "My neighbors also told me their boy talked to a fox in their yard. Scared them pretty badly."

"He's infected too?"

"Yes. His room's down the hall."

The doc nodded. "And you posit that the virus has connected Kyndra and the other children to the environment in some way. Have I stated it correctly?"

Luk's stomach flipped. *Here it comes.* "Yes. I do."

"Why?"

Had she not heard a word he'd said? "Because of all I told you," he said with a snippy tone.

"Again, Mr. Behn, I hear you. I'm willing to consider that this is a real possibility. I want to know why *you* believe it. A lot of other people who have gone through the same illness with their children still somehow conclude that it's all coincidental. I want to know why you don't."

He stroked Kyn's hair. "Because Kyn told me what it was. And I trust her."

The doctor looked at Sadie. "What about you, Ms.—"

"Schupert." Sadie stepped forward. "Please call me Sadie. Same reasons. I've seen most of the process firsthand. Been here through almost every step. I've heard Kyn talk about what's happening to her. She's not making it up. I can tell."

"Why don't you ask me why I believe it?" Kyn said.

"Okay." Parker addressed Kyn like she might speak to another adult, with respect instead of condescension. "What do you have to say about all this?"

Kyndra struck Luk as both vulnerable and mighty as she regarded the doctor.

"I don't know what the phage is, exactly. But I know what it's doing to me."

"What is that?"

Kyndra smiled. "It's making me better."

"You mean it's making you better now? Today?"

"Yes. No. I mean, I was sick *before* the phage came, but I didn't know it. The phage has been helping me get well since that very first day."

Understanding dawned on the doc's face. "You mean people without the phage are the sick ones?"

"Yes." Kyn's fingers played with the edge of the blanket. "Every day, it helps more kids start healing. There's a man you know, someone you work with who has blond hair."

Parker's frown deepened. "Yes."

Kyn tilted her head. "His little boy just started getting well, too."

The doc blanched. "Thank you for telling me. I'll let him know."

"I like you," Kyn said. "You don't want to kill it, even though the others want you to."

"You don't want us to kill it?"

"Why would I want that?" Kyn asked. "It's helping me. It's helping all of us."

"You don't think the other phage patients would want us to kill it?"

"No."

"I see." Parker nodded. "Doesn't it hurt you?"

"No. The phage didn't cut down the trees or kill that reef."

"But you feel those things. You said in the video that you feel those things like they're happening to you. Right?"

"Mm hmm."

"And that doesn't make you angry?" Parker asked.

"Not at the phage."

"What will you do if the doctors find a cure, Kyndra? A treatment that would put an end to the pain."

"I don't want it," Kyn said.

Parker's attention shifted to Luk. "Mr. Behn? How do you feel about that?"

"If she doesn't want it," Luk said, "I won't make her take it."

Doctor Parker gritted her teeth, looked away, then hit him with a cutting stare. "It may not be that simple. Please understand I'm not trying to change your mind, but you need to know that according to state law, it's your duty to see that your minor child receives medical treatment, especially in a life-threatening situation. If you refuse, the courts can terminate your parental rights and treat her anyway."

Kyn's eyes widened, and Luk glared at Parker. "Stop it. You're scaring her. She had a heart attack two days ago. She does not need this kind of stress."

Parker grimaced. "I'm sorry, I was out of line. I'm usually more involved in the research side of things and don't often get involved in direct patient contact and care. My bedside manner is rusty." She turned to Kyn. "I didn't mean to scare you, Kyndra. I'm sure your dad can manage whatever comes."

Kyn didn't respond at first. She examined Parker's face, seeming to read every twitch, every line. "You're an important doctor in all this."

"I—"

"But you're more important than you even know."

Parker glanced from Kyn to Luk to Kyn, blinking fast.

"She's telling the truth." His daughter flashed him a bright-eyed affirmation. "She does believe us. She wants to help, but she worries about her job. Her wife."

Parker's mouth fell open and she stepped back.

Kyn grinned at their guest. "You should know you aren't going crazy. The phage isn't God. At least, not the one you're thinking of."

Doctor Parker blinked at Luk and Sadie, her throat working as if she wanted to speak.

Luk shrugged. "You wanted to speak with her."

"I..." Parker closed her mouth, drew a long breath, and blew it all out. "Yes, I did." She nodded at Kyndra, then at Luk and Sadie. "Thank you for talking to me. I'll take some time to consider what you've said, and make notes. If I have further questions later, may I visit again?"

Luk agreed, and the doctor left. By the time she was gone, Kyn's eyes were closing.

"Good job, Dad."

Sadie stepped closer. "You gave her a lot to think about, girlfriend."

Kyn yawned. "It's stuff she already knew. I just reminded her."

Rhue Children's Hospital, Austin, Texas
Sunday, November 17, 12:45 PM

Number of infected: 1,600,053

Nadine pushed out of Zero's room and walked like a wooden doll down the hallway, rounded the corner on shaky legs, and made it to the elevators without the need to speak to anyone else. She pressed the call button and waited until the metallic doors slid aside. No one was aboard, and she entered the car alone. People passed by in the corridor while Nadine punched the "close" button over and over as fast as her shaking finger could work.

Then the doors closed and the car started to rise. At last, she could take a breath.

What in the nine levels of primary pasta preparation was all that?

Nadine had never put any stock in psychics and fortune-tellers and all that gas-ripened bull hockey.

Until today.

Those 3XG scans of Zero's brain had been taken how long ago? Two days? How many more new spindle neurons would have taken up residence by now? The way that kid talked, nothing in those images surprised Nadine. Seeing the neurogenesis on a computer screen and hearing the words it prompted in this eight-year-old were two entirely different kinds of sauce, one flavorful but thin and the other robust, substantial.

If there had ever been a doubt about what her decision might be, that child had blown it clean out of the blender.

Chapter 31

En Route to Nouméa Airport, Nouméa, New Caledonia
Monday, November 18, 11:05 AM
(Austin, Texas, Sunday, November 17, 4:05 PM)

Number of infected: 2,113,905

ISOBEL'S PACKED SHUTTLE PULLED IN past the graffitied wall at the access road to La Tontouta International Airport and stopped. Traffic clogged the way before them. She scooted forward in the middle seat. Passengers beside her offered a little space to move.

"Driver, is there no other way to the terminal?"

"No, Miss." The middle-aged man smiled at her over his shoulder, bright white teeth amid the brown of his complexion. Rimless glasses sat astride his nose, sun glinting on the lenses, and on his bald pate. He spoke excellent English, though his accent made it hard for her to understand him sometimes. "I am sorry."

She groaned. "Is this normal? This kind of crowd?"

"No. The tourists try to leave all at once because of the sickness. They fear for their children."

Isobel winced. That she understood.

Another passenger said something to the driver in French, and he responded. Others in the van talked among themselves. Outside the van, palm trees and other large-leafed tropical foliage lined the roadway.

She glanced at the couple behind her. A toddler sat in the woman's lap. Both of the adults looked frightened. She didn't blame them.

"How many are sick now?" she asked.

"Oh," the driver's whole face puckered, "more than two million. All around the world. You didn't hear the news?"

"No." Isobel frowned. "I've been out of touch." She pulled her phone from her pocket and began to scan headlines about the sickness. Tendrils of fear wrapped around her chest, squeezing tighter with each one. This is what happened to Claire. And no one knew what it was or how to cure it. One sick child in her family wasn't enough, it seemed. Cruel fate felt the need to afflict her other as well.

A new thought seized her. "They won't keep me from leaving, will they?"

The driver twisted in his seat. "I haven't heard that they were holding people in Nouméa, but I don't know for certain. I am sorry."

Isobel sat back and waited for the van to inch its way to the terminal.

Rhue Children's Hospital, Austin, Texas
Sunday, November 17, 4:36 PM

Number of infected: 2,795,131

Nadine stared at the computer screen with mixed emotions. None of her team's efforts had borne fruit, but she hadn't really expected them to. Mitch's unrealistic hope that they would have a therapeutic any time soon added fuel to her conviction that he was being irrational. It would be a year, at the least, with pharmaceutical research labs around the world working on the same goal before anyone found a working MCM, not to mention a vaccine.

A cure for patients who might not want it.

She didn't know how to feel about that. Mitch would say they were children with inadequate experience or wisdom to make such important informed choices in the first place. But he also would believe the neurogenesis was making them behave irrationally. Even more reason to kill this thing.

She rehashed her visit with Kyndra, the mind-boggling things that child had said. No doubt the neurogenesis was changing how she thought and spoke and behaved, but not in a deranged way. She had more to process, that's all. Kyndra could make *more* informed choices, given the fact that she appeared to have access to information the uninfected did not.

To tell the truth, Nadine no longer knew whether she wanted to find a cure. Not that it would matter. She wasn't in this alone, and someone somewhere would manage it, given enough time. What would happen to Kyndra and the other phage kids then? Any company who spent the time and resources to concoct an expensive treatment wasn't going to take lightly a response of "Thanks, but no thanks" from a majority, if not all, of their intended recipients. The pharma companies would push and push until governmental agencies stepped in and mandated the cure if they hadn't already by that time. What long-term effects would manifest in the phage patients if they were forced to surrender this unique connection they'd established with something larger than themselves?

Beside her computer, Nadine's phone buzzed. She glanced down. Mitch. She thumbed it on.

"Hey, boss."

"What's your team's status?"

"Hello to you, too. How's the wife? Good? Glad to hear it. What about your kids? Grandkids? All good? Great news. Me? I'm fine—"

"Not now, Nadine." Mitch sounded exhausted. "Status?"

She went quiet. "No new news. We're still working on it. I suggested they also try treating a selection of the virus samples with estrogen and testosterone, but they started that this morning. Too soon to know whether it'll have any effect."

"Worth a try."

"Yep."

Mitch hesitated. Nadine maintained the awkward silence. She used to be able to read Mitch Donaldson like a familiar recipe. She knew what he wanted from her before he did. This version? She had no idea. Best to wait and let him tell her.

"We need to update the public on what we've done to date in trying to nail down this virus. They're scared, and scared people can become a problem. It's up to us to calm them down. I've set up a press conference for tomorrow morning. I want you to handle it."

"By 'handle it,'" she said, choosing her words with care, "I take it you want to give them the decaf version. All is well, fear not."

"I'm asking you to do this because you've been involved with this virus longer than anyone. If you aren't up to the task, I'll transfer the conference to Atlanta and do it myself."

"I've got it. I just need to know where my boundaries are. You say I'm your first choice because I know the most about it, but there isn't a lot of hard science to share with anyone, and I'm confident you don't want me to spout my theories about this bugger."

"Absolutely not. Stick to what we know for certain. Tell them what we know about NJace itself and how it's shifted to a lysogenic mode, the new peptide, even the neurogenesis, and that we think it's the peptide provoking this neuronal growth. You can tell them we've tested ways to stop the phage, but without success thus far."

"That's the list of approved topics?"

"Jesus, Nadine." Sounds of drinking and swallowing came through the line. Probably bourbon. "Can you do this or not?"

Nadine's jaw clenched, and she worked it a few times before she could respond. "Okay. Where?"

"Right there at Rhue Hospital. Eleven tomorrow morning. You should touch base with Doctor Aimee de Verlaine, the hospital administrator. She'll fill you in on the details. She'd also like a copy of what you're going to cover by eight o'clock tomorrow morning, specifically the opening remarks you plan to make and what topics you'll include."

The administrator had good cause to be concerned about how this press conference would affect the hospital. "Of course."

Mitch paused again. "Can I count on you, Nadine?"

"Always."

"Good. Then unless something else comes up in the meantime, I'll speak to you afterward." Other voices came through the speaker, getting louder as if they were coming closer to Mitch. "Gotta go. Good luck."

He hung up and Nadine put the phone down on the desk nice and slow.

This was going to cost her.

Nouméa Airport, Nouméa, New Caledonia
Monday, November 18, 11:50 AM
(Austin, Texas, Sunday, November 17, 4:50 PM)

Number of infected: 2,994,127

At last, the van arrived at the terminal's drop-off station. Passengers exited, gathering their luggage from the driver at the rear. One glance at the doors sank her heart. Crowds mobbed the lobby inside, their numbers spilling out and onto the covered loading zone. Security officers spread out into a line along the sidewalk, preventing anyone else from attempting to enter.

Isobel stopped, staring. It would take as long to get into the terminal as it had taken them to get to the curb. Maybe though, since she wasn't flying commercial, she could bypass all the red tape.

She paid the driver, grabbed her large roll-around case, and made a beeline to one of the numerous security officers. Dressed in uniforms, they appeared as nervous as the others. The officer she approached, and those to either side, tensed as she drew near.

"Excuse me. I have a private plane waiting. I need to find out where it is and meet it without further delay. Can you help?"

The woman, a head shorter than Isobel and broad-shouldered, held her arms out to either side, curved toward Isobel as if to herd her in another direction. The woman spoke in rapid French and pointed at the end of the line.

"No, you don't understand." Isobel heard the desperation in her voice. "I'm not flying with them."

The guard's voice rose. Her tone sharpened. Another guard came closer, holding a nightstick down low.

Isobel's taxi driver materialized at her side and said something that calmed the guards, though they didn't retreat or offer to help. They answered, and the driver translated. "The officer is telling you there are no exceptions, miss. Everyone must go through the customs."

"But can you tell them I—" She almost identified her connection to Holschtatt, until she remembered Jake's phone call. That might not be a safe thing to do. "There is a private plane waiting for me? My children are in the United States, both of them sick. I'm dealing with an emergency. I can't take hours to catch that plane."

"Miss, look around you." The driver gestured. "All these people fear as you do. It is an emergency for everyone."

Isobel reached for her purse. "What if I pay them extra? What if I pay you extra?" She dug for her wallet.

The guards tensed further, and the woman pulled loose her baton.

"Miss." The driver's tone chilled by a few degrees, and he offered a polite, but cool smile. "I'm sorry. Any other time, we would be glad to take your money. Our families need it. But today we cannot help you. Please." He pointed, as the guard had done.

By now, several more vans full of passengers had unloaded, and the line wrapped down the sidewalk. This would take hours, time Isobel didn't have. Tears welled and she dashed them away with a huff.

"Fine." She shoved her wallet into her purse and grabbed her suitcase. She tried not to notice the travelers staring at her as she walked to the end of the row. She'd never seen anything like this. Never been stuck in a foreign country where her business contacts or her money wouldn't buy her special privileges.

As she went, she walked by the young couple with the toddler from her shuttle. They peered past her with concern, and Isobel followed their line of sight. Behind her, two security guards came fast, and two others behind them. Isobel stiffened, her heart hammering, until the officers stepped around her and took the young couple and their child out of the line. The other two guards approached a new group closer to the end of the line, three adults and two children. That family, too, was removed from the line and shuffled into an unmarked door to one side of the main entrance.

Isobel recoiled, shrinking from the guards. What were they doing? She dragged her focus from the door and scanned the line. There were no children in view. The others from her shuttle, who stood near where the toddler's parents had been, looked at her from faces blank with a shock that probably matched her own. She made herself continue to the end of the line.

Once she'd reached the end, she dialed Jake. He'd need to know she would be delayed a long while.

Rhue Children's Hospital, Austin, Texas
Sunday, November 17, 5:10 PM

Number of infected: 3,390,252

Nadine stood on the balcony garden chilled by the evening's coolness. She should have brought a jacket. She pushed the speed dial on her phone with fingers colder than the night's chill could explain. Her stomach rolled as the phone rang.

"Hey, beautiful," Nadine said.

"Oh!" Strange clinking noises sounded on Barb's end. "I didn't know you were gonna call." She sounded distracted.

"I wanted to surprise you. What'cha doing?"

"Ugh. Making cookies. For a potluck. Remy's bringing a pie, so I said I could do cookies. I thought, how hard can it be, ya know?"

Nadine imagined her wife on the other end of the line, sipping tea and making a mess in the kitchen. "Really? That's nice."

"I wish you were here," Barb said. "You'd do a much better job. I'm no good in the kitchen. Who knows what these'll look or taste like when they come out of the oven? Me and my helium-hand. What was I thinking?"

"You were being your beautiful self, volunteering to help. Every potluck needs at least two desserts."

"I suppose."

Kitchen noises filtered through Nadine's mobile. The clatter of a cookie sheet. The rattle of aluminum foil. The clacking of a wooden spoon in a glass bowl.

"How's the investigation going?" Barb asked.

Nadine snorted. "You haven't seen the news? I'm sure they're full of updates."

Barb dropped something, followed by a crash and an expletive. "I don't watch those bloodsuckers."

"Yeah. That's why I called."

The noises in the kitchen stopped. "What's wrong?"

Nadine almost said "nothing," then shut her mouth and mulled over how to say what she needed to. "Mitch wants me to do a press conference. He's already set it up. Wants me to announce our findings thus far."

"Really? Everything? I knew he'd come around, see you were right. That's great, Nadine!"

"Well," Nadine hesitated. "No. Not everything. He doesn't want me to tell anyone about my theory."

"Aw, honey, I'm sorry." Noises on the Atlanta end of the call resumed. "You wait, though. He'll come around."

"No, Barb. He won't."

"Why not?"

Nadine explained the recent announcement of the cooperative agreement in the works between Holschtatt Pharmaceuticals, the CDC, and the FDA. "As long as Holschtatt is holding a carrot on that stick and the CDC gets first crack at their Milani Syndrome research, they aren't going to burn that bridge. I have no doubt Mitch was given orders to hush up any potential bad press where Holschtatt is concerned. I'm effectively neutralized."

Barb muttered something very unladylike.

Nadine was about to make it worse. She closed her eyes. "Or at least, they assume I am."

"Oh no. No, no, no. Nadine, we talked about this. You promised."

"I did no such thing. I can't ignore this issue, babe. Kids are dying."

"And how is getting yourself fired going to help any of them? You told me yourself, you can't prove anything. If you go out there and spew that nonsense as if it's science, you'll blackball yourself, and no one will listen, and then where will we be? Hmm?"

"Nonsense?" Nadine frowned. "You said you believed me."

"Ugh. I do. But they won't, and that's the takeaway here. You can't do this, Nadine."

"Listen. I went to see Patient Zero earlier today."

"You did *what*?"

"Met her. Met her dad. Met a nice young woman named Sadie, probably dad's partner. They're good people, Barb."

"That's irrelevant, Nadine! Isn't personal contact with the patients verboten for your investigators?"

"It's not part of our team's normal process, true."

Barb muttered things Nadine couldn't make out. "Are you trying to commit professional suicide?"

"I'm trying to solve this medical mystery. I'm telling you, there's more going on here than a simple virus. This child, Barb...she was something else. A kid, but not a kid. She knew things she had no way of knowing. It has to be connected to the neurogenesis. And that is connected to the peptide. The virus is doing this to her, to all of them, on purpose."

"I'm sorry about that, Nadine. I'm sorry for those kids. I am. Truly." Barb's voice rose. "But you were specifically instructed to keep all that under your hat. If you do what I suspect you're planning, poof! There goes your retirement, your pension, your benefits, our entire support structure. I know you feel you're doing the right thing, but dang it, I don't wanna have to find a job at my age. I want those years of leisure we planned. I want to keep our things, our house, our lifestyle. Call me selfish, but I don't think it's too much to ask after all our years together. I'm begging you. Don't do it."

Nadine listened without interrupting. When her wife finished, she took a deep breath. "Barbara Parker, I love you more than chocolate. More than good red wine. More than the best baked Alaska I ever ate."

"But you're gonna do it anyway. Aren't you?" Barb said.

"I have to. I'm sorry for whatever fallout comes."

Barb didn't speak.

"You know—"

"I have to go." Barbara hung up.

Nadine sighed and left the terrace behind. Inside, Cagney, Lara, and Thom were murmuring to each other.

"Hey," Cagney said. "What's wrong?"

"Come with me." She passed them and entered the shared office. Yuka was at her desk, making notes. "Yook, where are Blondie and the others?"

"In the lab. You need them?"

"No. Let them work for now." Nadine sat on the edge of Yuka's desk. "I need to tell you all something."

They gathered around. She told them about Mitch's phone call, the boundaries he'd set around what she could and couldn't say, and what she planned to do. She left out the part about her visit with Zero.

"Oh man," Thom said.

"We're with you, Nadine," Yuka said.

Laura nodded. "Absolutely."

"Damn right," Cagney added. "He's asking you to obfuscate relevant data and omit germane findings. These details could be important to a solution, or at least a better understanding. Besides, you can bet other countries have found similar patterns. They won't ignore it."

"No," Nadine said, "you misunderstand my intention. I'm not telling you this to get you on my side, but because I don't want you to be blindsided when this bakeoff goes down tomorrow."

"Doesn't matter." Cagney shook his red head. "I won't let you do this alone."

Lara leaned forward. "*We* won't."

"Y'all don't get it. By this time tomorrow, I might be on suspension. I've risked all of your jobs and reputations by telling you what I intend to do. By all rights, you should call the main office and report this, although I'd be grateful if you don't. But if you stand with me, you might end up in the unemployment line, too." Nadine pointed at Cagney. "If the worst happens, you all need to stay on the team and test this hypothesis until we can prove it, or until someone else does. M'kay? And don't share this with the others. I'm risking enough as it is, and I don't know them well enough to trust they'll stay quiet."

The door opened right on cue, and Blondie came in, followed by the other three new researchers, whose names she could never remember.

Blondie stopped, regarded them. "Did we miss a meeting?"

"No. I was telling a joke." Nadine passed a secret wink at the others, and they all laughed.

"Sounds like it fell kinda flat," Blondie said.

"Say, Blondie," Nadine said. "You have a kid, don't you?"

"Uh, yeah. I do. Carl Junior."

That told Nadine Blondie's name. "How old is he?"

"Two." Blondie's suspicion grew. "Why?"

"I like to get to know my team members," she said, her voice as innocent as she could make it. She couldn't bring herself to tell him what Kyndra had said. "That's all. You married?"

"Not yet. Next summer."

Cagney picked up the thread. "We're all getting invites to the party, right?"

"Sure," Blondie said. "You bet."

Yook, Lara, Thom, and Cagney peered at her, confusion writ large in their expressions.

"Later," she murmured. She slid off Yuka's desk and grabbed her stuff. "I'm famished. Feel like I could eat a last meal, and it's close enough to my shift end that I'm gonna go. You all have everything under control."

"Hey," Yuka called after her, "can I join you for dinner?"

Nadine paused as if she were thinking about it. "Rain check? I'm beat. Gonna pick up a fast-food something, eat it while I finish some paperwork, then go to bed."

She tossed her backpack over her shoulder. She still needed to put her notes in order for the press conference, make a copy of the sanitized version for the hospital's VP of communications, and get to Rhue bright and early.

Tomorrow would be a long day.

Chapter 32

Nouméa Airport, Nouméa, New Caledonia
Monday, November 18, 6:15 PM
(Austin, Texas, Sunday, November 17, 11:15 PM)

Number of infected: 4,951,334

ISOBEL SHOVED HER THINGS INTO HER SUITCASE and squeezed it shut. Why couldn't customs agents take a few extra minutes to treat travelers' things with respect? She stood up after sitting on the case to work the latches and took in the long line of people behind her. It stretched out of the room and around the corner, probably all the way to the entry. Okay. Maybe she could understand their need for speed. This time.

She hurried toward the jetway that had been indicated by one of the beleaguered counter clerks. At the entry, a Holschtatt employee met her and took her suitcase.

"I'll be your flight attendant. Airport staff contacted us an hour ago and said you'd be through soon. How long were you waiting?"

"Over six hours." Isobel glanced aside at the other woman. "Is there wine on the plane?"

"Of course."

"I'm going to need a big glass."

They exited the jetway, crossed the tarmac, and climbed the stairs into the plane. Once they were inside, a man in his thirties pulled in the stairs, then closed and locked the hatch before nodding at Isobel.

"Good evening, Doctor Fallon. I'll be your co-pilot. If you'll take your seat and strap in, we'll be leaving as soon as the tower clears us on the runway."

Thank god. "How long until we reach Austin?"

"Give or take an hour or two for weather or other unforeseens and one stop to refuel, I'll guess twenty hours."

Isobel groaned. "We can't go any faster?"

He adopted a classic patience pose. "Well, this is a long-range aircraft and does have the capacity to fly straight to Austin. However, if we run into bad weather, need to circle at Austin, or meet headwinds along the way, we might cut it far too close on the aircraft's fuel margin. The pilot and I feel it would be safer if we stop and top off our tanks in Honolulu."

"Will we have to disembark and go through customs again?"

"No, ma'am. We can fuel up and depart again without leaving the plane."

"Good."

"Will that be all, Doctor Fallon?"

"Yes. Thank you." The man ducked into the flight cabin and Isobel followed the attendant. The front cabin held comfortable chairs with tables between for working or dining. The attendant led her past this to the rear compartment.

Here, carpet, molded leather sofas and chairs, and marble tables with brass accents all matched the cream-colored upholstery on the walls and ceiling. Recessed lighting ran in decorative strips down the length of the compartment, and a television adorned one end wall. She could see Neillsen traveling in something like this, but it was a first for her.

She selected a sofa seat and strapped in. The plane began to move, taxiing away from the terminal before she could even settle. With luck, things in Austin wouldn't get any worse before she got there.

Rhue Children's Hospital, Austin, Texas
Monday, November 18, 10:45 AM

Number of infected: 6,719,432

Nadine popped into the lab before the conference. "Checking in...any updates?"

Yuka and Blondie stared at his screen. Blondie crooked a finger. "Yeah. Take a look at this."

She peered at the display. "What've you got?"

"You asked me to treat some phage and peptide samples with a hormone cocktail?"

"I remember."

His screen was split into four sections. "I dosed each of these peptide samples with a single hormone—one each with estradiol, estriol, estrone, and testosterone."

"Estrone's not a sex hormone."

"No. But it is connected to the estrogen cycle. I wanted to cover all the bases."

"Okay. Good." She eyed the screen again. "Are these lined up in order?"

"That one," Yuka pointed at the top left image, "is estradiol, and that one," she pointed at the bottom right image, "is testosterone."

Nadine studied the images.

"Let me know when you've seen enough of these," Blondie said. "I have another set you need to see."

"It has to be quick. I'm due downstairs in ten minutes."

"Then let me give you the highlights. These two," he indicated the top two, "have both changed from their original states when the test started. I'm not sure how to quantify what that means yet, though."

He switched over to a new screen with four additional images. "I treated these phage samples," he pointed to the first three, "the same as I did the peptide tests. Their modification is greater than what I see in the peptide, but I'm not sure what to make of that." He pointed to the fourth sample. "This one got a shot of combined estradiol, estriol, and testosterone in a 40/40/20 mix."

The combo sample appeared to quiver on the screen. Nadine scowled. "What fresh-baked weirdness is that?"

Blondie shrugged. "You got me. I guess we'll find out."

"Any reduction in the release of interneurin in the phages?"

"Nope. Not a jot."

She observed the squiggling sample. Maybe Phagey didn't like the hormone blend. Could be they were watching it die. It was hard to unwind her feelings about that.

"Good job, Blondie. We'll—"

His phone rang, and he peeked at the number. "That's my fiancée. Hold on a sec."

He picked up the call. "Hey. What's—" He listened, his complexion paling. "When? Where is he?"

Prickles crept up Nadine's back and she shivered. Dollars to donuts she knew where this was going.

Blondie pushed the hair off his forehead. "Yeah. Okay. I'll get the first flight."

Nadine waited until he ended the call. "Your boy has NJace?"

"Yeah." His voice shook. "I gotta go."

Yuka's fingers pressed against her mouth.

"Understood," Nadine said. "Yook, do you know all the details on this test?"

She shook her head. "Sorry."

Blondie gathered his things. "I'll catch Thom up before I leave. He's already working with the other glove boxes. Maybe he can take this on."

Nadine nodded. He made it to the door before she stopped him. "Blon...Carl..." What could she say that wouldn't sound trite? They all knew what the boy faced. "I hope your boy's gonna be okay."

"Thanks." He left without further comment.

Nadine sighed, glanced at the time. Three 'til. She was going to be late.

Yook watched him go, then shifted her weight from one foot to the other in a sort of restless shuffle-step. "I wish there was something I could do, for him or for you. Good luck in your conference."

"Thanks. I'll see you when I'm done." Nadine ducked out of the lab, passed Blondie and Thom on the way in. Lara and Cagney stood at the elevator.

"What are you all doing here? This isn't your shift."

Cagney scoffed. "You think we're gonna let you go down there alone? Pfft."

Lara gestured as if Nadine didn't know the way.

"You don't have to do this. It isn't smart, you know."

Cagney tapped his wrist as if he were wearing a watch, even though she couldn't remember ever seeing one on his arm. "Tick tock."

"You're good eggs," she said. "Cracked, but good." They rode down together. Nadine didn't mention little Carl. That wasn't her news to share. Instead, she skimmed her sanitized notes once more.

Lara glanced at the papers. "That's what you're gonna say?"

Nadine winked. "More or less."

Rhue Children's Hospital, Austin, Texas
Monday, November 18, 10:59 AM

Number of infected: 6,798,514

"...and I ate the whole thing." Luk finished the joke with a flourish of both hands.

Kyn giggled. "Dad, that's silly."

His smile widened. That was more like his kid. They'd moved her to a step-down unit first thing this morning, and Luk tried to accept their good fortune and not to hold his breath, waiting for it to all start again. "I'm so glad you're feeling better."

She sobered. "Yeah. Me, too."

Sadie pushed past the curtain carrying two coffees. "Oh good! You're awake, sweetie! I heard the CDC is downstairs. They're about to give a press conference on the phage. Wanna watch?"

Luk took a cup. "Want to?" he asked Kyn.

"Sure. Let's see what she has to say."

"She?" Sadie asked.

Kyn smiled.

Sadie grabbed the remote. They'd not used the television even once before now, and she fiddled with the device until the TV came on. She flipped channels and found the local news program where they were winding up for the conference.

"Here it is."

All of them focused on the screen.

Rhue Children's Hospital, Austin, Texas
Monday, November 18, 11:02 AM

Number of infected: 6,798,532

On the first floor, the doors opened and Nadine led the way to the classroom repurposed for this event. Doctor Aimee de Verlaine, hospital administrator, waited outside with a short, bearded man in a designer suit. Both watched her approach.

"Thank you for allowing us to do this onsite," Nadine said. "It'll enable me to resume testing that much faster." Or at least allow the others to do so.

"You're welcome." De Verlaine looked like a woman who laughed a lot. Not now, though. A small crease knitted itself between her brows. "Although I must say this was an unusual request."

"These are unusual times, Doctor de Verlaine."

"Yes." The woman gestured. "This is Jorge Schirru, my director of public relations."

Nadine nodded acknowledgment. "Have you both had a chance to review my statements?"

The slender administrator and the stocky PR director exchanged an uncomfortable glance before Jorge spoke. "We have."

"And they're acceptable for you?"

Again that nonverbal exchange between them. De Verlaine touched her short twists, the only sign of her misgivings, then tucked her arm across her chest like a shield.

Jorge put on his best PR mask. "We were ... reluctant," he said in a smooth, slightly accented voice, "to reveal some of the details you intend to share. But Mitch Donaldson has convinced us that it would be best not to withhold this information."

They didn't know the half of it. Nadine shrugged. "The facts will come out eventually." More of them than they knew. Sooner than they expected. "Better they hear it from us instead of social media."

"Indeed," he said with a practiced smile.

She couldn't blame them for worrying about how this would affect the hospital. She understood all too well their concern for their jobs. But this pandemic was bigger than any one medical facility, or three professional positions.

"Well then, if there's nothing more..."

"When you've finished," de Verlaine said, "we'll take over to field any questions that might remain or to direct queries to the proper authorities."

"Of course. You'll need a chance to buffer the hospital from bad press."

"Precisely." Jorge motioned for her to proceed.

She looked over her shoulder at Cagney and Lara, at their angsty faces. None of them knew how this would turn out, but these two at least perceived the size of the tiger whose tail she was about to pull. She winked at them, then entered the room and went straight to the wooden podium positioned near the door. Schirru and de Verlaine entered behind her and stood just inside.

Nadine noted the numerous mics set up nearby, as well as all the cameras, streaming video equipment, and eager journalists. Rows of folding chairs filled two-thirds of the space, with aisles down both sides as well as the middle. Every seat held a fanny, and people stood in the available space at the back. Blended colognes, body heat, and a lingering trace of disinfectant crowded the room. Had they exceeded the fire marshal's occupancy limit? That might become an issue when the tomato sauce hit the fan.

"Good afternoon. I am Doctor Nadine Parker, EIS officer with the CDC. I would like to read a prepared statement without interruption if you please. After I have finished, I will open the floor to a limited number of questions."

Rhue Children's Hospital, Austin, Texas
Monday, November 18, 11:07 AM

Number of infected: 6,798,592

"That's the doctor who came to see you yesterday," Luk said, wide-eyed

Kyn pushed herself farther up in the bed. "Yeah. It is."

Luk and Sadie exchanged a startled look. Sadie came closer. "Did you know who she was when she was here?"

"Mmm... not exactly." Kyn grinned. "But I think she's about to surprise everybody."

Rhue Children's Hospital, Austin, Texas
Monday, November 18, 11:08 AM

Number of infected: 6,798,603

Nadine faced the reporters.

"As you already know, initial investigations into the children's ailment pinpointed a novel bacteriophage, unidentifiable as any prior known organism. The CDC has since designated the phage Novel Juvenile Cerebral Bacteriophage, or NJace. All victims of this disease have exhibited the same symptom of excruciating pain that appeared to be psychosomatic, which each of them attributed to damage inflicted on wildlife, plants, trees, or other humans.

"Three days ago, CDC investigators here in Austin discovered a previously unknown peptide, temporarily designated 'interneurin,' in Patient Zero's bloodwork and cerebrospinal fluid. We believe this peptide to be a neurocatalyst. Subsequent scans revealed rapid and expansive neurogenesis in the portion of Patient Zero's brain that is thought to control emotions, feelings of empathy, sensations of connectedness to others outside oneself. Those findings have now been confirmed in other patients around the world. We infer a link between these two things, that the peptide is promoting the unusual neuronal development in the brain, but are thus far uncertain as to why this is happening or what to expect next."

She raised her gaze to the crowded room. "Thank you for your attention. I'll take your questions now." Every reporter began to shout questions. She chose one at random.

"How did this happen?" the reporter asked. "Has NJace been here all along and for some reason now become infectious to humans?"

"Bacteriophages are presumed to be the most abundant organism on Earth, so it's likely been here all along and we never encountered it. We do know it has never affected humans in this way, not in recorded medical history. One hypothesis we're considering is that this particular organism's development is the result of an epigenetic modification."

"Can you define that term for our viewers?"

"Of course. When an organism's gene expression or cellular function is altered in a stable, persistent, and heritable way without actual changes to its original DNA, that is an epigenetic modification. These changes can be brought about by any number of factors. In this case, our hypothesis is resting on environmental changes."

She selected another from the shouting rabble.

"If the development is environmental, wouldn't that limit its spread to the region where conditions were ripe for its growth?"

"Normally, yes," Nadine said. "But since NJace cases have manifested worldwide, we have been forced to acknowledge that there may be a global trigger behind the emergence of this disease. We're currently testing this theory on samples of common phages in closed environments with elevated levels of heat, carbon dioxide, methane, and oxygen. Results are as yet inconclusive." She surveyed their waving hands and selected another. "Red jacket. Yes."

"The theory of epigenetic modification in mammals is still under debate. How do you justify using such a speculative direction in your investigation?"

"For one thing, a bacteriophage is not a mammal," Nadine said with a fleeting smile. "An epigenetic hypothesis will have detractors, no doubt. But it's the concept that currently fits best. We're hoping other scientists in the field will either confirm or refute our findings with further study." She selected another.

"You say NJace is changing the children's brains. Will this change be permanent or will a cure for the disease return them to their original states? If not, is the CDC working on a way to reverse the abnormal growth?"

"That's a difficult question, one for which we don't have answers yet," Nadine said. "If this virus is a result of epigenetic modification, then the children may also be regarded as so modified. Their changes fit the definition, although that particular detail has not yet been raised for debate in the scientific community. However, some epigenetic shifts in lab experiments have proven to be temporary, though subjects only revert to their prior states after a number of generations and the removal of the environmental stressor—in this case, the virus—which caused the shift. We'd have to find a safe way to artificially reverse the shift without physical removal of the new neurons. There is no way to know what sort of physical or psychological damage that would do to the patient. Nor do we know what further modifications may arise in the months to come."

"You mentioned 'generations,'" said another reporter. "Does that mean NJace effects in current patients will be passed on to their children?"

"That is a reasonable assumption at this time, yes."

"For how long?" asked the same reporter. "Is this a step forward in evolution for humans?"

Nadine took a breath. "Patient Zero's DNA tests show no remarkable change from earlier medical records before infection set in. Therefore, we conclude that this is not exactly an evolutionary step. However, as I explained, even if it is an epigenetic shift resulting from environmental stressors, the shift will not fade and allow the DNA to reassert control until the stressors are removed or stopped. As long as those continue, we presume these children will carry the disease."

"Will other children contract it, too?"

Nadine hesitated. "That is likely. Yes." She called on a new questioner, one who hadn't spoken yet.

"Why is this affecting only children?"

"We have two ideas on that, both of which are currently being tested by medical specialists. One, which has the least support in the medical community, is that it is something to do with the growth plates in an adolescent skeleton. Once those harden, they may prohibit development of the disease in some way. The problem with that explanation is that skeletal maturity comes between ages thirteen and seventeen. However, the oldest NJace child so far is eleven. We're now leaning toward a second hypothesis, that something in hormones associated with puberty inactivates either the phage itself or its peptide."

"Has the CDC tried using those hormones as injections to interrupt the phage's progress in the children?"

"That is currently under investigation in the lab. The hormones had some interesting effects on both the virus and the peptide, though we aren't yet sure what those changes mean. Unfortunately, the hormonal treatments did not reduce the production of interneurin. We are still trying to ascertain how NJace operates, what its mechanisms are. Until we know that, we can't know whether our hypothesis is correct in the first place and, if so, why these hormones failed as a means of halting the production of the peptide."

"What action is the CDC taking to create an antiviral that would kill the phage or interrupt its process somehow?"

Here was her point of departure. Nadine took a deep breath.

"Creating successful medical countermeasures, especially for a newly emergent virus, is a challenging prospect. Development is a long and complicated process that could take the scientific community months, if not years, to complete. We have tried a few preliminary tests designed to either eradicate NJace or the peptide, or interrupt NJace's production of interneurin in a laboratory setting. Every single one has had a negative result that would likely have been fatal to the patient, had the tests been human trials."

The room went quiet for about five seconds.

"That sounds like a self-defense mechanism," a reporter said.

"Yes, it does." Nadine braced herself. "From this evidence, and from several other behaviors exhibited by the organism, it appears possible that NJace may have intelligence of a sort."

The room exploded with noise, everyone talking at once. Nadine let it run. By the door, Schirru had one finger crooked over his mouth. De Verlaine stood rigid, her arms crossed, her narrow countenance closed. Nadine asked for quiet.

"This is, of course, a controversial premise, and I call on others researching in this field to test and either confirm or refute these findings. Yes." She pointed to a reporter near the front.

"Self-defensive actions alone are not enough to denote intelligence," the man said. "How is the CDC defining 'intelligence' in this case?"

"The presence of intelligence in animals is deduced from the observation of an animal's behavior and its ability to resolve challenges. In this case, the organism has produced 'tools,' if you will, by releasing interneurin to promote specific neuronal development, which seem essential to the organism's deduced purpose."

"Which is?" asked another.

Nadine weighed her response. "Let me express it as a series of hypotheticals and ask you to go along with me for the sake of argument. Let's say the organism did develop as a result of environmental changes on a global scale, as we suspect, and that development produced within the phage the ability to devise a means to communicate with humans. The form of communication NJace manifests is a symbiotic one that makes its victims empathic to such a degree that they feel, personally and physically, the pain of any damage to the environment. That would tend to make other humans more reluctant to do anything that would cause those children to suffer."

The room fell completely silent for maybe ten seconds. From the hospital bigwigs' expressions, someone would think they were standing barefoot on glass shards. She wouldn't have much more time before they would call a halt to this revelation.

"Our research has revealed strong indicators that support this hypothesis. Infection numbers and spread patterns from the start have paralleled the heaviest global patterns of pollution or ecological challenges. For every spike in crises among phage patients over the last ten days, we found a corresponding event that involved environmental damage, wildlife abuse, or habitat destruction." She considered mentioning the Holschtatt blast on that reef but decided that might put her in jail.

De Verlaine started toward the stand until another reporter spoke into the pause. Instead, the administrator spoke aside to Schirru, who hurried out.

"You're suggesting that this bacteriophage, this microorganism, is telling us to stop polluting the earth? To stop doing the very thing that, according to your conjecture, is what prompted its genesis in the first place?" The reporter's features creased in a disbelieving frown. "That makes the phage sound self-destructive to me."

"Not at all," Nadine said. "Even if we brought all our noxious emissions to a halt tomorrow, for example, the climate would continue to warm and change for some time. Some experts estimate as much as fifty years. NJace is in no danger from that front. It may even thrive in that changed environment. In addition—"

No one was going to like this news, but at least it was sanctioned. Nadine cleared her throat. "The phage has integrated its own genetic material into the normal flora of the patients' bodies in what is called a lysogenic cycle. Instead of being immediately copied and expressed, which would kill the host bacteria, NJace DNA recombines with the bacterial chromosome. It becomes part of the chromosome as a prophage."

She'd worded it as simply as she could, and yet faces in the audience folded into frowns or twisted into confused masks, either from the technical details or the shock of the news.

"What does that mean for the children?" someone asked.

"In the lysogenic mode, the prophage isn't active. It isn't producing new phages. However, it is being copied every time a cell divides."

"Will it become...active again," the same person went on, "in the future?"

"We don't know. Probably."

"But in the meantime, this disease is being written into the children's genetic structure?"

"Not their genes," Nadine corrected, "but in those of their normal flora, the beneficial bacteria present in their bodies all the time."

"But won't that make the phage nearly impossible to eradicate?"

Nadine wanted to shout *yes! Yes! It's here to stay!* Instead, she looked the woman in the eye. "Further interpretation of the known data is still open for debate."

Schirru returned and nodded to de Verlaine, who came forward and all but pushed Nadine aside. "Thank you, Doctor Parker, for that enlightening report. Now I'm sorry, but that's all the time Doctor Parker has for today. I will be happy to answer any other questions you might have."

Nadine slipped out of the room, chased by the near-instant clamor that erupted. Shouted questions followed her down the hall to where Cagney and Lara waited. A room behind them held a computer whose monitor showed the still-streaming coverage of the press room. Reporters clamored for recognition in a babble no human ears could make out. At least hers couldn't.

"Well?" she asked. "How'd I do?"

"You managed it well," Cagney said.

"It's not like this was any ordinary press conference." Lara grimaced at the roomful of shouting reporters. "Nobody knows what's really going on. The home office's decision would have kept it that way."

"Exactly. And people need to hear what you said." Cagney pointed at the room she'd left behind. "They can make sure that happens."

"I hope you're right. The rest of you may have to take it from here." Nadine nodded at the security guards who approached their little group. "I think my part is finished."

They twisted to see what she was watching. Both of them paled.

"Doctor Parker, the hospital administration has asked that you leave the hospital grounds and not return."

Huh. Took longer than she'd expected for them to show. Nadine's mouth puckered with the effort of stifling the laughter that would be as inappropriate in this setting as a Minnesota corn dog on a dessert table. "Okay. Can we go to the fourth floor first so I can collect my things?"

"Yes, ma'am, but we'll accompany you."

"Of course." She smiled. "Lead on, gentlemen."

Chapter 33

ISOBEL'S LIP CURLED AS THE CDC'S SUPPOSED EXPERT was crowded from the podium to bring that sham of a press conference to an abrupt and necessary end. What in the world did the woman hope to accomplish with such a ridiculous claim? The odds of the woman having a job at the end of the day were slim to none. At least real doctors in pursuit of actual science could hope that someone like this would be booted out of the field.

She switched off the television and walked around the cabin. They'd been on the ground for a while now, waiting their chance to refuel, and then to depart. The pilots said it would be at least another hour. This airport was as mobbed as the one in Nouméa, everybody in a panic and trying to get somewhere else. She knew that feeling well.

In her earlier call to Jake, she learned that Gabe had fallen several times over the last couple of days. He'd also developed a stutter. Claire had regained consciousness for short periods, minutes when she wept for dying fish and birds, wailed that she was choking on the dirty water and couldn't see the sun anymore. Doctors had increased her ketamine dose, but it hadn't stopped the delusions.

Isobel knew better than most of the parents how long it might take to find a treatment for the new disease. She'd been working on a Milani treatment for years, and that was with the added benefit of knowing exactly what she hoped to resolve. This...

She dropped into a seat in the center cabin, pulled her feet up into the chair, and regarded the aircraft queued up at the runway. Until the doctors knew what the hell this was and what it was doing to the kids, antivirals administered by the hospital might as well be candy. All they could do was treat the symptoms. Keep the patients sedated. Feed them intravenous fluids and nutrients. Collect their waste in tubes.

These delusions seemed so odd. She'd never studied that branch of medicine and assumed it was a symptom, like all the others. It had to be, since the patients' visions and claims all ran along the same lines. If she didn't know better, she'd think that crackpot on the TV was right, that the virus was connected to environmental problems somehow. As if that was even possible.

But that kind of conclusion was crazy. The virus was attacking the children's brains. That's all this was. As soon as the specialists figured out how it was doing that and what was causing the hallucinations, they'd figure a way to fix it. Then the seizures, pain, and delusions would disappear. Claire would be her normal self, assuming she lived through the process.

Except the world wasn't listening to reason. They would believe this "doctor" at the CDC. Even Jake had sounded like he wondered if there was a connection when he'd first told her about the fallout surrounding Holschtatt's reef work. He'd gone on to agree the public reaction was ludicrous, but for a second, when he'd commented that Claire's seizure had also happened at the same time as her blast at the Nlaan reef, he'd sounded as if he had a doubt.

She grunted. Just for grins, and to pass the time, she retrieved her laptop and called up a browser. Someone had to be sharing real science to disprove this kind of bunk, and it would no doubt be online somewhere. If not, she'd find some of her own.

She called up public access data on the spread numbers and patterns for the virus and compared them to ecological and environmental statuses of those geographical regions. Page after page showed that the areas with the worst air pollution, industrial waste issues, poaching numbers, or deforestation seemed to be the same areas hardest hit by the virus.

Isobel frowned. Coincidence.

The more she searched, the more support she found for the CDC doctor's claims.

That didn't make any sense. How could a virus, even one that was epigenetically modified—if that part of the CDC's theory was correct—be influenced by something totally disconnected from its existence? This went against every theory of viral spread she knew of. Not that she was a virologist.

She dug up the date of the earliest recorded cases of the phage. Odd. They'd started around the same time as her coral harvest project. The same day she took her first harvest and made the initial visit to the Nlaantu. What about the day of Claire's seizure? Was it really the same day she'd detonated explosives along the reef?

Jake said there were a bunch of cases in St. Ives that night. She reviewed the case numbers and compared them to the date of her explosions. The numbers of infected jumped from one hundred twenty-five thousand to two hundred seventy-nine thousand in under twenty-four hours. By yesterday, which marked forty-eight hours after her reef blasts, the numbers had surpassed two million and were continuing to climb at an alarming rate.

A cold chill twined up Isobel's spine and she wrapped her arms around herself. No. It couldn't be.

Her hands shaking, she reached for the keyboard once more and called up the blog for the Gaian Protectorate. It wasn't hard to find their videos on her harvest site. The page was full of them. She chose a random link and watched it through, then another, and another. Each showed enormous white clouds clogging the water, streaming away from the wounds she'd created and following the currents to drift over other reefs, other regions of the South Pacific. Even one taken earlier today, nearly three days after her blasts, showed heavy traces of the debris still floating in milky ribbons across the miles.

She picked one of the latest written reports and forced herself to read every stinking word. The Protectorate claimed that the reef Holschtatt—the reef she—had blasted had begun to die. Large chunks had broken off and drifted to the bottom, the attached animals all dead.

No. No! All those animals! Those beautiful colors, the fish that lived there...

She'd done that?

A tiny voice of logic whined behind the pounding guilt. What had she expected? Detonating explosives in such a delicate habitat was bound to have devastating consequences for the lifeforms around the blasts. Had she really not taken this into account?

No. No, she hadn't. Gabe had been all that mattered. She'd chosen between a fish and her son. If people didn't like her choice, they could stuff it.

But that choice had cost her more than she'd anticipated. Claire was sick now, possibly because of her actions.

What was she supposed to do with that knowledge?

When the flight attendant approached with breakfast, Isobel twisted aside, one hand pressed her quivering mouth. She couldn't stop her tears.

The attendant set the tray down and retreated without a word.

Chapter 34

Rhue Children's Hospital, Austin, Texas
Monday, November 18, 11:40 AM

Number of infected: 7,194,665

NADINE'S PHONE BEGAN TO RING when she stepped off the
elevator. She sent it to voicemail. One dismissal at a time.
Mitch would have to wait his turn.

Yuka and the others lingered in their makeshift office.
Yook had packed up Nadine's laptop and other belongings in
her pack.

Nadine slung the bag over her shoulder. "Thanks. How'd
you know?"

"Cagney called me. Nadine—"

"I knew I had a good team. Always looking out for one
another in our search for the truth." She winked at Yook.

The younger woman's glance took in the guards at
Nadine's heels. "I guess we won't see you in Austin again?"

"Probably not."

"In Atlanta, then? When we get to the office?"

Nadine chuckled. "I wouldn't count on that, but anything's
possible. You all have my number." She took in the shock and
confusion displayed by Thom and the other researchers.

Her phone rang again, and she sent it to voicemail.

"You know about Blondie's boy, I take it?"

"We heard," Yook said.

"Blondie was onto something with those hormone cocktails. The best way to help his family is to keep after his experiments. Include that data in your next update. Not sure who they'll send to replace me, but meanwhile, you guys are reporting to Cagney. Make sure he's aware of your latest results."

The awkward silence stretched out.

Nadine jerked a thumb at the guards. "Guess I better be on my way. I'm holding these fine gentlemen up." She extended her hand to each of her team members. Yuka, though, wrapped Nadine in a tight hug.

"We're gonna miss you."

Nadine patted her back. "Okay, now, don't make me cry. You'll spoil my thick-crust image. Besides, you have work to do."

Yuka withdrew, and Nadine held her at arm's length. "Keep working this to your fullest, you hear? Finish what we started."

Yuka nodded, her eyes glistening.

Nadine left the office with the guards in tow. Together they rode the lift in silence to the first floor.

Outside the elevator, Cagney waited with Lara. Nadine stopped them before they could start.

"It is what it is, y'all. Please don't drag this out. You know how to reach me later. Cagney, you're in charge until you're instructed otherwise by the main office. Do me proud, you hear?"

"That's a promise." Cagney's lip quivered.

Lara did not speak. Nadine winked at them, then preceded security to the foyer. Her ringing phone echoed in the glass-encased space. She knew who it was before she thumbed it on.

"Hello, Mitch."

"Goddamn you, Nadine, do you even realize what you've done?"

"I've followed the CDC pledge to pursue scientific data in an open and objective manner and placed the benefits to the public above those of our own institution. That's more than your bosses have done."

"Don't quote institutional platitudes at me. You have lost the high ground here. You took action that was in flagrant opposition to my direct orders. Rhue Hospital is threatening to sue. They've demanded that we find somewhere else to continue our on-site research. CDC PR is still trying to talk them down. You've endangered delicate negotiations between the CDC and numerous other organizations for critical research."

"Yeah." Nadine laughed. "I saw that online. Now who's the one stifling the quest for treatment in exchange for a buck?"

"Shut the hell up. You gave us the goddamn finger on live television. Our entire department will be a laughing stock."

"Oh come on." Nadine left the guards on the sidewalk with a wave and wound through the parking lot. "You can't possibly imagine I'm the only person who's come to these conclusions. It's a matter of time before my hypotheses are supported by other groups, other nations' health organizations. You should be glad that we were the first ones to say it out loud."

"You see?" Mitch shouted. "You don't quit, do you?"

"Not when I know I'm right." She approached her car, envisioning that vein standing out on his temple like it did when he was about to pop a seam. "Calm down, boss. You're gonna give yourself a heart attack."

She hit the clicker and tossed her bag in the back seat.

Mitch's muttering voice came from a distance as if he'd pulled the phone away from his ear, perhaps in contemplation of throwing it as hard as he could.

Nadine got in the driver's seat and strapped in but didn't start the car. No sense being in motion while she navigated the rest of this conversation.

His voice returned with a measure of control. "This was the last straw, Nadine. You're suspended, pending a labor-employee relations process, as is Squires and the rest of your team. You screwed it up for all of them."

"Now hold on a minute." Nadine's hackles went up. "You can't suspend them for something I did."

"You don't get to expect any consideration at this point. You're done."

"And I accept that. But even if Cagney and the others had anything to do with my decision to speak out—which they didn't—you're shooting yourself in the foot to can all of us. You'll have to send a whole new team, who'll have to come up to speed overnight. You're gonna make these sick kids pay, too?" She paused to take a breath. "Come on, Mitch. That's not like you. This isn't anybody's fault but mine, and you know it. I get that you're angry but be pissed at me. Leave the others out of it."

At first, sound from the other end of the call was limited to Mitch's heavy breathing. "True. Okay, but they are all on my watch list. If they step out of line even once after this, they're gone."

"Thank you."

"I didn't do it for you." Again with the yelling. Again with the heavy breathing. After a pause, he continued in a more reasonable tone. "I'll have someone contact your hotel and pay for your expenses through this minute. Anything after that is on you. You'll have plane tickets waiting at the airport. I suggest you don't linger, or they may expire."

"Okay."

"Don't bother coming to the office. I'll have your things delivered to your home. You'll also be hearing from CDC legal."

"Got it. You know, Mitch," she said, "despite this doughy mess, it was great working with you. I've learned—"

The connection clicked in her ear.

"Mitch?"

Nothing.

She slid the phone into her pocket. Barb would be next, she supposed. If only Barb would give her the cold shoulder for a day, but Nadine had a butter pat's chance in hot potatoes of that happening. Her wife would gnaw her like a piece of sugar cane and spit her out when she'd run out of juice.

Ah well. Nothing like a hot oven to make a fine baguette. She started the car and backed out of her parking space. Lots to do. She'd best get to it.

St. Ive's Hospital, Austin, Texas
Monday, November 18, 4:25 PM

Number of infected: 7,994,623

Reporters gathered near the entrance of the hospital. Isobel spotted them, tried to escape, but it was too late. They'd seen her. They rushed forward, microphones and cameras held forth like weapons. Isobel flinched. She'd spoken to the press before, but that had been in times of triumph. She'd been proud of her pharmaceutical accomplishments, medicines she or Holschttat had helped to create, and how they would benefit large numbers of patients.

What would it be this time? Claire? Or the coral harvest? She had a split second to prune her anxiety before they pounced.

"Doctor Fallon, what can you tell us about the coral harvest run by Holschtatt Pharmaceuticals on the Nlaan reef?"

"Doctor Fallon, isn't it true that mining in the Coral Triangle is illegal? Was Senator Rand O'Sullivan behind Holschtatt's mining agreement with Nlaan?"

"Doctor Fallon, the entheóphage didn't infect anyone until Holschtatt began mining on the Nlaan reef. Can you comment on the possibility of a connection between the two events?"

"Doctor Fallon, isn't it true that Holschtatt sent you to Nlaan to find a cure for your own son's Milani Syndrome?"

Tears sprang to her eyes and she struggled to maintain her composure. Questions came too fast to even think. She blinked and chided herself for not being prepared. She should've anticipated this. Bone-level weariness slowed her reflexes, muddled her thinking. She held up her hands, which made them shout louder and push harder. Damn vultures. She tried to walk around them. They followed her like a cloud of gnats with that annoying buzz.

Another voice rose over the rest.

"Hold it down. This is a quiet zone."

A few of the reporters retreated. The others pressed forward with more urgency.

The security guard, a tall, broad-shouldered man, waded through the reporters. He grabbed Isobel's elbow and shepherded her through the crowd. The microphones and cameras followed them all the way to the door, reporters calling so many questions at once Isobel couldn't have made them out if she wanted to. Inside, the sliding doors closed behind her, blocking the clamor.

She heaved a breath. "Thank you." Her voice shook, as did her knees.

Her savior smiled, a crooked shine of white teeth. "No problem, Doctor Fallon. You need to sit a minute?"

Oh, she wanted that more than almost anything, to sit and let the quaking in her knees slow and stop, to give her heartbeat a chance to settle. But those sharks continued to film her through the glass. Any weakness she demonstrated now would chum the waters. "No," she said. "I'll be fine. You have a good night."

"You, too. And hey, when you're ready to leave, let security know. They'll help you get out without a fuss like we do for Mr. Fallon every day."

She thanked him again. In the elevator, she leaned against the wall. The reporters didn't know how close they'd gotten to the same questions she was asking herself. How did this get to be such a mess?

The doors opened, and Isobel made her way around the central desk in ICU to Claire's room. The blinds were closed tight against the late afternoon sun. A nightlight on the wall by the bed cast eerie shadows across the room. Jake waited in the semidarkness.

"How is she?" Isobel asked.

Jake put a finger to his lips and they stepped out into the corridor. "She woke up, but they had to sedate her again."

Isobel sagged. "Still in pain?"

"Same delusions as before. We need to bring in a specialist. These doctors are taking too long."

"I don't know, Jake."

He frowned at her. "What do you mean you don't know?"

"I ran into a bunch of reporters on the way in."

"Nlaan again?"

"That and asking me whether there might be a connection between our Nlaan project and this mysterious illness."

Jake rolled his eyes. "That's ridiculous."

"Is it?"

"Don't tell me you believe that tripe."

The skin on her face felt hot, stretched taut over her bones. How did he always manage to make her doubt herself? "Did you see the CDC's press conference earlier today?"

"Hah." He paced a few steps closer to Claire's room. "I saw them usher that quack away from the mic in time to keep her from spreading more false facts."

"You think it's a coincidence that our daughter began to scream in pain about fish and birds and dirty water at the same exact time I was blasting holes in the Nlaan reef?"

He spun to glare at her. "What do you think, Bel? That our daughter and kids all around the world are suddenly and mysteriously psychic?"

When he said it like that, it did sound silly. But Isobel couldn't shake the reports she'd read, the vids she'd seen on the plane. "I don't know. The timing of it all makes me question whether we know as much as we think we do." She told him about the corroborating data, how it all added up to a whole string of dovetailing events that grew too large to ignore.

Jake drew himself up to his full six-foot-four height and peered down at her.

It was no wonder he ran such an efficient operation at Holschtatt. That athletic frame and that ice-blue stare made him an imposing figure. Few challenged him for long, not because he was a bully but because he oozed command. Usually, she found that sexy. Today, it annoyed her.

She waved at him. "Don't pull that daddy crap on me. I'm expressing an opinion and voicing my doubt about the validity of what we think we know to someone who's supposed to be on my side."

He deflated with a long, exasperated sigh. "What do you want from me, Bel? I can't pat your hand and tell you yes, you're right, the Earth elves are speaking to all the children of the world. I can't let you continue in that fantasy, because then you won't acknowledge reality. Which is that something is wrong. Claire is sick. It has nothing to do with Nlaan or Holschtatt, or anything other than a novel bacteriophage. Once some clever doctor or scientist figures out how to cure it, everything will go back to normal, and you can continue to focus all your attention on Gabe."

He might as well have punched her in the stomach. All the breath whooshed out of her along with the last shred of her patience before her eyes narrowed to slits. Her hands knotted into fists at her sides. "Oh," she grumbled. "You can be such a bastard sometimes."

He opened his mouth to respond but before he got out a single word she wedged her indignation under his guard and took a bite out of his arrogance.

"How dare you?" Her low voice trembled. "I have never neglected either of our children. Not once. Gabe's issue is a slow burn. Claire's illness is a raging inferno that may or may not be connected to something outside known medical science, a virus that will fry her in a month or two, for all we know, so that's my current priority. I'll do whatever it takes, follow wherever the trail might lead if it means finding a treatment for her, same as I did for Gabe. You always called me 'determined.' I seem to recall you liked that about me, but if you don't appreciate where it's taking me now, then step out of my way."

Jake heaved a breath. For the first time, she noticed he looked tired. She knew she was. She'd barely slept since the detonations at Nlaan.

"I'm sorry." He shook his head. "I didn't mean to say it like that. Make it sound like you're choosing between our kids. That came out wrong. I'm as worried about them as you are, and still trying to hold things together at work, for both of us. It's making me crazy."

"What do you mean, 'for both of us'?"

He grimaced, as if sorry he'd said that. "The board isn't happy with the way things were done on your trip. They've invested a lot in this project. In you. A great deal of money and estimations for the next year are riding on your shoulders, and you came home from this prospecting trip with holds two-thirds full of usable raw materials."

"And they're blaming that on me? I told you there was a typo in the processing notes," she snapped. "If it wasn't for that little mistake—made by someone Neillsen hand-picked—we would have had more in the holds. It took me more than a week to discover the glitch, during which I was wasting the samples on doomed tests. I don't suppose it occurred to you to share that info with them."

"They don't want to hear it from me, Bel." He held out his hand like a flag of truce. "I need you to pull yourself together. I'll help you with the kids, but you can't go around supporting this quack CDC doctor's version of the truth. You need to stick to the science. Finish what you started."

"Or what?"

Jake's jaw stiffened. "Or the board is likely to replace you with another project director. They'll take over your lab, work from your records. It'll be someone else who takes credit for the Milani treatment. Not you. I know it sucks, but that's how this business is. You knew that already. Please don't tell me you're surprised now."

She wanted to say he was wrong. To slap his hand and say Holschtatt could go screw themselves. But he wasn't, and she didn't. Instead, she took it in her own. "No. I'm not. But I'm still not convinced that the reef is unrelated to what's happening."

"If you persist in that delusion," he said, "our family will pay the price."

It wouldn't matter anyway. Not for this particular coral. They could still grow it in the tanks, true, harvest it from there. But star queen had never been found anywhere else outside the coral triangle, and Nlaan was now out of reach. She'd follow the coral project as far as she could, but it would be a slow process, waiting years for artificial reefs to fully establish in their new environments if they survived that transition at all. Neillsen may not mind that, since it meant he could charge higher prices for the small quantities of treatment as they became available. For her, it would be torture. She would have to watch Gabe die, as she did with Zoe.

Isobel sent Jake home for the night. When he was gone, she stood by their daughter's bed, where Claire twitched in apparent pain.

Had she done this?

"I'm sorry, sweetheart," she whispered. "I never meant to hurt you. I was trying to make that medicine I told you about for Gabe. Remember?"

Tears spilled down her cheeks. Claire might have gotten sick anyway. But harvesting that coral had been the only way Isobel knew to help Gabe, then or now. Given everything that happened since, would she make the same choice?

She couldn't answer that, but she knew one thing for sure. With Milani and this virus being completely different types of illnesses, she had little hope of finding a way to save both her children. There wasn't enough time. No matter what plan of action she chose, if she treated one, she would lose the other.

No mother should ever have to make that choice.

Chapter 35

Rhue Children's Hospital, Austin, Texas
Tuesday, November 19, 7:30 AM

Number of infected: 8,846,299

LUK AWOKE TO THE BUZZING OF HIS PHONE. He lurched to a sitting position and snatched it up.

Simon.

What a nerve. Luk almost didn't answer. He glanced at the bed, where Kyn lay watching him.

"You gonna get that?" she asked.

Still half asleep, he thumbed the call and held the phone to his ear. "Simon. This is a surprise. Shouldn't you be speaking to my attorney?"

"Already done. Both attorneys are in the process now of preparing and signing court documents to drop the suit. As soon as everything's finalized, you'll get a copy."

Shock did more to wake him up than a cup of Perkatory brew. Luk gaped at Kyn.

Simon went on. "Will Sato and I have come to believe we may have acted in haste."

"Um. Okay." Luk frowned. "May I ask what brought about this change of heart?"

"Several things." Papers shuffled at Simon's end of the call. "A CDC specialist made claims similar to your video in a press conference yesterday."

"Yeah. I saw that."

"So did a lot of other people. Even though the hospital and the CDC are refusing to confirm her findings, public reaction to your vlog post has done a complete one-eighty. Several large environmental groups have gone on record to support the claims you made and have shared your post over and over. Even YouTube is carrying it. Comments at each site I found were overwhelmingly positive."

Luk said nothing. How telling it was that public opinion played a bigger role in funding than doing the right thing.

"Have you seen BehnWerks stock values lately?"

"No. Why?"

Simon laughed. "It's up thirty percent in the last few hours. Market analysts are predicting it'll double that by the end of the day."

Luk covered the phone's mouthpiece. "You were right about that doctor."

"Told ya." Kyndra grinned.

"Simon, I appreciate the information, but I would have found out on my own by tomorrow at the latest. Why did you call me?"

The investor hesitated, building up his response as if the words he needed to say tasted bad. "Will and I hope you'll allow us to step in and repair our relationship with BehnWerks."

"Huh." The sound escaped before Luk could stop it. "I don't know, Simon. I still owe you a game. And I'll provide it as soon as I can. But I feel that any future working relationship will require a bit of consideration before I can trust you and Will again. My family is always going to come first, and I'm not sure you're willing to work with that. I'll need time to reassess our relationship."

"Fair enough. But you are willing to finish Hyde and Seek?"

Luk tensed. "As soon as Kyn is home from the hospital. Not before. In the meantime, I'll try to get someone at the office to set up pre-orders."

"We'll accept those terms." Simon's voice carried a forced grace, as if he were thanking a dentist for pulling a perfectly fine tooth. "How is she, by the way?"

Luk regarded his daughter. "She had a heart attack a few days ago, but she's better now. Out of ICU. Getting stronger every day."

Sadie popped around the curtain, two to-go cups and a small paper bag. She looked a question at Luk, but Kyn told her who it was. Sadie's eyes widened.

"Simon, I have to go. My breakfast has arrived. I'll keep you posted on Hyde."

When he finished, he hugged Sadie and ruffled Kyn's hair. "Lord Ganesha came through. Simon and Will are dropping the lawsuit."

"That's great news." Sadie put an arm around him and smiled.

He bent and kissed her. Just a little peck on the lips, but it was the first time for something like that. A little spark zipped through his belly and kindled a warmth in his heart.

Kyn hooted her approval. "About time."

Sadie laughed, her grip tightening around Luk as she sipped her coffee.

Luk wanted to surrender to the moment, but the last time he'd felt this happy, Kyn had a heart attack. He hoped there wouldn't be another shoe to fall this time.

Fallon Residence, Austin, Texas
Tuesday, November 19, 8:15 AM

Number of infected: 9,071,863

Isobel heard the screaming the minute she opened her car door in front of the garage. She kicked off her heels, ran across the grass, and raced up the brick steps. Yanking open the storm door, she bolted into the kitchen in time to see a salad bowl on approach. Without thinking, she ducked. The bowl crashed against the closing door, breaking the pane and raining pebbles of glass down on her back and on the steps behind her.

"What is going on?" she shouted over the din.

But a single glimpse was all she needed to arouse suspicion.

Can't be, said her clinical history, rejecting the visible evidence. Too soon.

Maria had cornered a flushed, screeching Gabe who snatched dishes and whatever else he could reach on the counter—thank god the knives were in a drawer—and swung them at the housekeeper, or threw them in a rage the likes of which Isobel had never seen.

Not in Gabe.

Maria tried to grab him, but he shoved her, slapped her, kicked her bent knees.

Maybe this was a normal tantrum.

Claire never did this. Zoe had.

If she could hold him, maybe—

Yes! That would fix it!

Isobel rushed into the fray, nudged Maria out of the way, and reached for her son. He had other ideas. He grew redder and slapped her even harder than he'd hit Maria. She recoiled from her gentle, good-natured, sweet Gabriel, and knew.

This was Milani, top to bottom.

Isobel did the only thing she knew to do. She dropped to the floor, grabbed his struggling body, and lay down, her arms and legs wrapped around him so rigidly he couldn't move.

Maria's eyes filled her ashen face.

"My office," Isobel yelled over Gabe's screams while she mentally chanted a litany of denial. *Can't be Milani. Can't be Milani.* "Top right desk drawer. The key's on my keyring. Bring me that little black box. Hurry."

It seemed she waited there for hours restraining her five-year-old, trying to calm him, though she doubted he heard her. He had never displayed an outburst like this. Ever. Not even during the terrible twos when most kids stamped their feet, yelled at parents, and threw their toys. Gabe never did. He'd always been sweet, loving, gentle.

This child wrapped in her limbs now, the one trying to bite her, the one leaving welts on her breasts and belly, was demon spawn. Acceptance took root and spread, despite the wails of negation that ricocheted in her mind.

Maria came running with the black box and dropped onto her knees beside them.

"You have to take him from me and hold him like this. Got it?"

She nodded, clearly frightened, and stretched out on the floor.

"Ready?"

"*Sí,*" Maria said in a shrill voice, barely audible over Gabe's fury.

Isobel took a breath. "Go."

Maria grabbed one of Gabe's arms. He snatched it away almost at once, the recoil nailing Isobel on the cheekbone.

Maria tried again. This time she succeeded and pulled the flailing child to her, one limb at a time, wrapping herself around him as tightly as she could. Even when Gabe headbutted her chin, Maria did not let go.

Isobel rose to her knees and grasped the black box with medicine Zoe hadn't needed until eight months before she died. The box Isobel had inherited, kept as a failsafe, and restocked two years ago. The box she'd prayed she would never need. Her thumbs punched in the combination. Throwing open the lid, she yanked out a hypodermic and a vial with clear liquid contents, shoved the needle in through the vial's seal, and drew back the plunger with care. Holding it up to the light, she thumped the syringe, squeezed the plunger until liquid squirted out the top. "Hold him still!"

Maria's embrace constricted until Gabe could not struggle. Zoe's fits had never been this bad.

Isobel yanked down one side of his pants, shoved the needle into his little posterior, and pushed the medication into his straining body. Once it was empty, she slid the hypo into the case. By the time the lid was closed and once more locked, he was calming. She smoothed her hair while he fell still in Maria's arms.

Isobel's breath rasped in and out in a panicked wheeze, a loud sound in the sudden calm. Her gaze met Maria's, which was wide enough to show the whites all around her irises. The woman still held Gabe like a vise, bracing his head to keep it from banging on the floor.

Ears ringing, Isobel scooted closer to take Gabe from the housekeeper, who relaxed her grip reluctantly as if afraid he would start again. Isobel rolled him over and peered at his now limp form. He appeared to be sleeping peacefully. This would keep him under for a couple of hours. When he woke, this would be over. Until the next time. She laid him against her shoulder where he drooped like a marionette freed from bondage.

Isobel focused on the frightened housekeeper who had risen to her knees. Strands of Maria's thick black braid, freed during the struggle, stuck out at odd angles. Slivers of glass sparkled on her clothing. Her skin was as pale as Isobel's own.

Isobel dropped her rear end to the floor. "Are you hurt?"

"No. *Lo siento, Señora.*" She babbled on in a mixture of Spanish and English.

"No, Maria. Don't apologize. This is not your fault. It's mine. This is probably part of Gabe's illness, but I never expected it this soon," Isobel said, still breathing hard. "Are you sure you're not hurt? He banged your chin pretty hard."

Maria touched her chin as if just realizing she'd been hit. Her fingers came away clean. The injury didn't break the skin. Still...

The housekeeper's big dark eyes locked on Isobel. "I don know what to do. He start screaming and throwing things like that." She waved around the room and for the first time, Isobel took in their surroundings.

The kitchen was wrecked. Some undefined brown fluid and what might be pasta sauce oozed down the front of the refrigerator and the wall beside it. Broken pottery and dishes littered the floor, along with pots, utensils, and everything else Gabe could reach. It looked like he'd upset the drying rack— that's probably where he got some of the dishes—and knocked everything off the table, which sat askew. Salt and pepper shakers lay shattered underneath the chairs, their contents spilled across the terazzo. Mail sat ruined in the mess. Some of the rubble was hard to identify.

Then she saw the blood. Smears that trailed from her heel. Gabe and Maria had been wearing shoes, but Isobel was barefoot in all this glass. The cut didn't hurt yet, but it would once the shock diminished. She'd worry about that later.

Isobel glanced at Maria's legs, her knees where the woman had knelt in all this glass. At least half a dozen small spots of blood dotted her khaki pants. Both her arms had spots of blood. How much glass would she have to dig out of her skin?

Her own legs and hip were similarly marked, all small cuts. They were lucky. This could have been much worse.

Damn it. She should have warned Maria this could happen. The woman was alone with Gabe much of the time. If she'd known, she could have been ready. Neither of them would be wounded. Isobel gestured at the housekeeper's legs.

Maria looked down at herself and began to chatter in Spanish, speaking far too rapidly for Isobel to follow.

Isobel shushed her. "Maria, I need you to stay calm and listen to me."

The housekeeper quieted.

Isobel took a breath. "Let's take this one step at a time. First, you should take off those clothes. They're covered in slivers of glass. Shower to remove any lingering shards and take care of those little cuts. Then we'll clean up the mess and I'll show you how to use the medicine that puts Gabe to sleep. Understand?"

Trembling, Maria nodded.

They'd also need to have a chat about what else to expect. At least then, poor Maria wouldn't be caught unaware.

"Where is Mr. Jake?"

"He go to work at seven o'clock."

That meant he wouldn't be home for hours. He'd need to be here for a conversation with Maria. She'd intended to come home, shower, and resume her vigil at the hospital. But waiting all day for Jake, followed by a lengthy discussion with Maria, meant Claire would be alone too long.

"Okay," Isobel said. "After you shower, can you call Mr. Jake for me? I need him to come home right now. Tell him what happened but speak slowly, Maria, so he can understand you. Comprendes?"

"*Sí, Señora—*"

"And please call someone to come and fix the door."

"*Sí, Señora.*" Maria got to her feet and hurried out of the kitchen toward her house, out by the pond. It wasn't until Maria had gone that Isobel's shakes began. It took her five minutes to get up from the floor. Another five to strip to her underwear and drop her clothes where she stood. Five more to get to the upstairs bathroom, where she stripped her boy to the skin and sat under the shower with him. Trickles of pink water trailed down the drain.

Gabe never woke.

Afterward, she dried them both, bandaged her cuts, and put on her robe before carrying him to his room. She dressed him in pajamas and laid him atop the covers, then threw a blanket over him.

If she didn't know better, she'd think he was merely sleeping, relaxed and calm, the picture of normalcy. Except the tremors had started a few months ago. Now the behavioral changes and mood swings, and Jake had said he was stumbling and stuttering. If those late-stage symptoms were showing up already—

Isobel raised a shaking hand to her mouth. The disease was progressing far faster in Gabe than it had in Zoe. They'd have less time than she'd hoped. Even once Travis got the coral harvest and live samples to Texas, Holschtatt needed time for developmental research to derive a testable medication. Human trials would take months. Maybe years. Gabe wouldn't have that long.

And yet the single treatment she'd found that might help him threatened her daughter.

She lay down on the bed, curled around her son, and wept.

Chapter 36

Parker Residence, Atlanta, Georgia
Wednesday, November 20, 10:30 AM
(Austin, Texas, 9:30 AM)

Number of infected: 10,000,027

AFTER THE INITIAL WHITE-HOT ERUPTION upon Nadine's early return, Barbara had barely spoken. Nadine had been home for almost two days now, and Barb still slept in the guest room. Nadine hoped a thaw lurked in her near future, but for now, she spent her time stress-baking in the kitchen. When her phone rang, she was elbow-deep in pastry dough.

"Barb? Can you please get that?"

No response.

Nadine glanced up. Her wife puttered around in the dining room with earbuds in, listening to some audiobook while she sorted paperwork for one of her charities.

"No, it's no problem." Nadine scraped off the messy batter and grabbed a kitchen towel. "I can get it, babe. No really, don't put yourself out."

Still grumbling, she walked to the dining room table and reached past Barbara to grab her phone. She recognized the number and picked up.

"Why Senator Lamont Moseley, what a surprise!"

A rich, resonant voice greeted her. "Hello, Nadine. It's been a minute since I've seen you. How're you doing? How's the wife?"

Nadine looked askance at Barb, who had removed one of her earbuds but was pretending not to listen. "Fit and feisty as ever. You?"

"Oh," he laughed, a mellow rumble that stirred fond memories. "Healthy as a horse. A little too well-fed, maybe."

"That makes two of us." Nadine laughed. "What occasions your call?"

"I wanted to let you know the big house has pulled together a special Senate committee to scrutinize the NJace work your team did in Austin. A little birdy told me this morning you're going to be called to testify."

"Really? Even though I'm in the doghouse?"

"You're being called *because* you're in the doghouse."

Nadine dropped her bulk onto a chair. "Okay. That needs some explanation if you have time."

Barb had removed the other earbud and was watching Nadine with a slight frown.

"Mitch Donaldson and his bosses submitted paperwork on your suspension a few hours before the U.S. was approached by a group of reps from other countries who all suspect the same things you disclosed in your press conference." He chuckled. "Congrats on that by the way. I'm betting Donaldson never saw that revelation coming, and he should have, with you in play. I have to admit, I laughed. Anyway, these other reps or their ambassadors saw your little Q and A and want us to cooperate with them in a global coalition on this NJace thing. Given the contradiction between your presentation and what Donaldson's office has claimed, we're supposed to listen to all the sides and make a recommendation on whether or not to collaborate."

"Well, bite my buns. Are you my invitation?"

"No, you know how it is," Moseley rumbled. "They'll make it all official. You'll be hearing from Health and Human

Services today because they want you in D.C. tomorrow morning. Testimony starts first thing. You're not on the docket until Friday, but your briefing with my staff is scheduled for tomorrow. As soon as you can get here and get settled, call my office. They'll fit you in."

"This is happening faster than a microwave minute meal, Senator." Nadine winked at Barbara who, by now, was hanging on every word. "Why the rush?"

"It's an urgent situation. Infection numbers are on their way to the ten million mark with no sign of slowing down. We need to get in front of this thing. If you're right—and for the record, I think you're onto something—then we need to figure out a way to pacify this virus, get it to at least slow down."

"Huh." Nadine ran a hand over her hair before remembering she still had traces of dough on her fingers. "This is official enough I should pack a bag?"

"If you're smart, and I know you are, you will."

Nadine grinned at Barb. "You made this happen, didn't you, Senator?"

"No. They would have called you anyway, given the purpose of the committee. But I made sure they knew that you would speak the truth as you saw it, not because you had nothing left to lose in the process but because you would naturally do the right thing even if it killed you."

For a second, the whole English language fled Nadine's tongue. That didn't happen often. As in never. At last, she managed to thank him.

Moseley cleared his throat. "We haven't always agreed on political issues in the past, Nadine, but I've always liked you. More to the point, I respect you. I trust you. If you say this NJace bugger is intelligent, well," he tsked, "I believe you. It's downright unprofessional the way Mitch treated you. If you're interested in staying on at the CDC, I'll see what I can do to dismiss this suspension and erase the smudge from your record."

"I'd sure appreciate it, Senator. After this mess is over and life resumes its usual chaotic normal, maybe I can make dinner for you one evening."

"That's the best offer I've had all week. I'll take it."

They chatted for a few more minutes. The instant she put the phone down, Barb's questions began. Nadine explained.

"You won't be fired?"

"Don't pull that cake out of the oven yet. This ain't a done deal. I still have to go to D.C. and testify, which isn't gonna make Mitch any happier."

"Well, yeah." Barb shrugged. "But if Senator Moseley has anything to say about it, Mitch's opinion about what you did won't carry much weight."

"Even if you're right, Mitch is still my boss. He can make my remaining days at the CDC a living hell. Assign me to the worst jobs, send me places he knows I hate, keep me on the road all the time."

"Only for a couple of years."

"Seven, babe. Seven years in hell could feel like twenty." Nadine pushed herself to her feet and went into the kitchen. Her dough had dried out. She'd have to start over. Figures. Just as well, though. She needed to pack.

Barb's arms came around her from behind. "You'll be the one giving them hell, Nadine. Trust me on this."

Nadine pivoted in Barb's embrace and kissed her wife on the cheek. "What happened to the hotheaded spitfire I've been living with the last day or so?" Nadine squinted past Barb as if expecting someone to walk in the kitchen behind her. "She was kinda cute in a scary way."

Barbara twisted her lips to one side and dropped her gaze for a second before renewing eye contact. "It's possible... possible, I say...that I was wrong."

Nadine struggled to maintain a serious expression. "I see." She nodded. "I may need to arrange for Senator Moseley to call here every time we fight."

Chapter 37

"No really." Sadie pushed the coffee into his hand and hooked her arm through his. "She's with Miss Green. They're chatting and having a great time. She won't even notice we're gone."

Luk glanced at the bed, where Kyn's physical therapy was getting started. Since she'd gotten better, Miss Green worked Kyn a little harder. Got her out of the bed and walked her around the room. Might be better if they weren't crowding the space.

"Okay."

He let Sadie pull him out the door, down the hall, and into the courtyard garden surrounded by lush greenery, a sloping lawn, and the tinkling sound of splashing water. One side of the garden held a brick wall but on the other three, windowed corridors offered views of this open-air space. He strolled with Sadie to the little bridge at the top of the waterfall. Below, the bottom terrace of the courtyard garden bordered the cafe on the first floor. Patio diners could listen to the waterfall or see the babbling brook that meandered through the patio.

Chittering birds and the murmurs of diners filled the space with a pleasant buzz of white noise that raised Luk's mood.

His gaze wandered over the colored tiles, winding waterway, garden plantings, noting details much as any game designer might do, filing them away for potential use in a future game scene. "Kyn would love it out here."

"Wouldn't she, though? Maybe later we can wheel her out here in a chair." Sadie took a deep breath of the fresh air. "Marin used to tell me that a garden could heal anything, even the soul."

As if summoned by the thought, one of Kyn's doctors called to them from behind. Luk and Sadie turned, instantly alert. "Doctor Engan... is something wrong? Is Kyn—"

"Kyndra's fine." Engan smiled. "We're encouraged by her progress."

Relief closed Luk's eyes for a second. "That's good news, doctor."

"Indeed. I wonder if we might chat." She looked from Luk to Sadie. "Am I intruding? We can do this later if you prefer."

"No, now is fine." Luk led them to a small table with chairs and an umbrella.

He remembered seeing Engan her first day on staff when he'd tried to get Sarsby and Whitfield to hear his report on Kyn's claims. Engan had been the only one he thought might have been willing to listen. She'd seemed regretful when the other doctors shut Luk down. He liked her compassionate and approachable manner.

"Mr. Behn, it's been a week since Kyndra's heart attack. Her pain has begun to ease. She's been awake and lucid numerous times since, and though she's still in some discomfort, it doesn't appear to be as overwhelming."

"Yes. She told me she still felt the pain, but that she was getting used to it."

"Mmm hmm," Engan said. "I've consulted with the rest of her medical team, and we agree it's time to start weaning her off the medications."

Luk's gut twisted. "What does that mean for Kyn?" He could already hear her screams. But they couldn't keep her numb for the rest of her life. Besides, she felt the pain anyway, even with the drugs.

"Well," Engan said, her head tipped to one side, "ketamine withdrawal has few physical effects on the patient, especially as administered here in a clinical setting. It's been used as a pediatric sedative and analgesic for more than twenty-five years, and since she's been receiving it in small doses for such a short time, we don't anticipate any drastic changes. She may be disoriented. You may notice some dissociation or confusion. But I don't foresee any problems. We'll taper her doses gradually to make it easier. I wanted you to be aware."

"Are you saying she's addicted?"

"Not in the same way a street user would be," Engan clarified. "Any sedative or analgesic we could have given her would induce dependence with continued use such as she has required, but ketamine is one of the safest around for this scenario. She's been under constant observation, her doses strictly regulated. Her withdrawal, if indeed there is any, should be gentle. Easy."

"Is there anything we can do to help?" Sadie asked.

"No. Just be there for her, Ms. Shupert. Like you have been all along."

"Does this mean..." Luk's words trailed off. He hated to ask. He felt torn, unsure which response he wanted from the doctor. Kyn wanted this change. Given that, he guessed he did, too.

"Yes?"

Luk squinted at the doctor. "Does this mean she's getting better? From the phage? Or is she still infected?"

Engan's face twitched. "I'm afraid the phage is still very much alive in her body. No one knows, yet, how to interrupt its progress, though medical professionals around the world are working on it." She leaned forward. "But she is better. Her pain is more manageable. That alone is a blessing. Unless something happens to set her back before then, we hope to send her home in the next couple of days."

Hope blossomed in Luk's chest. For the first time since this whole nightmare started, the future held hope.

"Doctor Engan," Luk said, his mouth widening in a smile, "that's the best news I've heard in weeks."

Engan rose. "I wanted to tell you how sorry I am that some of the other doctors here were … less than open to your concerns about Kyndra's claims."

Luk's jaw tightened. "I appreciate that. I can't express to you how frustrating that has been."

"I expect it has." Engan favored them with an open expression. "I'm not making excuses, exactly, but doctors in hospitals, especially children's facilities, see some horrid things. Situations you would never expect to see in this country. Some of the parents we deal with are…difficult. Less than truthful. Not all of them are concerned with their child's best interests."

Luk tried to imagine seeing that, especially in a hospital setting, and what that might do to a doctor's reactions to other parents, whether or not they were the same.

"Those doctors who've spoken out about their concerns over how you're raising Kyndra…" She wrinkled her nose. "Well. They've told me some real horror stories about other cases. They're predisposed to disbelieve anything that doesn't fit normal parameters. And you have to admit Kyn's claims seemed, in the beginning, to be abnormal. Did you credit them at first?"

Sadie squeezed his hand. Luk sighed. "No."

"There. The doctors couldn't have known then that she was telling the truth. This virus has presented quite an unprecedented scenario. The idea that it's sentient has yet to be proven, but the other doctors are starting to come around. Try not to be too hard on them." She walked away.

"Doctor Engan?" Luk called, stopping her halfway to the door.

"Yes?"

"Do you believe?"

Engan looked out across the garden, up at the sky, over at the trees, then smiled at Luk. "Yes."

Chapter 38

"ARE YOU READY?" HE ASKED.

Nadine glanced at Cagney, his spiked do as neat as it ever got. He fidgeted, checked his mobile, straightened his tie over and over. She understood his twitchies. She'd testified before Senate committees on numerous occasions. It was no big deal now, but that first time she'd been as jumpy as a drop of water in a hot skillet. Since she may or may not have a job going forward, though, Cagney would need to know the steps to this dance.

She got Moseley to ensure Cagney could sit in on the "murder boards" yesterday where senior officials role-played members of congress and threw questions at her as if they were on the committee. It was grueling. Exhausting. Stressful. The whole experience caught Cagney unprepared. Why not just tell the truth? he'd asked. How hard could that be?

How hard indeed. Every one of the committee members took a role in this inquiry not only to find answers or to adjudicate but also to gather ammunition for their political agendas. There were good folks among them, like Moseley. But the rest would not hesitate to use her discoveries or manipulate her responses to launch themselves into positions of greater power. Whatever they learned today would be used as leverage against their political adversaries.

Besides, Mitch and his superiors probably had a friend or two on the committee. They'd be trying to throw her off balance at every chance. It made sense to prepare this dough in advance.

This time Nadine would be reporting to a special Health and Human Services Committee. Their questions weren't going to be easy to answer, especially when her replies weren't what the committee—or anyone else—wanted to hear.

"As ready as I'll ever be," Nadine said. "Take notes out there in the audience. You'll need them one day."

"Gee, thanks."

She laughed, puckered, and whistled some classic soul about truth and honesty. She needed some Aretha about now.

The room where they waited was typical District of Columbia. Wood-paneled walls. Thick slate blue carpet that would appear elegant on television, but up close proved to be shabby and worn. Chairs that passed for official but wouldn't know comfort if it bit them on the leg. Nadine's caboose was numb from sitting in one of them. Was Mitch sequestered in a similar room or had he already testified? Would he watch her testimony from his hotel?

She stood and wandered to one of the framed pictures on the wall. Beautifully done, these portraits of famous men in U.S. history. Their luster bestowed a sense of heritage and dignity to the space, which had a stately air, like everything else. But government job notwithstanding, as far as Nadine was concerned, most of Washington was a cardboard set painted to seem real. If you peeled away the surface layer, you'd find nothing beneath but worms.

The heavy door opened and a huffy aide, his chest as puffed out as a sage grouse in a mating display, gestured. "We're getting started."

Nadine winked at Cagney, who brayed a nervous laugh, before she followed the aide to the Committee chamber. More aides filed in on one side with tablets, pens, laptops, and snappy fashion to hover around seats behind the row where the Committee members would sit. The diffuse glow of morning light seeped past plush velvet curtains at windows along the wall to her right. The rear wall, paneled in rich brown wood, stood in stately contrast to the beige—taupe, Barb would say—paint on the other three sides. It gave the room a bureaucratic feel that set Nadine on edge. She'd be lucky to get out of this hearing with her reputation intact. At least Moseley was in her corner.

Audience members poured through the doors opposite the bench, filling the chairs. Cameras and recording equipment lined the front and sides of her section of the room, and photographers roamed the space overall, snapping random photos. Bottles of water sat at each place along the bench. Her own space held one, too, along with a remote for the PowerPoint presentation she'd prepared.

Cagney came in, along with several others. Nadine nodded to him, then took her seat at a long, imposing table that smelled of lemon furniture polish. There she would sit alone, facing the committee. It felt like an inquisition of sorts. Maybe it was.

She flipped through her brief, ensuring for the twentieth time the pages were in the proper order. No guarantee she'd get to use them. But she'd prepared diagrams of the molecular structure of the interneurin, images of NJace, scans of several patients' brains with their neuron-packed insulae, and images of Zero's brain dyed to demonstrate how it'd begun firing on a whole new level. She also had visual overlays of NJace's spread patterns atop areas of highest environmental crisis. Visual aids like that might soften the hardest crust along the table.

Too bad she didn't have images of the latest changes in the environmental tests Thom had set up a week ago, the ones with the higher gas levels and increased temps. Cagney told her the samples were showing increased activity as if they were ramping up to do...something. Who knew what? But Cagney had decided—wisely so—that he would be overstepping his bounds to bring her images when she was technically suspended.

The Committee members began to shuffle in, and Nadine made herself sit still, hands resting atop her folder. Audience members still rustled about, talking among themselves behind her. The general murmur of a crowded room, like a busy restaurant, filled her ears.

Committee Chairperson Valerie Pratt called the hearing to order and outlined the basic procedure, then welcomed Nadine and stated the purpose for the hearing. It sounded to Nadine like the Chair was giving a speech that, in part, explained her own accomplishments in the field of medical science and research, why she was important enough to be a committee chair, and why she was specifically the best person to hear this particular matter.

Another committee member followed in the same format, then another. It was all Nadine could do not to roll her eyes. She hoped some real good would come out of this dog and pony show, but one didn't say "No, thanks," when a Senate Committee called one to testify. Besides, if it would make people hear what she was trying to say, it would be worth the drama.

When all the committee members' horns had been tooted, the chair introduced Nadine to the assembled committee, staff, and audience members, as if they didn't already know who she was. It always felt odd to hear a recitation of her achievements.

After the Chair had sworn her in, Nadine took the floor.

"Thank you, Madam Chair," Nadine said, "Vice-Chair Bradbury, distinguished Committee Members. As the Chair has already introduced me and listed my qualifications in the area of infectious disease, I will assume that those present here do not need me to repeat them. I would like, instead, to describe what is happening with affected patients, and what we might stand to gain from this organism."

She brought up the first slide.

"This is the Novel Juvenile Cerebral Bacteriophage that is infecting the children. We posit that the organism, which we are calling NJace, has provoked permanent change in the infected patients, which may well be heritable. Researchers around the world are still debating this and searching for ways to stop further infections as well as to reverse what has already occurred. To my knowledge, they have thus far had no success, though trials are still ongoing."

She changed slides to display a different image of the phage. "Evidence thus far indicates that NJace is not communicable from person to person. We believe it started as a common bacteriophage, yet that original virus's form has changed in its mutation chain to the degree that we are unable to identify its history. We are still debating the means for the infection's global diffusion and distribution since any localized bacteriophage is likely to have had a more limited presence. This mutation in a globally present phage and its close varieties may have been sparked or driven by global environmental changes. I understand now that our initial investigations into this mystery are beginning to show tentative results that may eventually lead to an answer.

"This experience has been horrifying for the parents and families of these children. NJace itself has thus far proven impossible to eradicate without using methods that would prove fatal to the patient. However, the CDC has also begun to investigate a peptide produced by the organism itself." Nadine switched to a new, animated slide that rotated forward and back for a simulated 3-D view.

"We first mistook this peptide for intermedin, a hormone naturally present in the body. Once we unmasked it, however, we began to research its effects on the patients and have come to theorize that the peptide, which we are calling 'interneurin,' is a neurocatalyst. Evidence suggests it is actively promoting the growth of new neurons in the brain, a process called neurogenesis."

She switched slides to show brain scans from several patients, then to the one of Zero's brain artificially colored to demonstrate its new level of activity.

"Neurogenesis in the human brain is a lifelong process, though it does slow as we age. Triggering or encouraging further growth can be achieved through exercise, proper diet, and other means. However, until the last eighteen months or thereabouts, medical science presumed contrived neurogenesis to be impossible. Even now, drug and gene therapy treatments to promote neurogenesis in Alzheimer's patients and those with similar conditions are in the early stages. The CDC's primary goal is to fight disease and support communities to do the same. With this in mind, we as medical professionals would be remiss to ignore the potential for good that could come of this discovery. I hope that through outreach with others working toward these or similar goals, we can find a way to control the NJace organism's growth while researching its peptide as a possible treatment for patients with brain disorders or injuries, and if those show promise, to produce an open-source set of formulae for clinical trials.

"Thank you for your attention. I look forward to your questions."

St. Ives Hospital, Austin, Texas
Friday, November 22, 10:20 AM

Number of infected: 13,090,347

Isobel sat in Claire's room. A nurse had come earlier, bathed Claire, and gone about her duties. The therapist came soon after, working Claire's joints and adjusting her position in the bed. A lab tech came next for Claire's daily blood draw. Isobel saw it all from the sidelines, her thoughts skittering from one topic to the next like a bee in a stiff breeze.

Now she stared at her computer screen, shoes off and feet tucked up in the chair. One Bluetooth earbud allowed her to listen to the Senate hearing on the phage without waking her daughter. Isobel wanted to hear what the expert had discovered but kept yawning even though it was shortly after ten in the morning. C-Span had a way of making the most intriguing topics boring.

She was half-watching when the CDC witness—the same woman Isobel deemed a "quack" in that initial press conference—brought up the image of the new peptide. Isobel could see how they'd been fooled at first. But when the image enlarged and rotated to views from various angles, the portion of the amino acid chain that distinguished this from intermedin became clear. It wasn't until the visual had completed its rotation and began to reverse to its original position that Isobel almost dropped her computer.

This neurocatalyst had the dangling amino acid she'd found buried in the coral protein. It was the same damn one, or so close to it, she couldn't tell the difference. Except this one wouldn't require as much processing to remove extraneous material. It might even lock on to the toxic Milani protein fragments as it was in its natural state.

Her mouth went dry. If she was seeing this image correctly, it could mean the disease that almost killed her daughter could hold the key to saving her son.

No. Impossible. She couldn't believe she would find such an enormous coincidence buried in this nightmare. There had to be some mistake. She pulled up a notepad on her MacBook and typed in the CDC witness's name. Isobel could contact her later and ask for a consult, assuming she could get near the woman.

Awake and on full alert, she watched as the testimony continued.

Chapter 39

NADINE OPENED HER BOTTLE AND TOOK A TINY SIP. Not too much. It wouldn't do to need a bathroom break in thirty minutes. The hearing would run at least another hour.

The Chair took first shot at the mic, as was her privilege.

Pratt propped her elbows on the desk, peering at Nadine with an apparent mixture of curiosity and caution in her light brown eyes. "I cannot speak for families affected by this disease. My children are grown, and my grandchildren are too old to be infected. But if the effects of this phage are, as you say, permanent and heritable in those infected now, that does not bode well for the children of my grandchildren. If we cannot find a way to prevent the transmission of this disease to unborn generations, I fear those carriers will be marked as outcasts and subjected to a new witch hunt in their adult lives. They may be confronted with a potential future of social and cultural isolation and ostracism. It seems doubtful that unaffected individuals would want them as partners for fear that their children would endure what we've seen in our hospitals over the last month. What efforts are currently being undertaken by the CDC to divert us from that trajectory?"

"As I stated before," Nadine said, "tests are underway for a means to reverse NJace's effects, but we have not yet been successful. We're also researching ways to inactivate the organism in the hope of stopping the progress of the disease. It's simply too soon to know."

"How long do you expect it will take to find those answers?"

Ambient light snuck past the nearest drapes in meager ghosts of shadow that danced like nefarious sprites across the wall behind the senators. Nadine tried to ignore them.

"I can't speak to that, Madame Chair." Did the woman think Nadine was a fortune-teller? "I can say that medical specialists and epidemiologists around the world are working on the same goal. I have high hopes."

Pratt nodded. "I assume standard antivirals have been ineffective?"

"That's correct."

"Has the CDC had any success testing therapeutics for this disease?"

"No, and even if we could find and rush one to development, there's no way to know whether it would work long-term, or what side effects might arise, either now or decades in the future."

The Chairperson's white bobbed hair framed her angular face. Grey might have suited her better, with that pale skin and minimal makeup. "Maybe I should have asked this first. Has the CDC tested any new medical countermeasures at all as of this date?"

"Yes. Our trials were intended to interrupt the organism's production of interneurin and discontinue the resultant changes in the patients' brains."

"What was the outcome of those trials?"

"As you know," Nadine said, "I've been out of the loop for four days now, but at the time I left Austin, we had tested three. All of them proved deleterious."

Pratt cocked one eyebrow. "Can you be a little more specific?"

"Of course. One trial killed the organism but also destroyed red blood cells in the sample. Another stopped peptide production but morphed what was already present into an unknown poison similar to tetrodotoxin. The third appeared to double the number of phages in the sample, all producing the peptide."

"Thank you," Pratt said. "The Chair recognizes Senator Gideon Bradbury from Oregon."

A bald, slender man took the floor. "Thank you, Madame Chair. Doctor Parker, I'd like to address the elephant in the room. You are on administrative suspension from your position as EIS officer at the Center for Disease Control in Atlanta, where you have worked for..." He consulted his notes. "...nearly thirty years now. Is that correct?"

"Yes, sir, it is."

"Would you please explain, in your own words, why you have been suspended after such a long and illustrious career with that fine institute?"

Nadine cleared her throat. "My supervisor assigned me to speak at a press conference regarding our team's findings on NJace and gave me a very strict boundary on the type of information I could divulge. I went beyond that limit during the televised conference and revealed more than I had been authorized to say."

"Didn't you realize your career would be at risk?"

"Yes, sir, I did."

"Then why do it?"

Nadine took a deep breath. "Because I believed the unauthorized information was crucial to understanding the nature of the virus, and to any workable plan on how to slow or even affect its spread patterns. The CDC is not working in a vacuum here, Senator. It is my professional opinion that if we don't share all the data, whether or not it is convenient or proven, we will be unable to stop this virus."

Bradbury's long fingers steepled before him. "You feel we should share the knowledge we've gained with other nations? Collaborate with them on this thing?"

"Yes. Absolutely."

"Why?"

"Because this virus and its effects are unprecedented. No one group knows the answer. But if we work together, pooling all the details of our research and building on one another's theories, we can find a solution much sooner."

"Thank you, Doctor Parker." Bradbury sat back with a satisfied grin.

Nadine squinted. He was up to something.

"The Chair recognizes Senator Wilson Farley from Alabama."

A pale, heavyset man moved closer to the mic, light glinting on his scalp through thinning hair. "Thank you, Madame Chair," he drawled. "Ms. Parker—"

Nadine leaned forward. "Excuse me, Senator Farley. That's Doctor Parker."

He blinked at her over his glasses and offered a smile that never touched his eyes. "Of course. Doctor Parker. I'm concerned about this global collaboration idea. Sharing sensitive information about United States citizens and U.S. medical technologies, not to mention our technical weaknesses, with other nations seems unwise. Any one of them could use that information against us in the future. Doesn't that concern you?"

Danged fearmongers. "Senator, I'm not talking about sharing national secrets. I'm referring to blind patient data and very specific medical results on tests related to a singular objective. The benefits we stand to gain far outweigh the risks."

"You really believe that?"

"I do," Nadine said. "While it's true that any data can be reverse engineered to the sharer's detriment, the gamble this kind of collaboration poses to our government, our medical science, or our national citizens is far less of a threat than the computer fraud and identity theft we already see on a daily basis. And yet people continue to release their personal details and credit card information online every day."

Senator Farley clasped pudgy hands in front of him on the bench. "Doctor Parker, the U.S. is arguably the most technically advanced nation in the world, especially in the area of medicine. What exactly do you expect these other countries to contribute?"

Nadine didn't miss his emphasis on her title. She forced a smile. "Sir, the notion of the United States as the most technically advanced country in medical science overall is debatable. It's possible the U.S. still leads in biotech, but we are certainly not ahead of the pack in areas of general medical tech. However, that is a subject for another day. Other countries, especially those who do not practice Western medicine, have already provided excellent insights over the last few days in online articles and discussions. Many of them are eager to collaborate in this way for the same reasons I've stated here. Any researcher can confirm that comparing notes and getting a fresh perspective on a knotty problem can help. If nothing else, it would save us the trouble of repeating someone else's mistakes and thus be a more efficient use of time, effort, and resources."

The Chair recognized a speaker in a navy blue blazer, Senator Joanna Pollard from Ohio.

"Doctor Parker," Pollard said, "you've stated that you concluded, based on your observations, that the neuronal growth in the children is connected to their apparent psychosis, and the empathetic connection they appear to be sharing with the environment. Have I stated it correctly?"

"Yes."

"And that growth is being promoted by this interneurin, which is produced by the NJace?"

"That is correct."

Pollard frowned, carving darker creases in an already lined face. "How likely is it that preventing the production of that peptide would cure the disease, or at least halt the development of new neurons?"

"If the peptide is in fact the catalyst," Nadine said, "it's conceivable that would serve the desired function, yes. But as I said earlier, we tried this. NJace reacted badly every time."

"Granted," Pollard said with a nod that swung her neat, corralled braids in a gentle arc. "But we're just starting our research, are we not?"

"That is correct."

The Senator's long fingers splayed as she gestured. A diamond in her wedding band flashed in the light. "Then if you were to find a way to stop it, is it possible that given some time to recover without the constant exposure to the peptide, the children's new neurons would shrink or disappear? Perhaps reverse the 'psychosis' the children are experiencing?"

"Given how little we still know about this organism and its effects, I would rather not speculate on that sort of possibility at this time."

"Very well. One more question," Pollard said. "You've posited the idea that interneurin might be successfully used to treat patients with brain injuries or disorders, which I took to mean dementia, stroke, and the like. Is that correct?"

"Yes."

"Isn't it possible that using it in that way, even with the best of intentions, could cause those patients to be subjected to NJace's less beneficial effects, as the children are now?"

Nadine knew this question would come up. The murder boards had thrown it at her in several formats. "We won't know until we run clinical trials, which are at least a year off even if we started toward that end today. Yes, there is a risk. But it seems to me that not to try at all would be even more irresponsible. Even if the United States doesn't make the attempt, I assure you someone else will. It should be understood that we are working at this time under the conjecture that hormonal changes induced by puberty would effectively make adults immune to NJace. That has yet to be confirmed. However, we have no way of knowing how the subject would be affected if interneurin is introduced outside the presence of NJace in the body. We won't know unless and until we pursue the research and run trials."

Pratt spoke up. "The Chair recognizes Senator Kevin Stalls from New Jersey."

"Thank you, Madame Chair," a slender, hawk-nosed man said. Numerous lines and more than one scar gave his features a hard look that Nadine couldn't read. She hadn't dealt with him before. "Doctor Parker, the pharmaceutical industry is a big part of my state's economy. Many of my constituents are heavily involved in that business. If the United States discovers the treatment to kill the phage or reverse its effects, sharing that information in an open-source manner such as you have suggested would harm them financially. Would you care to comment on that?"

Nadine bit down on the retort that sprang to her lips. This was not the time for snark. "With all due respect, Senator, the only thing an open-source agreement might compromise is the ability of individuals or corporations to profit from this crisis. I understand that you are trying to protect the best interests of your constituents. But we're talking about a global pandemic. I can't in good conscience recommend we refuse to share findings in any trials solely for profit's sake."

Stalls' jaw worked as if he wanted to say more. A lot more. But Senate Committee Hearings were broadcast live, and available for all to see online for months afterward. A descent into testiness here could hurt him in the next election. His glare, flinty and cold, made Nadine want to twitch. She was grateful when he glanced at the cameras and pushed away from the mic with more vehemence than seemed warranted.

Nadine struggled to maintain a professional facade. She wasn't entirely sure she succeeded.

The chair recognized Senator Lamont Moseley of Georgia.

"Doctor Parker, you said in your press conference last week," he said, "that you've seen reason to believe this organism knows what it's doing, that it's acting with a purpose."

Nadine cringed. Even though she'd seen this coming, her toes curled inside her sensible shoes.

"In fact," he went on, "it was this theory, in addition to your belief that the virus is intelligent, that your supervisors forbade you to reveal. Was it not?"

"That's correct, Senator."

"Do you still adhere to the premise that NJace is intelligent?"

"In a sense, yes. That is my supposition at this time." Nadine chose her words with care. Mosely had been generous enough to tell her she wasn't alone in that assessment, but this was not the time or place to reveal that information. "I strongly believe this warrants further investigation. One possibility is that when NJace is established in the human body, the relationship between the organism and the host could conceivably become symbiotic."

"Like partners?"

"Yes. Again, that's a suggestion for further examination."

The senator rubbed one hand across his close-cropped natural hair and gripped the back of his neck for a second. "Correct me if I'm wrong, but symbiosis usually garners positive gains for both parties. That's not what I see happening here. Our children are suffering. All they got was more brain cells and a whole lot of pain."

Nadine raised her chin. "As a matter of fact, the earliest patients' symptoms have begun to ease, which would be consistent with the symbiosis theory."

"How so?"

"In the case of a newly developed symbiotic partnership, especially one with such a profound engagement, it would take time for each symbiont to acclimate to the presence of the other. The beginning stages would be the most painful and arduous. As the relationship becomes more attuned, the connection clears and becomes smoother."

Moseley shifted in his seat. A fine sheen of sweat gleamed on his brow. "Are you saying the children will get better?"

"Based on our observations to date, that is our current expectation, yes. The pain felt by the first wave of patients in the earliest stages of the infection is no longer acute enough that they must be sedated all the time. We are cautiously optimistic that they will soon be able to leave the hospital and get on with their lives."

"What are the long-term effects of those new neurons in the children, Doctor Parker?"

"I cannot answer that question at this time. It could take decades for any such changes or results to manifest. Only longer study and better understanding will tell."

"I see." He tapped his finger on the desk as if thinking about her words. "If I understand you correctly, then, our children get redesigned brains and an emotional connection with each other and the animal kingdom out of this whole deal," he said. "But there's another question here that has not yet been addressed. What does NJace get in return?"

That's a question the murder boards hadn't foreseen. She had, but it did her no good now.

"Honestly, Senator," she said, "we just don't know."

St. Ives Hospital, Austin, Texas
Friday, November 22, 11:30 AM

Number of infected: 13,716,035

As soon as the Chair brought the hearing to a recess, Isobel closed her computer and checked on Claire. Still out.

Everything Parker had said fascinated Isobel, but nothing more than the details Parker had shared about the interneurin. This could be the basis of a treatment for Milani

Syndrome. If the introduction of the peptide did present the NJace symptoms in patients, Gabe's body would then produce the means to treat Milani all on its own.

It seemed too good to be true. Isobel might—*might*—be able to save both her children.

She whirled and grabbed her phone. A little after 11:30. What day was this? Friday. Oh yes. She knew where he would be.

After another glance at the bed, she was on the move.

Chapter 40

La Croûte Supérieure, Austin, Texas
Friday, November 22, 12:05 PM

Number of infected: 14,421,523

ISOBEL THUMBED THE BUTTONS ON HER PHONE, dropped it into her pocket, and surged out of her car at the valet station. She threw her purse over one shoulder and passed the staring patrons with a wave. Never once did she worry about her jeans and wrinkled sweater, the sneakers she'd kept for comfort, not style. She hadn't bothered to put on makeup. She advanced like a guided missile, and her target sat inside eating lunch.

The doorman pulled open the door and she swept into the foyer. Ahead stood a curved cherrywood podium in front of a matching partition that swept almost the width of the space in a graceful arc. Staff came and went from the dining room beyond on both sides, their soft soles swishing on the marble floor. The maître d' stood at his station, his dark silk suit, cranberry cravat, and greying beard impeccable. At the sight of her, his smile faltered for a second before he regained control.

"Good afternoon, Madame," he oozed in accented English. "May I—"

Isobel charged past him, almost colliding with one of the servers as she rounded the blind corner.

"Madame!" the maître d' shouted. "Madame!"

She did not slow until she entered the dining room proper. Christoph Neillsen had a standing lunch reservation here on Fridays. Good thing, too. The place was packed. She glanced both ways in the large open space before she spotted him. Behind her, the maître d' called for security.

Neillsen brought her here once when Holschtatt bought out Threet Research, her prior employer. He'd wanted to recruit her, keep her from bailing in solidarity with other Threet scientists they'd cut loose. The decor had been different then. Darker. Since that day, the dropped ceiling had been removed to reveal painted structural supports. Below those, a wide arc of that same beautiful cherry wood hung over the length of the dining area. Simple lights dangled from the arc like stars from the sky. Besides the arc and one wood-paneled wall, everything was soft beige, right down to the marble floor. The only other color came from potted plants placed at regular intervals down the aisles between banks of tables.

Patrons looked up from their coq au vin, crêpes, or soufflé as she passed, eyeing her like a piece of tissue stuck to their shoe. She ignored them and barreled toward Neillsen. She had to make him listen. The man sat at his table like he owned all of Austin, chatting with two other men. He hadn't seen her yet. She threaded her way between full tables and approached his party, one of whom was Jake, his cheeks shadowed, his skin dull. His late nights with the Laphroaig were taking a toll.

For the first time, her steps faltered. Had this been a mistake?

Didn't matter. Too late to back out now.

All three men saw her at the same time. Jake pushed out of his chair, a hint of panic leaking past the business mask he always wore. "Isobel, what's wrong? Is Claire—"

"She's fine. For now." Isobel regarded the board chairman, who had not risen. "Mr. Neillsen, I need to speak with you."

"You were directed to report to me when you returned to Austin. Since you did not, this will have to wait." He offered a polite smile. "I'm in the middle of a lunch meeting as you can see."

Sounds from behind drew her glance. Two well-dressed men approached—security, by the looks of them. They might have been wrestlers, for all their brawn. "No," she said. "This won't keep."

Jake started to appropriate another chair, but Neillsen stopped him. "This won't take that long. What is it, Isobel?"

The man cut another piece of his chateaubriand, dipped it in the wine sauce on his plate, then placed it oh-so-primly in his mouth.

"I'm not sure if you saw the video interview with Lukas Behn of BehnWerks Games. His daughter contracted the phage at about the same time we started the Nlaan project."

Jake closed his eyes.

Neillsen began to cut another bite. "Don't tell me you buy into the drivel that the two are connected."

"Behn's daughter went into cardiac arrest at the same time I blasted the reef." She saw Jake's wince but kept her focus on the chairman. "She's not alone. Other children in Austin, including my daughter, Jake's daughter, also went into crisis that night. A few died. At least one is on a ventilator and may not survive."

"Coincidence." Neillsen ate a mushroom.

Was his ignorance willful? "You can't be that obtuse. I won't let you. We are partly responsible for what's happening, for this disease that's killing children. The reef project was the trigger for the phage. Ramping it up was a tipping point. A final straw. The infection numbers support this theory."

"Ridiculous." Neillsen spoke around his food. "Surely you don't believe Holschtatt is the only company harvesting from reefs? Or cutting down trees? Or running factories that," he added air quotes, "pollute?"

"No. But Nlaan was pristine. Untouched." Her voice shook. She folded her arms over her chest. "Our actions started a collapse on that reef. News stories say the islanders have reported large fish die-offs and bleaching of the remaining coral. What if it spreads like a domino effect all through the Coral Triangle?"

"This was your idea, Isobel. You got what you wanted. Don't cry to me now about some sick fish."

She snapped at him. "Yes, it was my plan. Yes, I wanted a treatment for my child, but not at this price! Jesus—"

Neillsen looked around. Isobel followed suit. Conversation had died throughout the dining room. Everyone watched the drama playing out at this table. A voice at her shoulder snagged her attention.

"Ma'am, please come with us."

She braced herself against the table. "There might be a way to salvage this project without harming another reef. Without the need for more coral. If I'm right, it would be cheaper, cleaner, easier for Holschtatt to produce."

Neillsen turned a slow glare on her that should have iced her blood. She was too intent to care.

"I just saw a Senate Committee hearing with testimony from that CDC expert who spoke at the press conference a few days ago. One of her presentation slides showed a molecular diagram of the peptide they presume is causing neurogenesis in the sick children. It contains an amino acid chain that may work to treat Milani. Even better than what I found in the coral protein, and it'll be simpler to process."

With a delicate motion, Neillsen laid his fork on his plate. "Isobel, that's enough."

She leaned even closer and lowered her voice. "What if we could use it to treat Milani and the phage? Holschtatt could hold a total market share for both medicines."

Neillsen studied her. A shadow of a frown narrowed his eyes. "How?"

Isobel glanced at the security officers. Neillsen gave them a quick motion of his head, and they withdrew but didn't leave.

She set herself to convincing Neillsen, willing him with every breath to say yes. "The CDC already has strong indications that the peptide is the link between the virus and the brain changes in its victims. What if we could find a way to modify samples of the peptide and re-release it into the phage patients' bodies to neutralize those produced by the virus?"

Neillsen rested his elbows on the table, hands clasped before him. "Go on."

Jake and the other man also listened hard.

"I already suspect this peptide could be used to lock onto the toxic Milani shards. It's possible we could use that same methodology to lock the peptides onto each other. Make them larger, possibly ineffective at producing the neurogenesis. And we don't have to harvest anything except blood and CSF samples from the virus patients." She shrugged. "There seems to be a bountiful crop of those."

Neillsen regarded the other men, then noted the patrons who still watched indirectly. "Your actions at the Nlaan reef have put Holschtatt in a grim light. Assuming I agree to this mad plan, we'll need to delay its commencement while public outcry dies down before we can proceed."

Isobel leaned closer. "Not if everyone thinks you fired me. If they think I'm working on my own."

"I'm listening."

"It'll go faster if I can get a copy of the CDC's research."

"How?" He bent closer.

"I can go to this CDC person and convince her that you blamed the whole Nlaan debacle on me so Holschtatt could walk away clean. That would make her assume I have reason to retaliate against you. Maybe make her sympathetic enough to help poor little me."

Neillsen stared at her, his jaw clenching and releasing almost as if he were chewing a bit of his now cold meal. He peered again at the men across the table, then off into space. His clasped fingers fidgeted against one another.

At last, he nodded. "If you can do this without revealing that Holschtatt is behind it," he murmured, "I will support your plan. But you are on a slender leash, Isobel. If word gets out what this is about, if the press breathes one word of Holschtatt's involvement, I will blame this entire fiasco on you and hang you out to dry. Is that clear?"

"Perfectly, Mr. Neillsen." She glanced at Jake, who'd gone pale.

"You'll send reports to me through Jake. Do not come to the office," Neillsen said, his tone low. "We'll have to make this good."

"I understand."

"Very well. Here we go." He sat back and folded his hands in his lap. "I'm very glad you came today." This time, his voice carried to the nearby tables, and other patrons once more looked their way.

"You are?"

He smiled at her again and she felt the chill from his gaze as if this were real. "Yes. It will save me the trouble of calling you before the board. Your services are no longer required at Holschtatt Pharmaceuticals. You needn't come to the office for your things. They've already been boxed up and delivered to your home."

Isobel straightened to her full height. "You're firing me?" she said, pushing her shrill voice across the now silent dining room.

"I will remind you that your nondisclosure and non-compete agreements with Holschtatt will remain in effect for five years. If you discuss this project or its particulars with anyone outside Holschtatt Pharmaceuticals," he said, "we will prosecute to the full extent of the law."

He nodded to the men behind her, then cut another bite of steak.

Mouth agape, Isobel glanced at Jake. He sat speechless, as he always did when it came to defending her.

"Ma'am," the man behind her said again, "please don't make us call the police."

Jake never said a word.

"Well, then," she said to Neillsen. "I guess I know where I stand."

She jerked clear of the security officer, squeezed between the others waiting to escort her, passed the highly offended maître d', and barreled out the door. At her car, she removed the phone from her pocket, thumbed off the voice recorder, and dropped it into her purse.

When she had driven a mile, she finally let herself smile.

Capitol Hill, Washington D.C.
Friday, November 22, 2:10 PM
(Austin, Texas, 1:10 PM)

Number of infected: 14,996,202

Cagney's phone buzzed as they entered that same room where they'd waited earlier today. He pulled it out. "Squires."

He listened while a frown pushed creases onto his youthful brow. "Hold on. Let me put you on speaker. Nadine's here."

He sat the phone on a table. "Okay, repeat that, Thom."

"I was saying that those samples Carl tested with the 40/40/20 hormone cocktail have begun to mutate."

"Is it ongoing?" Nadine asked. "Or has it settled?"

"Ongoing. Remember how it was quivering when he first started?"

"Yeah," Cagney and Nadine both said at the same time.

"Still doing that. It's freakin' weird, man."

"He treated a bunch of samples with different hormone mixtures," Cagney said. "This is the only one that's changing?"

"Nope. The estradiol and estriol also show signs of mutation, but not to this degree, and not this fast."

Cagney glanced at Nadine, but she gestured for him to take charge. He nodded. "All of those samples are still in isolation?"

"Yes, in the second set of glove boxes Nadine had us set up."

"Good," Cagney said. "Keep them there. We can't risk them affecting the others."

"Got it. Yuka wants to know when you're coming back."

"Hopefully later today. Maybe tomorrow. I want to see this hearing through with Nadine."

"Understood. Good luck, Nadine."

The door opened and Senator Moseley entered with Senator Bradbury.

Cagney's eyes widened. "Thanks, Thom. We gotta go." He ended the call.

Bradbury came forward, his hand extended. "Doctor Parker."

Nadine shook and introduced Cagney. "Is the committee ready to reconvene?"

"Not yet." He waved at chairs. "Why don't we sit? I'd like to chat with you if I may."

She managed to keep a neutral expression, despite the thoughts whirling in her brain like nuts in a Cuisinart. "Of course."

"Lamont tells me you already know," Bradbury said as he settled at the table, "we've been approached by other countries who want to collaborate on a solution for NJace."

She flicked her gaze to Moseley long enough to see him wink. "That's correct."

"Did he also tell you they contacted us after your press conference?"

"He might have mentioned that, yes."

"Seems they agree with your theories. They also believe this thing is intelligent, that it's working with a purpose." Bradbury crossed his legs. His derriere had probably grown accustomed to numbing furniture like this after years in Washington. "It was this committee's task to decide whether or not to work with the other nations in this way."

In her peripheral vision, Cagney gripped the arms of his chair tight enough to splinter the wood. She almost laughed. Instead, she nodded. "Have you come to a decision?"

"We've concluded that this type of arrangement would benefit everyone concerned, our distinguished colleague from New Jersey notwithstanding." He winked. "We're going to agree to it. But we haven't yet decided who to select as our representative."

"I see." Nadine fought the temptation to clutch her own chair.

Moseley chimed in. "It would have to be someone we could trust. Someone who can commit to this as a humanitarian cause."

"A scientist," Bradbury added, "who's not afraid to speak the truth, no matter the consequences. Like you, Doctor Parker. Sound like something that might interest you?"

Interested? She'd trade all her secret recipes for the chance to pursue something this exciting. "Possibly. I'd want to know more. Mitch Donaldson will make noise." Oh, the face he would make when he heard, like they'd made him drink vinegar.

"Donaldson won't be a problem. Nor will any of his superiors at the CDC. If you agree, this would mean more than a departmental shift. You'd be working for a whole different branch of government."

"Would I keep my salary, my pension, and retirement?"

Moseley shrugged. "Well, we'd planned to offer you a substantial raise and more comprehensive benefits across the board, but if you'd prefer to stay at your current level…"

She couldn't stop her grin this time. "I could suffer through a raise, I suppose. If it's for the cause. But," she added, all seriousness this time, "I want a guarantee that I won't be shushed or muffled on any truth or strong evidence that comes up in this effort simply for the sake of convenience. You already know that's not how I work."

"Agreed," Bradbury said, "as long as you agree to check with us first and will accept our decision to stay silent on matters that could pertain to national security."

"Us?" Nadine said. "You two are going to stay involved?"

"Oh yes. All of us have been appointed to serve long-term as an oversight committee for this collaborative work."

Great. With Farley and Stalls, she'd have to fight every step of the way. She sighed. "Okay. One more thing. If you're pulling me out of the CDC, my team needs a new leader. I have an idea on that." She nodded at Cagney, who went whiter than ever. Made his hair look even more like a flame.

Moseley smiled. "We'll see what we can do."

Chapter 41

ISOBEL SAT IN CLAIRE'S ROOM, watching the announcement of
the United States' decision to take part in a global coalition for
research on the phage. A new Senate committee, established
to administer U.S. participation in the group, had named
Doctor Nadine Parker as their coalition representative.

What good fortune! Finagling a contact within the CDC's
team would have given her a chance to grab samples of the
peptide, as well as be in the loop with ongoing research. This
was much better. Instead of one group's research, she'd gain
early access to that of multiple nations and could pass it on to
the Holschtatt labs. Beyond that, she'd be among the first to
know if another researcher stumbled over interneurin
research Holschtatt could use in treatments for Milani.

If she could get Parker to help.

"Whatcha watching, Mom?"

Isobel's attention darted from the computer screen to the
bed where her daughter was awake.

"Hey, honey," Isobel said, her voice soft. She pulled the
earbud out—she could see the rest of the announcement and

its follow-ups later—and moved to Claire's bedside. "How are you feeling?"

"Tired," Claire said, her voice hoarse, trembly. "When did you get home?"

Isobel smiled. "Almost a week ago."

"A week? I've been asleep that long?"

"Mm hmm." It had been ten days, but she didn't need to know that.

Claire tried to push up in bed but couldn't manage it without help. "Shouldn't I feel more rested?"

"Not necessarily. You've been pretty sick. Healing like that takes a lot of work. The doctors have begun to wean you off the sedatives, but everybody reacts differently to that sort of thing. Besides, you know how sometimes you study hard for a test, then you go to bed and sleep, but your mind is still working on the subject you were studying? You dream about it and everything."

"Yeah."

"Well, that's what's happening now. Except it wasn't a test. This time it's the phage." Isobel sat on the side of her bed. "You've been dreaming a lot, haven't you?"

"Boy have I," Claire said. "One of them, it's like I was flying over the Earth, far above the trees and the oceans and the mountains."

"Oh! That sounds nice."

"It was, at first," Claire said. Her nose wrinkled. "Then I flew closer and saw big patches of brown in the forests or huge empty gaps where the trees had been cut down. There were gouges in the mountains like the holes in Gabe's sandbox when he's been digging down too deep, and the rock was cut and ripped and aching." Her lip quivered. "When I was over the ocean, I saw a big school of fish near the surface. I flew toward it to watch them swim. But when I got close enough, I saw that they were dead. Lots of them, all floating belly up."

Claire's voice thickened, and she dropped her gaze.

Isobel grasped her daughter's hand. "Don't think about that, babe. Focus on something happy."

"If I were walking down the street in our neighborhood and came across a cat that had been hit by a car, should I walk off and leave it there to suffer? Not think about it so I won't feel bad?" Claire stared at Isobel as if she were searching for something. "Wouldn't it be better to call someone, try to get help for the poor thing?"

Suitable answers fled, leaving Isobel's mind empty, echoing.

"What if another person was hurt," Claire went on, "or even dead, and I didn't do anything to fix what hurt or killed them, wouldn't that make me a bad person?"

"Honey, you are not a bad person. You could never be a bad person."

A tear ran down Claire's cheek. "Then how can I ignore mangled forests and hollowed mountains and whole schools of fish dead? Won't that make me as bad as the people who hurt them?"

Shame tore at Isobel's insides, pushing against the coffee she'd finished not an hour ago and threatening to bring it back up.

"I know you did it, too," Claire said, almost whispering. "But you didn't understand that what you were doing was killing the reef."

Isobel gasped. "How do you know that?" she demanded in a shrill voice. Tears welled and she let them trace a path to her chin.

Her daughter shrugged. "I just do. You aren't the only one. It's happening everywhere. That's what my dreams are telling me. And I feel it, the same as if someone was hurting me."

Isobel tried to stifle the sob that escaped anyway. She twisted her upper body to one side, her eyes closed against the truth laid naked by her child. It didn't help. She could still see that blast at the Nlaan atoll in horrific clarity, enhanced by visions of whole schools of dead fish from Claire's dream.

Her grand plans to save Gabe had exploded right alongside that reef. Holschtatt was doing what they did best— prioritizing the bottom line. But Isobel's actions were no better. She'd ignored the potential for damage to the reef as if it were a piece of furniture. Her single concern, until Claire got sick, had been getting that coral. It had never occurred to her that a dead fish, give or take a few hundred or thousand, would affect her family. Now, both her kids would pay.

Unless her new idea bore fruit.

"Mom?"

Isobel wiped her tears and tasted the bitter lump in her throat. "Sorry," she croaked. She tried to say more, but the words wouldn't come. Her daughter's thin body lay beneath the blanket, her eyes huge wells of innocence and pain that tore at Isobel's fragile calm.

"This happened because you wanted medicine for Gabe, right?"

"Yes."

"If you stop, Gabe will die?"

A hiccup—part sob, part wail—belched from Isobel's lips. She looked for a moment at the ceiling, at the equipment attached there. All of it so clean. So sterile. So opposite this mess she'd made of their lives. "Not if I can help it, honey. As long as he's breathing, there's hope."

"You know the reef won't survive what you did there."

Isobel croaked a response. Nodded.

"Then can I ask you something without you thinking I'm a smarty pants?"

"I don't know. That depends." Isobel took a deep breath and blew it out nice and slow. "But I'm not likely to take away your Xbox or anything. Not today, anyway. Ask me."

"You always tell me that our actions have consequences." Claire clutched the top of the blanket. "Now that you know what you started, now that you know what's happening everywhere, what will you do?"

Isobel gathered her child in her arms. "I've stopped working on the reef. I have another plan. I'm going to save you both."

Rhue Children's Hospital, Austin, Texas
Sunday, November 24, 11:30 AM

Number of infected: 18,761,011

Luk came into the room to find Sadie and Kyn packing up. After living in it for three and a half weeks, the room looked as naked as a bigtooth maple in winter. He'd taken home most of his belongings yesterday. Kyn's blanket from home had been folded and stuffed in the suitcase with the last of his clothes and her bathrobe. Luk tried to sort his mixed feelings. He hated this room. He'd come to feel comfortable here, and that alone frightened him. But it was also the place where his daughter had grown wings, in a way. He was still sorting through that.

"Ah, coffee!" Sadie reached for the cup he carried.

"This is a switch, me bringing you a bean fix." He handed over the goods. "It's not a Seventh Level Brew, but it isn't bad."

"Right now it's nectar of the gods. Thanks." Sadie took a sip and gave him a thumbs-up. "We're almost done."

"Good." Luk kissed her, then sat on the sofa. The last couple of days had been blissfully uneventful. Relief and exhaustion wrestled in him. He couldn't wait to get his daughter home. He could sleep for a week, but that would be time lost with his kid. No way he was going to give that up.

Kyndra went around the room pulling down the rest of the drawings sent by her classmates. She examined the last one, a colored pencil sketch of a funny Thanksgiving turkey sent last week. She looked so serious. Introspective. "I'm sorry I made us miss our November feast."

The idea that she would be sorry for anything at all right now stung. He swallowed the lump that tried to grow in his throat.

"Come here, kiddo."

Kyndra stood by his knee.

"I don't care about a date on the calendar. You are the most important thing to me ever, and you got strong enough to come home. That's all I care about." Luk touched her cheek. "We'll have our feast in a few days, after you settle in."

"Okay. Maybe Sadie can join us."

Sadie met Luk's eyes across the room. "Oh, you don't have to—"

"I love that plan," Luk said. "Do you want to join us, Sadie?"

"Sure." Sadie's smile, tired but radiant, set a tiny tingle alight in his belly.

"Cool." Kyn nodded. "When we light Shiva's diya, can we light some extra candles for all the kids who won't be going home?"

"Absolutely."

She looked down at his jeans. Her fingers toyed with a loose thread in the seam at his knee. "You know Zach's not going home, either."

Luk's face fell. Zach had been on life support since the night of Kyn's heart attack. Just over an hour ago, Rachel and Joy had made the gut-wrenching decision to power down the machines. Luk hadn't had the heart to tell Kyn, but he should have guessed she would know. He peered at her. "Yeah. Did you want to go see him before we leave?"

"No. He knows I'll miss him." Kyn pulled at that thread. "Besides, he isn't really there anymore. I mean, his body is there, yeah. But Zach went on ahead."

Sadie's eyes widened. Luk could almost feel her thoughts because they likely paralleled his own. Is this what it was going to be like from now on? Living with a child who was connected in such an intimate way to the world around her was bound to introduce a few surprises. Kyndra would never be "normal" again. Or maybe it was that she'd raised the bar on what that might mean.

But at least they knew now what was happening. She seemed to be coping much better. No more seizures, no more headaches. Only an occasional wince. Once, yesterday, she'd gone really quiet for almost ten minutes. When he pressed her to know what was happening, she'd given him a quick, tight smile and assured him she was fine, that it would pass in a few minutes. She'd been right.

Still, Doctor Engan had written her a prescription for sedatives and calmatives in case things got bad again. There wasn't much more anyone could do. People around the world were still trying to figure out this new medical mystery, but until they did, those affected had to learn to live with it.

For herself, Kyndra wanted no part of a cure. She'd entreated Luk and Sadie to support her in that, saying she felt more awake, that she wanted to show other people what it meant to be a part of Nature, instead of apart from it. Luk and Sadie had agreed, though he knew that would be a hard promise to keep, both personally and legally, if Kyn's life were once more on the line.

His daughter watched him. "I had that dream about Mom again last night," she said. "But this time she looked like that green goddess in the picture books she used to read to me. She had flowers in her hair, and vines, and a ladybug."

"You mean Green Tara?"

"No." Kyn gestured. "The one that makes the flowers grow."

"Gaia?"

"That's the one."

"Did she say anything?"

"No. But she smelled like Ms. Rachel's garden after the rain. She hugged me, and I knew she was proud of me, happy that I was feeling better." Kyn's mouth puckered. "I miss Mom sometimes, even though I don't remember a whole lot about her."

Sadie started to leave them alone, but Luk waved her close. She sat beside him on the sofa and smiled in a way that warmed him all the way through. She was family. She should take part in these exchanges now.

"Dad, why are people calling this disease the 'entheóphage'?"

"Didn't the co-op study Greek and Latin earlier this year?" Sadie asked.

"Yeah," Kyn said. "I kinda know what the word means, but why are they calling it that?"

"Well," Luk said, "why do you think?"

Kyn twisted her lips to one side. He could always tell when she was figuring out a riddle. "Because they think it knows what it's doing?"

"Probably."

Sadie leaned into his shoulder.

"I guess I understand." Kyn perched, light as a butterfly, on his knee. She tired easily. "But that's not actually true."

Luk frowned.

"What do you mean?" Sadie asked.

"Well," Kyn said, picking at that thread on Luk's jeans again. "I mean, it does know, because there's something behind it, teaching it. You know, like dandelion seeds. When you blow them across the yard, they know how to grow wherever they land. But it's the plant they came from that told them how."

"Then the phage is like a seed?" Sadie asked.

"Sort of," Kyn said. "Something taught the phage, and now the phage is teaching us like a new dandelion would teach its seeds. But I don't know why the nurses are surprised about the phage being smart. I mean, isn't everything? Plants, animals, fish, birds, even bugs. They might not think like we do, but they know what they're doing, right? They want to live and grow and be happy, the same as we do. We—the phage kids—feel it."

Wow...what would that be like? To feel all of that without losing touch with what it means to be human? How could he offer adequate emotional support for his daughter when he couldn't even begin to fathom what she was going through?

"You believe me, don't you, Dad?"

He put an arm around her. "Yes. I do. And guess what?"

"What?"

"I've started notes for a new game, one you inspired since you got sick—I mean since you started getting well."

Sadie grinned. "Really? Tell us about it."

He grabbed his laptop, always the last thing to get packed, and opened the document he'd started after her heart attack. He told them what he'd written already. "What do you think?"

"Players would start in a polluted site," Sadie suggested, "where picking up trash is the first level. Players get points for everything they pick up and throw away."

"Or recycle. Or compost," Kyn added. "Did I say that before? I can't remember."

"You did. What else?"

"The next level could be things like planting trees," Kyn said, her voice bright, "or helping to rehab wildlife."

"Ooo," Sadie said. "Good one. He could even add levels where players learn to clean up toxic spills, like oil in the water, or help to reseed reefs. There are already companies doing that sort of thing, deliberately sinking old ships or dropping cement rings or tubes corals can use for a base."

She and Kyn rattled on with ideas, while Luk set his phone to record the conversation so he could remember it later. His imagination whirled with possibilities that sprouted in the background—more advanced levels where players could net big point margins by designing sustainable communities, or environmental cleanup strategies. AI functionality in more advanced versions could transform it into a real-life simulator where higher-level players could create beyond the ability of the basic program itself.

What if he could add incentives beyond winning to spur interest? Free access to their next new game or a paid registration to a science convention in that player's region, for feasible new eco-solutions designed as part of a player's strategy. Adult levels of the game might be made available online in multi-player format so that players could collaborate worldwide on large-scale solutions.

BehnWerks could even partner with engineering companies so game solutions that were implemented in the real world could pay percentages of profits directly to the player or net a potential design job with one of those companies. BehnWerks could even help the player fund patentable designs.

Kyn tapped him. "Earth to Dad?"

They were staring. "Sorry. Got caught up in all those great suggestions. Soon as I can finish Hyde and Seek and deliver it to Simon, I'll start coding this new one."

"You should find new investors," Sadie said. "Some person or group who won't be unreasonable over a delay due to a critically ill child. Besides, I'm not sure your Hyde investors would find this new game very exciting. Others will, though, especially now."

"Good idea." Yet another detail he'd need to research. "But for now, we should come up with cool names. By the time it's ready, we'll need to have one picked out."

"I know." Sadie's smile crinkled the corners of her eyes. "How about 'Kyndred Spirits'?"

"Well?" Luk asked Kyn.

"It's perfect." Kyndra pulled him and Sadie into a hug. They hunkered there like that for a few minutes before Kyn squirmed free.

"Okay, Little Miss Mystic." Luk chucked her under the chin. "Let's get you checked out of this four-star hotel and go home."

Chapter 42

Rhue Children's Hospital, Austin, Texas
Tuesday, November 26, 9:25 AM

Number of infected: 22,116,322

"WHY SHOULD I OFFER YOU ANY PROFESSIONAL COURTESY at all?" De Verlaine sat behind her imposing desk, her expression as flat as a brand-new baking sheet. "Rhue Hospital welcomed you and your team into our facility as a courtesy with the goal of allowing your team to render a more efficient resolution that would help these sick children. You betrayed that courtesy by lying to me, to this facility, by omitting critical information from your press conference packet which you knew I would not approve."

The woman had a point. Nadine nodded. "I admit I may have been out of line. But it's worth mentioning that my action is what sparked the other nations to invite U.S. participation in a new coalition. That collaborative effort will be essential to understanding NJace, not to mention finding a solution that will help all your patients." She gestured, half a shrug. "Had I waited for your permission, it wouldn't have happened."

"The end justifies the means?"

"Let's not get philosophical. We both have a lot of work to do, and I can't stay all day. Will you allow me onto the Rhue campus to do coalition work now and in the future?"

"Will you guarantee me there will be no repeats of the behavior you demonstrated at the press conference?"

"I will promise to be honest with you to the extent allowed by the committee," Nadine said. "That will have to do. My guarantee to national security and the committee's internal affairs comes before my promise to any one hospital. If that doesn't work for you, it's no problem. I'll stay out of Rhue. But you should know that as the coalition's representative, I require access to the teams staffing the labs. If Rhue refuses, I'm sure the coalition would be able to shift their Texas satellite lab to St. Ives, or perhaps another city. Dallas, Houston, Fort Worth."

De Verlaine scowled. "This is a private facility, Doctor Parker, which relies largely on support from private funders. We have to be cognizant of our reputation at all times. Your little stunt at the press conference has cost us dearly in negative repercussions and lost donors."

"Which you will no doubt make up in support funding from the coalition for Rhue and all the other hospitals that agree to host satellite labs for this endeavor. That doesn't even take into account the new donors you'll acquire once this program gets off the ground." Nadine gave the woman a moment to consider these points, then went on. "Here's the deal. Neither I nor my team will be working here full-time any longer. You'll see me maybe a half dozen times each year. Most of the interaction between the researchers in this satellite lab and the Atlanta office will occur via phone, internet, or video conference."

De Verlaine sat stiff as a mannequin in her executive chair. Her gaze, sharp enough to chip ice, bored into Nadine. At last, she nodded. Once. Already, she looked regretful.

"Good. I'm glad we could reach an accord." Nadine got to her feet. "For what it's worth, we may disagree on many things. And you don't have to like me. I can accept that. But never forget that we are on the same side in this thing, and we are both determined to do whatever it takes to help these children." She extended her hand.

De Verlaine glared at it before she stood and shook. It seemed to take every ounce of her control and professionalism to remain cool.

On her way out, Nadine whistled some blues and waved at the security officer who had escorted her from the front entry. She still had a task here before she could go home to Barb.

In the CDC's makeshift office, Cagney sat at her old desk, engrossed in something on his laptop. The others on shift were still working on their various parts of the project. None of them knew that they were about to be homeward bound.

Yuka saw her first. "Nadine!" She leaped up and hugged Nadine.

This time, Nadine reciprocated. "Hey yourself."

"This is a surprise." Cagney's smile almost split his face in two. "I thought you were unwelcome at Rhue. What's going on?"

"Hospital administration had a change of heart. And home office says to move this test kitchen to Atlanta. Better facilities, more comprehensive. More focused."

Happy surprise got them chattering. Thom pumped his fist.

"We're abandoning the Rhue frontier?" Cagney asked.

"Nope. The big boys are sending a new team here, and to other select hospitals around the country, to set up satellite offices. You," she said, gesturing, "are moving up to a higher level of research. Same topic, but you'll be sandwiched between samples sent in from the satellite labs and the higher-end coalition tests."

Cagney gasped. "You got the coalition job."

"Yes," Nadine said. "I did. Meet the new U.S. representative to the Global Research Accord for Collaboration on Entheóphage. GRACE, for short."

Squeals and congratulations hit her from all sides. She breathed in the moment. Sweet as fresh-baked cinnamon rolls.

"Nadine, that's fabulous news!" Yuka clapped. "We're happy for you! Details, please!"

"Not much to tell yet," she said. "First thing is to get a written Accord all parties can agree to. That might be harder than treating this danged bug, but they hope to have a ratified agreement by the end of the year. I just reviewed the latest draft. It's getting there."

"Are you excited?" Cagney asked.

"Hmm. Am I excited at the chance to collaborate and brainstorm solutions with scientists around the world who've been studying this thing? Exchange ideas and see what they've come up with that we missed? Or to show them what we found that they didn't?" Nadine's eyes cut to Cagney. "What do you think?"

"This is huge. What did Barb say?"

"Hell. The damn Accord hasn't even been signed yet, and my wife's already planning a dinner party for GRACE's first meeting in Atlanta."

Her team—correction, Cagney's team—laughed.

"Your next order of business," she said, "is to pack up all your stuff, set Rhue's equipment to its original status, and then get checked out of your hotels and catch your flight to Atlanta. I'll want to see you there bright and early the day after tomorrow. We'll continue this project from there. Or, rather," she grinned at Cagney, "you will."

Cagney clicked his tongue. "It'll be good to work in our own labs. We—" His response snapped off like a light switch. "Wait. What?"

"You heard me."

Understanding spread over his face like molasses over a hotcake. "I got the job?"

"Yep."

"I'm being promoted?"

Nadine rolled her eyes and walked to the whiteboard that still held notes from their last meeting. She swiped it clean, then drew a stick figure flow chart with Mitch at the top and

Cagney's name next to the team leader stick figure topped with red spiked hair, followed by the other investigators below his spot. When she'd finished, she spun with a flourish, à la Vanna White. "Never underestimate the power of the diagram."

"OMG." Cagney stared at her while he fanned himself.

"That's all you can say? 'O-M-G'?"

He laughed. Honest-to-god jumped up and down. "Are you kidding me?"

By now, everyone was in stitches.

Cagney's demeanor went flat as if suddenly aware of his new "boss" image. "You aren't kidding, are you? Tell me you aren't kidding."

"It's legit. I swear. Starting immediately. Paperwork should come through by December 15."

The beaming grin reappeared, and he held the sides of his head as if to keep it from exploding. "Then no, that's not all I can say. This is incredible! Thank you, Nadine." His excitement grew as the reality set in until he did a little dance right there in front of everyone. When he finally stopped, he gave her a weird expression that combined joy and something like disappointment. "Aww. You know I wish you the best. But damn, the job's not gonna be the same without you."

"We'll still work together all the time, just in a different way. You'll do fine. With that hair, how could you help but be fabulous?"

Thom clapped him on the shoulder. Yuka hugged him. The others congratulated him.

Cagney laughed. "I still can't believe it."

"Why not?" Nadine said. "Isn't this what you wanted?"

He gawked. "Yes! Definitely. But I didn't know it would come this soon."

"What soon?" Nadine shrugged. "You've worked your coppertop off for this position. And you're ready."

"I hope you're right."

She laughed. "Fake it 'til you make it. That's what I do."

"Oh yeah. I'll buy that. Thank you again. For everything. You've been a great teacher."

"Teachers can't do much without a willing and capable student. Remember that and pay it forward. Now. I need to be in Atlanta by tonight, but I have a little while before I have to catch a plane." She surveyed the room. "What can I do to help?"

Cagney waved. "Nothing. We can get this."

"You sure?"

"Yeah," Yuka joined in. "Go catch your flight."

"You want me to call you when I get home?" Cagney asked.

"No. I'll see you in the office day after tomorrow." She winked at the others. "It's not too late, you know," she told Cagney, "to get out of this business. It does tend to interfere with holidays and vacations."

"Please." He smirked. "I'm exactly where I want to be."

"Good answer," she said on her way out.

She traipsed through the carpeted corridors to the elevator. It opened right away, and she stepped in. She should be thinking about Barbara. About their celebration dinner tonight. About the crowd that would fill their house two days from now for Thanksgiving. And she was. Except NJace wouldn't leave her alone. Such a fascinating organism, and so much still to learn about it! She did hope they could find a way to prevent it from infecting new kids. She'd do everything in her power to help figure out what this latest change meant, as well as how to reverse its effects. But a small part of her— okay, maybe not small, per se—was curious to see what would happen if they didn't eradicate it. If, instead, they could make it work for them. *With* them.

The elevator pinged at the third floor and the doors slid open to reveal a couple of families, complete with kids carrying balloons and small suitcases. Cagney and his teammates weren't the only ones going home today. That knowledge warmed her. She nodded to the families and stepped aside so they could join her on this joy ride.

Nadine had asked Senator Moseley over dinner, after the committee had adjourned following the announcement of their decision, what he thought about all of this.

"All what?" he'd asked. "The phage?"

"Yeah, all of it." She gestured with her fork. "The timing of its emergence, the way it's affecting its victims, its apparent intelligence." She stabbed another bite of potato.

"I think," Moseley began, his words slow, "that the whole thing is an intriguing mystery, like many other things in the natural world. Whether or not I switch that from a lower case 'm' to an upper case one remains to be seen."

"Do you believe it could be divine intervention?" Nadine had been friendly with Senator Moseley for years now. As far as she could remember, they had never discussed faith, religion, or spirituality. The nature of existence. Any of that deep doo-doo.

"Can't say." He sipped his wine. "I'll need a few more promotions before I'm privy to the mind of God. But that's as viable a possibility as anything else we're evaluating thus far."

"Do you think we should kill it?"

"That depends." He cut a bite of steak. "A wild tiger is a beautiful and majestic beast. I'm content to marvel at its power and place in nature all day. But if it starts stalking me or another person, I will always choose a human life over that of the animal." He put the steak in his mouth, still gesturing until he could speak again. "This NJace phenomenon is a story still unfolding. Intelligent or not, sentient or not, if it keeps killing kids, yeah, I say we destroy it if we can. But if there is peace to be had between it and us, I think we should consider it."

The Senator's description, mystery vs. Mystery, seemed apt. She had to admit to a little guilt over the feeling that NJace was the most exciting thing to happen in her career in...ever. Kids like these with her in the lift had endured excruciating pain and now faced a challenging life. Others had died. Yet the prospect of chipping away at this puzzle every day, of being among those who figured out its secrets, ticked up the pace of her imagination. What the hell was it? If indeed it proved to be sentient, even sapient, what was its real purpose?

This would be a bigger thrill than baking a perfect puff pastry on the first try. If she could see a clear indication of communication from these organisms, she might come one step closer to admitting the possibility of a higher being. Who defined what that was, anyway? Maybe God was just a level up from humans, and there was something above that, and something else above that. Or maybe God was a camouflaged element of science, after all, found in the connections that appeared to underlie much of reality, of causality. Because it seemed that the emergence of this organism, which rewired its hosts to feel empathy with creatures of all types in the environment, at this exact time in history when climate issues were teetering on the brink of unstoppable...

Well. She no longer believed it was a simple coincidence. Not that she was convinced it was God, either. At least, not yet. Zero had said it wasn't, or at least not the one Nadine thought, whatever that meant. Still, God or no, there seemed to be some reason, some logic behind this whole disaster. Something that might change this course of events to a good outcome.

On the first floor, Nadine stepped out behind the families. As she crossed the lobby a woman with long dark curls came forward.

"Doctor Parker?" the woman said. "I was on my way upstairs to ask your team to help me contact you."

Nadine waved her off. "I have no time today for an interview. If you have questions or concerns, please direct them to the CDC's Atlanta office." She kept walking.

The woman fell in beside her, matching her stride. "No, I'm not a reporter. I'm Doctor Isobel Fallon."

Nadine paused. "The same Doctor Isobel Fallon who ran that reef project in the news?"

The woman stopped, grimacing. "Yes."

Nadine started walking again. "I don't want to talk to Holschtatt Pharmaceuticals either."

"I'm not with them any longer," Fallon said behind her. "They fired me."

Nadine grunted. That's what she'd expect from a big pharma company. Literally muddy the waters, then pin the blame on someone dispensable. Not her problem. She passed into the foyer, already deciding what she wanted for lunch at the airport.

"My daughter has the phage," the woman called.

Nadine wanted to keep going. Instead, she sighed, stopped, and turned around.

Fallon caught up to her. "I was behind the whole thing from the beginning. Harvesting that coral was my idea, but I never meant to hurt anyone. I never meant to kill the reef." The woman shook her head. "We didn't know this would happen. When I realized what was going on, I told them this was all connected, but they wouldn't listen to me."

"Did you come to me for absolution?" Nadine squinted at her. "Because that's outside my purview."

Fallon made a strangled sound, raised her clenched fists in front of her, then let them fall to her sides. "No," she said, keeping her voice under control with obvious difficulty. "I came to you because of that peptide diagram you shared with the Senate Committee on C-Span. I wonder if I might have a closer look at it?"

"Why?"

"Because part of its amino acid chain resembles what we were after in the coral on that reef. I'd like to see if it could be the basis of a treatment for Milani Syndrome."

Nadine rolled her eyes and kept walking. "Sounds to me like you're still working for Holschtatt."

"I'm not," the woman called. "But my son has Milani."

Nadine whirled. "Your son has the disease that sent you to the reef, and your daughter has the disease that scared you away from it."

"That sums it up."

"Doctor Fallon, you have about the worst luck of anyone I ever met."

"Maybe not. My daughter made it through the crisis thus far. And if I'm right, that neurocatalyst could save my boy's life."

"And if it gives him the symptoms of the NJace disease?"

Fallon sagged. The skin puffed beneath her eyes, as though she hadn't had a good night's sleep in weeks. "At least that's survivable."

Nadine weighed Fallon's proposition while other people flowed around and past them, coming and going on whatever business drove them. The concept boggled Nadine's mind— that the phage might provide solutions to two somethings doctors hadn't yet discovered a way to fix. Growing new neurons on demand, and fixing Milani. Which made sense. Milani was a genetic disorder that affected the victim's brain. How many other neurological disorders might be repaired or treated as a result of or with byproducts from the phage?

It was far too early to tell if this woman knew what she was saying. But if she was correct, curing the phage too quickly might remove any chances to find out. Talk about tough choices.

What would the coalition think about this? Its purpose was to work on NJace-related issues. If this didn't qualify, Nadine didn't know what would. Even before—or while—they worked on a cure for the disease or a reversal of its effects, they could test interneurin for use in developing treatments for diseases and conditions like Milani. They could make the Milani treatment open-source, too. Once they could establish the formal group, she could suggest it.

An odd realization raised a crooked smile. What was that she'd been pondering moments ago about coincidences?

Nadine pulled her mobile out and glanced at the time. Her plane didn't leave for almost two hours. She dropped the phone back in place and resumed walking, waving Fallon to follow.

"I have a plane to catch, but I'll give you what time I can before I have to board. We'll have to talk at the airport after I get checked in. You can buy me lunch," Nadine said. "No, on second thought, let me buy you lunch. You said you were unemployed?"

Isobel tagged along, parting company to find her car and meet Doctor Parker at the airport. When she was alone and en route, she grinned.

This might be easier than she expected.

Chapter 43

IN THE DARK BEDROOM, LUK STARED INTO THE SPACE above the bed. Kyndra lay asleep in her room—he'd already checked on her twice—but his mind refused to shut up. He turned his head to watch Sadie. Even in sleep, she was fun to look at. Her hair tumbled across the pillow behind her. Those cute freckles across her nose shone even in this dim light. He conjured the memory of her expression when he'd asked her, that first day Kyn came home, to stay the night—but only to sleep. She hadn't believed him. Not then. Later, after they were in bed fully clothed, she'd laughed.

"You were serious?" she'd said.

Some things, he'd told her, were more important than sex. He had not wanted to be alone with Kyn freshly home from the hospital. Everything had finally started to go right again, and he hadn't wanted to rush his budding relationship with Sadie. Good things, he'd told her, take time.

So he'd kissed her, really kissed her, for the first time. They'd cuddled for a long while until she had fallen asleep with her head on his chest. It had been nice to lie in bed holding someone again. Sadie's body felt different from Marin's, thank goodness. He didn't want it to be the same.

Now, two nights later, Sadie was still here. He smiled in the shadowed room and thought about next steps. But not now. Not yet.

He slid out of bed trying not to wake her, made his way through the room to the hall, and pulled the door mostly closed behind him.

Luk padded to his daughter's door and peeked in at her. She flipped over, one arm flung out, hanging off the side of her bunk. She twitched and murmured. Was it a bad dream? Or did she feel something else? Something hurtful? His breath caught. But soon her features relaxed, and he exhaled, long and slow.

He went to the living room. Scattered across the tables lay the remnants of last night's November feast party—Shiva and the diya at center stage surrounded by tea lights in colorful glass holders Sadie had found at a big box store sale. A Fritos bag and a dip bowl, both of which had started the evening full and now sat empty. They'd put on some tunes while the three of them ate munchies and played Hyde and Seek, which Luk had delivered yesterday. Simon wanted to keep that original name on the final product, and to keep him happy, Luk agreed.

After, they'd gone outside to stargaze. All evening, they laughed in each other's company. Even the few times Kyn's jaw tightened had not been enough to dampen their fun.

But underneath the joy lurked anxious compassion for his daughter's plight. She'd been changed, rewired to feel every human slap in Nature's face. There was no way to stop it, either her transformation or the ongoing cause for her pain.

Luk and Sadie kept watching the news for hints that the phage's effects on millions of children, or at least the many deaths, would bring some of the major global industries into the light with promises to change their ways. It was still early in the age of the phage, granted, and such turnarounds might grow more prevalent with time. As yet, though, only

Holschtatt had announced big changes in their corporate practices. In the weeks since the news exposed the company's reef debacle, protestors and accusations in the court of public opinion piled up until Holschtatt had called in all their PR gurus, made a few promises, and managed to rally. Almost certainly, their words were empty, meant to deflect blame and cast them in an innocent light. Oh, they'd funded a philanthropic branch of their company whose purpose was to clean plastics out of the oceans and recycle them into things like medicine bottles and other medical devices. Definitely a good thing. But why had it taken so much tragedy for something like that to happen?

He gathered the empty tea-light tins and other recyclables along with the trash and carried them into the kitchen. There, on the counter, rested the purchases they'd made in the last two days—reusable straws and produce bags, cloth napkins, even a living composter, set up last night and full of the squirming wigglers that had already begun to consume their kitchen scraps. Kyn's new Rothys sneakers, made by an eco-conscious company from recycled materials, still sat in the box near the door. She'd loved them as soon as she put them on. They'd talked about other ways to scale down their waste with things like bamboo toothbrushes and dryer balls instead of those little sheets.

The smell of change permeated the house, its scent lingering with a sense of permanence. Marin would have been proud of their daughter for coming through this experience stronger and wiser, as well as for embracing the transformation. For seeing what it—and she—could do for others in the larger scheme of things.

Even if the doctors could find a way to reverse the effects in the phage kids, Kyn said she wouldn't go back. Whatever was happening to her, she welcomed it. He could force the issue, but he wouldn't. He'd spoken to his lawyer on the legalities of refusing treatment, but that would take a while to figure out or, if necessary, challenge. Kyndra had always had

Marin's sensitivity, her drive to do the ethical thing. He and Sadie both felt proud of Kyn, but her determination to keep her phages meant her life—all their lives—would never be the same.

How many of the other kids felt that way? It might be a good thing to know. Maybe the phage kids needed regular contact with one another, like a support group where they could socialize with others who understood what they felt, what they endured. Maybe BehnWerks could design a new social media platform especially for them, with no charge to join. They could support the program with ad income from companies and products that met a strict guideline for green or even circular practices. He would run the idea past Kyn. See what she might add. Something like that would take time, though. These kids would need support long before any new platform was ready for extensive use. Their parents would too.

The powers that be who ran the major podcasts and local news stations probably would let him speak about this on-air, which would help him get the word out. BehnWerks games were marketed at kids, young and old. His voice might be "heard" more than someone else's. He shuddered at the anticipation of standing again in the spotlight but if it could help Kyn, if it could help all the phage kids, he could at least try. If enough of them felt like Kyn and wanted to keep their phages, they might be the ones to effect the necessary changes in how people did things with regard to the environment. Somebody needed to do it, and these kids could literally feel their way through to the best practices.

He grabbed his laptop, went to the living room, pushed the remaining party paraphernalia to one side, and re-read his notes for the new game he'd started. Yes. These gave him a perfect starting point. He opened his coding program and started writing the platform. After a couple of hours, he reviewed the progress, pleased with this plan.

Now he needed to find new investors. Sadie's suggestion had been a good one. This new project needed a different focus, as well as funders with a little more compassion for what the phage kids were going through. With all that had been in the news, and the phage kids such a novel phenomenon, the timing was perfect to move on this new game. He should jump on it quickly before someone beat him to it because the sad truth was that making green solutions profitable might be the only way they would ever gain any real foothold in this world.

So, fine. Kyn's idea for this game could be a seed. If they were lucky, and if the phage kids had the new influence he suspected they would, maybe it would grow into an industry to promote practices and lifestyles that protected, rather than destroyed. This could be the first step along the way to involving everyday citizens in something that would benefit them all. If BehnWerks could model the behavior and encourage others to follow their example, Luk would feel as though he'd done something to help Kyn. To help all the entheóphage kids, current and future.

The thrill of starting a new and exciting project, especially one with such outstanding potential benefits as this, tickled him. Luk dove into the design program and continued coding. He couldn't wait to show Kyn a playable alpha.

Chapter 44

JAKE MET THEM IN THE CURVED DRIVEWAY and opened the passenger door to help Claire out of the car.

"Welcome home, sweetheart," he said, sweeping her into an enormous hug.

"Thanks, Dad," Claire said. "I'm glad to be out of that hospital room."

Isobel grabbed her keys and climbed out on her own. She popped the trunk and went to gather their daughter's things. There wasn't much left, just a suitcase, which she set on the pavers, and a gigantic teddy bear. Isobel had sent most of the other belongings home last night with Jake. She closed the trunk and rolled the case to the driver's door, where she reached in one more time and grabbed the bag from the pharmacy with Claire's meds, then bumped the door shut.

"Let's get inside," she said across the top of the car. "We don't want her getting overtired. She needs her rest."

"Definitely, because we're having a late Thanksgiving dinner tonight. Maria's been busy all morning." Jake guided Claire up the drive and in the front door, chatting every step of the way.

Isobel trudged after them with Claire's things. The suitcase wheels made a clackity sound against the gaps between pavers, which somehow comforted Isobel.

Inside the house, the smell of roasting turkey and baking pies made her mouth water. Gabe's squealing voice echoed down the hall. Isobel dropped the suitcase and the bear at the foot of the stairs and carried the meds into the kitchen, where they could be stored out of reach of her youngest. Maria stood by the sink wrapped in Claire's embrace. Morning light from the window behind Maria lent a seraphic glow to her profile.

"I don't know if I ever told you, Maria," Claire said, her voice muffled against Maria's breast. "I love you. I'm so glad you're part of our family."

Maria's smile lit the room. She squeezed Claire, staring at Isobel. All the while, Gabe chanted Claire's name like a litany.

Isobel flushed at the sight of tears on the housekeeper's cheeks. How telling that it had taken all this to make one member of the Fallon family say what should have been said long ago. Perhaps it was a sign of the changes to come.

Jake stuck his hands in his pockets. "She's right, Maria. We'd be lost without you."

Claire hugged Gabe, too, but when she tried to stand up again, he didn't want to let her go. Isobel dropped the bag of meds on top of the fridge, then rescued her daughter.

"Come on." Isobel pulled Gabe into her arms. "Give Claire a little space. She's been really sick. We need to help her out for a while. Deal?"

His lips began to quiver. His face crumpled. A storm brewed there. Isobel forced her features to brighten and grinned as if she'd had a great idea.

"Hey, I know! Do you want to help me get her settled into her bed? Then maybe she can read you a story. One. Story."

Gabe looked at Claire, his lip still trembling, but the storm began to lift.

"Yeah, Gabe," Claire said. "That'd be fun. Or we could play a game. Come on."

Gabe struggled to get down. Isobel put him on his feet.

At the stairs, Claire tried to grab her suitcase but couldn't lift it.

Jake snagged the case and gestured to his daughter. "After you."

"Thanks." Claire gave the teddy bear to Gabe on her way up. Isobel and Jake followed.

Inside her room, Jake sat her case in the rattan chair in the corner. Gabe held out the bear, but she pushed it back at him. It was almost as big as he was. "No, that's yours now. You keep it in your room."

He squealed and hugged the bear tight.

Claire laughed. "Which one, Gabe? Book? Or game?"

"Two by Two!" he yelled.

"Okay. Bring your tablet. We'll play in here."

He hurried out. Claire kicked off her shoes and slid, jeans and all, between her red blanket and rainbow-striped sheets.

"You know the man who owns the gaming company for LeapFrogge and Two by Two?" Isobel said. "His daughter has the phage, too."

Claire's expression grew distant as if she were searching across the city to see Lukas Behn's child.

"I figured you might want to know. You don't have to pacify Gabe right now. Take it easy. If you're too tired—"

"It's fine." Claire sounded like she meant it. "I want to do it. I missed him. He missed me. Besides, we don't know how much longer I'll have the chance to play with him. I can rest later."

Jake made a guttural sound.

Isobel ignored him. "Well, don't overdo it." Gabe came in with his tablet. She stroked his hair. "Be nice, now," she said in her mom voice. "Claire's tired."

"Okay." He sounded more amiable than she'd expected.

"Claire, your father and I are out in the hall. Call if you need us."

"Thanks. I'm good." Claire helped Gabe remove his shoes, then settled him under the covers with her and opened the game.

Isobel watched them until Jake put his arm around her shoulders. She shrugged him off and ducked out into the hall. He followed.

"Bel, I don't know what you want from me."

"I want you to champion my agenda," she said, continuing their discussion over her agreement with Neillsen. "I want you to remember why I'm doing it."

"I've always supported your projects in the past. You know that. But this one could land you in jail." His eyes pleaded with her. "Don't do it, Bel."

"You're saying I should stop trying to save our children?"

"That's not what I meant. But can't you find another way?" He huffed a heavy breath and waved a hand at Claire's room. "They need both their parents, and that won't happen if you're caught."

"Then what, Jake?" Isobel planted her hands on her hips. "Without more research, I won't find a long-term solution outside the star queen to help Gabe, and Claire will still have the phage. The CDC, or its new coalition, isn't likely to give their notes to a pharma executive if they know I'm planning to privatize any of it. And if Neillsen is going to honor his agreement with me, I need to procure that data. I don't know why it's hard for you to understand that."

"Someone will find out," he said through clenched teeth.

"So? That coalition has vowed to make their findings open-source. I don't think they could come after me later, even if Holschtatt makes a sellable product from it."

"That depends on their open-source agreement. It's possible they could prohibit that on the part of anyone who participates in brainstorming new solutions while working with them."

She waved away his arguments like they were bothersome flies. "You're being paranoid. We've taken every possible precaution. Neillsen will set me up with a private lab, separate from their main facilities. I'll have my own staff. The only contact between me and Holschtatt will be you."

They stood in awkward silence. The game sounds from Claire's room drifted into the space between them.

"Tell me who I'm speaking to. My wife? The mother of those two children in there?" Jake said, pointing. "Or Holschtatt's new corporate spy?"

"Jake," she almost shouted. She glanced at Claire's room. "I'm all of those people," she said, her tone softer. "I can't leave one on and shut the others off. I'm not wired like that."

"Then this conversation's over." Jake brushed past her and crossed the landing into their room.

Isobel sighed. Such a useless argument. How could he not see that she was doing this for their kids? Finding some path through all these obstacles to get them through today? And tomorrow? And all the days that followed? Because if someone didn't do it, Claire might still die. Gabe certainly would.

She followed him into their en suite. "Don't you even want to know my plan?"

He turned away with a grunt. Folded his arms. Met her eyes in the enormous mirror over the vanity and nodded.

"That interneurin is key. I know it. If I can figure out how it works, I could find a way to stop the infection altogether or hamstring the virus by interrupting its production of the peptide."

"The CDC already tried that. The results would have been deadly in a live patient."

"I'm not them," she said to his reflection. "But they do have a running start. They're out in front already. That's why I need access to their research."

"And they're going to give you that data? No questions asked?"

Isobel wavered on the edge of a decision. Lead him on with confidence? Or admit to him that it wasn't yet a done deal? Her talk with Nadine Parker held promise, though where it would go from here and what part Isobel would have to play in it remained to be seen. Nadine had talked about possibilities and said she'd investigate further, that her first responsibility was the coalition's work on the phage. No wiggle room there. But if Isobel could help, maybe...

"I don't know. But just in case, I'm going to have to play the injured party for them to accept me."

Jake spun and leaned against the counter. "What if you can't synthesize the peptide?"

"We'll harvest it from patients."

"Then you risk triggering a fatal response from the virus." He blinked at her, disbelieving. "You would take that chance with the phage patients?"

Isobel tsked. "Then I'll infect lab mice with the phage and harvest it from them."

"Won't that cause pain for the phage kids?"

She stared at her husband. "I didn't think you believed those things were connected."

"Claire convinced me." His jaw clenched and unclenched. "I don't want to cause her even more pain than she's already been through. More than she'll confront in the weeks and months to come, even without this kind of exacerbation."

"Lab mice can breed by the thousands. It isn't like I'll be torturing them."

"Won't you?" He shook his head in slow motion. "How do you know they won't feel the same kind of pain Claire does?"

"I don't." She'd thought this through. "But it would be short-term. Only until we can find a way to resolve the virus in the children. Once we mitigate the peptide's effects in humans, the mice won't be a problem any longer. We'll maintain an adequate supply of specimens to continue production of the treatment. Who knows whether this thing will resurface down the line?"

"Isobel, I love you. I love our kids. I want to do what's best for them. For us." He regarded her as if weighing his options.

"But this is wrong. You need to find another way. A legitimate one that won't cause more pain and suffering."

"There is no other way. Medicines are tested on animals all the time, Jake. You know this. Would you rather we experiment on the children? Keep a few of them in labs to produce the peptide for a continual harvest-ready crop?"

"Now you're being ridiculous." He paced away, awkward silence again filling the space between them. "You know someone will find out eventually," he said. "You can't hide something like this forever. It's going to bite you, Isobel. It might eat us all alive."

She shrugged. "I'll deal with that if it happens."

"How? Neillsen told you that if the press breathed a word, he would hang you out to dry. You know he'll fire me, too. Who'll pay for the medical bills then?"

"He won't fire either of us." The mental image of Neillsen threatening her or her family almost made her laugh.

"How can you be sure?"

Isobel pulled out her cell and brought up a recording. She fast-forwarded a bit, then let it play. Color drained from Jake's face as Neillsen's voice came from the phone's speaker, evidence that revealed Neillsen had gone along with the corporate espionage idea from the start, as well as his promises to pin it on her if anyone else found out. She tried to imagine the man's smug look crumpling if he ever heard this.

Jake stared at her as if they were strangers. "You're going to blackmail him."

"If he threatens me or tries to fire either of us, yes." She paused the playback.

"That'll drag me into the news, too," he whispered. "You'd do that?"

That was coming anyway, but he didn't see it. Yet. She pushed her mobile into her pocket. "It won't come to that. If he comes after me, I'll play this ace in private first. Neillsen's not going to sacrifice Holschtatt over this, not after they finally managed to salvage it from the gutter. He's more interested in helping himself and the company than in hurting me."

"And if you're wrong?"

She crossed her arms. If she were wrong, her family's future would get even rockier than it already was. But she had to take the chance. This project was too fat a carrot to ignore, especially in light of how it might help both her kids. If she ended up in jail, but her kids got the help they needed, she could live with that.

"I have to try, Jake," she said, trying to keep the pleading tone out of her voice. "I owe it to Zoe, and to our kids. Please try to understand."

"Great," he muttered. He paced a few steps, stopping as if he would comment. No words came. They stood like that for a couple of minutes before Jake took a deep breath. "I need some space while I mull this over."

"Okay." She fought the urge to continue the argument. "I'll leave you to yourself today."

"I'm gonna need more than a day, Bel."

Isobel frowned. "How long?"

He looked at his feet. Stuck his hands in his pockets. "I don't know. But I can't stay here."

Her mouth fell open. "You're leaving me?"

"No." He grimaced. "Of course not. We need to put the kids first right now, and they need us both here. I'll move into the guest room for a while."

An empty feeling sprouted in her gut. Apparently, the virus would take her marriage, too. She was doing her damnedest to fix what she could. Why did that upset him so?

A tear leaked out and crawled down her cheek. She didn't even swipe at it. Instead, she gulped a deep breath and nodded. She and Jake needed to be the adults here, even when that was hard to remember. Especially when it was hard to remember.

"Okay. You want some help?"

"No. I've got it."

She straightened her shoulders, wiped her tears, and left the room.

Chapter 45

Fallon Residence, Austin, Texas
Wednesday, December 11, 3:17 AM

Number of infected: 59,941,807

ISOBEL RAISED HER HEAD FROM THE PILLOW. Moonlight peeked through the slitted blinds, casting strips of dim light in the dark room. She glanced at the clock and listened for whatever it was that woke her.

Nothing.

She lay down and almost dozed off before she heard it again.

What was that?

She pushed the blankets aside and sat up in the dim light. This room, where she and Jake had conceived both their children and spent many happy times, now felt alien. No valet stand. No cufflinks or tie clips on the dresser. Open space gaped like a wound in the alcove where his stationary bike had stood. Its absence still hurt.

The sound came again. Isobel grabbed her robe from the hook by the bed and padded barefoot across the room. No movement in the shadowy hallway.

She frowned. Could it be Claire?

Claire!

Isobel hurried to her daughter's door and opened it as quietly as she could. No, Claire tossed in her bed, either dreaming or feeling something that caused her discomfort. Maybe she'd been murmuring in her sleep?

Was that what Isobel had heard?

Claire had been home a little over ten days now. Talking in her sleep had not yet manifested, as far as Isobel knew, but it wasn't beyond the realm of possibility.

She checked on Gabe, too. He was sleeping curled around the bear his sister had given him. Isobel tiptoed out of his room and closed the door.

In her room, she heard it again. It was coming from the backyard.

Her heart leaped into her throat, and she rushed at the window, then stopped short. What if someone was out there? They'd see her.

Instead, she went to the guest room door. She tapped, a soft rap that she hoped would not wake the kids.

"Jake?" she whispered.

He didn't respond, and she huffed, exasperated. He always was a heavy sleeper.

She pushed open the door. His blinds were pulled up tight to the top of the window frame. Light from the full moon shone through the glass and glowed on the white carpet, illuminating the whole room. Jake was not there.

Isobel blinked at the empty room, her hand still on the doorknob. Where—

He'd gone downstairs for a drink or a snack. Or he'd gone out to his gym above the garage and started the elliptical. Was that what she'd heard?

No, that noise came from the yard.

She went to the top of the stairs and called down in a hoarse whisper. "Jake!"

Still no answer.

Isobel muttered under her breath and tiptoed down the stairs, trying to be as quiet as she could. He was not in the living room, the office, or the den. He was not in the kitchen.

She stood by the kitchen door in the dim light. Where could he be? Jake's routine never wavered. Up at five a.m. Workout in the garage. Record voice memos while on the treadmill.

Then half an hour at his computer, responding to email and voice mail. Shower, dress, hit Holschtatt for ten hours, and home in time for supper. Help the kids with homework. Spinning on the bike in the bedroom—the guest room now—during the news. To bed no later than eleven p.m. In all the years she'd known him, he'd never wandered the house at three in the morning.

Mired in confusion, Isobel searched the room as if some random clue to where he might be would leap out and be recognized. Her glance flitted across the window above the sink, but something wrong, something out of place, drew her eye to the glass pane once more. Beyond lay the yard. And at the far end near the pond stood Jake, his white pajamas almost glowing in the dark.

She raced to the sink to see better. Life hadn't exactly been comfortable of late, for either of them. But that wouldn't make him... He wasn't going to... *Oh god...*

She didn't bother to check the gun safe. Instead, Isobel hurried through the closest kitchen door, down the brick steps, and across the patio in her bare feet. Nightgown and robe billowing behind her, she bolted out onto the wet grass toward her husband.

He never moved.

She slowed as she neared him, but the closer she got, the more confused she grew.

"Jake?"

"Shhhh," he hissed. "You'll scare her."

"Scare who?" No one else stood in their yard except Maria, who must have heard him, too. She stood on the stoop of her house, a wraith in the darkness.

He waved in Isobel's direction but did not look at her. He pointed. "Her."

Isobel's gaze followed the direction he indicated. There, at the edge of the tall brush around the pond, hunkered a grey fox.

Isobel froze. Her heart did somersaults in her chest. Her mouth went dry. "Jake, honey, back away before she attacks you."

"She won't."

"You don't know that," Isobel reasoned. "She might have kits nearby. She might be rabid. You don't know! Come here. Let's go in the house."

"She's not rabid. No kits. Too early in the season. She's hungry."

Isobel inched closer. The fox watched her. Jake watched the fox. When Isobel was close enough, she peered up at her husband. He was wide awake. Not drunk.

"I'm trying to tell her we have food in the kitchen. I could bring her something. But she doesn't trust me enough yet to wait. No problem, though," he said, an odd smile on his face. "She will, soon enough."

A chill crept up Isobel's spine, followed by goosebumps. She gripped his arm. "Jake, how do you know this?"

At last, he turned to her.

"I feel it."

Afterword

THE IDEA FOR ENTHEÓPHAGE OCCURRED TO ME in early 2019. Dreams, conversations with my First Reader (a.k.a. The Hubenstein), and random notes followed until the story concept solidified. It wasn't until June of that year that I began the medical research necessary to bring Phagey (thanks, Anna!) as close to reality as I could. That summer was filled with e-mails and Twitter messages to relevant medical professionals I'd found online, searching for resources who could clarify the many fuzzy spots in my plan. No actual story content had yet been written; the story was still all concept.

Fast forward to September, when I attended a small writers retreat. One of the young ladies at that event convinced me to try my hand at National Novel Writing Month. So all through October, I gathered my notes and made last-minute contacts to compile further data. On November 1, I sat down and began writing the actual story. By November 30, I had written nearly sixty thousand words. I finished that first draft a few days into December and set it aside to percolate.

Later that same month, the first hints of what became a very real pandemic began to surface and by January of 2020, COVID-19 was at least in the back of everyone's minds.

In the beginning, I didn't see any real connection between what happens in Phagey and what was happening in the world around me, so in March of 2020 I passed a new draft of Phagey off to my first round of beta readers. I don't think any of us knew, at that point, how bad the COVID pandemic would get. By the time I got comments back from that round of readers, it was in full swing. Lockdowns and face masks were a reality for everyone. At first, I couldn't even bring myself to work on this story. It hit too close to home. By the time I got past that block, COVID had become, to some extent, a real-life experience that influenced my manuscript. Maybe you saw some of those details in these pages, but keep in mind that Luk's, Isobel's, and Nadine's story takes place in a world where there was no COVID to inform their processes. I wanted to keep that sense of discovery—not just of the phage but of the process that occurs during unprecedented medical crises—thus I deliberately left out some of the detailed steps the world has developed during COVID's unfolding.

So many times, during the process of bringing this book to your hands, I have seen things in the world around me—not just the pandemic, but in the many global environmental crises surrounding all of us—that have made me grateful to whatever Muse first whispered this story concept in my thoughts. Writing it has changed the way I see the world.

I hope reading it will do the same for you.

— Drema Deòraich

Acknowledgements

NO WRITER WORKS IN A VACUUM. Support, encouragement, and assistance come from often unexpected quarters. *Entheóphage* is no exception. A great many people contributed to this story along the way—too many to name them all—but a few stand out in my mind.

My special thanks go out to:

Deb Brown, Deborah Cohen PhD, Erik Erkenbrak, Lee A. Everett, Katie Frooman, Nikita Milani, Matthew Moore, Athena North-Henderson BSN/RN/CPPS, Melinda A. Smith PhD, Kelly Ann Staso, and Ernest Williams IV MPH for helping me get the medical science and other technical details as close to right as I could. Any errors in the medical or science-y portions of this book are on me, not them.

Sean Bai for helping me with gaming technologies; Melissa Gillikin Rolaf for her help with homeschooling details; Rob Verger, author of "How Do We Prep for the Next Pandemic?"—*Popular Science*, Fall 2020; and anyone else who contributed to the realism of this project.

Becky, Chase, Cyndi, Dixie, Dylan, Jane, John, Katie, Reid, Sarah, Shawn, Tammie, Vince, and William for their honest opinions on early readings, their suggestions on improving each draft, and their help in polishing the story.

Lydia Netzer, writing teacher and enthusiastic supporter, for shooting down all my bad ideas and insisting on excellence in my work.

Anna "Anner" Kaling, dinosaur fan, shark lover, cat lady, and Mentor Extraordinaire, who turned my Pitch Wars learning experience into a blessing.

My editor, Lauran Greathouse Strait, who not only sharpened the story's focus, but helped me see which words I love most.

Duncan Eagleson, of Corvid Design, who read the story and created the perfect cover.

My little brother Jimmie, who always encouraged me to follow my dreams, even when the prospect scared me.

And last, but certainly not least, my husband, for listening endlessly to my meandering thoughts since the moment this story's concept entered my head, for reading draft after draft and offering sincere and helpful feedback, for making sure I ate and slept, and for doing all the necessary adulting in our household so that I could focus on this manuscript. I love you, Silly Man.

About the Author

DREMA DEÒRAICH IS A LEGAL ASSISTANT, sometime gardener, spider savior, Nature-lover, cat mom, and writer of speculative fiction. While her short stories have appeared in Mithila Review, Electric Spec, All Worlds Wayfarer, and other zines, *Entheóphage* is her first published novel. She is currently hard at work on her next project, *The Founder's Seed* trilogy, and plans to release the first book in early 2023.

A long-time resident of Southeastern Virginia, Drema lives with her husband, two rescued felines, and all her other characters. When she's not writing, she recharges with quiet moments spent among trees, surrounded by Nature.

You can subscribe to Drema's blog at https://www.dremadeoraich.com, or follow her on Facebook (https://www.facebook.com/NiveymArtsLLC) and on Twitter (@dremadeoraich).

Keep up with the latest news about Drema's releases at www.niveymarts.com.

Don't miss out! Sign up for The Quill, Niveym's monthly newsletter (https://niveymarts.com/newsletter/), to get environmental news and tips on ways you can make a difference! Subscribers are the first to receive announcements about upcoming book releases, cover reveals, news on progress of our various projects, or other juicy tidbits from Niveym Arts.

Did you enjoy this book? Please leave a review on Amazon, GoodReads, your blog, or wherever potential readers might gather. Thanks so much!